own. BEYOND MIDNIGHT is a gripping and chilling page-turner . . . outstanding reading!''

''Spectacular! A terrific story that had me anxiously turning the well-written pages.''

—The Literary Times

''Ms. Stockenberg does it again! She's written a story that keeps you so involved, you can't put it down.''

—Bell, Book and Candle

''Ultimately satisfying, mystically entertaining, and a perfect book to take to the beach.''

—The Time Machine

''If you are in the mood for a little spine-tingling, this is for you.''

—The Belles & Beaux of Romance

TIME AFTER TIME

''A richly rewarding novel filled with wrenching loss, timeless passion and eerie suspense. A novel to be savored.''

—Romantic Times

''As hilarious as it is heart-tugging . . . Once again, Antoinette Stockenberg has done a magnificent job.''

—I'll Take Romance magazine

''Antoinette Stockenberg is a superb contemporary writer . . . TIME AFTER TIME is that rarest of works—a satisfying treasure for a vast variety of palates.''

—Affaire de Coeur

EMBERS

''Stockenberg cements her reputation for fine storytelling with this deft blend of mystery and romance . . . Sure to win more kudos.''

—Publishers Weekly

A Charmed Place

ANTOINETTE STOCKENBERG

St. Martin's Paperbacks

A CHARMED PLACE

Copyright © 1998 by Antoinette Stockenberg.

ISBN: 0-312-96597-4

Printed in the United States of America

St. Martin's Paperbacks edition / June 1998

St. Martin's Paperbacks are published by St. Martin's Press, 175 Fifth Avenue, New York, NY 10010.

10 9 8 7 6 5 4 3 2 1

For Jennifer Enderlin,
dreamshaper

Chapter 1

"He'd look perfect tied to my bedposts," Norah decided.

Joan lifted the binoculars from her friend's grip and focused them on the lighthouse at the tip of the windswept peninsula. After a minute, she said, "They'd better be pretty strong bedposts."

She held out the binoculars to Maddie Regan, who, as always, was the first to show up at Rosedale, her family's summer cottage on the Cape. "Here, Maddie. Have a look."

"Thank you, no," said Maddie, walking away from the kitchen window with her box of books. "Unlike the two of you, I happen to have a life."

Norah arched one perfectly shaped eyebrow. "Well, la-di-da. Doing what? Spending another summer on the Cape, watching the beach erode? Get with the program, Maddie. Women our age have to keep their eyes open. Especially women our age in Dulltown."

Maddie managed a wry smile and said, "There's nothing wrong with Sandy Point. It's where I want to be every year come June. It's where I want a teenage daughter to be. It's quiet; it's safe; it's—"

"Dull. Let's face it. It's *dull*. We aren't the Hamptons. We aren't the Vineyard. We aren't even Newport. There's nothing to do in Sandy Point, and no one rich to do it with."

Joan, still focused on the peninsula, said, "This one could change your mind, Norah. No kidding. Wow. Killer aura.

He's standing in front of the lighthouse, looking out at the ocean. The wind's blowing his hair around. You can't mistake the guy. It really is him. Sure you don't want a peek, Maddie?''

Maddie shook her head and kept to her box of books.

Norah took Maddie's refusal personally. "You do understand our situation here? Three women, nada men—none worth bringing down from Boston, anyway? How are we going to network? This is turning into a serious dry spell, Maddie. I'm still separated. Joan's still single. And you're still—''

"All right, all right. Divorced," Maddie conceded. "But unlike you two, *not* dribbling with lust.''

"Why should you be?" Norah shot back. "Your ex has a condo two miles away, and he's willing to bed you any time you want.''

"But I don't want.''

"I've never really understood that," Joan admitted. "Michael's always been so kind, so considerate to me.''

"So considerate to *everyone*," said Norah with a caustic smile. She repossessed the binoculars from Joan and aimed them on her prey. "Nuts. He's gone. No, wait. Here he comes out of the lighthouse—with a basket of laundry. Good Lord. Dan Hawke is going to hang his own laundry. Dan Hawke!''

Joan, as usual, had a theory. "He's a war correspondent. He's probably used to washing his socks in some dead soldier's helmet.''

"Joannie, the way you put things. Okay, here we go. First item out of the basket: jeans. I'd say a thirty-four waist, thirty-six, tops. How cute—he's holding the clothespins between his teeth. Oh, Maddie, you *should* look. He looks nothing like he does on TV.''

Maddie dropped another box of books onto the kitchen table and began unlocking its cardboard flaps. "How would you know, Norah? You never watch CNN.''

Without taking her focus away from the lighthouse, Norah said, "Now, now. Just because I sell shlock art for a living, it doesn't mean I don't watch CNN.''

"Have you ever actually seen him in a broadcast from a war zone?"

Norah shrugged and said, "No. But it doesn't mean I don't watch CNN."

"Well, *I* watch it," Joan chimed in, "and I can tell you, the guy makes an impression. It isn't his tousled hair or his flak jacket; they all have that. And he's not especially to-die-for handsome. It's more his air of—I don't know—reluctance. As if he can't stand what he's doing but he does it anyway because somebody has to, and he can do it better."

"Bullshit," Norah argued. "War pays his bills."

Joan, less assured but more introspective than taller, thinner, richer, red-haired Norah, decided to dig in her heels. "He hates his work. I'll bet my house on it. He's come to Sandy Point because he's burned out."

"Pillowcases," said Norah, looking up from her binoculars and flashing the other two women a knowing grin. "That's a good sign. He's only been renting for a couple of days. He must be fastidious."

"Fastidious!" Joan had another theory. "That's the last thing he'd be. War correspondents eat leaves and grass if they have to, and sleep in the crotches of trees."

"A waste," said Norah with a snort. "He should be sleeping in another kind of crotch altogether."

"Norah!"

Maddie said it too sharply for someone who wasn't supposed to be listening. She looked away. Norah was being outrageously—well—Norah. It didn't mean anything.

Norah seemed oblivious to the scolding. A second or two later, still gazing through the binoculars, she said, "One, two three, four, five, six hankies. How quaint: he uses handkerchiefs."

Joan had theories for that, too. "Of course he uses handkerchiefs. Do you really think he can buy purse-sized Kleenex in the jungles of Guatemala? Besides, they make good tourniquets."

She added in a thoughtful voice, "I remember one of his reports from Chechnya. There were half a dozen rebels huddled around a campfire, trying to keep warm, and most were in rags. He wasn't wearing anything better. I suppose he bartered his jacket for information.''

"Whatever.'' Obviously Norah wasn't listening. Her high cheekbones had become flushed with the first faint sign of her formidable temper. Maddie braced herself.

Norah turned to Maddie in a fed-up way and said, "You know what your problem is, Maddie Regan? You're too damned prim. You're too damned proper. And you're too damned passive.''

She handed off the binoculars to Joan and launched into an all-too-familiar lecture. "You assume the Right One will just drop in your lap while you're sipping iced tea on your patio.'' She folded down one of the box flaps over Maddie's forearm, forcing her to pay attention. "And meanwhile life is passing you by. You've been divorced for four years, Maddie,'' she added, sounding extremely annoyed about it. "You're almost forty. What're you waiting for?''

Maddie reached into the box and pulled out a hardcover. "I'm waiting for this guy to make the *New York Times*,'' she quipped, waving a Horston novel in front of Norah. "He's vastly underrated.''

Norah responded with a stony look, so Maddie gave her an honest answer. "I'm not waiting for the Right One . . . or the Wrong One . . . or anyone, Norah. I have my hands full with all the relationships—''

"None of them sexual!''

"—that I can handle at the moment.''

Nudging the cardboard flap open again, Maddie lifted Guterson's best-seller out of the box, and one by Oates, and Vonnegut's way-too-old *Cat's Cradle*. This was the summer to revamp the Freshman survey in contemporary literature that she taught. She'd meant to do it last summer, but last summer she was still caught up, along with the rest of her family, in shock. No one did much of anything last summer.

"And I'm not prim,'' she threw out over her shoulder.

Passive, maybe. Proper, obviously. But not prim.

"Of course you're prim!'' snapped Norah. "Who the hell

else could resist gawking at a bona fide celebrity who's spending the summer a few hundred yards away from her?''

"The man is renting a lighthouse," Maddie reminded her friend. "In a backwater summering hole. It's obvious, at least to me, that he wants privacy."

"It's obvious that he *doesn't* want it. He went and became a celebrity of his own free will! If you had a shred of decency in you, you'd be fawning over him like the rest of us. He's entitled to it!"

"Oh, pooh," said Joan in a disappointed voice. "He has a woman with him."

"What? Let me have those," said Norah, snatching the binoculars back from Joan with such vigor that she knocked Joan off balance.

"Watch it!" Joan snapped. The edge in her usually soft-pitched voice was a clear sign, at least to Maddie, that Norah had gone over the line again.

He has a woman with him.

Norah stared intently through the binoculars. After a thoughtful silence she said, "Hard to say. If she's his lover, she's not a recent one. They seem too used to one another. She's leaning against the mud shed with her hands in the pockets of her sundress, mostly listening to him—the wind just blew her dress up; *great* legs—and nodding once in a while. I get the sense that she's just soaking him up. As if they go back together."

Norah looked up for a moment. "I'm right that he never married?"

Joan said, "Not as far as I know. He made *People*'s most-eligible list a few years ago—after the Gulf War—but then he kind of faded. So it's possible he went off and did something stupid, but I doubt it. We would've read about a wedding, in *People* if not in *Newsweek*. I imagine he was just living with someone. Probably her."

Joan rose up on tiptoe, trying for the same vantage over the café curtains that Norah had. In heels, Joan was able to manage an inch or two over five feet, but today she was wearing sandals. She was short. Her two best friends were tall. It made her peppery sometimes.

"Norah, would you mind?" Joan asked in a dangerously mild voice. "They're my binoculars, after all."

She reached for them but Norah shooed her away with her elbow, the way she might a pesky terrier. Maddie stepped in, as she always did, to keep the peace. She took the binoculars.

"All right, you two clowns. Have a little dignity."

With Norah, dignity was always in short supply. She proved it now by nodding slyly toward the lighthouse. "Check it out—if you're not too prim."

Probably she'd used the exact same line on half the men she'd dated; Norah had no reason to be shy. With her knock-out figure, creamy skin, red, red hair and full red lips, she was the kind of woman who made men take off their wedding rings and hide them in their hip pockets.

But Maddie was not, and never would be, Norah.

"Why are you being such a pain, Nor?"

"You're abnormal, you know that? Anyone else would look. Prim, prim, prim."

With an angry, heavy sigh, Maddie accepted the binoculars and aimed them in the general direction of the lighthouse. Her sense of dread ran deep. She did not want to gape at the man and did not want, most of all, to gape at the woman. What was the point? It would be like staring into her own grave.

"Yes. I see him. Yes. He looks like on TV." She held the binoculars out to Norah. "Happy now?"

"What about the woman? What do you think?"

"I didn't see any woman," said Maddie, grateful that a billowing bed sheet hid all but a pair of slender ankles from view.

"No, she's there, Maddie. I can see her now, even without the binoculars. Look again," Joan urged.

It was going to be so much worse than Maddie thought. She sighed and tried to seem bored, then took the glasses back for another look. This time she was spared nothing. A slender woman of medium height was facing squarely in their direction, laughing. The wind was lifting her blunt-cut hair away from her face and plastering her pale blue sundress against her lithe body. She was the picture of vitality and high spirits. And the sight of her filled Maddie with relief.

"It's obviously his sister," she said.

"Ah, his sister. Wait—how would you know?" Norah demanded.

She walks the way he does . . . throws her head back when she laughs the way he does . . . does that jingle-change thing in her pocket the way he does. Who else could she be?

Maddie spun a plausible lie. "I overheard it in the post office yesterday. I remember now."

"I don't believe it. She's half his age."

"I doubt it."

The two were five years apart. But the sister looked young for her years, and the brother carried thoughts of war and savagery with him everywhere he went. Joan was right: he looked burned out. Maddie could see it in the apathetic lift of his shoulders after the woman said something. It was such a tired-looking shrug.

Norah was watching Maddie more carefully now. She folded her forearms across her implanted breasts and splayed her red-tipped fingers on her upper arms. "What else did you manage to . . . overhear, in the post office?" The question dripped with skepticism.

Maddie met her friend's steady gaze with one almost as good. "That was pretty much it. It was crowded. You know how little the lobby is. They took the conversation outside."

"Who were they? Man? Woman? Did you recognize them from town?"

"Two women, as I recall. I didn't bother turning around to see who. As I've said, I'm not really interested."

Norah cocked her head. Her lined lips curled into a faint smile. Her eyes, the color of water found nowhere in New England, narrowed. "Really."

"Okay, they're getting into the Jeep!" Joan cried. "Now what?"

"We follow 'em. Let's go!"

Maddie stared agape as the two made a dash for the half-open Dutch door that led to the seashelled drive of the Cape Cod cottage. "Are you out of your minds? What do you hope to accomplish?"

Norah slapped the enormous glove-soft carryall she'd slung over her shoulder. "I have a camera," she said on her way out.

"You're going to photograph them?"

"If we don't, the paparazzi will!"

She had her Mercedes in gear before Joan was able to snap her seat belt shut. The top of the convertible was down, of course, the better for Norah to be seen. Maddie watched, boggled, as the two took off in a cloud of dust, Norah pumping her fist in a war whoop the whole time.

The episode bordered on the surreal: an educated, beautiful forty-year-old woman and an even more educated thirty-eight-year-old one, tracking down a media celebrity like two hound dogs after some felon in the bayou. All they needed was Maddie in the rumble seat and there they'd be: Three perfect Stooges.

She closed the lower half of the Dutch door, and then, because she felt a sudden and entirely irrational chill, closed the upper half. June meant nothing on the Cape. June could go from warm and wonderful to bone-chilling cold in the blink of an eye.

June had done just that.

Chapter 2

Maddie Regan woke to the sound of rain drumming on the roof of her gabled bedroom. She had told herself many times during the long, snowy winter that it wouldn't matter whether her first morning in Rosedale was bright or dreary, warm or wet; she would love it just the same.

But she was wrong. It might as well have been raining volcanic ash. Her mouth felt dry, her brain, incapable of reason. Like some villager caught in the shadow of a violent eruption, she had become paralyzed by events.

She simply could not make herself move. The usually jolting aroma of Starbucks coffee drifting up from the kitchen did nothing to pry her from her bed, nor did the awareness that the new lace curtains on the windows were getting soaked by the rain.

Why him? Why here? Why now? The questions rolled with numbing repetition through the haze of her thoughts.

Aiming those binoculars at the lighthouse yesterday had been one of the most painful things that Maddie had ever done—nearly as painful as identifying her father. She had no idea, even now, why she'd let Norah goad her into it. Until then, Maddie's plan for dealing with Dan Hawke had been simple: ignore him. Smile, if pressed, and say good morning, evening, whatever. Be civil. No more, no less.

She could do that. She had convinced herself that it was entirely doable.

But then she had focused the binoculars and was nearly knocked down by the wave of resentment that roared over her. Twenty years of insulating herself—where had they gone? Twenty years of burying the memory of him under layers of birthdays and marriage and teaching and babies and summers and colds and tuition and car pools and death and divorce. Twenty years. A lifetime of layers, stripped away by the simple sight of him standing in front of the lighthouse.

Yesterday the depth of her resentment, the sheer rawness of her emotions, had amazed her.

And today she couldn't move.

I'm like some trauma victim. I'm lying here waiting for an ambulance to arrive.

But ambulances did not come running for flashback victims. That's what psychologists were for. Maddie could mull over her feelings with a professional for two hundred dollars an hour—or she could save herself some cash with a little common sense.

Get your butt out of bed and get on with your life. What're you waiting for? A special invitation?

But still she lay, listening to the rain, trying to focus on the twenty years rather than those twenty weeks.

Eventually Maddie was forced out of bed by the deep chime of the doorbell. She glanced at the clock: nine-thirty. Norah and Joan weren't due until lunchtime. Probably a couple of college kids, offering to clean house for the summer.

She waited. The chimes sounded again. Would Tracey possibly rouse herself from sleep to get the door? Would any teenager, on a rainy Saturday morning?

Grabbing a robe of daffodil yellow, Maddie made her way down the painted white stairs. She opened the door to see Trixie Roiters standing under a huge black umbrella and holding a Cruller's bakery box tied with a narrow red ribbon.

The rain bounced on the umbrella and rolled off in a dozen different streams, but the sixty-five-year-old woman standing underneath was both cheerful and dry. A warm smile pushed plump cheeks nearer to her startlingly blue eyes as she said, "Oh, dear, still in bed? I wanted to catch you before you went out on errands, but . . . should I come back another time?''

''Hello, Mrs. Roiters. No, no, I should be up and about, anyway. I . . . I thought I might be coming down with something, that's all. But I'm sure I'm fine. Come in.''

She accepted the bakery box with thanks as the older woman collapsed her umbrella, shook it free of rain, and dumped it in the Chinese porcelain stand near the paneled front door.

''When does your mother arrive?'' Mrs. Roiters asked as she followed Maddie into the kitchen. ''I hope she's doing well,'' she added in a kindly voice.

''She's coming along,'' said Maddie. ''I plan to drive up to Sudbury next weekend for her. I need to drop by the university in any case, so it'll work out well. Coffee?''

''Only if you have time, dear. Will your brother be coming to Sandy Point anytime soon? Or is Claire too far along?''

''The baby's not due until September. I'm expecting George and Claire to arrive in time for the fireworks, the same as usual.''

''Good. Last year we hardly saw any of you.''

''Yes . . . last year. But we're all hoping that this summer will be more normal.''

''It's bound to be,'' said Mrs. Roiters in her reassuring way. ''And Tracey? How is she? I thought of her last September—starting prep school, meeting a whole new crowd, and having to deal with your awful tragedy all at the same time. Is *she* all right?''

From anyone else, the endless questions might seem prying. But Trixie Roiters really did care. Underneath her curiosity was old-fashioned, neighborly concern. The woman was a fourth-generation Sandy Pointer, the official welcoming committee to every new year-round and summer resident alike. You simply couldn't not answer Trixie Roiters.

Maddie sighed and filled a stoneware cup with coffee. ''It was rough,'' she admitted. ''You know how girls are at that age. They cringe if they're the center of any kind of negative attention, and it doesn't get much more negative than murder." She had to steel herself to say the word.

Mrs. Roiters pressed four fingers into her cheek and shook her head. "Dreadful . . . dreadful. Well, it's behind you now."

The cup was too full; coffee slopped over as Maddie set it before her guest. "But it's not behind us, really, is it?" she said softly. "It never can be."

"Well, I know . . . in the sense that they haven't found out who murdered your father, but . . . I mean, time *is* passing. And time heals all wounds, so they say."

"So they say." And damn them—they lied.

Mrs. Roiters dipped her paper napkin in the saucer to siphon off the coffee puddle lolling there. "I don't suppose the investigation has turned up anything lately?"

Maddie shook her head. In a flat voice, as though she were reciting the Pledge of Allegiance, she said, "But the case is still open. Sometimes these things go on for years before the police catch a break. It hasn't been that long, really. Fourteen months. The investigating officer is very dedicated. He hasn't given up by any means."

"Carjackings! I'm sorry I've lived long enough to see them. We may as well be living in the Old West. To tell the truth, I'd feel safer in a stagecoach than I do in my Buick."

Maddie had to smile at the thought of Mrs. Roiters cowering in her Buick as she drove around the village. "But you live in Sandy Point, Mrs. Roiters. Most of us don't even lock our doors. I've summered here all my life, and I can't remember a single serious crime being committed."

"I suppose you're right. After all, your father was nowhere near here when he—"

"Yes," said Maddie quickly. The veil came down again. "Nowhere near."

Maddie refused to go into all that again. The details of the murder had unfolded in agonizing bits and pieces, and it seemed to her that for the last year and two months, she'd had to talk about it—at times like these—in similar bits and pieces: her dad's brand new Accord, discovered in the Norfolk parking lot of the Boston T; the continuing nightmare of his disappearance; the eventual discovery of his body in the ditch off a winding country road nearby; the relentless lack of clues. The discovery of the crime had dragged on, and the mystery of it was dragging on still.

Suddenly Mrs. Roiters pulled out a Kleenex, dabbed at her baggy eyes, and blew her nose loudly. "I'm sorry, dear. I got such a vivid picture of him at Town Meeting, arguing against that developer. It came on me sudden. He was such a good speaker. I always said, he should've run for office."

"He always told the truth," Maddie said simply. "He never played politics. I imagine he would've made a terrible official."

"He was a good man. You must miss him."

Maddie nodded. After a minute she made herself say, "The cardamom cake is wonderful. I wish I had their recipe."

She may as well have been chewing on a handful of Tums. It didn't seem possible that her mood this morning could get any lower, but there it went—sliding, sliding into a deeper pit.

Mrs. Roiters cleared her throat and said, "You know, I have a reason for barging in on you so soon after your arrival, Maddie. Ordinarily I would work things out for myself, but this case is a little tricky . . . he's a little tricky."

"Who is?"

"Dan Hawke. I've heard that he wants to keep a real low profile this summer, and that's fine, but . . . well, you can see that I would need an interview with him for the *Crier*. Just a little one would do. What kind of credibility would the *Crier* have if I ignored his stay here? He's a high-profile visitor."

Maddie refrained from pointing out that the *Sandy Point Crier* was regarded by the summer colonists with more affection than respect and said faintly, "I don't see where I fit in."

"I've heard," Mrs. Roiters said with an oddly tender smile, "that you once knew him."

Maddie blinked. "Whoever gave you that idea?"

"Oh," said the older woman, bobbing her head from side to side, "you know how people talk."

People talked? But who could possibly have known? He'd only stayed in Sandy Point for two weeks. He'd been just another college kid, part of a summer painting crew. Maddie had talked to him in front of the lighthouse a total of three times. They hadn't started dating until they were at Lowell College, and even then she'd kept it secret. Her mother would not have approved of a man like Daniel Hawke.

Twenty years ago. It was downright scary to think that someone could've remembered them talking in front of the lighthouse an entire generation earlier.

She tried to phrase an acceptable lie. "Mrs. Roiters, I don't know who told you that Dan Hawke and I are friends, but we're not."

It didn't work. Mrs. Roiters sighed and said, "You know, I'm not surprised. He travels; he's famous. Friends like that have a tendency to get out of touch."

Maddie shook her head doggedly. "It wasn't a question of getting out of touch. He is not my friend. He never was my friend."

Things had roared along too fast to have paused at friendship.

"I don't blame you in the least for being hurt, dear. He has no right to have a swelled head just because someone began aiming a camera at him. It happens all the time, I suppose. But frankly, I'm disappointed. I assumed he was better than that."

"No, that isn't what—"

"Mom, I *really* don't want to stay in the attic bedroom this summer. I *know* there's bats in the other half."

Her daughter was up. And running.

"Hello, Tracey!" said Mrs. Roiters in an overly cheerful way. "My goodness, how you've grown!" she added as she sliced a second, more generous chunk of coffee cake for herself. "You must be taller than anyone else in your class."

Reddening, the girl mumbled, " 'Lo, Mrs. Roiters," and turned back to her mother. "Why can't someone else take that room this year?" she said in a petulant, sleepy croak. "I was up all night, listening to stuff. Why do *I* always have to be the one who gets stuck with the worst of everything? Dad says—''

''Honey, why don't we talk about that later? We have a visitor right now,'' Maddie said in mild reproach.

Tracey acted, of course, as if she'd been slapped. Her eyebrows, pale and unshaped, slanted upward in a tragic way, and her cheeks puffed out from the force of her sigh. She gave her mother a burning, stricken look—and waited.

She was so very good at it. In the last year or so, Tracey had perfected sullenness to an art form. She was convinced she was ugly—and when she assumed that infuriating look, Maddie was tempted to agree.

As with most teenagers, Tracey's hormones were running wild. The growth spurt was only the tip of the iceberg. Her skin had begun to flare up, which made her give up chocolate and soon all food altogether. Getting her to eat was a constant battle in any case; she'd become obsessed with her weight. She should've had braces a year ago, but a year ago, they were all too busy avoiding the press. After seeing herself on page one with her face twisted in grief, Tracey had begged her mother to wait on the braces. They were still waiting.

''All right,'' Maddie said at last. ''Take your grandmother's room. She's been complaining about the stairs anyway. I'll clear out the study for her to use if—when—she comes down from Sudbury.''

Tracey said reproachfully, ''Too bad you had to wait 'til I unpacked.'' With a brooding look, she dragged herself out of the kitchen.

She was somewhere in the hall when Mrs. Roiters said with affection, ''She's so tall. And her nose, oh dear, it's still too big for her face, isn't it? You see it so often in girls her age.''

Maddie heard her daughter's pace quicken on the checkerboard floor of the hall and then the tragic stomping of feet up the stairs.

After a disastrously long pause, Mrs. Roiters added, ''Still, once she gets through that ugly-duckling phase, she's going to be a real beauty. She'll have her father's good looks—blond and loose and elegant. You'll see.''

This is going to set Tracey's therapy back half a year, thought Maddie, wincing inside. Not that it mattered. Counseling didn't seem to be helping at all. The murder of her grandfather fourteen months ago had delivered the knockout blow to Tracey's innocence—but Maddie's divorce from Michael, three years before that, had delivered the first hard punch.

Dear God, what are we doing to our children? Maddie asked herself with a shudder, not for the first time. She rallied to her daughter's defense. "I remember when I was a teenager. It was a homely, awkward time."

"My dear, *I* remember when you were a teenager, and I thought you were wonderful: a regular young lady, even then. Very well brought up. Enterprising, too. I can see you still, walking half a dozen dogs at a time for the summer folks. And you always cleaned up after. Very nice. Children today, well, they're not the same."

Mrs. Roiters cast a longing glance in the general direction of the coffee cake, then sighed and stood up. "So when do you think would be a good time?" she asked Maddie.

"To—?"

"Take a walk over to the lighthouse," said the irrepressible woman. "If you truly don't want me to come with you, I suppose you can just give him my card and plead my case for me. Tell him I only need half an hour. An hour at most. Maybe two. No, better not say two."

From the back of the rush-seated chair she unhooked her purse, then fished around in it. The card that she handed Maddie said

The Sandy Point Crier
Trixie Roiters, Editor & Publisher

All the News That's Fit to Print—
And Some That Isn't

"He's here to write a tell-all memoir, you know," she told Maddie in an undertone. "I understand that Ted Turner,

among others, is going to be taking it on the chin. And Mr.
Hawke will have something *very* interesting to say about Wal-
ter Cronkite. . . .''

Maddie was agape. ''Who on earth is telling you all this?''

Mrs. Roiters flicked a wrist at Maddie and said, ''That's
confidential, dear; you know that.''

A smile, a hug, and she was off, leaving an amazed Maddie
to wonder whether Sandy Point had been infiltrated by the
C.I.A.

Who was the source of all the gossip? Who knew both
about her past with Daniel Hawke and the chapter headings
of his memoirs, for pity's sake? Maddie racked her brain,
trying to remember who could have seen her, a college freshman, clamming on the beach in front of the lighthouse those
two or three times.

Jimmy Gordon saw her. She remembered envying the local
quahogger as he waved, then raked in quahogs by the bushel
from his work skiff while she poked laboriously at every air-
hole on the beach, struggling to gather a decent quota so that
her dad could make chowder for the Labor Day picnic.

Would Jimmy even have noticed when Dan Hawke first
wandered down from the lighthouse during a break from
whitewashing it, saw her Lowell College sweatshirt, and chatted her up?

Jimmy wouldn't have noticed. Jimmy wouldn't have cared.
And Jimmy certainly wouldn't have remembered if he had.

Who else? The Lawsons? They were relentless busybodies
and they had a view of the lighthouse. The Tilleys . . . the
Nichols . . . the Wrights. Those were the only families still
around from back then, and Maddie was willing to bet a
whole bushel and a peck of clams that they'd seen nothing
then, and had said nothing now.

Could Dan have told his sister—if that's who she was—
about Maddie and him and the disastrous event at Lowell
College? It didn't seem likely; he guarded his personal life
fiercely. Once, anyway.

Unless . . . was he trying to get some buzz going about the
memoirs he was planning to write? In that case, he'd be more

than happy to give Trixie Roiters an interview for her community rag. And Mrs. Roiters wouldn't need Maddie at all.

She sat back down and reread the card.

> All the News That's Fit to Print—
> And Some That Isn't

Too much. Because of Dan Hawke, Maddie had stopped watching CNN. Now she'd have to stop reading the charming, silly, folksy *Crier* as well. She broke off a corner of coffee cake and popped it into her mouth.

It still tasted like Tums.

Chapter 3

By noon the rain had let up; by one, the sun was out. It was hard not to be happy in Rosedale Cottage when the windows were thrown open to the garden, and Maddie found herself humming a tune as she put on a hat and went wandering through her perennials, snipping and pruning and inhaling deeply from old world roses that tumbled over the knee-high picket fence.

The heavy work—the weeding, the mulching, the early spring pruning—had already been done, compliments of a maniacal neighbor with too small a yard of his own to keep himself busy. All that remained for Maddie to do, basically, was to enjoy one of the prettiest gardens in Sandy Point.

She brought out wonderfully beat-up rattan chairs and arranged them around a makeshift table fashioned from an old, round, ironbound shop shingle that she'd found years ago at a yard sale. The shop's name, HMS *Bliss*, was written in ornate script on a background of hunter green. When she'd first dragged it home to clean it up and attach short legs to it, her father had mocked her scavenging ways. But after she set it up, if the weather was fair, he'd invariably have his lunch on that shop shingle, and he always drank his tea there.

It was an annual tradition with Maddie to wonder what kind of wares a shop called HMS *Bliss* would carry. Chocolates? Nautical supplies? No matter. For now, the name fit her mood. And in her bliss, she was extravagant: she cut a huge

armful of roses, whacking off whole branches of the flori-
bundas, letting the unopened buds on them go to waste.

No matter. Life was short.

She was standing at the cedar potting table alongside the
house, stripping the roses of their thorns, when Norah Mills
roared up in her milk white Mercedes with Joan MacDonald
hard on her heels in her dark blue Jeep. They were an hour
and a half late, but Maddie didn't mind at all.

Norah was first out of her car. The mood on her face did
not match the mood of her T-shirt, which proclaimed, "Life's
a Beach."

"Maddie! Where the hell were you? We cooled our heels
through two cocktails and a salad. Where were you? We
called three times!"

"Really? I guess I didn't hear the phone," Maddie confessed.

"I guess you didn't *want* to hear the phone!"

True enough. "I thought you two were coming here to pick
me up."

"That was Plan A," said Joan, freeing a pale pink rose to
slip through her straw hat. She sniffed the rose and smiled,
and her joy made her round face pretty. "Plan B was you'd
come meet us in your own car, because you didn't want to
go antiquing with us this afternoon. Remember?"

Actually, Maddie had been too upset to remember much of
anything yesterday, but she had no intention of admitting it.
"I do remember now. Sorry about that. Are you both stuffed,
or shall I make you something?"

No one was stuffed, not on a salad, but Norah would wire
her jaw shut with her own hands before she'd eat anything
substantial. Thin and rich, that's what got Norah's respect.
And Joan—Joan, who was neither thin nor rich—wanted Norah's respect, so she declined Maddie's offer as well.

"We stopped by to drop off Joannie's Jeep, that's all,"
said Norah with a queenlike wave of her hand. "We'll come
back for it later. Ciao."

"Oh, but—so soon?" The words fell from Maddie's lips

before she had a chance to snatch them back. "We've hardly had a chance to talk."

"Darling, that's what lunch was for. Two of the dealers are by appointment only, and we're late." Norah blew Maddie a kiss and turned to her sidekick. "Got your Visa?"

Short, dark-haired Joan patted the place where a six-shooter would hang and said, "Yup. Let's go." She loved shopping, loved it to the point that she'd maxed out her credit cards and had to resort to an equity loan to keep up with Norah.

Joan joked that shopping was cheaper than gambling as a hobby, and maybe she was right. But what she really wanted—what she'd made no secret of wanting—was a husband, two kids, and a cat. So far, all she had was the cat.

Maddie stood at the potting table, watching and smiling as the two women prepared to go off on their frivolous mission. She lasted until Norah turned the key to the ignition, and then she yielded to wretched temptation.

"Wait! You never said what happened at Annie's with Dan Hawke!"

Did it sound like an afterthought? She hoped so.

Norah said gaily, "Oh, that? It was a disaster. We went up to him, all polite and properly starry-eyed. I was on my best behavior, swear to God. After exchanging two sentences with us, he said, 'I'm sorry, but I'm having a private and rather important conversation. Would you mind? Thank you so much.' "

Joan covered her face at the memory, moaned, and said, "I've never been so embarrassed in my life."

Norah threw her head back and laughed, displaying a graceful curve of throat. "Joannie!" she hooted. "Who cares? The man puts his pants on one leg at a time, the same as everybody else. He's not worth blushing over. Oh, and Maddie? That was his sister, I'm sure of it. She was delivering some kind of good-natured harangue when we walked up to them. I doubt that a lover would dare."

With that, Norah threw her Mercedes into fast reverse, sending white quahog shells spinning beneath its tires. Maddie stared at the ruts created in the rain-soaked drive and shook her head. Her father would've felt vindicated: he'd wanted to go with asphalt.

But Maddie had overruled him, because she was a romantic. A cottage called Rosedale deserved a drive paved with seashells, she'd said. She remembered the wry look on her father's face as the dump truck rumbled up the sandy, pot-holed road past the ten other laid-back cottages that made up Cranberry Lane, and then emptied its load of horrendously stinky clamshells onto their driveway.

"The smell will go away," she'd insisted. And it had. But her father had never lived to know that.

Maddie sighed and tried not to look at the lighthouse as she carried the flower clippings out to the compost bin. She felt a sudden surge of indignation over Norah's driving. Really, the woman was impossible. From now on, Maddie would make her park in the lane.

All day, he'd had glimpses of her. In the garden; at the mailbox; coming and going past her kitchen window. But he hadn't yet got a good look at her, and it was killing him.

From where he was positioned—at a bedroom window that looked over a small bight of water toward her cottage—he could tell that she looked much the same. The granny-print dresses that were all the rage back then had made a comeback; she was wearing one now. And her hair—it was still the same reassuring warm brown, thank God, and not fashionably streaked with blonde. It was shorter now than waist-length, of course; less obviously erotic. When he saw her for the first time yesterday, he felt a pang that she'd cut most of it off. But by today he could see that she'd done the right thing. She wasn't a kid anymore.

And neither was he. That was the hell of it. Neither was he.

Were her eyebrows still thick and straight? Her eyes still denim blue? Did she still have that oddly lilting laugh? Had she had that chipped tooth capped? These were questions that consumed him as he worked ineffectually at the well-worn oak desk that came with the lightkeeper's house.

Her breasts, he remembered, were slightly uneven; she had been comically tragic about that. He prayed with all his heart that she hadn't gone and done something stupid to make them match.

He remembered all the rest of her body as well, but it was hard to tell now if her hips were the same, if her waist was as slender, if she'd gained or lost weight. The dress she wore was anything but revealing. It was a hell of a lot easier to see, for example, that the tall, flashy redhead had a dynamite body and that her short, dark-haired friend didn't.

He'd been able to see them clearly enough as they got into the Mercedes, though he scarcely remembered them from Annie's. But Maddie? Blocked by the damned house. For two cents he'd bulldoze it. Make her homeless. Make her seek comfort and refuge in the keeper's house. Make her seek him.

At least then he could see her up close. He had the profound sense that if he could just see her, up close, he would know. He'd know if she had the answer to a question he couldn't begin either to ask or to answer: Are you sorry?

He saw movement in the kitchen again, but again, he couldn't see a face. It may have been the girl, home now from an outing with her friends. How old was she? Fourteen? Fifteen? Where was he that many years ago? He thought about it and came up with a place: Africa, covering yet another civil war . . . yet another famine. People dead and dying . . . bodies everywhere . . . children too starved to cry.

God, how he hated it. Hated himself. Hated life.

He began instinctively to reach for a cigarette, and then, less instinctively, he resisted. He'd made a promise.

It was dusk. He couldn't keep up the pretense of reading if he wasn't going to turn on a light. Reluctantly, he lowered the ratty wood blind, turned on the green-glassed banker's lamp, and opened a political biography he had no desire to read. He stared at the same page for a full eternity, until it felt as if his eyes were beginning to cross.

"Damn," he muttered. He threw his head back, closed his eyes, and gulped a long, deep draft of air, then let it out in a brief explosion.

He turned off the lamp, pulled up the blind, and lit the cigarette after all. At least now he had some of what he craved: comfort and darkness. He pushed his chair deeper into shadow; it made a loud, scraping sound against the battered plank floors, jarring the stillness in the sparsely furnished room.

He smoked another cigarette, then a third, watching the windows of the cottage, thinking thoughts he had no right to think. It hadn't been so bad when Jess was there. She'd dragged him through an endless round of shopping, hitting every domestics department between Sandy Point and Boston. She seemed to believe his life wouldn't be complete without a sink rack, bathroom curtains, and a soup ladle, not to mention a thousand other gadgets and doo-hickeys without which the modern homemaker could not, apparently, survive.

But he was no homemaker. He couldn't see how he'd ever be a homemaker. Too much water had flowed under that bridge, carrying with it all those basic instincts to couple, to breed, to nurture. Maybe once . . . ?

But he doubted it.

He reached for the cigarette pack, then remembered—not that he'd actually forgotten—that it was empty. Jessie had made him promise that this pack would be his last, and he had honored all her hard work of the last three days by agreeing, again, to quit. In a way, he really did mean to. He had come back to this place, to this hallowed shore, armed with a fierce desire to get things right, whatever the hell that meant.

He smiled wryly to himself. Twenty years earlier, another nonsmoker had challenged his habit.

How can you smoke these things? she'd asked as she hunted down half a dozen butts from around the rock on the shell-strewn beach.

They clear my head, he'd replied. From his perch on the rock, he'd watched her groom the beach in front of the lighthouse before the tide had a chance to. She had rolled her pants up above her knees, but one of the cuffs had come undone and was sodden; he remembered it well. Her hair was so long that it grazed the water when she bent over to pluck a stray butt from an outgoing wave. He had a vivid picture of the way the chestnut strands floated like a silken starburst on the seawater. Venus Returns to the Sea. If it wasn't the name of a poem, it ought to've been.

She loved poetry. And he loved to hear her recite it. The stuff was harmless enough, if irrelevant, so he used to seek out quiet corners with her on the campus green where he could listen to the rich, low caress of her voice without the chatter and clatter of students around them.

She liked the pre-Raphaelites. And he, who had no room in his curriculum for bullshit like poetry, went out and bought a leatherbound, slender volume of their verse for her. He'd intended to give it to her for her birthday, but they never made it that far. He had the volume still, and he knew every single poem in it by heart. The book was ragged now, and falling apart. The leather had turned out not to be leather at all and he took the fraud to be symbolic. He just wasn't sure of what.

He sighed again, frustrated beyond measure with the general state of his ignorance, and reached for the pack of cigarettes.

Empty. Right.

He had an unopened pack in his overnight bag. He got up from his desk to retrieve it.

"Hey, gorgeous! How's my favorite woman in the world?"

"Dad! Hi! Where are you?"

"Right in town. At Annie's."

"Cool. Are you coming over?"

"That depends entirely on your mother. Is she around?"

Tracey's voice fell to a conspiratorial whisper—the tone she used whenever the subject was her mother. "Mom's out doing a stock-up. I have to stay home for when Mr. Chaves comes; we don't have any hot water."

"Bummer. That old house is a real bag of bones, isn't it?"

"Yeah, it sucks. Those bats are back in the attic—didn't I tell you they would be? And the roof's leaking over the bathroom ceiling again, so there's flakes of paint on the floor all the time, and when you walk in there barefoot, the flakes stick to your feet and you almost need tweezers to get them off. It's like, so totally gross. And it's *boring* here.'' Her voice trailed off in a tragic wail. "I can't believe we're back for another whole summer.''

Michael Regan laughed and said, "You used to like it well enough when you were a kid, Trace.''

"Yeah, when I was a baby. But, like, I'm *fourteen*, Dad. There's just nothing, nothing, *nothing* to do here. It's not like Boston. I wish I was back in Boston.''

"I wish you were, too, puddin'. I miss our routine when you go down there for the summer. This should've been our weekend.''

Tracey's sigh was loud and heartrending. "I don't see why you can't stay here some of the time. I mean, you're family, no matter what. And all the rest of the family gets to come and go. Why should Uncle George be able to stay here and not you? I mean, who cares about Uncle George? He drinks and he's mean and he makes fun of me. It isn't *fair*.''

"Honey, we've been through all that. You know that if I could, I would.''

"No, I *don't* know," she said petulantly. "Juliette's parents are divorced, and *her* father gets to stay over sometimes.''

"Well, your mother and I are not that kind of divorced.''

"How many kinds of divorce are there? It's not like Mom's seeing anyone.''

"You mean, at all? What happened to Eric?''

Her voice was a shrug. "He doesn't come around any more.''

"And that other one you talked about, the new guy in her English department—Gerald?''

"Oh, Gerald. I'm pretty sure he's gay.''

"You are, are you. Well. Since you're the expert—''

Tracey giggled and said, "I'm not an expert, Dad, but really. I'm pretty sure.''

"Well, I'm just glad I have you there to watch over your mother for me, Trace. I mean it. You're a sharp observer.

"I get that from you, Dad, don't I? That's what Mom says."

"She says that?"

"Well, yeah. And that we're both moody."

"So she still talks about me?"

"Of course! You're my father."

"Well, I'm glad she hasn't put all thoughts of me out in the recycle bin with my photographs."

"No way! She even has some wedding pictures, you know. A bunch! I found them in her room."

"Really. Now that's interesting. Huh."

"Dad?"

"Hmm?"

Tracey's voice dropped even lower. "I really need you to be here lately. I mean, Mom is just coming down on me so hard. The older I get, the more she comes down. Like, I wanted to go to Great Woods to see Jimmy Buffet with a bunch of other kids? They were mostly older, but Juliette's my age. And like, it was Jimmy Buffet, not Nine Inch Nails. Like, it would've been so . . . so . . ."

"Innocuous?"

"So innocent. She just won't trust me!"

"Never mind, honey. The next time he has a concert there, I'll take you myself. Promise."

"Yeah, but it won't be the—well, anyway, if it was up to you, I could've gone. Right?"

"Probably."

"Y'know, I bet I *still* wouldn't have a pierced navel if it wasn't for you."

"Hey, no one sees a navel. I say that's your own private business. Your mother overreacted on that one."

"She overreacts on everything, Dad! That's just it!"

"I know. I know."

"It really isn't fair. She's so uptight."

There was a grudge in his voice as he said, "Tell me something I don't know, honey."

"I mean, every time she uses the word 'teenage,' it always has something bad after it. Teenage drinking, teenage drugs,

teenage sex. She's always lecturing. I was taking off nail polish the other day? She starts nagging about not sniffing the
remover. Sometimes I think she watches too much television.
It's warping her brain.''

Michael laughed and said to his daughter, ''An interesting
point of view.''

''And she's been so weird since we got here. First she's in
a sucky mood, then a good, then a sucky. I mean, she calls
me temperamental. Da-ad! Do something!''

''All right. When I see your mother I'll—''

''Oh! Doorbell! It must be Mr. Chaves. I gotta go. Come
over now, Dad, please please please!''

She hung up without waiting for his answer, confident, no
doubt, that her dad was as good as on his way to Rosedale
Cottage.

Michael let his hand linger on the receiver of the wall-
mounted phone; he was tempted to call his daughter back and
caution her that he had to go through channels.

Channels! It was idiotic to have to ask Maddie for permission to see his own daughter. Four years of that crap had left
him doubting his own competence as a father. All that bowing
and scraping, just because some goddamned judge had decreed where and when he'd have access to his own child!

He frowned, then stepped around a huge hanging pot of
ivy and scanned the café's checker-clothed tables. His back
had been to the tables while he was talking with Tracey. Now
he noticed that Trixie Roiters, Town Busybody, had stopped
in for coffee. The woman had ears like an elephant; no way
was he going to humiliate himself in front of her by calling
Tracey back.

Piss on it, he thought bitterly. I can see my own daughter
if I want to. He made up his mind to go straight to the cottage.

Chapter 4

By the time he arrived at Rosedale, Maddie was there, unloading groceries from her Taurus.

He pulled in behind her on the crunchy drive and emerged from his car with a smile. "So you went with the quahog shells after all."

Her return smile wasn't hostile, but it wasn't warm and fuzzy, either. Somehow he'd convinced himself that Maddie would be pleasantly surprised, rather than merely surprised, to see him.

"Hello, Michael," she said. "Are you in town on business, or on pleasure?"

"A little of both, actually. My tenant vacated the condo early. I had to come down to check it out and decide what to do about his deposit."

She nodded in sympathy. "Will you be able to rent it for July and August?"

"Without a doubt. And they tell me summer rents are out of sight this year," he added with a grin. He looped his fingers through six of the heaviest plastic bags of groceries that lay sprawled in the back of the wagon and lifted them out with a grunt.

Hoisting several others, Maddie said, "In that case, I guess you'll be giving your tenant back his deposit."

Michael declined to tell her that he had no such plans. He followed her inside and stood in the kitchen while she unpacked, watching the play of sunlight on her hair, catching a scent of her perfume as she passed under his nose for another bag of groceries to put away.

As always, their talk turned to Tracey. As always, he had to watch what he said. "I thought, since I was in town, that I'd take Trace out for a burger and a movie, if that's all right with you." Beg, grovel, *damn* the judge to hell.

Maddie was arranging cans of tomato products in a pyramid of big to small: whole, stewed, sauce, and paste. "Sure," she said. "What's playing? I haven't paid attention."

"Some Mel Gibson thing. She still likes Mel Gibson, doesn't she?" he asked, handing his ex-wife a couple of overlooked cans of plum tomatoes.

Maddie stepped down from the wood footstool and turned to him with an on-second-thought look on her face.

"It's a thriller, isn't it?" she said quietly. "They're always so violent."

"It's a shoot-'em-up cartoon, is all it amounts to," he answered, defending his choice.

"Bullets are bullets."

She was thinking of one bullet in particular, he could see.

"For God's sake—they use *blanks* in the movie, Maddie!"

The look in her eyes—stricken, combative, aloof—made him say quickly, "I'm sorry. I didn't mean to snap."

"You never do."

"I'm sorry, honest."

Where the hell was Tracey? He cocked his head, listening to the rush of water through the plumbing in the kitchen wall. "Still showering," he said with a look of wonder. "I can't believe your well doesn't run dry."

Maddie laughed and said, "The furnace was out. We had no hot water all morning. It turns out that a fuse shook loose above the boiler, but we needed a plumber to figure that out for us. It took him two seconds. Dad would've—anyway, Tracey was forced to go four extra hours without a shower. Naturally she needs to compensate."

They exchanged a wry look of commiseration. On this, at

least, they were agreed: their little girl had a daunting standard of hygiene.

His gaze drifted from Maddie's blue eyes to Maddie's blue jeans. She filled them out well. She had always filled them out well. He shifted his focus. If she saw him staring, she'd terminate the visit on the spot. He decided, arbitrarily, to admire a hand-thrown mug in the dishrack.

"Is that new?" he asked, pointing to it. He'd taught a pottery course or two before he began teaching painting, so the question was more or less reasonable.

Maddie lifted the green-glazed cup from the sink and swung it by its loop. "Is that a hint?" she asked with a wry look. "I was about to put on a pot."

"Yeah . . . thanks. I could use some."

He pulled out one of the rush-seated chairs and sat down on it. He missed this. Missed the kitchen. Missed the way late-morning sun poured in, washing the pickled-pine cabinets and red country wallpaper in clear, bright light. Some kitchens—this kitchen—begged to be filled with family. He felt right, in this kitchen.

He drew an imaginary outline of Maddie's face on the tabletop as she moved around the room on automatic, putting together Starbucks and Melitta. They shared that, too, he realized: a love of high-octane coffee.

While Maddie chatted on about the new head of her department, he decided that they shared—or had shared—a lot of things. Food, sex, a kid, college, Sandy Point, sailing, books, most movies—they'd done them all in their fifteen years of marriage. Trouble was, he'd gone and done a little extra.

She should've been more forgiving. She's had lovestruck freshmen hanging on her every word in class, too. It comes with the territory. She knows that. Banging a student doesn't mean a thing. If she didn't know that, she should have.

For Pete's sake—he was an *art* professor.

Besides, that was over now. He'd lost his taste for wanton sex—maybe because now he was free to have all the wanton sex he wanted. Or maybe it was the headaches. They seemed to be coming more frequently now, and staying longer. Some days—especially if they'd kept him late at the lab the night before, testing him—he wanted nothing more than to go home, put up his feet, and close his eyes. It was all he could do to make it through his posted office hours, never mind making the effort to seduce a student during them.

Damned headaches. Seized by a dread of one of them returning, he rubbed his forehead with his fingers and grimaced, baring his teeth in the process.

"What's wrong, Michael?" she asked, watching him warily. "Headache again?"

"No, just the fear of one."

"You should see a doctor about them. You never used to get headaches. Maybe you need glasses."

"Come on—at my age?"

She smiled at that. "It's been known to happen, after forty."

"Well, it's not going to happen to me."

Her smile turned wary. "Michael, you can be so—"

"Spare me the 'immature' speech, please! I know it by heart."

She stiffened, as if he were a stranger who had stepped too quickly into an elevator she was taking; and then she walked deliberately out of the kitchen to the foot of the stairs.

"Tracey!" she called up. "Your father's here."

Michael Regan.

Christ, he hadn't changed. He was the same fair-haired preppie, straight out of a Lands' End catalog. Christ! Didn't that type ever age?

Hawke grabbed the binoculars from the bedroom desk and zeroed in on his old classmate. He was wrong: time had made at least some inroads. There was a certain puffiness around the jowls, a certain thickness under the pale blue polo shirt. He felt a surge of petty satisfaction seeing it. Nonetheless, Michael Regan was the kind of man that a woman might say was "still good-looking."

Shit.

It gave Hawke no pleasure to watch Michael wave to Maddie, hold the door open for the girl, and get behind the wheel of the vintage Beemer.

Michael would be back. He had visitation rights, obviously, and he would be back. The good news was, Mike and Maddie were divorced. The bad news was, they had a family. They shared common ground.

Were they divorced? The evidence said yes. Hawke had looked them up in an an on-line directory for Sandy Point and found her still listed at Cranberry Lane, but him on Overlook Road. But whether they were divorced or not, his own mission would've been the same: a return to this sacred place, to where it all began.

Without thinking, Hawke swung the glasses from the Beemer to Maddie. At the same moment, she turned to stare in the direction of the lighthouse—it seemed to him, to stare at the second floor window of the keeper's house.

There she was in his field of view: close enough to touch. It gave Hawke a jolt; he put down the glasses and retreated farther into shadow. He had vowed not to use the binoculars on her. He had vowed to let her have at least an iota of privacy.

For now.

From the brick patio they had a perfect view of the setting sun. The scene was textbook New England: a faded sky dissolving into a cauldron of liquid amber behind a brooding sea. Overhead, half a dozen sea gulls arched, their graceful flight at odds with their shrill, warlike calls.

Between the sea gulls and the sea, between Maddie and the setting sun, stood the keeper's house and its attached lighthouse, topped by a darkened lantern that no longer warned mariners away from the shallow, treacherous run of coast.

Was Dan home? Maddie had no idea; she could see only a bit of the lighthouse itself from the patio, and not the keeper's house to which it was attached.

She fingered the condensation on the glass of her rum

punch and tried to seem enthusiastic about Norah's latest find: a Tiffany bronze and favrile crocus lamp, poised on display in the middle of the HMS *Bliss* table. Norah owned a contemporary house on the water, sparingly furnished. But she collected Tiffanies the way some women collected Hummels, and she was especially pleased with this one.

Joan hadn't come back empty-handed, either. She held on her lap a Ruskin Pottery stoneware vase glazed in a mottled oatmeal color. It was plain, it was chipped, but it was something. She'd come back with something, and that's what mattered to her. She propped the vase on her knees, much the way she would a year-old baby, and made cooing sounds of pleasure while Norah held forth on the exploding value of Tiffany art.

Sundowners at Rosedale. It should've been fun. But Maddie's thoughts were somewhere else entirely.

He's in there now. I know he is. I can almost feel his presence. The keeper's house has had tenants before; that's nothing new. But it's not the same. I've never felt such fear before, such apprehension.

The hair on the back of her neck was literally standing on end. Earlier in the day, as Michael was loading Tracey into his BMW, Maddie had felt a tremendous, almost preternatural pull in the direction of the lightkeeper's house. Against her will she'd found herself staring at one of the second-floor windows, though she knew that the room behind it, the shabbiest in the house, had always been used for storage. It was the other two bedrooms that had the spectacular views. So why was she so convinced that Dan Hawke had been in the one that looked back at her cottage?

Because my heart began beating in a new rhythm altogether, she told herself. For no more reason than that.

Her thoughts were sliced abruptly in half by a single, knife-like word: lighthouse. Norah was talking about it.

"It's painful to watch. One or two more hurricanes," Norah was saying, "and the house and tower will be swept out to sea like a box and a styrofoam cup."

Joan stirred the grenadine at the bottom of her rum punch;

the drink turned from the colors of the sunset to a solid, garish pink. "Don't be silly. It's been there a hundred years."

"And we're losing beachfront at an average rate of half a foot a year, even without hurricanes. Look where it's standing even as we speak. Do the math, Joannie."

"I teach history, not algebra. You do the math."

"I have," said Norah. "And I say the lighthouse is doomed, unless . . ."

Maddie was grateful that the talk was of the lighthouse and not its tenant. "Unless what?"

"We save it. You and Joan and I, and others who love it as much as we do. We have to save it. Let's face it: the owner's not going to. He doesn't have the money. Very few people do, and the ones that do aren't about to throw it into what is basically a hole in the ocean."

"So how do you propose we save it?" asked Joan. "Pile sandbags in front of it?"

"*Très amusant.* No, we do what everybody else does when their local lighthouse is at risk: we form a nonprofit foundation. We'll call it Friends of Sandy Point Light, and we'll raise the funds to move the house and tower inland a few hundred yards. Simple."

Norah leaned back and drummed her fingertips on the shop-shingle tabletop. Napoleon had probably struck a similar pose when he decided to move his army across Russia.

"Wow. Move the lighthouse. Wow." Joan, at least, was impressed.

Maddie, not so much. "Oh, sure, just like that," she said with a breezy snap of her fingers. She cocked her head appraisingly and added, "But let me ask you, Norah: why now?"

"It's pretty much now or never," Norah said, surprisingly serious. "I have a friend who was involved in the effort to move Southeast Light on Block Island. He thinks we've waited too long as it is. You can't decide to go ahead when the waves are lapping at the tower. I mean, look at the rock out there—the one all by itself in the water. They tell me that

that rock was once high and dry on the sand, and not all that long ago, either.''

"It was about twenty years ago," Maddie said quietly. She knew the rock like the back of her hand. It had a hollow on the top of it where a man could sit and smoke a cigarette, if he were so inclined.

And he had been inclined. No matter how much she'd teased and chided and coaxed, he had been inclined. He hadn't stopped smoking for her. She'd never really had that much influence over him; she realized that now. She'd thought for a while there. . . . when he had seemed to respond so positively to her poetry readings, to life's quieter pleasures . . . . But it hadn't lasted. He was a firebrand and a hothead, and he had ruined a family with his impulsiveness.

A whole family.

"Maddie, c'mon! It's not that bad an idea," Joan said, coming to Norah's defense. "You look as if you've just been asked to mail a letter bomb."

"No, no, not at all," Maddie said, rallying what enthusiasm she could. "It's just that . . . Norah, a *foundation*? The only foundations I know about have cement in them."

"No-o problem." Norah hooked a sandaled foot under a nearby wicker ottoman and pulled it toward her. Crossing her ankles demurely on it, she locked her hands together in front of her and stretched her arms out full length. Her private smile became a quiet boast as she fastened her Caribbean-blue gaze on Maddie.

"I have a gentleman friend," she explained.

That's all she had to say. Maddie and Joan exchanged looks. Norah had a gentleman friend for every conceivable situation. If you needed a stone wall built, an airtight will drawn up, tickets to a Bulls' game, or a man's legs broken, Norah had a gentleman friend who could do the job, and probably gratis. God only knew how she enslaved such a wide variety of talent, but enslaved they were. In Norah's mind, at least, the lighthouse and the keeper's house were as good as moved.

"It won't be easy," she admitted. "We'll need everyone's

cooperation. Old man Mendoza will have to sell it for a song—which is a song more than he'll have if the whole property washes out to sea. And we'll have to get variances from the planning board. That shouldn't be hard. We have a dearth of tourist attractions—one, to be precise—and this is it.''

Warming to the concept, Joan said, ''Maybe we can get the town to buy it outright?''

''Probably not. This town hasn't been able to float a bond since Admiral Nelson went to sea. No, what we need is a single fat contribution to establish credibility, and all the rest will follow. Leave it to me.''

With a mixture of interest and dismay, Maddie had been watching Norah gather steam. Now she said bluntly, ''Okay, Norah. What's your agenda?'' Because everyone knew that Norah always, always had an agenda.

Norah favored her with a bland look. ''I have no idea what you mean.''

Maddie wasn't fooled. Norah loved power, money, and men. Saving the lighthouse with Dan Hawke still in it combined all three.

After a pause, Norah said, ''Someone will have to approach Dan Hawke about the relocation effort, once the time is right. We don't want the landlord being the one to tell him. Mr. Mendoza isn't the most congenial man, and Mr. Hawke might refuse to cooperate, depending on his lease, I suppose.''

''You can persuade him if anyone can,'' Joan said.

Norah batted her lashes once or twice and said, ''I may have to do that.''

Dan Hawke and Norah Mills: they were a daunting thought. Well, it couldn't be helped, Maddie decided. Sooner or later they were bound to find one another. Reckless meets Abandon—they were a match made in romance novels.

Think about something else, she told herself, shutting her eyes against the image of them together. Someone else. Anyone else.

Maddie stood up and said, ''You know what? I'm going to have to leave you two to finish off the pitcher on your own. If I don't get a bed moved into my father's office by the time my mother arrives, I'll be the one untangling bats from my hair.''

The mention of her father struck a sober chord. The two women decided to pack up their treasures and shove off, leaving Maddie to ponder a whole new set of concerns.

Save the lighthouse from being washed away? She was still trying to save herself and family from being washed away. Who had time to go door to door selling raffle tickets and chocolate bars? And if she did get involved, what then? There was simply no way that she'd be able to avoid Dan.

She glanced through her kitchen window at the lightkeeper's house, dark against a dark sky except for two rectangles of light that issued from it. One of them was from the storage room. That light had gone on and off at regular intervals since her arrival. Like Morse code, it seemed to be blinking a message. Or so she fancied. Her preoccupation with the white gabled structure was making her thoughts just a little on the strange side.

The Venetian blinds in that window were closed now, but earlier they'd been drawn all the way up. Earlier, she'd assumed that he'd needed good light, maybe to pick through the stored odds and ends that could be found in every house that was rented furnished. Now she wasn't so sure. Why would anyone bother to lower the blinds in a storage room?

And why on earth should she care? She was obsessing over trivia, acting more like a teenager than any teenager she'd known.

Idiot! Let it go!

The phone rang, making it easier to put an end to the idiocy. Maddie answered with a distracted hello.

After the briefest of pauses, a male voice said, ''Tracey?''

''No, this is her mother. Can I help you?''

The party quietly hung up, setting off at least one alarm in Maddie's vast array of them. The voice had sounded too old to be a boy Tracey's age, and too . . . at ease, somehow, to be a stranger. An older boy from a prep school, maybe? If so, it was an older boy with very bad manners.

Maddie would certainly ask Tracey about it, but the odds were slim that she'd get an answer.

Chapter 5

Surprisingly uneasy about the call, Maddie put away all evidence of her round of sundowners with Joan and Norah—the less drinking paraphernalia that Tracey and her friends were exposed to, the better—and crossed the hall, passing through French doors into her father's snug study. It wasn't the first time she'd been there since her father's death, but it was the first time she'd had no choice but to tackle his papers and personal effects. God knew, no one else was going to do it.

Sarah Timmons, leveled by grief, had scarcely stepped foot in the room since her husband's murder over a year ago. Looking around, it was easy for Maddie to see why. Grief was an odd and quirky thing. Sarah was able to sleep in her husband's bed and eat on his plates. But look at his handwriting on notes and papers? She simply couldn't do it.

Maddie's brother hadn't been any more anxious to clear out the study; but then, George was a man. Men didn't deal very well with death and loss. Like most men, George was keeping his feelings corked up in a Scotch bottle. He'd been aghast at the thought of counseling, and he'd turned thumbs down on the idea of a one-year memorial. But he brooded a lot, and he sniped at the family.

George was hurting too.

Maddie's sister certainly couldn't pack up the study. Suzette lived in France. She had flown over for the funeral, wept with them, and flown back. Suzette loved them all, and they all loved Suzette. They kept in touch. She had visited twice since the funeral. But . . . France.

That left Maddie. Maddie the middle one, caught between an overachieving brother and an underachieving sister. Maddie the loyal. Maddie the sentimental. Maddie the reliable. Maddie the traditional.

Maddie was closer than either of her siblings to her father. He had meant everything to her, and she was his darling. They had the kind of bond that Kodak was forever portraying in its commercials, and it had lasted until the day of his death.

She'd followed in his footsteps, taking her degree at the college where he'd taught, then going on to teach at a college herself. She loved Rosedale Cottage as much as he did; that also pleased him. And the lighthouse, too. They shared a life-long fascination with it. He had made some maudlin paintings of it; she had written some maudlin poems about it.

The two of them cared equally about Sandy Point. Whenever his wife wouldn't come to Town Meeting, Edward would drag his middle child along instead, teaching her how to be a good little citizen. He'd taught her to stand up for her principles, and always to do the right thing. Everyone had known that Maddie was his favorite, and no one had begrudged it.

But they did expect her to clear out the study.

Maddie took one of the empty cardboard boxes left over from her recent unpacking and set it down on the desk, then began emptying drawers. The desk was massively built of mahogany, its top scarred over the years by hundreds of embers that had flown from her father's pipe. She could picture him now, puffing it into life before tackling a pile of term papers or cracking open the spine of a book he had agreed to review. She fingered one of the deeper burn marks, and smiled at the memory of her mother's chronic scolding.

"You'll burn the house down one of these days, Edward," she'd say. "Can't you just *chew* the tobacco?"

And he'd answer, "My dear Sarah. The tobacco is not the point. The ritual is the point. Tamping the tobacco in the bowl, the feel of the wood cupped in my fingers, the flick of

the match, the puffing into life—*that's* why I smoke a pipe.''
Then he'd smile and blow his wife a smoke ring, and flick
another ash from the top of his desk.

Embers. Would they ever be extinguished? Maddie sighed.
How did you get over a murder when the murderer was still
out there somewhere? She shuddered, then resolved not to
think about it until she was done packing up the study. It was
such an impossible goal that it ended up being possible: Maddie simply shut down all of her brain except the part needed
to match boxes with contents. Heavy books—strong box. Unbound papers—shallow box. Paperbacks—beer box. Awards
and citations—the seat of the chair.

Late in the afternoon, Tracey phoned for permission to go
miniature golfing after the movie. By the time she got home,
Maddie had made a noticeable dent in the orderly chaos of
her father's private world.

''Did you have a good time?'' she asked her daughter,
intercepting her on the way upstairs.

''Sure.''

''What movie did you end up seeing?''

Tracey snorted. ''Something PG, you'll be glad to know.
Dad was afraid to take me to a PG-13.''

''Tracey, I never said you couldn't go to a—''

''Yes, you did! You always do!''

''I'm sorry you feel that way, honey. I think you're being
unfair.''

''*I'm* being unfair!'' Tracey rolled her eyes melodramatically and raised her arms shoulder high, then slapped them
against her sides. ''Fine. *I'm* being unfair. Fine!''

Without waiting for a response to that—and Maddie had
none—the girl burst into tears and ran the rest of the way up
the stairs to her room.

Sighing, Maddie tried to convince herself that Tracey's reaction was just another example of hormones gone amuck.
She went back into the study, determined to work off some
of her frustration over her daughter. But something had
changed. Maddie's thoughts, having been interrupted, were

not her own to control anymore. She actually began paying attention to what she was packing.

And what she was packing made her snap to attention.

It was a slip of paper, tucked too completely in the leather side pocket of the desk blotter to have been visible before. If Maddie hadn't stood the blotter on end against the wall, the corner of the paper would not have dropped into view. She pulled out the folded slip and read, in her father's handwriting, an hour and a date: 10:00, April 6.

There was no year, so it could have been any April 6, she supposed. But that didn't explain the pounding of her heart. On April 6, her father had disappeared. It was too uncanny to be coincidence.

She turned the paper over. Nothing. It was maddeningly cryptic.

It was easy to see how the police had missed the note, despite several passes through her father's effects. Maddie hadn't seen it, either, when she'd searched the room during the agonizing days before and after they found him.

Her first thought was to phone Detective Bailey about the discovery. She had his home number in Millwood and she had his assurances to call anytime. But those assurances had been given long ago; by now the detective's priorities had moved on.

It was late. Maddie decided to call him in the morning. It would give her time to consider whether the note was significant or not. But the night brought her no comfort, only a thousand dark corridors of possibilities. She wandered down every one of them before waking up tired and none the wiser.

She dreaded having to tell her family about the note. If her father *had* had an appointment on April 6, none of them knew about it. The police had questioned each of them thoroughly, as much to establish their alibis as to find out anything helpful regarding her father's whereabouts.

All that the family knew was that Edward Timmons had planned to spend the day ''bumming around Cambridge,'' which he did regularly. His typical routine was to visit the

Harvard Coop, buy a book or two, have coffee, take in the scene, and pick up pipe tobacco.

As always, he'd left Sudbury at six in the morning so that he could get a jump on traffic. No one had thought to question him thoroughly before he left. No one had thought they'd need to know.

And now this.

The disturbing note sat propped up against a Nantucket pepper grinder on the kitchen table while Maddie cooked up a batch of hollandaise sauce for eggs Benedict, Tracey's favorite breakfast. Every once in a while she'd glance at the slip of paper. Was it a clue—or wasn't it?

When the juice was poured, she yelled up again to her daughter. "Trace! Last call for breakfast!"

She heard the toilet flush and Tracey's voice come drifting down the hall stairs in a moan.

"I can't, Mom. I'm sick, really sick. I think I ate something funny yesterday."

Surprise, surprise. It was one of Tracey's favorite excuses for avoiding meals. "Shall I come up and take your temperature?" Maddie asked, knowing the answer full well.

"No . . . that's all right. I'll be okay in a little while."

Right. As soon as you hear the dishes being done.

Maddie sighed and went back into the kitchen to eat alone. Short of feeding her daughter intravenously, she had no real idea how to get food into her. There was a time when Maddie would have told herself to relax, that Tracey wouldn't let herself starve.

But she didn't necessarily believe that anymore. Two of Tracey's girlfriends were undergoing treatment for anorexia, and most of the rest were obsessed with being thin. Food was all they talked about, always in terms of how to avoid it.

It was sad and dangerous and all so wrong. What had happened to the outgoing little girl who used to play ball like a boy and had built her own treehouse? Overnight she'd turned into a melancholy bundle of anxiety. Granted, it could have been because of the slaying. But most of her friends shared the same mindset. What was their excuse?

Maddie's own mournful thoughts were interrupted by a knock at the kitchen door. She hadn't heard a car; the visitor must have come on foot. Outside the morning was cool and foggy, hardly the weather for a stroll. Something in Maddie went very, very still as she hesitated with her hand on the doorknob, then pulled it toward her.

"Ah. Good morning."

"Hi."

She didn't ask why Michael was there again; her face, she knew, showed the question.

He held up a brown grocery bag with its top rolled closed. "I was going through the condo storage bin and found this," he said with a sheepish smile. "I don't know how long it's been there, but I remember the uproar when Tracey thought she'd lost it."

He handed the paper bag to Maddie, who opened it and peered down into it. "Mr. James!"

She took out the scraggly teddy bear by one of its resewn arms and went suddenly teary-eyed, remembering the sweet sorrow Tracey had felt when she had discovered him gone.

"I found him in an Igloo cooler. You know how she took him everywhere. He probably got left there after a picnic. Do you think Tracey cares anymore? She seems so grown up."

"To you, maybe. The jury's still out as far as I'm concerned."

Michael grinned. "Mr. James will be glad to hear it. Maybe she still has room for him at the foot of the bed. He's very depressed, you know," he added with a whimsical smile. "It's no fun being cooped up in a plastic box for four years."

"Not that long, surely," said Maddie.

He said softly, "We've been apart four years and two months. And one, two . . . three days."

"Oh . . . then I guess you're right."

"Time flies when you're havin' fun," he added with a sad, droll look.

He stood respectfully on the stoop, obviously waiting to be asked inside. Maddie had completely mixed feelings about inviting him in again, but she did. He was her one open line of communication with Tracey. It was amazing, it was infuriating, but it was true. Maddie had to be able to put her pride to one side in order to hear what Michael could tell her about their child. She wasn't going to find out anything from their child on her own.

"Are you hungry?" she asked him. "I have a plate of eggs Benedict going untouched. Tracey claims to have a stomachache from yesterday."

Michael threw up his hands in mock self-defense as he stepped over the threshold. "Don't blame me. I took her to Bingham's Family Restaurant, and she ordered mashed potatoes and roast chicken. That's as down home as it gets."

"She ate that?" Maddie was amazed. Bingham's served massive portions, laden in gravy and fat.

He shrugged as he took a seat and said, "I didn't pay much attention. We were too busy gabbing."

Gabbing. It seemed inconceivable that Tracey ever gabbed with anyone old enough to be out of school, much less a blood parent. Not for the first time, Maddie wondered about her daughter's Jekyll and Hyde personality. How could she gab with her father and yet so despise her mother? Was it because Maddie was the stern one? Because Maddie was the one who made her make her bed and be in by nine?

Or was it—it had to be—because the divorce had been Maddie's idea. Maddie had never said a word about Michael's chronic faithlessness. She'd tried, maybe too well, to explain the breakup to Tracey in vague terms of incompatibility.

She might as well have said that she and Michael had split up because they couldn't agree on a color scheme for the living room. Tracey would never forgive her for divorcing so arbitrarily; Maddie could see that now. She sighed with frustration. Maybe she should've told Tracey the truth, poisoned her mind, and been done with it.

Michael had been following Maddie's "eat—it's getting cold" command. But he stopped in the middle of his second egg and said, "Why are you angry? What did I do?"

He'd always been able to read her mood down to the smallest nuance, and now was no exception. She shied at having been caught feeling jealous and hostile again—it felt too much like the old days—and said quickly, "My fault. I have a lot on my mind today. More coffee?"

"I'll get it," said Michael, pushing his chair back.

"No, that's all right."

Maddie got up for the pot and when she turned around with it, Michael had the note in his hand. She saw at once that he recognized the date on it. His fair skin was flushed with distress and his blond brows were drawn down hard over his green eyes.

"What's this?" he asked.

"I found it in Dad's desk blotter when I was cleaning out his study."

"It's in his handwriting."

"Yes. It is."

"Good lord." He ran his hand through his moussed hair, which ended up taking an odd little turn away from his temple.

"So you think it's that April 6?"

"What else could it be?"

Maddie came over and sat back down in her chair. "I haven't told anyone about it yet. Mom would go all to pieces again, and George . . . well, you know George."

"Yeah. More likely than not, he'll blame you for bringing the whole thing up again."

"Exactly. But I plan to call Detective Bailey after breakfast and see what he says," Maddie said, taking the note back.

"He'll want to examine it," said Michael. He lifted it out of her hand for another look.

"Why? It's not as though he's going to carbon date it."

"Hmmm? No," he said, staring fixedly at the slip of paper. "But maybe they can tell something we can't."

Maddie watched his eyebrows twitch down a little harder as he turned the note over just as she had, then read the date again, just as she had. His lashes were light, giving him a look of wide-eyed innocence—very effective with coeds away from home for the first time.

He turned those artless green eyes on her again. "Income

tax? Could he have planned to see someone about income tax? The timing would've been right. There's an H & R Block in Cambridge.''

''Dad did his own taxes. You know that.''

''Maybe he wanted them to check it over. Had he filed by the sixth?''

''No. The returns were sitting on his desk when—''

''That could be it, then!''

''What could be it, Michael? The returns were on his desk.''

''He could've taken a copy with him.''

''No, there weren't any . . . when they found him he didn't have any income tax returns on his . . . No.''

''Maddie, you're doing it again. Closing yourself off to a possibility.''

She said stonily, ''I'll see what Detective Bailey says.''

''Sorry,'' he said, his voice dropping suddenly soft and low. ''I was barging. I do that. You know how good I am at it. Will you allow me to apologize one more time this weekend?''

He looked so genuinely sorry that Maddie found herself saying in a reassuring voice, ''No, you're right. You've always been more intuitive than I, and usually, well, often— sometimes—you're right.'' She sighed and said, ''This could be one of those times, I suppose. I'll leave it up to Detective Bailey.''

''Do you want me to take this up to him?''

''No, that's okay,'' she said with a wan smile. ''Finish your breakfast. Now it really is cold.''

On an impulse she reached over and straightened the hank of hair that had gone awry on his head. She did it not so much because it bothered her, as because she knew how much it would bother him if—when—he looked in a mirror later.

Surprised, he smiled, then laid his hand over hers on the table. ''I wish I'd been able to be there for you, Madsy. It was a hideous time, I know.''

Her smile was more quivery than his. ''Yes . . . thanks.''

They heard a sound in the hall and turned at the same time to see Tracey, dressed in drab, standing with a startled look on her face. "Dad! I didn't know you were here." Her glance took in the relative positions of her parents' hands.

Gently, Maddie slid her hand out from under Michael's.

"Hey, Trace," Michael said, flashing his daughter his earnest smile. "Your mom tells me you're feelin' punk."

He got up and walked over to her while Maddie began clearing the table. Placing a graceful hand on the girl's brow, he said, "Aw, baby, you're hot. Maybe a touch of the flu?"

Maddie laid the plates a little too hard in the sink and came over herself to check her daughter's temperature. Tracey pulled back a fraction, as if it were her mother who was contagious, then submitted with sullen meekness to her touch.

"You're fine," Maddie said. "Sit down and have some cereal."

"Mom, I *told* you."

"And I told you. Eat some breakfast or you're not going anywhere."

Tracey gave her father a tragic glance before she stomped over to the cupboard and took down a box of shredded wheat. Trying hard not to seem to be standing guard, Maddie busied herself with the dishes. She heard a single clunk in the cereal bowl, then the milk jug being waved over it before almost instantly being returned to the fridge.

The contretemps ended with Michael saying with forced cheer, "Hey! I almost forgot!"

Maddie watched her ex-husband take three loping strides across the red and white checkerboard floor, scoop up Mr. James from the top of the breadbox where Maddie had tucked him, and wiggle the long lost teddy bear in front of his daughter's face.

"Oh, Dad," said Tracey. "Where did you find him?"

She said it in such measured tones that Maddie found herself turning around and staring, just to divine the teenager's mood. Was she pleased? Was she not?

But Tracey's expression was as careful as her voice. She

wasn't going to give her mother the satisfaction of catching her red-handed with enthusiasm, that was for sure.

Maddie sighed and stole a peek at the frail old bear: Mr. James looked alone and forlorn, and desperately unloved.

Chapter 6

With every passing day Maddie became more aware of him. She saw him leave at eight in the morning (she began getting up early just to see him do it) and strike out for town on foot. At eight-thirty she saw him return, a loaf of French bread sticking out of his backpack, a newspaper under his arm. At ten he left in his red Jeep. At twelve he returned in his red Jeep.

After that, the pattern broke down. Sometimes she didn't see him all afternoon. Sometimes he puttered outside. For one devastating thirty-six-hour period he and his red Jeep were gone altogether. But then Maddie saw the car turn up again around midnight, and the light go on in the storage room— obviously his bedroom—and she found herself bowing her head in the dark and saying, "Thank you, thank you, thank you."

And that shocked her.

The next day, Maddie chose not to sit in the patio chair that looked out at the lighthouse; she sat facing her roses instead. It was Norah who took the chair that faced the tower. She was in an especially gleeful mood, and it made her blue eyes sparkle.

"Fifty thousand," she said, triumphant color flagging her cheeks. "That should get people's attention."

"Fifty!" Joan was clearly astonished; she could go antiquing for the rest of her life. "You got that ancient old man to pledge fifty thousand dollars? But what does he care if the lighthouse gets moved or not? He could be dead by the time that happens."

Norah smiled her special smile, reserved for occasions like these. "He took a little—very little—persuading." She lifted her chin and ran a slender index finger along the line of her throat. "I may have to drum up another fifty," she said, pursing her lips. "But for now, fifty is fine. It proves we're not in it for the parties and the cocktail weiners. It proves we truly care."

If Maddie had learned one thing in her ten-year friendship with Norah, it was that she never rallied to a good cause just because she felt obliged. Norah was motivated to do things by one of two impulses: boredom, or curiosity.

"I keep meaning to ask you, Nor, how's the gallery doing this summer? Is Cheryl working out?"

"Yes, thank God. The woman is determined to have a gallery of her own someday. I may just sell her the Seaside at a bargain price."

Yes. Just as Maddie suspected: boredom.

"Now that I think about it, you don't seem to be spending much time there," Joan chimed in.

Norah shrugged. "Been there, done that, you know? Besides, the gallery doesn't maximize my greatest skill."

"Which is?"

"For squeezing blood out of a rock," said Norah, laughing. She surprised them by adding, "No, seriously, I guess I'm tired of the gallery because it doesn't seem—" She frowned, struggling for the right word. "Significant enough. Maybe it's because I chose not to have kids; but I feel a need to leave something . . . I don't know . . . of *me*. I guess that's it. Cheap egotism, isn't it? To want to leave something of me?" She added softly, "But saving the lighthouse would—might—satisfy me that way."

Coloring again, Norah turned away from them to gaze at the lighthouse. It was so unlike her to sound deep that Maddie and Joan were left exchanging a long, wordless look.

"But! That's not today's problem," Norah said more

cheerfully as she rose to her feet. "Getting the reclusive Dan
Hawke to come out and play: that's today's problem."

Joan smiled and said, "Hey, take a walk on the beach top-
less. That oughtta do it."

Norah batted long lashes at Joan and said, "You're warm."

She peeled off the yellow knit sundress she'd been wearing
and revealed an eye-popping yellow bikini underneath.

Joan said with respect, "You've been working out."

"Have to," Norah said as she laid the sundress over the
back of her chair. She picked up her canvas beach bag, rooted
around in it, and came up with a hefty screwdriver.

"Hide this," she told Maddie, handing her the tool. "It's
evidence."

"What the hell are you planning to do?" blurted Maddie.
She was scandalized at every one of the possibilities that had
begun lining up in her brain.

"I'm going windsurfing. And somewhere in shouting distance of the lighthouse, the fin is going to fall off my windsurfer and I'm going to have to call for help. If no one should
come out to save me, I'll end up drifting helplessly out to
sea. Does that answer your question?" she asked with a guile-
less look.

Joan blanched. "Oh, don't do that, Norah, don't! It's too
dangerous. You could be swept out to sea. Oh, Norah, don't.
Please don't!"

"Joanie, I'll be fine," Norah said with a squeeze of her
friend's hand. "You know I'm an excellent swimmer; where
do you think all this definition comes from?" she said, flexing
a slender but tight upper arm for Joan to see. "This'll be fun.
You can watch me from here. I guarantee I'll flush the son
of a bitch out of his lair. That brooding author routine of his
is beginning to get tired."

"Leave him be, Norah!" said Maddie. She was appalled
by the tension in her own voice.

Surprised, Norah said, "No way, darling. If I'm going to
save the lighthouse, I'll need his cooperation. The man
doesn't really have a choice. Besides—why should you
care?"

"I don't," said Maddie quickly. "Go right ahead and make a fool of yourself."

"Thank you. I reserve that right, though I don't usually take advantage of it."

A light bulb seemed to go on over Joan's head. "Norah! Do you really want to save the lighthouse, or do you just want to get this guy in the sack?"

"Wouldn't it be nice," said Norah, slinging her beach bag over her shoulder, "if I could do both?"

They watched Norah cross the lane and head for the beach by ducking down a right of way that ran alongside the shingled cottage opposite Rosedale.

Joan turned back to Maddie. Her expression, normally open and naive, was pinched with dread. "It's a horrible idea," she said, shaking her head. "She could fall off."

"Of course she'll fall off," Maddie said with a reassuring laugh. "That's the whole point."

"You know what I mean. She won't be paying attention; her mind will be on trying to get his attention. She could . . . anything could—"

"Nothing will, Joan. Truly."

"But it's blowing out," Joan said, standing up so that she could monitor Norah's progress better.

"You're making too much of this, Joannie."

Joan scarcely heard her. "Where are your binoculars?"

"Uh, let me think."

They were sitting on the lowest shelf of the cupboard to the right of the kitchen sink window, from which Maddie had a view of the lighthouse. Could she direct Joan there without drawing down suspicion?

"I saw a Blue Indigo feeding on the ground in the front yard the other day," she lied, "and I've been keeping the binoculars handy in case it comes back. Look around in the cupboards by the sink. I think that's where I left them."

"I'll see."

Even without the binoculars, Maddie was able to follow the progress of the bright pink and magenta sail as Norah kept a steady course for the water directly in front of the lighthouse. Norah being Norah, she wouldn't fall until she had to. And even then, she'd probably keep her hair dry.

Poor Dan Hawke. He didn't stand a chance. For one brief moment, Maddie put aside her resentment and longing and actually felt sorry for him. A genuine siren was about to come calling.

She has it all. Looks, money, brains, and confidence. Why didn't she ever have children? What an odd, odd thing.

Maddie thought of her own adored child (she did adore Tracey, despite the widening gulf between them). And she thought of Joan: everyone's favorite aunt, longing to have children of her own.

A mother's love. Was there anything stronger on earth?

"They were right where you thought," Joan said, reappearing with the strap of the binoculars looped around her neck. She refocused the lenses and peered in her nearsighted way at the horizon. "Is that her sail? The pink striped one?"

"Yes. She's fine. Although, why she expects him to realize she's in trouble after she manages to lose the fin is beyond me. He won't be able to see her if he's working at his desk."

Joan looked back at Maddie. "How do you know where he works?"

"I . . . often see a light on, on the side that faces my house. I assume he has an office set up there."

"Really. That's strange. You'd think he'd want to look out at the sea."

Maddie had had the same thought herself. Over and over again. "Maybe it's too big a distraction," she mumbled. "Anyway, Norah can sound like a banshee when it suits her. He'll hear her, even if he doesn't see her."

Maddie watched with her heart bouncing around in her throat. If someone offered her a million dollars to describe her own feelings at that moment, she'd have to pass, because she didn't have a clue.

Joan gave Maddie a blow-by-blow account of Norah in action. "Okay, she's down. She's just stepped off the board, kind of casually. You wouldn't call it a fall."

"Her bikini wouldn't take the force of a fall," said Maddie.

They laughed together. Joan's mood was less tragic now, and Maddie was glad.

"I wonder if Norah can actually pull it off," Joan mused.

"If necessary," Maddie deadpanned. They laughed again.

"Okay, she must've got the fin off. Now she's climbing back on the board. Now she's standing. The sail's lying flat in the water. What great balance she has. If it were me. . . . Now she's cupping her hands, yelling at the lighthouse."

"I think I hear her from here."

"I wonder if he's even home. Just because the Jeep is there . . . . And in the meantime, she really is drifting away fast. Oh, why did she pick a day when the wind was blowing offshore?"

"Joannie, think about it. It wouldn't make sense to pick a day with a sea breeze nudging her gently back onto the beach, would it?"

Joan sighed and said, "No . . . but . . . she's getting farther out. He won't be able to hear her, not with the wind blowing her cries away from the lighthouse. Oh, Maddie, we should go! We can knock on his door, point her out to him. Oh, let's," she begged.

"We'll wait a little longer," said Maddie, but even she was getting nervous. It really was far windier on the water than it was in her sheltered garden.

"He may not even know how to use the boat that's moored in front of the lighthouse. We're just assuming!"

"Joan, shh-hh. Just . . . wait."

They watched in silence as Norah, still standing, waved her arms in wide, crossing arcs, her cries for help a mere sigh in the wind. Her image became smaller . . . and smaller . . . and smaller, until at last Maddie said, "Damn it! We'll have to find somebody else to tow her back, or she's going to end up on Bermuda. Of all the dumb stunts!"

She went inside for her car keys, and when she came out again, Joan was grinning. "Look for yourself," she said, handing Maddie the binoculars.

Maddie held them up and readjusted the lenses. Norah was tiny, even through the glasses. But if a woman in a bikini on a broken windsurfer drifting out to sea could be said to look relaxed, then Norah looked relaxed. Very relaxed. Maddie panned to the left. Oh yes. Now she saw why. There he was in the skiff, full steam ahead for the damsel in distress.

"She did it," Maddie whispered, almost in awe.

Joan sighed with relief and said, "She can do anything. They'll be bonded now."

"Won't they? It's a regular Hallmark moment," said Maddie dryly. Inside her heart was being squeezed. It was like watching the *Titanic* converging with a certain iceberg.

Why had he come to Sandy Point at all? Not to see Maddie; that was obvious by now. If he was there to write his memoirs, then Norah Mills would make a darn interesting footnote to them.

Maddie handed Joan the binoculars. She couldn't bear to watch. "Let me know if we have to call in the Coast Guard," she told Joan briskly. "I've got work to do."

Dan Hawke had waited as long as he possibly could for someone else—anyone else—to come to the lady's rescue. But no one had and so here he was, circling like some shark in the water, trying to figure out how the hell to lasso a windsurfer with a missing towing ring.

No good. He was going to have to wrestle the thing bodily into his skiff.

After he wrestled *her* in, of course. She was incredibly voluptuous; he actually had to avoid looking at her while he tried to figure out how to untangle the sail from the mast, the mast from the board, all with her lounging on the board as if it were a Victorian fainting sofa. Hell!

Flat stomach, firm breasts, limbs that went on forever— she didn't look real and maybe she wasn't; he'd had the impression, when he talked with her in Annie's that day, that she'd been under the knife for cosmetic surgery. She looked no more than thirty, but his sense of her was that she was closer to forty than not. It wasn't so much the way she looked—he was staring at her now in the brutal midday sun and she looked phenomenal—but the way she was. She had an edge. She'd been around. She gave the impression of someone with nothing to lose.

He held the sailboard in an awkward grip to keep it from drifting away. "Okay, just step from there into the skiff," he commanded.

Or not. "That looks tricky," she said, demurring. "Why don't I wait in the water for you to load the sailboard, and then you can help me into the boat."

"Suit yourself." Which one was she, anyway: Joan or Norah? Surely the Norah.

The board was heavy. He wondered who had launched it for her. With a grunt, he pulled it out of the water and into the skiff, then turned to her.

"Okay, alley-up." He hooked his hands under her arms, trying not to notice her glistening breasts floating more or less free of the tiny top she wore.

Gripping the side of the hull, she ducked low in the water for momentum, and then rose up like a goddess, letting him help her, unnecessarily, the rest of the way into the boat.

"Very nice," he said. Even he didn't know what he meant.

"I don't know what I would've done if you hadn't come out to get me," she said, flashing him a dazzling grin.

His own smile was sardonic. "Something tells me you'd have managed."

"Probably," she agreed, not bothering to seem humble. After he shifted the boat back into gear, she stuck her hand out to him and said, "Thanks. Now tell me why you're avoiding us all."

He shook her hand and said dryly, "How so? I make a point of nodding to every person I pass."

"Mr. Hawke, you know what I mean. You have the whole town too intimidated to approach you."

"Except you, apparently."

"I'm special."

"Apparently."

God, this isn't what he wanted at all. She was some mind-boggling diversion thrown in his path when all he wanted was to get to Maddie.

Norah shivered and moved her butt closer to his on the center thwart. "It's still so cold this time of year," she said with a much too innocuous smile.

He'd been nudged meaningfully by women before. She was coming on to him, he couldn't imagine why.

He was still trying to figure it out when she cut to the chase. "I gather that Mr. Mendoza has told you about our interest in acquiring and moving the lighthouse," she said forthrightly. "Does that present a problem for you?"

He shrugged. "Not once I'm out of it. My lease is only for four months."

She shaped her lips into a fetching pout and said, "But that's just it. We can't really get a nonprofit foundation up and running without potential donors being able to go through the property and see its historic value. They'd want to touch the merchandise, so to speak." She smiled under lowered lashes. "You can understand why."

You betcha, he found himself thinking.

His glance slid from her to the sweep of horizon, then came to rest on little Rosedale cottage with its knee-high picket fence, just then coming into view. The endearing image, as precious as a picture postcard, was burned into his brain by now. He was as amazed as anyone that it held more allure for him than the seductress at his side.

The thought of Maddie standing by her roses made him impatient with distractions, no matter how worthy or well shaped. "What is it you want from me, Mrs. . . . Mills?" he asked as her last name popped into his head.

If she was put off by the formality, she didn't show it. She nuzzled her hip a little closer into his and said, "What I— we—envisioned is a series of fundraising events. A wine and cheese gathering at the lighthouse with a couple of speeches . . . a picnic or two on the beach, each with a tour . . . a morning coffee? They're all the rage in Washington—"

"No. No, no. No series of events. One event. An opener. That's all. Cocktails and a tour and out they go. Anything else would be massively disruptive."

She didn't ask what they'd be disrupting, and he didn't

say. The fact was, he hadn't done shit since he'd arrived. Trixie Roiters had blithely announced in her little chat-rag that he was there to write his memoirs. What a laugh. If he'd had any thought at all of writing, it was to try to pen a novel.

But he hadn't done that either. All he'd done was obsess over Maddie. He hadn't had the guts so far to confront her, because if she spurned him a second time he'd probably exile himself to Antarctica.

Amazingly, he hadn't known her father was murdered. Now, after spending a few mornings in the library, he did. The knowledge made everything ten times harder. So, yeah, sure they'd be disrupting him: disrupting his hard-earned paralysis. He couldn't have that, could he?

"That's quite a sneer on your face, fella," Norah said, giving him a sideways look. "If your writing is *that* important—"

"Forget it. All right: two fundraising events. But that's it. Pick a day in July and one in August. Give me plenty of warning."

She beamed him another dazzling grin and said, "Two events, then. It's a start." She added, "Those don't include the fireworks, naturally."

"What fireworks?"

"Come on. You didn't know? Every Fourth of July, the town sets off fireworks by the lighthouse. You're on a peninsula, which makes it a safe spot for launching them. But first we gather on the beach there, and we have an evening cookout for everyone. It's in your lease. You really didn't know?"

"Who the hell reads leases?" he growled.

The whole damn town in his front yard! Whose bathroom did they plan to use?

"Traditionally, the tenants in the lighthouse throw open the downstairs to their neighbors," Norah said, reading his mind. "The fireworks committee pays for a cleaning service to come in afterward, of course."

"Of course." Damn. Where had he got the notion that

lighthouses were isolate, private places? He may as well have taken up residence in a ferris wheel!

Cursing himself for having let the naked creature beside him con him into opening his door, twice, minimum, to the world, he eased the flat-bottomed skiff into the shallow water of the beach from which Norah had launched her sailboard.

By the time he hauled her gear out of the boat and onto the beach, she'd disappeared and reappeared again, this time wearing a yellow dress over the yellow bikini. The wet bathing suit left three telltale outlines in the dress. He tried not to see them.

"Thanks again," she said, extending her hand once more, this time not letting go of it. "Now, come have a drink with my friends and me. Trixie Roiters has just dropped by with one of the town selectmen. The house is right across the street," she said, eyeing him all too speculatively. "And don't worry about not having a shirt on. Dress is casual. Will you come?"

"I'd like that," he said with a bland smile.

About as much as boiling in oil. "The thing is, I . . . ah . . . had something in the oven, which is probably catching on fire right about now."

It was the best he could do. He backpedaled into the water, yanked up the grapnel, and tossed it into the bow of the boat. Then he mounted the skiff like a cowboy his pony, and he didn't look back until he was out of bullet range.

Not now. Not with half the town looking on.

The question was, when?

Chapter 7

"We checked with both of the H & R Blocks in Cambridge, Mrs. Regan. They have no record of your father showing up on April 6, either by appointment or as a walk-in."

Maddie couldn't hide the disappointment in her voice. She wanted the note from the desk blotter to have an innocent explanation. "I was hoping . . ."

"I know," said the sympathetic detective at the other end of the line. "I know."

She slapped at a mosquito parked on the wall above the phone. Blood. Damn.

"Since my father didn't go to H & R Block, and he wasn't meeting any of his friends that day, as far as we've been able to tell, what should we make of the note I found? Should we take it seriously? Or do you think it could be from some other year altogether?"

She could tell by the hesitation in his voice that Detective Bailey was choosing his words carefully.

"It's been my experience," he said, "that coincidences don't happen as often as people would like to believe. I've also learned that people don't necessarily tell their families everything that's on their m—"

"Oh, but my father would tell my mother if he were meeting someone," Maddie said, interrupting. "Really he would! They were very close; they shared everything. You must've seen that in your investigation. He and my mother loved one another deeply.''

Sarah Timmons had loved her husband so much, in fact, that she still hadn't come down to Rosedale cottage from Sudbury. She'd pleaded a summer cold, but Maddie knew better. Her mother was still drifting aimlessly in her grief, like a boat without oars.

Maddie had hated telling her mother about the note. Believing that Edward Timmons was a victim of random violence had been hard enough. Being told that he had an actual appointment with his slayer had sent Sarah on a whole new downward spiral of grief. The idea that her husband may have kept secrets from her was bound to be even more unthinkable.

''You're not saying that my father was having an assignation with some woman, I hope,'' Maddie said bluntly. It was the only secret she could think of: an illicit one.

The detective let out a wry chuckle and said, ''Believe me, Mrs. Regan, a man wouldn't need to write that down. No, my thinking is that your father made the appointment at least a week in advance—the note didn't say 'Tuesday,' after all, it said a date. Edward Timmons was retired, so he wasn't the one with the full calendar. It must have been the person he was meeting. A busy person. A professional, probably.''

But Maddie had another thought. ''You said he was meeting a person. What if he were planning simply to be at a place? A morning recital, maybe, or a lecture. He often attended those.''

''He wouldn't have mentioned that to your mother?''

''Oh,'' said Maddie, crestfallen. ''Yes. In all likelihood.''

''My gut tells me it was a person.''

Your gut hasn't found out a thing, she thought with a flash of bitterness.

''What's next, in that case?'' she asked him, trying to subdue her frustration. Detective Bailey was a hard-boiled sweetheart of a family man with four kids. He knew more than most what it meant to have a parent ripped away from the hearth.

The detective blew air through his nose and said, ''I have

a call out to your dad's primary care physician. It's a long shot, but it's conceivable that your father had arranged an appointment at ten in the morning on the sixth that he didn't want any of you to know about.''

A terminal illness? It didn't seem possible. ''Wouldn't the doctor or his staff have come forward with that information?''

''They might not have made the connection. He would have cautioned them against calling your home, and when he didn't show, they wouldn't have followed up.''

She turned the idea over. ''At least it would account for the note,'' she said, nodding her head. It amazed her to realize that she was actually rooting for a scenario in which her father may have had cancer.

She said, ''If it's all right with you—I know you don't have the resources to devote to this case anymore—I'm going to try to find out what events were scheduled in and around Cambridge at ten o'clock that day.''

''If he was planning to be in Cambridge,'' the detective reminded her.

''That's right,'' she said, taken down another peg in her determination. ''We don't even know that.'' Damn the note!

''Mrs. Regan,'' the detective said, suddenly earnest, ''I want you to know there's not a day goes by that I don't think about this case. I'm always open to new angles, and—''

''Oh, I'm sorry; I have another call,'' said Maddie, expecting to hear that Tracey was ready for a ride home. ''Can you hold?''

But they were done for the moment. The detective hung up and Maddie punched in the new caller. It was Michael, phoning about the note. Had she heard anything?

''You really are psychic,'' Maddie said, hardly surprised. Michael had always had the peculiar ability to clue in on a subject that interested him. When they were dating, he often picked up the phone just as she was calling his number. She used to interpret it as proof of his love. Now she knew better. It was a trait he possessed, like being double-jointed. It didn't prove love at all.

She told him about the phone call she'd just had, all except her own insistence that her father wasn't having an affair, which was too ludicrous to bother mentioning.

And yet in the next breath, Michael had her wondering again.

He said, "Do you suppose—you're not going to like this suggestion, but—do you suppose your father may have thought he had a sexually transmitted disease?"

"Michael! You knew him. How can you possibly suggest that?"

"No, you're right, you're right. It's a dumb idea." He backtracked into safer territory and tried to put a positive spin on the whole affair.

"It sounds as if Bailey thinks the note could be perfectly innocent," he said. "Maybe not income tax, but something just as legitimate."

"I didn't get that feeling at all," Maddie argued. "I think he sees a definite connection between the note and the murder of my father."

"There you go again, Maddie," Michael said, irritated now. "Looking for goblins where there are none."

"And there *you* go again, trying to pretend that all's right with the world. All isn't right, Michael. Take off those rose-colored glasses, would you for once?" she snapped.

"Maddie, you're out of control on this. I know how hard it is to have an unsolved crime lying around like an unexploded grenade, but—"

"Someone's here," she said, relieved to hear knocking at the kitchen door. "I have to go."

"Maddie, don't hang up," he pleaded. "It's probably the paper boy or something. I'll wait."

The knocking resumed. "Look, I—oh, all right. Hold on."

She slammed the receiver on the counter and marched over to the big Dutch door, feeling as if they were all walking around with their hands slapped over their ears.

We want to know; we don't want to know, she decided, swinging open the top of the two-part door.

Swinging it open to Daniel Hawke.

Twenty years. She stood there. Twenty years. Her heart lurched violently in her chest and began a wild knocking. She opened her mouth to say something, but nothing came out. Daniel Hawke. He was there. Close enough to touch. Her eyes stung with tears. She felt a surge of deep, wrenching distress, a pain so deep that it made it hard to breathe. She tried to say something again, and failed.

She tried again.

"Why . . . ?"

The wonder in his face seemed to mirror her own. It was as if he had no idea why he was standing there. And yet there he was. His brown eyes were as deep, as luminous, as intense as ever she remembered them. It astonished her that she remembered every little thing about his face: the wide, straight eyebrows; the sharply defined, aquiline nose; the broad space above his upper lip just crying out for a mustache; the stubble beneath his lower lip that never seemed to hook up with a razor blade. His cheeks were as hollow, his hair as unruly, as twenty years earlier. Time had left lines, especially around his eyes, and time had left scars: a small nick in the left eyebrow; a ragged line like a thin arrow across his cheekbone, pointing toward the nick.

He was there. Daniel Hawke. He was there.

"Maddie. Hello."

His voice, too, was the same. Deeper, softer, but the same.

"I heard you were in town, Daniel," she said, and immediately she cringed at how inane it sounded; she wanted to sound clever. She tried a smile and cringed at that, too. She knew the smile was crooked and trembly, and she wanted to look beautiful.

Clever and beautiful and young. And she was none of those things.

They both began to say something: he, to explain; she, to query. And then they stopped at the same time, and chuckled the same ghastly, bleak chuckle.

She recovered first. "Yes?" She sounded almost shrill to herself as she said it, as if he were holding a gun aimed at her belly.

He held up a Pyrex measuring cup. "Sugar?" he said, with a loopy, sickly smile. "Do you have any to spare?"

She stared. Whatever it was he had come for—money, jewels, silver, sex, forgiveness—she did not expect it to be sugar.

"I don't understand," she said humbly. Her mind and her heart were in turmoil. It was much worse—the face-to-face meeting was so much worse—than in her most anguished dreams.

"Here, take it," he said, thrusting the cup into her hand. "I don't want the damn thing. I just . . . .I had to . . . I didn't know how . . . Maddie. *Maddie*."

It was that second "Maddie" that was her undoing. A tear rolled down her cheek. "Why are you here?" she whispered. "Why?"

"Let me in," he said, his voice hoarse with emotion. "Maddie, let me in."

How could she? It was so much worse, so much worse: seeing him again, flogged by the years, lost years, years they'd never get back. And it was worse even than that. Despite the years, he looked so like himself that she was flung violently back to their last meeting. Her head began to ring with the sound of her own furious reproaches, hurled at him like so many javelins.

She remembered them all, every last one of them. Did he?

"We have to talk," he said.

His words brought a startled laugh to her throat. "Don't you think that ship has sailed?"

"If it has, it's gone round the world and come home again," he said with a burning look.

But she stood her ground, refusing—unable—to open the door to him.

He reached over the lower half of the Dutch door and unlocked the door on her side, letting himself in. Maddie watched, mesmerized, as he did it. Dan Hawke: intense, impatient, undisciplined. Dan Hawke: leader of a ragtag band of student radicals. Dan Hawke: bad boy of the campus.

There wasn't a door built that could keep him out.

Now that he had gained access to her kitchen, some of the

fierceness seemed to slide off him. "You look the same," he said. His gaze swept her from head to sandals and came back to rest on her face. "Like the girl next door."

"I *am* the girl next door."

He smiled at that. "I was counting on it when I signed the lease."

She pretended not to understand the implication. "Are you starting a second career in the Coast Guard?"

"No."

"Then a lighthouse is an odd choice of digs."

He gave her a raw look that instantly put her back on her guard. "You know why I'm here, Maddie."

"Actually, I've been wondering for a couple of weeks now," she shot back. Immediately, she wanted to retract the words.

"I know. I should've come over sooner. But you're rarely alone here. People seem to come and go constantly."

She said, "I have friends here. Family here." He wouldn't understand that. He was a lone wolf.

"I'm jealous of every one of them," he admitted.

That surprised her. Once when they were in bed together, he'd said, "You're all I need. Everyone else is clutter."

Except for his sister. He did admit to caring about her. But he claimed to have no use for his parents and no love for his other relations. She wondered whether he still felt that way.

"I can't imagine you being jealous that you're not surrounded by a crowd," she said without smiling. "It was never your style."

"No, that's not what I—" His face took on a sudden, puzzled frown. "Did you know your phone's off the hook?" he said, pointing to the counter.

Maddie whirled around. "Oh, my God." She snatched up the receiver and said, "Hello?"

She was amazed to see that her ex-husband was still on the line. "Who're you talking to, for God's sake?" he demanded to know.

Without thinking, she answered, "Dan Hawke."

There was a pause, and then Michael said, "Hawke? What the hell is he doing there?"

"He's staying in Sandy Point for the summer," she said, turning away from Daniel in a laughable attempt at privacy. "It was in Trixie's newsletter."

"Who reads Trixie's newsletter? What's he doing in your house?"

She said grimly, "He came to borrow a cup of sugar, Michael." In a lower, grimmer voice she said, "Is it really any of your business?"

"Yes, it's my business! I don't want that bastard near my family."

"Michael, this is not the time!"

But Michael didn't agree. "Jesus, Maddie! I don't care if he's there selling Girl Scout cookies. The guy brought an unbelievable amount of pain down on your father, on all of you. How can you—? Let me talk to him. Put him on the phone."

"No, I won't do that. Good-bye, Michael."

"Wait, wait—where's he staying?" Michael got in.

"In the lighthouse," she answered grudgingly.

"The lighthouse! That's ballsy."

"If you say so. I really have to get off the phone. Tracey should've called by now."

"You have call waiting, Maddie. What's the problem?"

"Michael, please. Good-bye." She hung up, aware that once again she'd let Michael go too far, too long. All for Tracey's sake.

She was about to explain to Dan that she was expecting a call when the call she was expecting came mercifully through. Maddie took it while a bemused Dan Hawke, arms folded across his chest, leaned back on the Formica counter and waited patiently for her to finish.

She hung up and turned to him, grateful for the chance to cut and run. "I'm sorry. I have to pick my daughter up from the Bowl-a-rama," she said.

He broke into a grin. "The Bowl-a-rama! Is that joint still there?"

"It's candlepin now," Maddie said. She wanted to wipe the grin off his face; it was bowling her over.

"I remember knocking off from work with a couple of the guys and playing a few lanes while we had a beer or two. It was fairly seedy then. Have they added ferns and made it all gentrified? Like Annie's?"

"I'd forgotten," she said, hurled back in time again. "Annie's used to be Anthony's Pizza back then. They had a great onion pizza; they—"

She brought herself up short. The one thing she did not want to do was to stroll down memory lane with him. It wasn't enough to peek behind the velvet curtains when you did that. You had to turn the rocks over, too. And she didn't want to look at dark things scurrying. Not now. Not ever. She had no more room for any more horror.

"I'm sorry," she said, looking away from him. She turned the cowardly act into a scan of the kitchen for her handbag. "I really have to go."

She found the bag next to the microwave. Scooping it up in a swoop onto her shoulder, she said as gaily as she could, "I guess you're right; it is a bit of a madhouse around here. My brother's arriving tonight with his family and I've got shopping to do. Please don't think I'm rude—"

"Not rude," he said, stepping between her and the door. "Afraid."

"Don't be asinine," she said flatly. Her cheeks burned from the dead-on accusation.

"You can't expect this to be the end of it, Maddie," he said in that urgently persuasive voice of his. Once it had rallied a band of idealists into doing wildly destructive things; she couldn't forget that.

"This *is* the end of it, Dan."

"I didn't come here just to pay my respects," he said, spitting out the word. "I came here to—"

"To what?" she cried. "To thrash it out, once and for all? Because *you* decided the time is right? You want me to drop everything—drop my life—and listen to what you in your accumulated wisdom have to say?'' She let out a harsh and bitter laugh. ''I don't think so.''

It shocked her, the depth of her anger. She tried to brush past him through the wide door, but he grabbed her arm to hold her back. The act infuriated her; she yanked herself from his grip and jumped away, like a cat, and then lashed out at him.

''You want my forgiveness? Fine! All is forgiven. My father's dead now; the chapter's closed. There. Feel better? Were you haunted by the memory of what you did to him? Did you need my forgiveness to make your glorious life complete?''

Her voice dropped to a menacing whisper as she said, ''Oh, yes, I—we—forgive you. But if you want me to forget, then *you* can forget it, Daniel. It's not going to happen. Good-bye. Lock the door on your way out. There are crazy people out there.''

Shaking with emotion, she forced herself to walk deliberately to her car. Without once looking at him, she backed the Taurus out of the drive, sending quahog shells flying in every direction.

Chapter 8

That night, he dreamed about her.

He dreamed that she was naked, and he had her in his arms. He was kissing her passionately, thrusting his tongue into her mouth, willing her to love him. But she was resisting; she kept telling him, "Don't you get it? It's over. It's over." At last she broke away, and she ran for the door. But he was faster than she was, and stronger. He slammed the door closed and locked it with a key that wasn't a key, but a rawhide dogbone. He could see outrage in her face as he turned and began to walk steadily toward her. She began to back away from him, not so much in fear as with revulsion. That infuriated him—and it turned him on.

He grabbed her and threw her across the bed, only it wasn't a bed, it was the top of the lighthouse tower, and as he plunged himself into her, the water around them kept rising. Only he didn't care; he kept driving himself into her, because he was convinced he could make her love him. And when the water level rose above her face she stopped crying, and he took that to mean she loved him. But the water kept rising; he could feel his mouth and nose go under, and he could feel the water filling his ears. . . .

He called out, and his own voice woke him from the nightmare. He sat up in bed, convinced he was sitting on top of the light tower, and looked around in the hushed light of dawn. No, he was in his apartment, all right: the same two-bedroom flat, carved from a once-elegant rowhouse in Boston's Back Bay, that he'd lived in since Maddie threw him out four years ago.

The bedroom was a mess. His dirty clothes, weeks of them, were everywhere—draped over the chair, the bedposts, the closet doorknob. A red tie hung limply from one of the rabbit ears on the small TV that crouched on a bureau. (When had he last worn a tie? He couldn't remember.) The blinds, broken on both windows, hung in the same cockeyed disarray that had recently prompted a neighbor to leave a note in his mailbox offering to buy him new ones.

Canvases on stretchers, some of them blank and the rest of them failures, were stacked up against the wall opposite his bed, flaunting his collapse as an artist. Once upon a time his canvases had served him well. "Come and see my paintings," he'd suggest to an aspiring student, and into the bedroom she'd stroll. But these were a joke. He'd die before he'd show them to anyone.

He rubbed his temples. The headache was back and he was due at the lab. He was convinced that his headaches were psychosomatic nowadays; whenever he knew he was going to be tested, he felt one coming on. Still, he was also convinced that he could make it go away. It was just a question of mind over matter, and he knew that his mind was more powerful than most.

That's what they're paying me for, he told himself grimly as he threw back the covers.

He went through his morning routine, unable to shake the sickening sensation that he'd just raped his ex-wife. When he wiped away the steam on the bathroom mirror, the haggard face that stared back at him looked guilty. After breakfast, when he caught a glimpse of himself in the hall mirror: guilty. In the rearview mirror of his beloved BMW: guilty. Even in the glass doors of the Brookline Institute of Research and Parapsychology, the face that looked back at him as he grabbed the door handle said guilty.

"Good morning, Mr. Regan; hot enough for you?" asked

the department secretary as she nudged the visitors' book toward him.

He had no idea whether it was hot or not. He glanced back through the glass doors out at the parking lot across the street. The cars looked hot.

"A real scorcher," he said with an amiable smile as he signed his name.

He walked down one of several long halls, all of them painted dreary mint green and separated from beige linoleum floors by mopboards of black vinyl. The off-putting smell of disinfectant persisted as he pushed through swinging steel doors into a lab whose purpose seemed vague. There were no porcelain-topped tables, no sinks, no Bunsen burners. Nothing but four steel desks, each of them accompanied by a small cart and two chairs with plastic seats and metal legs.

An EEG machine standing next to the middle desk, a computer on the same desk, and a video camera mounted high on one wall were the only electronics in the room. Everything else was surprisingly low tech: green boards, washed clean of chalk, on the long wall; folding screens stacked in a corner; a brown metal locker that Michael knew held printer paper and other stationery supplies.

The room was windowless. Only the wall opposite the swinging steel doors had any glass, and that glass was tinted. Michael had never been on the other side of that wall, but he knew that he'd been observed during every one of his tests by someone or other—faculty; parapsychologists; government observers.

Call it intuition, he thought with grim humor.

With an upward nod of his head he greeted the lab assistant seated at one of the middle desks. "Hey, Stuart. How's it hangin'?"

The goateed grad student, scruffy in jeans and a Grateful Dead T-shirt, grinned and said, "Higher, after last night."

"Hot date, hey?"

"Cookin'."

"Good for you. Well, what's on my plate for today?" Michael asked, wanting to get it over with. The testing, once fascinating to him, had seemed numbingly repetitive in the last few weeks. The initial excitement was fading, replaced by the growing realization that success would be neither overnight nor automatic. It was a little like being in third grade again, and having to do multiplication tables over and over and over until he got them right.

And they wanted him to get it right. He had no illusions about that. Geoffrey Woodbine, Director of the Institute, had impressed upon him how important it was that he, Michael Regan, get it right. The Institute was testing half a dozen other subjects with supposed psychic powers, and of them all, he, Michael Regan, had consistently scored the highest.

He wasn't surprised to hear it. All his life, he'd been aware that he was psychic. He had never done much with the gift; the circles he moved in were too cynical for that. But in the last several years he had read a lot, and had tested himself, and had gone so far as to respond to a discreet ad placed in the *Journal of Psychic Phenomena* seeking subjects for various studies.

Call it middle age, call it the millennium—but here he was. Was he good enough for the Pentagon to keep the spigot of funds flowing? Absolutely.

"We're going to work with lights today," announced Stuart, dropping Michael into an instant funk.

Lights. Lights were the least exciting of all. On. Off. On or off. On, on, off, off. That was it. Try to visualize the little red light on the panel behind the tinted windows as either glowing or dark. That's all he had to do. After the first fifty or so responses, he would find it almost impossible to keep his attention keyed up to the level necessary for testing his psychic powers. Had the great seers in history squandered their gifts divining about lit and unlit candles?

I think not, Michael decided, allowing only a lift of an eyebrow to express his boredom and displeasure.

Nonetheless, he let himself be hooked up to the EEG electrodes that would read his bodily functions while he tried to identify the status of the little red light on that panel behind the glass.

"We're going to do it a little differently today," Stuart said as he taped the last electrode to Michael's forehead. "The light will be triggered by random number generating software rather than manually by another research assistant."

"Whose idea was that?" Michael asked, surprised.

"The government's. They want to tighten our methodology. Dumb shits. What do they know about methodology?"

"I take it they're not here today?" Michael said with a gingerly, wired-in nod toward the tinted glass. Stuart wouldn't be so candid if they were monitoring his remarks.

"They'll be here, don't worry," the graduate student said.

Michael frowned. Why change the game plan now? If the Pentagon were satisfied with the progress of the project so far, they wouldn't be tinkering with the setup. It could mean only one of two things: either they thought the results were *too* impressive and were trying to break him, or they were wildly enthusiastic and were trying to hurry the project along.

Either way, he wasn't worried. He had what it took.

Stuart placed the counting device on a low table to Michael's left, asked if he was comfortable, and then walked over to the door of the windowed wall, opening it to murmur something to someone in the viewing enclosure. After that he came back and locked the door from the lab into the hall, took a seat at the desk, and with one eye on the wall clock, said to Michael, "Two minutes."

They sat in silence with Michael centering his thoughts during the countdown. He closed his eyes and kept them closed. He pictured the red light on the panel, pictured a small red glow. He pictured the small red glow, then the glow being extinguished. He felt his heartbeat slow and his mind begin to enter a zone barren of any other image but the red light on the panel. His breathing slowed and his mouth fell a little open, to draw in air more easily. He became utterly relaxed, as if he were floating in a warm, dark place. From a great distance he heard Stuart's voice, soft, feminine, almost erotic, say softly, "Begin."

His mind stayed blank, a dark and formless place. For a

long while it stayed that way, and then . . . a small red glow. He saw it. He could *hear* the color red, broadcasting in the dark cavern of his mind. He pressed the counter, and when the dull red light faded to black, he drifted back into darkness.

And waited.

An hour later, Michael Regan, free of electrodes and free to go, stood up on shaky legs. Stuart said something to him, but Michael had no idea what. He was, as usual, entirely disoriented and more than a little afraid. He had been to a place where no man was, and the profound and deadly isolation had unnerved him. Alone, so completely alone . . . he couldn't bear to be alone like that again. He would not submit to testing again.

"Hey!" he heard Stuart yell.

Dazed, Michael turned around in the hall and came back into the lab.

"Didn't you hear me?" the grad student asked. "Dr. Woodbine wants to see you in his office—which is that-away," he added, hooking his thumb down the hall.

"I know the way," Michael mumbled. He reversed direction and started off toward the office, trying hard to shake off the oppression he felt. It takes a few minutes, he reminded himself. But the oppression seemed deeper, the recovery longer, every time he was tested.

The Director's office was a soothing oasis of books, plants, and mahogany in an otherwise sterile environment. Velvet moss green drapes with nothing to do but look good hung alongside lowered wood blinds that were themselves doing a fine job of blocking the summer sun. A dark hued Persian rug, undoubtedly of value, added one more layer of dignity to a room that was already intimidating, giving it the look and feel of a psychiatrist's office in a venerable building in downtown Boston. The room commanded respect and demanded confidences. Michael distrusted it.

He sounded to himself like a schoolboy summoned to the principal's office as he said to the director, "Stuart said you wanted to see me."

Woodbine's answer was pleasant, even jovial. "Yes, that's right, Michael. How goes the battle?"

"You tell me," said Michael, refusing to be condescended to. He saw the computer printout opened on the desk and had no doubt that it contained the results of the morning's work. Woodbine had a remote hookup in a small closet adjacent to his office.

"Today was . . . interesting," the director suggested, tapping the printout and hedging his answer.

If he was disappointed, he was far too good an actor to show it. Tall and fit, with a chiseled, handsome face topped by a mane of wavy silver hair, Dr. Geoffrey Woodbine had always struck Michael as the perfect candidate to play a patriarch on a daytime soap.

"Interesting how?" Michael prompted, after a pause that went on a heartbeat too long. He hated that, hated the way he always leaped headlong into that trap.

Woodbine was candid. "It won't surprise you that the results today were . . . well . . . less than we had hoped. After all, the test was administered by computer. You and I both know that remote viewing depends very much on your being able to key on to a target. A human being administering the test makes a viable target, whether I'm doing the testing or someone else is. You can't be expected to score as well when that connection is severed in favor of a machine."

Michael couldn't understand it. "I felt right on top of it today, Geoff. How much off last week's results was I?"

"It's irrelevant, I'm telling you," the director said impatiently. "The important thing is, I've managed to make our friends from Washington understand that they've just thrown a massive bureaucratic wrench in the project."

He scanned the printout in front of him with obvious distaste, then looked up. His eyes, movie star blue, looked troubled. "You know, we're so close . . . so close. If those idiots hadn't tacked on this contingency," he said, smacking the printout with the back of his hand, "we'd have moved on to the next phase of testing today."

"But they're paying the bills," Michael acknowledged.

The director didn't need reminding. "Let me worry about that, Michael," he said coolly. "They have some excellent data in their hands right now, and once we deep-six these ludicrous results, we'll be back on track. I have no doubt, none at all, that the funding will be renewed next month."

Michael wanted to know what the next phase of testing was, but he knew better than to ask. It would taint the credibility of the project if he were to be told. In any case, he almost didn't care. As long as they were done with the little red light. The director got up from his desk and put his hand on Michael's shoulder, guiding him with reassuring words to the door.

"They're anxious, Michael. Extremely anxious." He lowered his voice and murmured, "They have something definite, something important, in mind for you. They need to know about you—and all of our test subjects, but really, you're the one who's front and center now. The thing is, they need to be convinced beyond a doubt. We're almost there, Michael! Almost there!"

His voice betrayed a passion that Michael had not heard before. But the director quickly dropped back into cordiality and asked, as he always did, after Michael's family. Were they coming along, after the tragedy?

"Without the press hounding them at every turn, they seem okay," Michael answered, still bitter over the way reporters had ridden roughshod over his daughter's feelings.

Woodbine shook his head. "That was a nasty crime, nasty. So Tracey's back to normal?"

"All things considered," Michael said halfheartedly.

"Good. I'm glad to hear it." He paused, then said, "I have a reason for asking, as you well know."

Michael did know. The Institute had received funding, this time from a private source, to study children with apparent psychic abilities in an effort to find out the effect that popular culture had on those abilities. But first the Institute had to line up a few children with psychic abilities.

Months ago, Woodbine had suggested a preliminary interview with Tracey. Then, and on two other occasions, Michael had refused. Now he was forced to do so again. .

"I don't see my daughter as possessing any special pow-ers," Michael said carefully. He had no desire to alienate Woodbine, but he had even less desire to deliver Tracey as a subject for testing. Who would be in the viewing room, any-way? The thought of strange men observing his little girl through a one-way window gave Michael the creeps.

Urging his case, Woodbine said, "Surely you realize that gifts like yours run in families."

"Not in my family," Michael said flatly. "I saw no evi-dence of it in my mother, and I never heard it said of my father. We've been all through this, Geoffrey," he added, edgy now in his exhaustion. All he wanted was to get out of there.

"You're right, you're right," said Woodbine, slapping him on his shoulder in farewell. "But I want you to think about it. At least let me do a preliminary interview. If I could just—"

"I said can we drop it, Geoff?"

Woodbine pulled up short. "Of course," he answered with a cool nod of dismissal. He turned back to his office, and Michael, still bothered by the apparently disappointing results of the morning's testing, headed for the lobby to sign out.

It wasn't until he was back in his car that he remembered, out of the blue, his phone call to Maddie on the day before.

Maddie with Hawke! A surge of ugly, devouring jealousy rolled over him. How had he managed to put the thought of them together out of his mind all day? Obviously he'd been distracted, first by the nightmare, then by the test, then by Woodbine's pressure tactics. But all that was behind him for the moment, and the realization that Daniel Hawke was living in the lighthouse just a stone's throw from Maddie began to eat at him in earnest.

Michael clamped his jaw tight. He decided that he must be pretty damned good at remote viewing after all, because he could picture, vividly, Maddie and Hawke together in her country kitchen.

Vividly.

Chapter 9

"Hot, hazy, and humid, right through the Fourth—perfect!" said Joan, zapping the TV on Norah's granite counter into silence.

She lifted the designer tea kettle off the Viking range and poured boiling water over a tea bag nestled in a china mug. "Of course, the high rollers won't be drawn unless the fireworks are spectacular," she told her two friends. "Which poses a problem. All we have is eight thousand dollars in the kitty, and for what we want, the Domenico Brothers would need thirty-five—and that's with a discount because one of them just married Trixie's cousin."

Joan was Chairperson of the Committee for an Old-Fashioned Fourth; she should know. Maddie was vice-chairperson. She'd signed on when Dan Hawke was still dodging bullets somewhere back in Albania, and she was much too far along to bail out now. Besides, she wanted to do right by the town; they deserved a Rilly Good Shew, as Ed Sullivan would say. And Tracey seemed to get a kick out of her mom being almost in charge of the fireworks. Apparently it gave her serious clout with the boys in her crowd.

So Maddie planned to be on that beach by the lighthouse if it killed her. All she could do about Dan Hawke was hope and pray that he'd stay in his corner of the playground during the festivities.

"I think I can scrape up another thousand for us," she

volunteered. She'd just have to hit the phones a little harder.

"Not enough," said Norah, tapping a pencil on her kitchen table.

She chewed on her lower lip for a moment, then said, "Okay. Here's what we do. Put me down for two thousand. Tell the Brothers D. that they'll have ten more by the end of the week and the last fourteen before they light the first rocket. Tell them to make it big, make it bold, and make it red, white, and blue. No greens and no golds. We want to keep this as patriotic as possible. That way we'll draw the Republicans as well as the preservationists."

As glorious as it all sounded, Maddie felt obliged to sound a note of caution as they relocated with their coffee and tea to the deck of Norah's villa.

"Thirty-five thousand dollars is a huge amount of money for a town our size, Nor. Wouldn't we be better off putting it directly into the lighthouse foundation's coffers? It would help give us the jump start we need for the project."

Norah was spinning her Rolodex like a Hollywood agent with a mortgage to pay. "Maddie, Maddie, Maddie," she said, flipping through the B's, "don't you know yet that you have to spend money to raise money? Keith Barnett. Yes!" she said, yanking the card from the Rolodex spine and moving on to the C's.

Truly, the woman was a wonder. Peering over her shoulder, Maddie muttered, "Is there anyone in that thing who's poor?"

Norah laughed and said, "Sure: my cleaning woman; my pool man; my first husband."

"Since when is a veterinarian poor?" asked Joan, dunking her tea bag.

"Since the divorce," Norah said without looking up.

Shaking her head, Maddie went over to the wall of French doors and pressed a button, activating a massive roll-out awning to shade them from the rising sun. After that she settled in one of the deeply cushioned redwood chaises that were arranged facing the sweeping expanse of ocean that lay to the south of Norah's ivory-stuccoed, glass-walled, multilevel,

multiwinged behemoth of a summer home, so totally at odds
with the town's original and quite modest gray-shingled
houses. Worse, she had started a trend: every new house to
the west was as ostentatious as hers.

Five years earlier, Norah's third husband, Maximillian
Mills, had built the house as a birthday present. Max was a
very rich Texan who had never quite connected with the low-
key sensibility of the Sandy Pointers. Max had wanted a palace for his new bride, and that's what Norah had got.

But the marriage went south and so did Max, to Palm
Beach, where he felt more at ease among the cap-and-polo
set. His fancy new pals spent their summers in the Hamptons,
of course, so naturally Max did too. Norah, on the other hand,
stayed faithful to her friends, opting to summer in sleepy, not-
so-fancy Sandy Point.

But that didn't mean she was thrilled about it.

She continued to flip through the alphabet of her Rolodex,
muttering nonstop about her misery the whole time.

"This backwater hole . . . we can't compete . . . Nantucket's bound to do a better show . . . Osterville, too . . . Marion
has money . . . Marblehead has mansions . . . we have squat
. . . no one's going to pledge . . . hmm, my good friend Sen-
ator Haskins from Connecticut—would he kick in? Probably
not. They have their own lighthouses to worry about . . . ah,
Billy Bob Jordan! Billy Bob owes me; we'll pull him
out. . . ."

Little by little the stack of cards piled up on the patio table's glass top as the Rolodex came full circle. In the meantime, Joan was happily leafing through her fireworks catalog
(Maddie, who hadn't known there was such a thing, had already shown it to Tracey and her friends, pandering shame-
lessly for their good will).

While Norah flipped and Joan thumbed, Maddie reflected.
She sat back on the chaise, cradling her coffee, breathing deep
the combination of Starbucks and salt air. She smiled at the
reassuring sight of Tracey and her girlfriend Julie sunbathing
at the far end of Norah's beach—and wondered what was
missing from the friendly, comfortable scene.

Well . . . Maddie's father, for one thing. How much better, if he were perusing the science section of the Tuesday *Times* and enjoying his own coffee back at the cottage right now. A wistful sigh escaped her. She missed him.

She missed her mother, too. Sarah Timmons should be at the library right now, organizing the used book sale, not brooding alone in Sudbury.

And finally, painfully, ultimately—Dan Hawke. Was it possible to miss someone, not during the twenty years that he'd been out of your life, but after he showed up again?

It was. Her gaze slid to the east. She saw the white cone of the lighthouse, aglint in the morning light, practically daring her to walk along its sandy beach. Once, the morning walk would've been part of her daily regimen. No more. It was yet another part of her life that she'd had to shut down because of him.

I miss you. Damn you.

Out of sight, out of mind, went the old saying, and for twenty years it had proved more or less true. But after the scene in her kitchen, Maddie was being forced to deal not with the memory of Dan Hawke, but with the man himself: with the nick in his eyebrow, the scar on his cheek, the utterly electrifying way he said her name.

I miss you. Damn you. I miss you.

She closed her eyes and sighed deeply. The memory of him was one thing, the sight and scent and sound of him another thing altogether.

The soap bubble of her thoughts was pricked by Joan, who said, "Hey, I almost forgot. Trixie finally wrangled a telephone interview out of him."

No need to ask who "him" was. Maddie mumbled "Good for Trixie."

"Interview!" Norah said with a snort. "I heard about that interview. He answered all twelve questions with yesses and noses. Max's cockatoo has a bigger vocabulary." Her voice turned low and musing as she added, "Still, he does seem to be coming around. I have hopes."

"I'll bet you do," said Joan, giving the redhead a sideways look.

Norah shrugged. "I admit it. The man intrigues me. There's something so remote about him . . . he's like the lighthouse, surrounded on three sides by water. But he's not yet an island. I can reach him. I *will* reach him."

Joan nodded gravely, as if Norah had just announced an all-out drive to save the rain forest. She sneaked a quick glance at Maddie before immediately returning her attention to Norah.

Norah pounced on that glance. "What's up, Joan? What is it you want to say?"

Joan's cheeks got red. "Well, nothing . . . I mean, if Maddie has nothing to say about it. . . ."

Norah said, "Maddie? *Do* you have something to say about it? Or do you plan to go all summer without telling us what the hell went on between you and Dan Hawke?"

So. The moment of truth had arrived. It was idiotic to think that Norah hadn't got wind of Maddie's connection to Dan Hawke. Maddie had been subjected to enough odd glances and pointed questions around town to know that her past—some version of it, anyway—was making the rounds. The jig seemed to be up.

But instead of answering Norah, Maddie turned to a thoroughly sheepish Joan and said calmly, "I'm curious. Tell me how you claim to know about Dan Hawke and me."

Joan stared into her teacup like some fortune teller at a strip mall. "Trixie told me," she said without looking up. "She said that you and Dan Hawke were once—you know— a pretty hot item."

"And how does Trixie claim to know this?" Maddie asked, still managing to sound casual.

Joan looked up. Her brown eyes became two slits of concentration. "I just want to make sure I get this straight. It was Trixie's brother's . . . boss's . . . hairdresser's cousin, I believe. I might have missed a career in their somewhere. But I know it started with this cousin who used to work as a groundskeeper at Lowell College, and he said that you and Dan used to . . . to . . . He saw you two, uh . . . he saw you doing it behind the bushes once!'' she finally blurted out.

Maddie gasped. ''He said that? He saw that? Oh, my God. I don't believe it. He said that?''

Now what? Confess? And stop where?

Best to keep on denying. ''I don't know what he thought he saw,'' Maddie said firmly, ''but he didn't see *that*.''

Joan looked uncertain and so did Norah. Maddie should've quit while she was ahead, but she proceeded to go and blow it.

''Besides,'' she added, ''he may be able to remember Dan Hawke's face, but he can't possibly have a clue who I am. It could've been the Queen of Sweden behind that shrub, for all he knew.''

Joan looked hurt. ''Oh, Maddie,'' she said, ''you don't have to lie to us. We're your friends.'' Before Maddie had a chance to deny the lie, Joan added, ''The reason everyone figured out that it was you is, the groundskeeper said that Dan Hawke carved both your initials in a tree after . . . it . . . took place. The groundskeeper remembers thinking how old-fashioned it seemed, carving initials in a tree. He remembered the initials. D, H, M, and T. He remembered they sounded like 'dammit.' ''

Their initials. Maddie hadn't forgotten them, but she hadn't thought about them for many years. Out of sight, out of mind.

''The tree is gone,'' she said quietly, caving in at last. ''It was cut down the following year.''

''After your wickedness, you mean.'' Norah seemed positively joyful at the sight of Maddie squirming. ''My, oh my, proper Maddie Timmons, banging in the bushes with Dan Hawke? Gee. Who would've guessed?''

Maddie managed a small, wry smile. ''But you'll notice I got right back on the straight and narrow: I married into an old Boston family and went directly to Bermuda for my honeymoon.''

''Dummy.''

"Not so dumb," Maddie said with a flash of heat. "I wouldn't have had Tracey otherwise."

Norah, childless, had no comeback for that. She softened and said, "So are you going to tell us about the guy, or what?"

Tell us about the guy.

It sounded so tempting. For twenty years she'd kept him hidden in the hollows of her heart. It was hard not to share someone like Dan Hawke. And yet . . .

"There's not a whole lot to tell," Maddie said, glancing back at the lighthouse despite herself. "It was a wild college fling. We were so young . . . so different from one another. Maybe that was the attraction. But there was nothing substantive to it," she insisted. "It wasn't the kind of relationship you could build on, have children from. We were just too different."

Norah wasn't buying it. "Why are you so reluctant to tell us about him, if it was just one of those flings?"

"Well, look at you, now that you know," said Maddie with an edgy laugh. "You're going to be a hopeless pest about him."

"True." Norah flashed her infamous grin. "So-o-o? Curious minds want to know: how was he?"

"At?"

Norah snorted. "Picking pineapples."

"Norah!" cried Joan, coming to Maddie's defense. "She can't possibly remember; it was decades ago. Can you remember your first time?"

"Of course I can!"

"Who told you it was my first time, for pity's sake?" Maddie said, sitting up in the chaise.

Blinking like an owl, Joan said, "I suppose I just figured it out for myself. You once said that you were still a virgin in your junior year, and the groundskeeper only worked at Lowell College for a year—your junior year, I figured out—so either you became some kind of nymphomaniac overnight, or—"

"Good God, Joan! Don't you have anything better to do

than to work out the dates of my sexual portfolio?''

Stung, Joan snapped, ''It's your fault, Maddie; you're the one who's clammed up good about him. You were the same way when you were splitting up with Michael. Maybe if you weren't always so private about your sex life—''

''My sex life is my own business, damn it!'' .

''No, it's not. I repeat: how was he?'' said Norah.

Completely exasperated by now, Maddie flung her hands in the air and said, ''Great! He was great! We went at it day and night! He had a dick the size of a musk ox and it never went down between bouts! Is that what you wanted to hear?''

''No kidding?''

''Oh, for . . .'' Maddie let herself drop back on the chaise and covered her face in her hands. She sucked in a big breath of air, pulled her fingers down to her chin, and let out the air in an explosive sigh. She looked at the sea. She looked at the lighthouse. She looked at her friends.

''All right,'' she said at last. ''I'll tell you what happened. And then we'll never speak of it again. And that includes both of you—to one another or to anyone else. Do I have your word?''

Joan nodded gravely; Norah, amused, smiled an assent.

''I met him here, the summer before my junior year. He was part of a crew that was painting the lighthouse, and one day when I was quahogging on the beach, he happened to notice that I was wearing a Lowell College sweatshirt. He'd transferred to Lowell the preceding semester, and naturally he commented on the coincidence.''

Joan nodded and said, ''It beats the old 'What's your sign?' ''

Maddie snorted. ''I'm not so sure. His exact words were, 'Boyfriend go there?' ''

''Ouch,'' said Norah.

''Yeah. I often think that if he hadn't been such a chauvinist, if he'd just said something conventional like, 'Hi, I go there too,' I would've just smiled and been on my way. Because he really wasn't my type; I could see that at a glance. I've never been big on rebels. I mean, he was such a stereotype. He even rode around on a motorcycle. God, that Harley,'' she said, laughing softly at the memory. ''How it set my parents' teeth on edge.''

''Ah, they knew him, then,'' said Joan.

Maddie shook her head. ''Not socially. My mother would never acknowledge someone who stored his cigarettes in the sleeve of his T-shirt. Not then; not now; not ever.''

''So how did you two hook up?''

''I told you. He pissed me off,'' Maddie said simply. ''You know how we all were back then; we didn't let anyone get away with anything. I took him on after that opening crack about a boyfriend, and somehow one thing led to another, and we ended up . . . well . . . behind the bushes. Among other locations.''

She ran a finger around the rim of her cup and said in a faraway voice, ''He was as quick and charismatic as a man could be, you know. A natural leader. But he was from a dirt poor background, and he never let anyone forget it.''

''He bragged about how far he'd come on his own, you mean?''

''Not at all,'' Maddie answered, shaking her head. ''It was more that he resented anyone who didn't have to make the same trip.''

''That would include you, of course.''

A rueful smile. ''No, he said he'd make an exception of me.''

''What a hypocrite!'' cried Norah, laughing.

''That's what he felt, too. It really bothered him. As for me, I didn't care if he was rich or poor,'' Maddie added softly. ''I was crazy about him.''

Still puzzled, Joan said, ''But your parents never knew?''

''Never.''

''How could the groundskeeper know, and not your father?''

''Dumb luck. My father worked and taught in the physics department, and Dan and I were in liberal arts—Dan was in journalism, I was in literature. Our paths just never crossed with my father's. Plus, my dad was flat out busy with his research when . . . well, he was flat out busy at the time,'' she added, not wishing to go down that road.

And yet it turned out that she had no choice. Joan was processing information with the efficiency of a computer. She said, ''What did break you up, then? Not your parents, since they didn't know. Not the differences in your background, since you seemed to be working around them. Did he take off again? Maybe leave Lowell for an internship with some newspaper or something?''

''He didn't exactly leave,'' Maddie confessed. ''He was . . . pushed.''

''Bad grades? Didn't study?''

''You really don't know?'' Maddie asked, surprised for no logical reason. After all, neither Norah nor Joan was from the Boston area, and even if they had been, they might not have been tuned in to yet another mess on yet another campus. Back then, student protests were still fairly routine.

But still. The tragedy had been so central to Maddie's life that it was impossible for her to believe that Joan and Norah were in the dark about it.

Maddie looked from one friend to the other. They seemed to understand how hard the going was for her, and they waited with puzzled patience for her to continue. She gazed at the reflection of a stone urn in the pale blue water of Norah's Olympic-size pool for a long, long moment, and then she spoke.

''Dan and I had been inseparable the entire fall of my junior year,'' she began. ''I was serious enough about him that I wanted to bring him home and introduce him to my parents. Dan turned the idea down flat. Finally I accused him of being afraid to face my mother.''

Joan was agog. ''What did he say?''

Maddie shrugged. ''What could he say? It was true. Oh, he hemmed and hawed and tossed off some rhetoric about taking a stand against the privileged class, but I was convinced he was afraid of sitting down to dinner with my parents and picking up the wrong fork during the fish course.

He was incredibly sensitive about dumb little things like that."

"Lots of people are insecure socially," Joan said.

"True. But they don't barricade themselves in buildings to get out of putting on a tie and making small talk at dinner."

"He didn't!"

Norah was incredulous. "All this, to get out of a meal with your parents?"

"Believe it or not, I thought so at the time," Maddie said. "I was young. Emotional. Stupid. Now I see that the timing was pure coincidence. At the time, Americans everywhere were protesting nuclear energy. Lowell just happened to reach critical mass around Thanksgiving, when Dan led the students into taking over the physics building."

"Surely Lowell didn't have a nuclear facility."

Maddie shook her head. "But one of the professors was overseeing an experiment in which several of his students were working with nuclear energy," Maddie explained.

"The actual work was being done in a lab off campus, but it's hard to take over a nuclear lab. Not so the faculty offices; they were in a quaint old Victorian mansion with lots of stained glass. The building was pretty to look at, but not at all secure."

"I assume that's where he spent Thanksgiving?"

"Most of it. The point is, my father spent Thanksgiving there, too, negotiating with Dan and the protesters, while the rest of the family sat around a twenty-five-pound turkey pretending nothing was wrong. My mother was the perfect hostess, despite being in a cold fury. But I was sick with anxiety. It didn't seem possible that Dan could have sabotaged our relationship any more thoroughly."

Maddie gazed at the lighthouse to their east. "But I was wrong," she said softly. "The day ended up so much worse than in my wildest scenario."

No one spoke. After a long moment, Joan whispered, "What happened?"

"Things got . . . out of hand. Equipment was destroyed. Files were scattered. And then someone—they never did find out who—started a fire with them. The building was evacuated, but not everyone ... made it out safely. My father was in the building. He tried to retrieve some of his research. Back then it wasn't like now—you couldn't put a life's worth of accumulated data on a couple of floppy disks and then in a crisis stick them in your pocket and run.''

Maddie wasn't looking at either Norah or Joan now. She was somewhere else altogether: back in Sudbury, forcing down a slice of pumpkin pie while her brother George answered the phone.

She took a deep breath and went on. "My father was overcome by smoke before he could make it with his armload of files to the door. Fortunately someone was aware that he'd rushed into the building, and they were able to rescue him, but by the time they found him, part of the building had collapsed on him. They weren't able to save his arm—or his research, needless to say.''

Joan was stunned. "He lost his arm in a fire? I thought it was ... on a safari," she said, realizing her naiveté.

Maddie smiled. "That's what he used to tell everyone: that his arm got crushed by a charging rhino. You actually believed it?''

"Oh, Maddie, I'm so sorry," said Norah. "What a ... bummer.''

Maddie nodded and said, "It was a long time ago. Lately it hasn't seemed that long.''

"Was anyone ever arrested?" asked Joan.

"Oh yes. Dan, and as many of his followers as the authorities could round up. But a lot of the charges were dismissed. For one thing, the school was in violation—the sprinkler system was defective. The legal tangle ended up a real mess. I think eventually he was given probation. I really don't know. By then we were out of touch," Maddie said dryly.

"You dumped him," ventured Norah. "As you should have.''

Again Maddie shrugged. "It was mutual.''

At least, that's what she used to tell herself. Dan had not

said a word in his defense as she railed against him after the fire. When he walked away, it was forever.

Until now.

"I'm sorry," said Maddie. "I didn't mean to rain on our parade this morning."

"That's all right; you didn't get anything wet," Norah reassured her. "It's over. Ancient history. You all moved on with your lives."

"I feel so bad," Joan admitted.

"Sorry," said Maddie with another wan smile.

"Don't be sorry, Maddie. And don't look back."

Confession was supposed to be good for the soul, but Maddie's soul was unconvinced. Dragging out her relationship with Dan and dusting it off for her friends to see only made the loss of it that much worse. The initials on the tree, for example. She had almost forgotten about them.

She tried to forget them again, as she worked on the new curriculum for the fall semester. When the phone rang, she reached for it almost absently.

But Tracey had picked it up before her. She heard Tracey's teenage voice, bored and brief, say, " 'Lo?"

"Is this Tracey?"

Very definitely, it was a man's voice, friendly and casual. Maddie held her breath, eavesdropping without a second's worth of guilt.

"Yes, this is Tracey."

"Tracey, you don't know me—" he began.

"Tracey, get off the phone! Right now!" Maddie blurted, rearing up to protect her child. Immediately the caller hung up. Maddie ran down the stairs to find her daughter, who was sitting in front of the television with the receiver still in her hand, a baffled look on her face.

"What did you do that for?" she asked her mother.

"Did you recognize the man's voice at all?"

"How could I? You interrupted him right away."

"This isn't a joke, Tracey. I mean it: *did you recognize his voice at all?*"

Tracey rolled her eyes and hung up the phone. "No, Mother. I did not recognize his voice at all."

Maddie had no reason not to believe Tracey, who seemed to have little interest in either the caller or her mother's concern. Nonetheless, she sat down on the spot and read her daughter chapter and verse of the dangers of having anything at all to do with strange men.

"If he calls again, I want you to tell me immediately. Better yet, let me answer the phone from now on."

That brought a look of outrage from which Maddie quickly backed down. "All right, you don't have to do that. But you do have to tell me if he calls again. Or if you notice anyone— anytime—watching you. Anywhere. Are we clear on this?"

"Yes, Mother. We're clear on this."

Maddie hated having to provoke the "mother" treatment, but she had no choice. There were strange and twisted men out there.

Chapter 10

Jittery and demoralized, Hawke paced the bedroom in an endless loop. He knew enough about his smoking habit—and his previous attempts to stop that habit—to know that he was in the acute stage of nicotine withdrawal. Add to that the fact that he'd seen Maddie go off with some jerk in a Corvette that afternoon, and he was ready to spit nails.

Was she back yet? Who the hell knew? He'd purposely moved out of the bedroom that faced her cottage and into the one that faced the sea, telling himself . . . telling himself what? That he was going to respect her space? Respect her sincere wish never to see him again?

That he was going to do his best to get over her?

Screw that, he thought for the thousandth time since the Corvette. Nothing and no one was going to dictate to him, and that included her.

On fire with jealousy and filled with self-loathing, he decided that he needed another bottle of sparkling water. The gum hadn't worked and neither had the hard candy. Sipping seltzer seemed to be helping, although he'd already drunk enough of it to float his bladder up around his tonsils.

Shit! If this didn't work, he was going to be forced to go on the patch. Beholden to some doctor for a nicotine fix—he detested the thought of it.

His mechanic had told him just that morning that he'd kicked his own cigarette habit by sipping seltzer. The guy had a bottle of Poland Spring, its label grimy with oil, sitting on his littered desk even as he spoke. He was big, burly, a smoker for thirty-five years. And sissy seltzer had worked for him.

Never mind that the presence of gas fumes all around should've been more than enough of a deterrent to lighting up. If seltzer worked for Richie, then why the *hell* shouldn't it work for Danny?

Hawke stomped down the worn wood steps to the dismal kitchen and flung the fridge door open with enough force to rip it off its hinges. One bottle left. And he wouldn't have his car until late the next morning. And he'd thrown out his Marlboroughs in town in a burst of heroism. And if this wasn't the dumbest, stupidest, most shit-headed predicament he'd ever put himself in. He was on the verge of hysteria because he was running out of *seltzer*, for pity's sake. . . .

He twisted the cap, jumpy with anticipation. Already he was becoming addicted to this new thing, this pathetic substitute for the tobacco drug. He'd come to depend on the feel of the plastic cap tearing from its seal; the sound of carbonation fizzing out of the bottle; the wave of bubbles flushing down his throat.

Forget the sipping shit—he was ready to shred the plastic bottle with his teeth. He drank long and hard, a series of swallows without air. After draining half of it, he let out a belch a frat man would be proud to call his own. One more "sip" like that and he'd be officially out of everything.

He glanced at his watch: 9:00 P.M. The damn town was rolling up its lone sidewalk right about now. And no car to get to the Store 24. Now what?

He could wander over to her cottage for the second time since his arrival. He mulled that one over. She might be home. He didn't have a snowball's chance in hell of bumming a cigarette off her, needless to say, but maybe, who knew, she'd have a bottle of seltzer to lend him. He pictured himself, cap in hand, at her back door and laughed out loud—a short, bitter, thoroughly savage laugh.

She's going to punish me until the day I die.

And the hell of it was, he deserved it.

He prowled his kitchen in bare feet, clutching the bottle like a wino, trying to find some way through his misery.

He was sick of his self-imposed confinement in the lighthouse. He'd arrived without a plan, stayed without a plan, and would no doubt vacate without a plan.

Maddie. *She* was the plan. It was as simple as that. After Albania, after his overwhelming experience in Albania, he'd hightailed it back to the States and straight to her. He wanted, needed, couldn't not be with, her. Her. Her.

Ah, Maddie. Jesus! Can't you see that?

Amazingly, he felt his eyes sting over with tears. He staggered back as if someone had thrown acid at his face. Cry? Him?

Oh, great. Why not just shoot me?

He snorted again. In Albania someone had done exactly that. And the bullet had turned his spiritual world upside down and then right side up again, like a little snow globe, with Maddie appearing smack in the middle of it. So here he was, because he had no choice. He had come for Maddie. Destiny had decreed it.

The crone who had rescued him and patched him up in her country hovel had said it best: *This is not your fight. Go home. Start over. There is still time.*

At least, that's what he thought she'd said; his command of Albanian was iffy at best. Often since then he wondered whether he'd simply heard what he wanted to hear, or whether the tea had been drugged, or—

A sharp sound from the adjacent lighthouse got his attention. Coming on the heels of his flashback, it sounded ominous. Hawke's mind was still full of snipers and random fire, and it occurred to him that he hadn't been making a habit of locking the door to the tower at night.

He slipped barefoot into a pair of deck shoes sitting by the entrance to the breezeway that connected the keeper's house and the tower, then took up a heavy metal flashlight to use as a billy club. Granted, if it was a raccoon, he was going to feel mighty silly; but if it wasn't some cute furry thing. . . .

He crept through the breezeway, which was lined with old wooden trunks that held old iron tools, and with utmost care he laid his hand on the doorknob to the tower. Silently he turned it, then threw the steel door open as he flipped on a switch, filling the tower with bleary light.

Aha! Not a cute furry thing at all—but not a sniper, either. Four teenagers, standing on various treads of the open metal staircase that spiraled from the base of the tower to the lantern room at the top, turned as one to stare at him. The smell of pot wafted up his newly sensitive nostrils at about the same time that he noticed an array of airline-size bottles of booze on the bottom stair. They even had a lantern. He was impressed. They were well-equipped little delinquents.

For some reason—maybe because he was jumpy from nicotine withdrawal, maybe because they were having more fun than he was—he exploded.

"What the f—hell are you doing in here?" he yelled. His voice bounced and soared up the metal cone, startling him as much as it did them.

Four deer, trapped in the headlights of his rage: that's what they looked like. One of the boys held a reefer the size of a Cuban cigar in his hand; the other clutched a small bottle that he made a pathetic effort to hide behind his saggy, baggy pants. Two girls—both of them known to Hawke—stood on the stairs between the boys.

Not a one of 'em said a word.

"Names, please," he said, stalling for time. What was he going to do with them all?

For an answer he got four identical sullen stares. He moved in front of the bottom tread, the better to prevent them from flight, and tried again. Zeroing in on the younger of the boys and carefully avoiding the girls, he said, "We can do this nice, or we can do this with cops. Name?"

The kid hesitated, then opened his mouth to say something, but the older boy said quickly, "You don't have to tell him, Ross."

All rightee. So the older one wasn't too bright. That was good news and bad news. Hawke shuddered to think what the older kid could do with—or to—a girlfriend. Pray God the girlfriend wasn't Maddie's daughter, who at the moment was sneaking frightened looks at the nincompoop.

He turned his attention back to the younger boy. "Listen to me, Ross," he growled, "you've got yourself in a whole passel of trouble."

The older boy snorted in contempt, maybe because of the word passel. Fine. Hawke rephrased. "You're in deep shit, kid. Massachusetts has stiff drug laws; I can't believe you don't know that."

Actually, Hawke didn't have a clue how the state felt about drugs. At the moment he was only a user of seltzer.

He noticed that the older boy looked like the younger one; he took a wild shot and said to Ross, "Your brother's a real smartass, but trust me, an ass feels a lot less smart sitting in a chair across from a probation officer. Assuming you're lucky enough to get probation."

He turned his attention at last to Maddie's daughter, the tallest of the four of them, and said, "What made you think you could camp out in the tower? Did you honestly think I wouldn't hear you?"

Her answer was a resounding silence. She didn't even give him the courtesy of glaring at him any longer, but simply attempted to look through him.

Like mother, like daughter. Physically she resembled Michael more than Maddie, but there was something unyielding in her eyes that he recognized. The funny thing was, it made her seem all the more vulnerable.

Like mother, like daughter.

He sighed, then immediately realized they'd take it as a sign of weakness, so he put more bluster into his next question. "You," he said, pointing to the girl with the porcelain skin and made-up face. "Would *you* like to tell me why you chose my lighthouse to flaunt the law in?"

She shrugged. "Your car was gone; we thought you weren't home."

The older boy did it again: "Man, Julie—!"

Dumb, or just stoned?

So, okay, they had a Ross and they had a Julie so far. Five more minutes, and he'd know the combinations to their school lockers.

It never came to that. About the time that Hawke began wishing fervently that they'd all just go away, the older brother suddenly jumped over the railing, dropped down to the floor, did an end-run around Hawke and took off, never bothering to look back. If he had, he'd have seen his kid brother Ross right behind him.

That left the two girls. Julie eyed the door, then half-started for it.

Automatically Hawke caught her by the forearm; he didn't want two young girls running around loose on the Cape at night.

"Touch me and you go to jail," the child said with impressive calm.

Yikes! What did they teach these kids? Hawke dropped the skinny arm from his grip and said warily, "Come on. I'll walk you both back to Rosedale cottage."

For the first time, Maddie's daughter spoke up. "We can find it ourselves," she protested.

He shrugged and said, "Go ahead, but I'll be right behind you. Is your mother home?"

She didn't want to answer that; but after exchanging some kind of secret signal with Julie, the girl said, "She called to say she'd be late."

Well, he couldn't exactly blame the kids. As a boy he'd done the same thing when, for a depressing variety of reasons, one or both of his parents would fail to show at night.

The point was, single mothers were not supposed to go off joyriding in Corvettes.

"Let's go," he said, signaling the two to precede him.

Before Hawke left, he stopped to grind the smoldering joint into the floor. He knew his marijuana, knew by the smell of it that this was damn good stuff. God. How did parents cope?

He let the two girls get a discreet distance ahead of him while he followed them down a sandy footpath under a hazy, half-starry sky and then down the road that led to Cranberry

Lane. There was little traffic on Water Street. The night was black and eerily quiet, with only the sound of crickets and the sporadic murmurs of the girls to break the monotonous hiss of flat waves rolling on the beach somewhere behind them.

It occurred to Hawke, really for the first time, how vulnerable kids were. There could be bogey men, there could be perverts, there could be boys with six-packs in those occasional cars that drove slowly by. He had a sudden, overwhelming urge to stick the two girls in a convent somewhere in the Alps. Anything to keep them sheltered and safe.

He was surprised when Maddie's daughter pulled up short and let him catch up to her. In the dark she sounded scared and guilty but not necessarily sorry as she said, "You don't have to tell my mother, do you, Mr. Hawke?"

"You know my name," he answered. "I think I should know yours."

She sighed in a way that made him feel like a hunchback paying court to a fairy princess. "My name," she said, "is Tracey Regan."

"Tracey, how do you do?" he said dryly. "As for letting your mother know that you were drinking gin and smoking dope, well, what do *you* think would be appropriate?"

"But I didn't get a chance to drink anything!" she said, sounding almost rueful. "And I only took one drag on the doobie, and it was my first time ever, and it made me cough. I didn't like it, really I didn't!"

Sure, sure. You say that now.

"I'm sorry, Tracey. Don't think I'm looking forward to this, because I'm not."

"But you don't understand. My mom doesn't trust me as it is!"

"Well, duh. I wonder why?"

"Please, please don't tell, Mr. Hawke!" she begged him. "My father would never tell!"

That pretty much clinched it for Hawke; now he was damn well going to tell. One way or another, he planned to make sure that Maddie got her daughter under control. How she was going to do that, he had no idea. But he didn't want Tracey turning into a female version of her slick and evasive father. He wanted Tracey to turn out, well, like Maddie. Maddie without the Corvette, anyway.

Since he hadn't responded to Tracey's last gambit, the girl repeated it. "My father understands me," she said in a plaintive wail.

"Yeah, but I'm not your father."

She sucked in her breath. "No, you're just like my mother!" she cried, and ran ahead to rejoin her friend.

"Thank you, Tracey," he said into the darkness behind her, and he meant it. In profound ways, he and Maddie *were* alike. He knew it once; he remembered it now. Their hearts and souls were carved from the same chunk of the cosmos.

If only he could make Maddie see it.

He shepherded them down Cranberry Lane. As they got nearer to Rosedale cottage, he saw that every light in the house was on. There were only two possibilities for that: either Tracey was afraid of the dark, or her mother was afraid of Tracey being out in the dark.

In the next thirty seconds, he had his answer. Maddie came flying out of the house, leaving the door open behind her, and ran into the street. She was little more than a dark shadow as she stood in the moonless lane, but he was able to hear the tension in her voice as she spied Tracey and Julie and called out to them.

"Tracey? Is that you?"

"Yeah, it's me, Mom," the girl said, glancing behind at Hawke as she answered.

"Why are you outside? Didn't I tell you to—"

Maddie stopped short. She could see him walking behind the two girls; Hawke had no doubt about that. Whether she recognized him or thought he was a stalker was another question altogether.

He kept on approaching as she said to her daughter, "Inside. *Now.* Julie, you too. I'll take you home later."

And then there were two.

Chapter 11

Before he was able to get close, she said, "If you've come for more sugar you're flat out of luck; my daughter's put us on Sweet'n Low."

He wanted to smile but he did not. He said, "No, it's your daughter I've come about."

The breeziness in her voice evaporated. "Tracey? Why?"

Boy, this stinks with both socks on, he thought. He'd never ratted on anyone in his life. Still, what he'd just seen had left him appalled. He might as well have been watching the girl holding a grenade with the pin pulled out. Maddie would have to be told.

"Were you home earlier?" he asked, though he knew she wasn't.

"No . . . my car was here, but I was off at a planning meeting with one of the contributors in the lighthouse project. He got a flat on the way back and didn't have a spare, so we had to wait for a tow truck. I called Tracey to tell her we'd be late. She was supposed to stay inside; I'm very annoyed that she didn't."

Hawke didn't hear anything after the word contributor. Contributor! A surge of almost inane relief went through him, but it made it even harder to say what he had to say.

He decided to give it to her straight. "Look, I'll be the first to admit that I don't know what goes and what doesn't go with parents nowadays, but I'm pretty sure that kids, drink, and drugs are still a no-no.''

Her response to that was a complete blank; she didn't know what he was talking about.

He was only an arm's length away from her now. He felt his blood run predictably faster at the nearness of her.

But he was there for the sole purpose of giving her really rotten news, so he plowed on stoically. ''I just found Tracey and Julie and a couple of kids—brothers; the younger one's name is Ross—in the lighthouse tower, having a little picnic. They had everything but the ants,'' he added, hoping she'd get his drift.

She did. ''Alcohol?'' she whispered, stunned. And then, without waiting for his answer, ''Which drugs?''

''Pot, as far as I could tell. I didn't frisk 'em.''

Not for a million bucks, he thought, thinking of Julie's savvy comeback.

''I see.'' In a voice that was trying hard to stay calm, she said, ''The lighthouse. . . . It's always been a favorite place for the kids to hang out. Whenever we have a community beach cleanup, that's where we find the most empty liquor bottles—you know, the airplane-sized ones? Somehow we've never found any half-smoked joints, though,'' she added in a painful attempt at levity.

It was her way of absorbing the hit—rattling on about the lighthouse instead of her daughter. Although he knew it was small comfort, he said, ''It's a rite of passage for some kids, Maddie.''

She let out a sharp sigh of distress. ''But the kids do it so much more . . . so much younger. . . . God, I can't believe this! I—''

She checked herself and said in a numb tone, ''I was hoping it would never come to this. I was hoping so much.''

Her voice was filled with such sudden, bewildered emotion that he wanted to take her in his arms on the spot and tell her he'd make it all better, which would be a little like a stagecoach driver offering to fly a 747. All he knew about kids was what he knew about himself as a kid, and since he'd chosen to forget most of his childhood, that wasn't a whole lot.

He stood there feeling helpless as she murmured, "I can't go in there now; I can't. I feel too much like shaking her until her teeth fall out. I have to calm down . . . have to stay cool . . . or we'll end up bitter enemies."

"Walk with me," he said on the spot. "We'll work on a plan."

Her head shot up. In the dark, he could only imagine the frown on her face. The skepticism came through in her voice, though, loud and clear. "You don't have children, do you?"

"You know I don't," he said tersely. Actually, there was no reason for her to know one way or the other.

She seemed to falter, then suddenly got defensive. "Well, take it from me: every parent in America is wrestling with this problem."

"Every parent?"

Just as suddenly, her bravado collapsed. "No . . . not every one," she said. He could hear tears welling in her voice. "Sometimes I wish it *was* all of them. I'd feel less of a failure then."

"That's nuts," he said, amazed to hear her talk that way, especially now that she'd explained about the Corvette. Hawke had followed her comings and goings close enough to know that she carted Tracey and her friends around everywhere and then remembered to pick them up again. That put her way ahead of any mother he ever knew.

Nonchalantly, he began to mosey down the flower-filled lane, praying that she'd fall in with his step. She did, and his heart went cartwheeling down the path ahead of them. Maddie was close enough to touch; Maddie was walking alongside. Maddie was talking with him again. Maddie, the one, the only, the great, great love of his life.

Maddie, my Maddie. I love you.

Convinced for a second that he'd said it out loud, he felt his cheeks do a sudden burn and was grateful for the cover of darkness that was wrapping them both with its warm, honeysuckle breath.

Tongue-tied out of fear of saying something that might make her skitter away, he waited for her to speak first.

"I don't know what happened," she said in an achingly frustrated voice. "One day she was a sweet, outgoing, loving kid, and the next day—this. I blame the divorce, I blame the murder. I can't blame her."

The allusion to her divorce cut through Hawke like a blade; she shouldn't have married anyone but him. He put the thought aside and concentrated on the rest of her remark. "Maybe she knows that she has immunity," he suggested. "Maybe she's testing it."

He saw her turn toward him in the dark. She said, "That's very perceptive, coming from a nonparent."

He shrugged, pleased to be considered a perceptive nonparent. "I know how it was with me, although in my case the immunity came from the fact that my parents didn't give a shit."

"I remember," said Maddie. "You said they weren't around much for you."

"Not at all."

They walked along in silence for a bit, with Hawke getting newly drunk on the sweet scents around them. How had he not noticed the overwhelming fragrance during the parade down to her house?

"Honeysuckle," he said, as though he were laying a bouquet of it in her arms.

"And wild roses."

He smiled. He was so happy. They walked a little farther down the lane, which was about to end in the blacktopped road that led to the lighthouse. Why did they make dead-end lanes so short?

He slowed to a crawl.

She matched his pace.

Her voice became low and musing. "You never married, then."

"Married?" he repeated, rather stupidly. "Who?"

"Whom," she corrected, and he heard the first smile she'd allowed herself since seeing him.

"Whom. You're right; I screw up my whoms in broadcasts all the time." It made him joyously, deliriously happy to have his grammar corrected by her.

As an afterthought, he came back and answered her question. "The right one never came along, I guess." *Actually, she came along but then she went.*

"Maybe because you're always on the move."

"And maybe not."

He sensed her stiffen and immediately cursed himself for being a blockhead. She didn't want to hear about him and her and what they used to be or might have been. She wanted to solve the problem that was Tracey. And he, big shot, had promised her a plan.

"Peer pressure is everything at that age—don't you think?" he suggested.

"But Julie's the one that Tracey hangs around with most, and Julie's not wild."

"She struck me as a little more street smart than your daughter," he hazarded.

"Oh, that's just the black nail polish and all the bracelets. She's really fairly sweet."

Or a damned good actress, he thought. He said, "Do you know her mother?"

"Definitely. She's a stay-at-home mom, very dedicated."

"Divorced?"

"Do you think it makes all that much of a difference?" she asked a little testily.

It was hard for him to say, "A bit," but he did.

"Well, we can't all be the Waltons," Maddie answered, more in sorrow than anger. "And besides, Julie will have a stepfather and a stepbrother soon; her mother's getting remarried."

"Great," Hawke said with faked enthusiasm. In his mind, merged families meant a whole new set of problems. "And the boys, the brothers—what's the deal with them?"

"Well, Ross seems harmless enough. He and Tracey took sailing lessons together at the Boys and Girls Club last summer. But Kevin . . . Kevin's fifteen going on twenty-one. I can't pin it down, really. It's not as if he has a rap sheet or anything; it's more an attitude.''

"Oh, yeah. Kevin had plenty of that.''

It occurred to Hawke that he may have seen a little too much of his own attitude in Kevin for him ever to trust the boy. When Hawke was fifteen, he was—what? Cooling his heels in juvenile court for smoking dope. Was that before or after he'd got thrown out of school? He had to think.

Before. After he was thrown out, that's when he was arrested for car theft.

Maddie sighed and said, "I won't let her see Kevin anymore, naturally. That should be more than enough to put me in her all-time Witches' Hall of Fame.''

She had another thought. "Were you able to tell whether Kevin was more interested in my daughters or in Julie?''

"Couldn't say,'' he answered honestly.

What he could say was that Tracey seemed a little more star-struck than Julie, who had no doubt promised her heart to a thirty-year-old pen pal in a federal prison somewhere.

They had arrived at the dreaded blacktopped road; it was either turn around and retrace, or part company.

Call it the honeysuckle or call it the roses, but by now Hawke was fairly pulsing from the nearness of her. Her favorite perfume used to have a flowery scent, and he had come to associate flowers with making hot, sweaty, mind-bending love. In the past two decades he'd had sex in many gardens, trying for that ecstasy, but it was never the same.

Tonight, it could be the same. He was overcome with a surge of desire so strong that it left his voice shaky as he said, "Maddie, have you ever wondered—''

"Dan, no,'' she whispered, cutting him off at the knees. "Please don't.''

Too soon. He knew that; he knew that, and yet he'd let himself be pulled along by his dick.

Shaking for another reason altogether now, he said lightly, "Don't what? I was going to ask if you've ever wondered how they get those model ships inside those little bottles.''

Her laugh wasn't a laugh at all; it was a small sound of

sorrow. "Thank you for bringing Tracey back . . . and for not calling the police—"

"I'd never."

"And most of all, for letting me vent. I feel a little better now. It really does help to talk about it."

"Even with a nonparent?" he asked, his smile as mournful as her voice.

"Even."

"Well." He bobbed and shucked like a country boy, then said, "Good night, then."

"Good night."

She turned and walked resolutely away while he waited for a car half a mile down the road to go by before he crossed. He was watching her, watching the way she held her head up and kept her shoulders back just the way she always did. He knew her so well. He loved her so much.

Sweet dreams, Maddie. Dream, dream of me.

When he couldn't see her anymore, he struck off in the direction of the lighthouse. It was only then that he realized he hadn't thought about nicotine since finding the kids in the tower.

Maddie was in turmoil. Dragging Dan directly into a family crisis was so much more boorish than ignoring him as a neighbor. She was deeply grateful that he'd handled Tracey with a firm but discreet hand, but she was mortified that he'd had to deal with Tracey at all. And it wasn't fair to him. Was there anything more awkward than having to tell a former lover that her daughter was a disobedient little shit?

And worse: it felt natural talking with him about Tracey, easier, in some ways, than talking with Michael about her. With Michael, every time that Maddie admitted to either failure or frustration, it was one point to him. But Dan didn't have an agenda. He was nonjudgmental; at least, he acted that way.

Funny, how Michael's name never came up between them. Maddie had made the one quick allusion to her divorce, and Dan had let it go by. He never did trust Michael back in college, probably because Michael was a Boston Brahmin. But there were no I-told-you-so's just now, and Maddie was grateful to Dan for that as well.

Her thoughts veered back to Tracey's wrongdoing and then, after a moment of hurt and anger, veered right back to Dan again.

She remembered, out of the blue, her wedding. She still had no idea how Dan had found out about it. The sterling candlesticks from him had arrived from London beautifully wrapped and with a gracious note. After one shocked glance at his handwriting, Maddie had tossed the card. The candlesticks she donated to a charity auction. She'd felt guilty about doing that—he'd had so little money back then—so she'd sent him a thank you card with her formal signature and nothing else. It might as well have been a bill of lading.

And that was the sum total of their communication until now. Yet he knew about the divorce. Did he understand Michael well enough to know why it happened? She'd never been able to talk about Michael's faithlessness with anyone. But she could've talked about it tonight with Dan.

She could have walked to Provincetown and back with him—just for the pleasure of his company.

And the realization shocked her.

It was Tracey's fault. Tracey's little escapade had caused Maddie to drop her defenses. There had been no such distractions when Dan had walked over to Rosedale the other day for—for what? Maddie still didn't know. Whatever his motive, she had sent him packing. She'd been able to do that because she'd been able to focus on her hostility. Not so tonight.

Tracey.

She felt her blood pressure rise at the thought of the coming confrontation with her daughter. What was she going to do about Tracey? Punishment didn't work; scolding didn't help. She'd sat Tracey down, despite the child's bored looks, and tried as reasonably as possible to explain the dangers of drink, drugs, and sex. She'd even made a point of not villainizing marijuana. So what did Tracey turn around and do?

A number.

Maddie was so caught up in her thoughts that she didn't pay much attention to the dark sedan that drove down Cranberry Lane, except to get out of its way. But the car came back quickly; it was then that she recognized that it belonged to Julie's mother. Julie was in the front seat. Deborah sounded a friendly toot-toot on the horn and kept on going.

After tonight Maddie had to consider whether Julie was trying to pull a fast one by having her mother whisk her away. If so, the girl was only postponing the inevitable by about fifteen minutes.

Maddie found her daughter in her oversize pajama T-shirt, sitting cross-legged in bed with a book by Cynthia Voight in her lap. Fuzzy Mr. James, looking cozy and well-loved, was snuggled on the pillow beside her. A glass of milk sat on the marble-topped nightstand by the white iron headboard. It was a scene right out of Normal Rockwell, and the heartache of it was, Tracey looked exactly right in it.

"Mr. Hawke told me what he found," Maddie said in her most authoritative voice. "Would you care to offer your side of the story?"

Tracey's face had a kind of puzzled innocence which tore at Maddie's resolve as she said at once, "I'm sorry, Mom. I know it was wrong."

Wow. If it was possible for a horror story to have a happy ending, then this was it. Maddie's emotions were a mess by then, anyway. Having her daughter apologize without being goaded made Maddie want to hug her till she burst.

She sat down on the same side of the bed as Mr. James, all too aware that Tracey might feel pressured if her mother got too close. Very calmly, she said, "Do you want to talk about why you did that?"

Tracey made an unhappy face and said, "It kind of just happened. I didn't know they were going to have that stuff with them."

"What did you plan to do in the lighthouse in that case? Sit around sharing a Pepsi?"

Too suspicious. Back off.

"Well . . . by then I knew. But it was my first time with, with, um, marijuana, Mom. Honest."

"Did it bother you that you were going to try something that you're maybe too young to handle?" She threw in the "maybe" for Tracey's benefit.

Tracey stared at her book. "I was nervous, yeah," she admitted, fanning the corner pages.

"And excited?"

Tracey looked up. Her eyes, blue like Michael's but darkly lashed like Maddie's, searched her mother's face, trying to fathom a correct answer there.

"A little excited, maybe," she confessed.

"Well, there's no doubt about it. The first time for anything can seem nervous and exciting, especially when it's against the law. But—"

"But I didn't drink anything tonight," said Tracey, eager now to please.

Tonight? Maddie's heart sank. "This time, you mean? Have you drunk anything before?"

Please God, let her say no.

"Yes," she said with downcast eyes. "At a party once." She looked up again, and volunteered a time and place. "At Mark Menninger's birthday."

"That was during your father's weekend, wasn't it?"

Maddie saw a veil come down over those blue eyes. "I don't . . . maybe. Yeah. I guess it was."

Maddie let it go at that for the moment. "You know, Mr. Hawke could've simply handed you all over to the police. Trespassing, underage drinking, illegal drugs. You broke a lot of laws at once tonight."

"Well, he's the one who left the door unlocked!"

"It's still trespassing, Tracey," Maddie reminded her without sarcasm. "I know I've said this so many times that you hardly hear it anymore, but truly, you can get into so much trouble drinking or doing drugs. I don't just mean with the law.

"I'm talking about when you lose control over your ability to make a decision," she went on. "Don't you know what happens then? Someone else—someone who doesn't necessarily care about your best interests—is going to make your decisions for you. And that's not fair to you. You're too smart to put your future—maybe your life—in someone else's hands.''

Tracey put down the book and picked up her teddy bear, idly pinning Mr. James's ears back against his head. She murmured, ''I wasn't going to lose control, Mom. Honest, I wasn't.''

''Honey, you have to trust me on this. When you drink or when you do drugs, you are not in control.''

The girl yanked the bear up by his ears. ''How do you know?''

How indeed? It wasn't the time to tell Tracey that Maddie—and Michael—and Dan—and just about everyone else she knew back then had at one time or another drunk to excess and experimented with pot.

So Maddie said simply, ''I have a certain amount of experience, and I know people with even more experience than I have, and what I'm telling you is fact.''

''All right,'' said Tracey with a shrug. ''I won't do that anymore.''

So that was that, for now. The trial appeared to be over. All that remained was the punishment.

Maddie grimaced apologetically and said, ''You know you're going to have to be grounded for this.''

''I figured,'' Tracey admitted.

''And I'm going to have to insist that you not see Kevin again. At least not for a while.''

''*Not see Kevin*?'' Tracey cried.

It came out as a shriek of pain. Immediately Maddie knew she'd struck a raw, raw nerve. ''Tracey, you don't have to act so shocked. If Kevin is going to drink and smoke pot—''

''Mom, that's not fair! I said I was sorry! You're grounding me! Why do you have to keep the punishment going forever? That's not fair!''

''Look, Kevin is too old for you—''

"He is not! He's fifteen!"

"He's an old fifteen—"

"Fifteen is fifteen! He doesn't even drive! How can he be too old?"

"It's not just the number of years. It's attitude . . . experience. He's an old fifteen; you're a young fourteen."

"Of *course* I'm a young fourteen! What do you expect? You treat me like a two-year-old!" she cried, sending Mr. James sailing across the room.

Maddie eyed the teddy bear on the edge of the braided rug. "That's because you have a tendency to act like a two-year-old," she said with a dangerous edge in her voice. She stood up, determined to leave while her temper was still in one piece.

For the rest of her life, Maddie wished that she'd walked out of the bedroom on the spot.

Because Tracey wasn't through. "Well, I'm just *about* grown-up, whether you like it or not! I've been in the papers, I've been on TV, and I know more about the homicide department than anyone else in school!"

And then came the final shot, straight for the heart: "And when I live with *Dad* instead of *you*, I'll be able to act my age for a change!"

Chapter 12

"Live with your dad instead of me?" Maddie was almost afraid to say the words out loud.

She wanted to shout, "How dare you say that after I carried you in my womb and nursed you and went sleepless when you were sick and taught you to speak and sing and play and be kind and be fair and gave you birthday parties and sewed your torn clothes and helped you with homework and went to every one of your school events and drove you everywhere and never, ever stopped loving you even for one tiny second, even now, when you're trying your best to hurt me as deeply as you can—how dare you?"

But she settled for saying, "I don't think so."

"I can if I want to," Tracey said with a dark look. "You can't stop me. I'm old enough to choose who I want to live with and I want to live with Dad. He'll be home more than you anyway now that he doesn't have a job, and—"

"What do you mean, doesn't have a job? What're you talking about?"

Caught betraying a confidence, Tracey folded her arms across her rib cage and said defensively, "He quit. He said he doesn't need the money. He said he's just going to work on his paintings from now on, and other stuff. So he'd be better for me to stay with. Because at least he'd pay attention to me."

Maddie was flabbergasted. Michael hadn't said a thing

about giving up his professorship. "You misunderstood him, Tracey. He must be thinking of taking a sabbatical for a year, that's all."

"He quit," she insisted. "He told me. He sent them a letter." Now that the cat was out of the bag, she became even more forthcoming. "Someone left him some money in their will and now he doesn't have to teach anymore."

An inheritance? Who could've died? His great-uncle Winthrop?

"Dad said he's going to hire a maid. I wouldn't even have to clean my room!"

"Oh, *there's* a good reason to move in with someone," Maddie said sarcastically, though she realized that men did it all the time.

"And he said I'll be able to go to any college that I want because he can afford it. Dad tells me everything," Tracey added with a sniff. "*He* treats me like a *friend*."

"If you were a true friend, you'd be able to keep something in confidence." Maddie had never pumped her daughter for information about Michael, and she didn't plan to change that policy now.

She surveyed the clutter in the high-ceilinged room with its cabbage rose paper and braided rag rug. It was a typical teenage mess, with cleaning enough for two maids.

So. Suddenly Michael seemed to be holding all the cards: money and time and Tracey's devotion.

"Good night, Tracey," Maddie said, closing the door on her way out. "We'll talk more about this tomorrow."

Tracey didn't respond.

As she dialed the number of Julie's mother on the phone in her own room, Maddie entertained a new and depressing suspicion. What if Tracey's milk-and-teddy-bear setting had all been staged? Because it certainly was true that once it didn't work, Tracey reverted instantly to form. And all because of Kevin.

Kevin! The boy was a toad. If Maddie could, she'd ship him off to a penal colony; anything to get him away from Tracey. Michael, Julie—everyone seemed to be a bad influence on the girl. And yet Maddie couldn't just lock her daughter up in a bomb shelter somewhere. Tracey had to go out there, make mistakes, fall down, get hurt, and get back up again. Maddie had to advise her the best she could, and then step back and pray.

There was no answer at Julie's house; Deborah must have stopped somewhere with her daughter. It was just as well. Maddie was tired of playing the Sheriff of Nottingham. She kicked off her low-heeled shoes, took off her black silk dress—finally—and changed into a white batiste nightgown. Without emptying the dishwasher or folding the laundry, she peeled back the cotton blanket on her walnut sleigh bed and lay down wearily in it.

What a night. Hours of forcing herself to care about Corvettes, fending off an awkward pass, a flat tire, fending off another awkward pass, the shock of seeing Dan shepherding Tracey and Julie home, the exquisite agony of walking off her anger in his company, and now this.

When I live with Dad. . . .

Not if. When.

Girls should adore their dads. That wasn't the problem. But Tracey living with her father . . . that wasn't an upbringing at all. Michael would never agree to rein her in. Their daughter would run free, which was fine for a Disney movie where the featured creature was an Orca whale, but a disaster when the creature was a teenage girl.

Michael was so apathetic. Either that or at best he was overly trusting. In Maddie's view, trust was something you earned. You honored it, and then you were given some more of it. But Michael believed that trust was something you got a whole lot of up front, until you did something to have it taken away.

They didn't agree at all about trust.

Maddie stared at the ceiling, seeing nothing. Maybe Michael was right. Maybe she was being too hard on Tracey. Maybe—was it possible?—she was actually forcing Tracey into reckless acts of rebellion.

Another thought occurred to her, even more painful: Was

she taking out her feelings about Michael's unfaithfulness on Tracey? Was what Maddie considered common sense parental caution really a fear of being taken advantage of again? For the first time since the divorce, Maddie had to consider whether she was the obvious choice to have custody of their child. Could Michael do better?

It was hard to believe that. Pushing the thought from her mind, she rolled over onto her side; her stomach; her other side; and then onto her back again. It was a warm night. Maddie made herself get out of bed and open the third window, trying to coax the faint sea breeze. She moved the lace panels aside, hooking each of them behind a metal tie-back, and stared into darkness, hearing the gentle hiss of the black, brooding sea rolling over the beach across the lane. A whiff of honeysuckle drifted through the window screen, maddening and elusive.

Honeysuckle. Dan.

Something else ruined, she thought with a sigh. Soon she'd have to leave the Cape altogether.

The phone rang. Deborah? Maddie was reluctant, but she made herself answer.

"Maddie."

Not Deborah. "Hello, Dan," she whispered. The darkened room filled with the sudden scent of honeysuckle.

His voice was low, tentative. "I, ah, was wondering how things went between Tracey and you."

Maddie laughed bleakly and said, "She's alive and I'm still here; they haven't hauled me away in handcuffs."

"Good. I know you can be—"

"Righteous?"

"I seem to remember that," he admitted, a smile in his voice.

"Believe me, I'm having second thoughts about it. In fact, I'm having my first crisis of confidence about being an adequate parent."

"You're doing just fine," he said stoutly. "Trust your instincts."

"My instincts say I'm in trouble." She meant it in so many ways.

After a pause he said, "Well, I won't keep you. I just wanted you to know that I, ah—"

Care? That you care?

"That I think Tracey may not have a clue how lucky she is to have you for her mother. But she will. Maybe not tonight or tomorrow . . . but she will."

"I hope you're right, Dan," she said with quiet intensity. "You don't know how much."

They said good night and Maddie went back to bed feeling immensely comforted. There was a time when his was the last voice she'd hear before drifting off into deep, satisfied sleep.

Her sleep that night wasn't exactly satisfied, and it definitely wasn't deep, but at least it was sleep.

The next morning, Tracey declined to meet her mother in neutral territory, the kitchen, so Maddie had to go up to Tracey's room to pronounce her punishment: no going out except under adult supervision for the next four weeks. The length of the grounding matched Julie's exactly; Maddie and Deborah had agreed on it half an hour earlier.

Four weeks. Maddie might as well have told her daughter four years. The sentence was received with stony silence.

"I'll be busy today with the cookout and fireworks," Maddie added, "and I've promised to go to the fund-raiser at Norah's house afterward, so I won't be home until late. Uncle George and Aunt Claire will bring you and your grandmother home, but they're going out again afterward. Will you be all right here alone with just Grandma?"

Or do I have to hire a security guard?

No answer.

"I'll take that as a yes," said Maddie quietly, and left.

The smell of charcoal grills being fired up on the town beach carried all the way to Rosedale cottage. Despite the standoff

120 ANTOINETTE STOCKENBERG

with Tracey, Maddie found her spirits lifting. It was the Fourth of July, after all.

Dressing was the tricky part. Norah's wine and cheese fund-raiser was scheduled to follow directly after the fireworks, and shorts just didn't seem right. So Maddie donned a flowing sundress in sea foam green, and around her neck she hung a pendant of pearlized teardrops made of vintage Japanese glass. She surveyed herself in the full-length mirror, turning round and round and round, fretting over every angle, despairing of getting her hair just right. Her hair! She pinned it up. She took it down. She pinned it up; she took it down. Up, down. Up? Down. With every rearrangement it became more limp until finally she cried, "Enough!" and left it down.

She was ready.

She left her car on the seashelled drive, opting to walk to the lighthouse. Her daughter was at the cookout already, presumably wailing with Julie over their plight. But Deborah was there, too, and that made the outing supervised. Score one for the jailers.

The crowd milling on the beach was large. There were many faces that Maddie knew and many more that she didn't. Volleyball, badminton, beach soccer—all the usual nets were strung, with players hustling for good shots and bystanders cheering them on. Dogs were everywhere, Frisbees too. A fire engine was parked near the lighthouse, looking official and dismaying kids who had sparklers hidden in their knapsacks.

Old people sat in their folding beach chairs, keeping an eye on their Igloo coolers and rubbing themselves down with repellant. All around them, kids darted in and out on secret missions known only to them. Teenage girls sat on their blankets, giggling and eyeing the boys. The boys, desperately nonchalant, sneaked hurried looks at the girls.

Maddie wandered through the crowd looking for Tracey and Julie, and found them with three other friends and no Kevins in sight. She breathed more easily, waved to them all, and made her way to the lemonade stand. Joan was there, ordering up drinks for Norah and herself. She added another lemonade to her tab.

"Hello, hello," she said to Maddie. "I'm surprised you didn't get here sooner."

"Why?"

"To take a pee—what do you think? And check out the lighthouse. But there's a line now."

"I've peed, thanks," said Maddie, smiling.

"All the rumors are true. The house is a pit. Or, as realtors like to put it, 'It just needs a woman's touch,' " Joan said, crooking her fingers into quotation marks.

She added, "I sure hope we're not biting off more than we can chew. Norah's worked up an estimate for the rehab once they get the house and tower moved. Sixty thousand just to make the house habitable, she says, and that's without the granite countertops she prefers. Then, too, we'll have to find and pay a permanent lighthouse keeper to live there and conduct tours—"

"Norah's been through the whole place that thoroughly?"

Joan blinked. "Sure. You know Norah."

"Oh, yes."

That was the problem. Maddie did know Norah. Norah was spearheading the lighthouse project, so it was perfectly reasonable for her to have gone through the property. But when Maddie tried to imagine Norah with the lighthouse committee in tow behind her, all she came up with was Norah with Dan in tow behind her.

Joan handed Maddie one of the lemonades. "Michael's here, you know."

"Is he?" Maddie said, still distracted by the thought of Norah running around the keeper's house holding up paint samples. Dan wouldn't be interested, of course; what did he care what color they painted the baths? But Dan would be there. Day and, of course, night.

"He's such an interesting person," said Joan.

"I suppose. He's had an interesting job, after all. It's taken him all over the—Dan?"

"Dan? Michael!"

"Oh." Maddie saw the look on Joan's face and recognized it at once. She'd seen the same dreamy, smitten look on many of the coeds that Michael taught. Used to teach. Had he made a move on poor Joan as well? Joan, a little too short, a little too stocky, a little too owlish and much, much too good for someone like him?

Probably not. Probably she'd fallen under his spell without his even trying. There was just something about a man who could knock off a flattering sketch of a woman in fifteen seconds. Maddie should know.

She sighed and threw her arm around Joan's shoulder in a hug as they moved away from the lemonade stand. "Joanie, he's not the one. . . . Trust me. For either of us."

An embarrassed flush darkened Joan's cheeks. "All I said was that he's an interesting man, not that . . . that I've fallen in love with him!"

But she looked and sounded much too flustered for someone who wasn't falling in love. Maddie sized her up. Joan had taken more care with her makeup than usual, and the peach tunic and stirrup slacks that she wore were as flattering as could be.

Obviously aware of Maddie's scrutiny, Joan busied herself with sucking lemonade through her straw. "Michael was talking to me just now about fireworks and smoke," she said offhandedly to prove her point. "Did you know that white smoke makes a better screen than black smoke? It scatters light and confuses the observer."

"Michael's an expert at that," said Maddie, dismissing him in one quip. She added, "I'm surprised he came down for the fireworks show. As good as ours is going to be, it can't hold a Roman candle to Boston's."

They were wending their way through the crowd, looking for Norah and not finding her. Joan said, "Didn't Norah tell you? Michael's just pledged two thousand dollars to the lighthouse project. Isn't that great? I guess he's about to come into a bit of money—but you already know that."

"Yes." Thanks to Tracey.

After one more pass, they spied Norah by the tower,

schmoozing it up with a couple of Texans. In their ten-gallon hats and cowboy boots, the men stuck out from the crowd of New Englanders like rhinos in a petting zoo.

"Uh-oh," said Maddie. "Five'll get you ten they want to buy the whole shebang and move it to Amarillo."

"Wasn't it Texas that bought the London Bridge?" asked Joan, taking Maddie seriously.

"I dunno. One of those states out there."

Maddie didn't care about the Texans. She and Joan were near Dan's front door, where a dozen people were lined up patiently, waiting to use the bathroom inside. Trixie Roiters had appointed herself Official Bathroom Hostess and was shepherding guests in and out with ruthless efficiency. All perfectly routine for the Fourth of July in Sandy Point—but would Dan think so?

Maddie pictured him at his desk trying to write to the sound of endless flushing, and she smiled. The Fourth was a funky, friendly holiday in Sandy Point, as endeared to its citizens as cotton candy on a boardwalk.

She scanned the second-story windows. Was he even inside? A part of her soul felt suddenly, wistfully alone, convincing her that he was somewhere else.

She turned to see Norah dragging the long tall Texans over to meet them. Introductions were brisk. The men had money and were willing to spend it, that's what came across.

Almost at once Norah said, "Dan's off with one of the men in search of more charcoal; some of the bags got soaked in yesterday's thunderstorms."

"Charcoal, on the Cape, on the Fourth? Lotsa luck," said Joan.

Norah shrugged and said, "He told me that I should give the tour to anyone who was interested. Jake, Cliff, and I are just going over to join half a dozen other contributors for a tour of the place. Come join us. You'll be surprised to see who one of them is."

Maddie didn't want to. It didn't feel right to go through Dan's house—it was his house, after all, and not a public exhibit—without Dan being there. And besides, she was getting anxious about the rest of her family. George had called to say they'd be late, but not this late.

Joan jumped at the chance to sneak a look at Dan's library, so Maddie wandered off on her own again, rationing her lemonade because the lines at the stand were getting long now. The sea breeze had died to a whisper, leaving a hot, clear evening, perfect for enjoying skyrockets, pinwheels, Roman candles, and burned hot dogs.

But who to enjoy them with? On a good day, Tracey would be mortified to have her mother share her blanket with her—and this was hardly a good day. If George made his way through the bottleneck on the Bourne Bridge in time, Maddie would no doubt be watching the display with her mother, him, and Claire.

But Maddie wanted . . . more.

Granted, fireworks at the lighthouse were a family affair, as old a tradition as Christmas. But this year's show was going to be special, and Maddie wanted someone special to share it with. Call it selfish, but she had reached the age in her life. . . .

She stood at the edge of the crowd, watching the old and the young and wondering where the ones like her, the ones in the middle, fit in. When she was a child, her mother had sat her on her lap and together they'd oohhed and ahhed at the bright bursts of colors high in the sky. Later, when she was a young mother herself, she'd sat Tracey on her own lap, and together they'd oohhed and ahhed at the bright colors overhead.

But Maddie's kids had their own friends now, and Maddie herself was forty. How many more fireworks would there be in her life? A Fourth of July here, a Labor Day there . . . and pretty soon, she'd be opting to watch the show through her bedroom window . . . or worse still, just wishing the noise would get over with so she could stop feeling guilty for not going.

Don't let that happen to me, she prayed, suddenly leveled by dread. Please . . . let me hold on to the magic.

"Maddie! Maddie Regan!"

She turned around, disoriented by the voice; it didn't belong outside on a beach. She saw a man that she recognized, but he was wearing clothes that she didn't: a green knit shirt over rust and blue plaid shorts; white socks pulled up tight to the knees; and spit and polished black loafers.

"Detective Bailey—what're *you* doing here?" she blurted.

Chapter 13

Detective Bailey hitched his sagging shorts back up to beer belly height and gave her an off duty smile. "I've got family in Wakeby, and I brought the wife and brood down for the day. Matter of fact, the whole gang's coming here later for the fireworks, but I decided to get a head start on 'em. I figured I'd touch base with you and enjoy a little peace and quiet all at the same time," he said with a chuckle.

"You've found something, then," Maddie said eagerly. "What? Tell me what!"

The smile fell away. He shook his head. "Nothing so far, I'm afraid. You?"

Maddie sighed and said, "I've been working my way backward through every calendar of events I can get my hands on, but nothing jumps out at me for April 6. I was hoping that since my dad was a gardener, it might be the date of a flower exhibition. But April 6 is too late for the indoor show and too early for an outdoor one. It's frustrating."

"Yeah, tell me about it." Bailey looked around and said, "So. They selling beer at this thing?"

She offered to accompany him to the concession stand, and they commiserated for a minute or two in their frustration over the unsolved murder. They talked about the note, and Maddie realized that though she wanted the slip of paper to have an innocent explanation, Detective Bailey did not. For him the note was a clue, possibly the best one they'd found so far.

He said, "The more I think about it, the more I'm convinced that ten o'clock on April 6 ended up being an appointment with your dad's murderer.

"The carjacking theory never sat too well with us, you know that," he reminded her. "There were just too many loose ends: the cockeyed attempt to remove the sound system; the fact that the car was locked when we found it; the half-removed license plate. Someone was trying to suggest a theft—and maybe slow down our ability to track the owner—but I guarantee that the man who was in the car with your father was there at your father's invitation."

"I guess the killer had to be a man, didn't he?"

"Probably. I don't picture a woman pushing your father out of the car that way. Either way, after that the killer drove to the T parking lot, dumped the car, hopped a train, and was home free. He could've connected to practically anywhere. Now, a busy parking lot might seem like an easy place to be noticed, and if your dad had been driving an orange Jaguar, that might've been true. But a silver Accord? There are half a dozen in every lot. It was a reasonable risk, especially in a lot like Norfolk's, which isn't too visible from the road."

"Could there have been more than one assailant, do you think?"

The detective shook his head. "One man, and your father knew him. They left together from the same place in your dad's car; that's my gut talkin'."

He offered to treat Maddie to a beer. When she declined, he held up a forefinger to the vendor, then turned back to her and said, "Another thing bothers me, we never did find your father's address book."

"I've thought about that a lot," she said. "Why would someone steal it? Just because they also stole the wallet? I mean, it's not as if my father knew a lot of movie stars and millionaires. Who would want it?"

The detective took a long, thirsty slug from the plastic glass and said over a discreet burp, "If the killer stole it, it's because his name was in it. If it really is gone, that's a significant factor. But I'd like to make sure it's gone. It could be somewhere still in your family's possession. It doesn't help the case so much if it is, but we gotta know."

Scanning the crowd the way a Secret Service agent might, he said, "That's what I came here to see you about. We never found it in your parents' house in Sudbury, but you did say that your father came down to Sandy Point occasionally in the off-season for a quiet place to work. Could he have left the address book in Rosedale cottage and then forgotten about it?"

Maddie shrugged. "I suppose. But I would've seen it when I packed up his study."

"Well, maybe it's not in the study. Maybe it's in a bookcase in another room. A magazine bucket in the john. Wherever. My point being, since I'm down here anyway, would you mind if I took one more look around? Right now or even tomorrow morning, if you can stand my poking through your rooms real early. Unfortunately, I plan to hit the road back to Millwood by eight."

"Oh-h . . . You know, maybe that's not such a great idea. My mother's due here any minute for the first time this year. She's been dreading the visit for months. That would surely make it worse."

The detective's face showed his disappointment. Maddie felt it, too. Here was someone willing to work on his own time for them, and she was telling him not to. She imagined her mother sitting in her robe in a state of anxiety while the determined detective searched under the beds and behind their clothes hampers.

No. It would be too painful for her mother. Maddie couldn't let it happen.

"I'll take the house apart room by room myself, starting tomorrow morning, I promise," she said with an apologetic smile. "I'll go through every box that I've packed."

"Okay . . . well . . . just thought I'd try." A resigned but compassionate smile flickered on his round, scarred face as he looked away, hiding behind his uplifted beer.

Maddie was so touched by the detective's concern that she threw her arms around him in an impulsive, affectionate hug and kissed his cheek. "Thank you for everything so far," she whispered in his ear. "We owe you so much."

The detective, clearly embarrassed by the public display of emotion, patted her gingerly on her lower back with his free hand as he muttered something about a job and just doing it.

"Hey, hey—that's my woman you're messing with, mister!"

Caught off guard by the crack, the detective stiffened. Maddie released him and turned in annoyance to her ex-husband, who was standing behind her holding three helium balloons: a red, a white, a blue. He handed them over to Maddie with a grin as he said to the detective, "How goes the battle, chief?"

"Never ends," said Bailey with a cool look.

"That's what they say. Maddie tells me you have a hot new clue. Anything going on with that note?"

Maddie hadn't told Michael a damn thing—he'd read the note on his own. She resented his implying that they were still intimate, and took it on herself to cut him off at the pass.

"Whatever the note leads to," she told her ex-husband, "I'm sure Detective Bailey will keep me informed."

She glanced up at the balloons that Michael had thrust in her hand. "You'd better take these back," she said, handing him the strings. "They're bound to be in my way when I do the macarena."

She saw the flash of annoyance in his eyes, but his grin was cheerful as he turned to a mother who was walking past just then with two young children.

"Excuse me," he said, offering them to her. "I have extras. Do you think you can put these to good use?"

Surprised but pleased, the mother accepted them with thanks and walked off, dispensing the balloons to her little boy and girl as they went.

The detective said to Maddie, "I'll be in touch." He nodded to Michael. "See you around."

He was barely out of earshot when Maddie turned to Michael and said, "You can be insufferable, you know that?"

Michael folded his arms over his head in a comical cringe. "Whoa, whoa! What'd I do now?"

"You embarrassed him, and you embarrassed me. And I really won't stand for it any longer, Michael. Stop making assumptions about you and me. Stop implying to everyone else that we're still a couple. We are not."

He cocked one eyebrow. "What brought this on, darlin'? I'm behaving the same as I always have."

"No, you're not," she said automatically. "And if you are, it's time to change. We have Tracey in common, Michael. And that's all."

"Bullshit! We have a marriage in common."

"That marriage is over. How many different ways do I have to say it?"

"What's the matter?" he asked with sudden insight. "Am I cramping your style?"

She didn't dignify the remark with an answer. Instead, she asked him a question of her own. "Have you seen Tracey yet?"

"No," he answered, a little sullenly. "I was foolish enough to want to see you first."

"Well, you're bound to get the tragic version of events when you do, so I'll give you the real version first."

She described the gathering in the tower, and Tracey's apology afterward, and the terms of the grounding. She was gratified to see the expression on Michael's face turn more and more grave.

"My God. Already?" he said when she was through. "I know they all do it—"

"That's just the point, Michael. They don't all do it. We want to believe that—it gets us off the hook—but most kids don't drink or use drugs, and we have got to make sure that Tracey doesn't either."

"Well, yeah, obviously. We'll keep her away from this Kevin character for starters. He sounds like bad news."

"Which reminds me: Does the name Mark Menninger ring a bell with you?"

Michael furrowed his brow. "Should it?"

"Tracey went to a birthday party at his house and drank there as well. You didn't smell it on her breath in the car when you picked her up afterward?"

"Did I pick her up? I can't remember."

"God, Michael! You've got to keep on top of these things!"

"But I'm always dropping her off somewhere or other," he said in his own defense. "Who can keep up? You know how they are at that age—totally wired. They can't sit still, not if they try. Maddie, Maddie, don't beat me up over this. I love Tracey; I'd do anything for her. Let's just be glad she didn't experiment with something worse. Let's just stick together and do what we have to do to keep her out of harm's way."

How could Maddie argue with that? Relenting, she said, "All right. As long as we're consistent. Please—*please*—don't let her go off scot-free on your weekend."

"Absolutely not. I'll make that clear to her today. Maddie?" he said, fixing his gaze on her. "I mean it. We have to stick together on this."

"I agree," said Maddie. And yet something in Michael's tone was too intense, too ardent, for her to agree with any enthusiasm.

"I'm gonna see what she's up to right now," he said, heading off in an arbitrary direction. He came back half a minute later. "I meant to ask, how did she get in the lighthouse?"

"The door was unlocked."

He frowned. Obviously, he didn't like that answer. "What made you go to the tower looking for her?"

"I . . . I didn't. Dan found her and brought her back."

He didn't like that answer any better. "Jesus! Who the hell does he think he is?"

Maddie said with spirit, "What would you rather he did—let her loose without saying anything? Or maybe have the police round them all up; would that have pleased you more?"

"Hey. I'm not the villain in this piece. I'm not the one

who left the door to the tower unlocked. Doesn't he know what a hangout the tower is?''

''How could he? He's not a local.''

''It doesn't take a genius, Maddie. And as I recall, Dan Hawke was exactly that, back at Lowell. Ace student, raging idealist, leader of men, and biker to boot.''

His voice became filled with innuendo, almost leering. ''It couldn't have got any better than Hawke, could it?''

''Just drop it, would you, Michael?'' she snapped.

Michael hunched his shoulders and leaned over her, a profile in menace. ''Just keep him away from my daughter, that's all. Does the rest of your family know he's living there?'' he added, yanking a thumb at the lightkeeper's house.

For whatever reason, Maddie felt obliged to answer him. ''I don't remember mentioning it.''

''I'll bet. Well, maybe you ought to. I'd be interested in hearing what Sarah has to say about having Dan Hawke for a neighbor—and your brother, too—although, why should they mind?'' he asked sarcastically. ''It's been twenty years since the trial. Probably George has forgotten all about assaulting Hawke in the courtroom.''

Michael had landed the punch squarely on her conscience. Maddie was all too aware that she should have said something to her family by now. At first she'd remained silent because she didn't want to distress them. Lately she hadn't said anything for the simple, stupid reason that she didn't want them boycotting the fireworks because of Dan.

And where had it got her? Her family was probably going to miss the show anyway, and resent her hiding the news about Dan besides.

''Do me a favor, would you, Michael? Let me tell them about Dan. You're right,'' she admitted humbly. ''They're bound to be upset.''

Instantly Michael's manner toward her softened. His shoulders relaxed and his smile, always rueful, became tender. ''Maddie, I'm sorry . . . I shouldn't have thrown him in your face like that. I'm just rattled, I guess. It's weird, him being here. And him crossing paths with Tracey that way, that was weird, too. Hell, maybe I'm still jealous,'' he admitted with a soft laugh. "You always did prefer him over me."

"I married you," she murmured. "I had your child."

He grinned. "Yeah. You did." He dropped an unexpected peck on her lips and said, "Speaking of that child, I'm off to find her and give her what-for. Wish me luck."

"You won't need that, Michael. She'll listen to whatever you have to say."

He grinned and said, "You're probably right. Okay, where is she? Wait! Don't tell me."

He closed his eyes and Maddie knew he was trying to "sense" Tracey's presence. It bothered her more and more, that conviction of his that he was psychic.

"Michael, really. Must you?" she said, tense and put off by his manner.

"That way," he said, ignoring her reproach and pointing vaguely in the direction where Tracey had set up her blanket. He plunged into the crowd.

It wasn't until after he was gone that Maddie realized he hadn't brought up the subject of his windfall. It didn't seem possible that he didn't want her to know about it; he'd blabbed to too many people around her.

Michael's motives had always ranged from arbitrary to inscrutable, but one thing Maddie did know: he wasn't trying to hide his money from her. It was one of the reasons she didn't hold him in such bitterness as some of her friends did their ex-husbands. So many bruised feelings were really about dollars. That wasn't her problem at all.

Maddie continued to scan the crowd for the rest of her family, but without any luck. Hungry now, and feeling more adrift than ever, she joined the crush around one of the barbecue grills. This was new, this long wait for a complimentary hot dog. Too many people. She wondered whether the food would ever again have the charm of being free.

The grill she'd chosen was manned by big Mickey Baretsky, a local butcher and donator of the hot dogs in question. Mickey, who looked amazingly like Dom DeLuise, was a driving force behind the barbecue every Fourth.

"Maddie, m'dear!" he cried, waving a giant fork in the air. "What'll it be? One dog or two?"

"One's fine, thanks," she said, lifted on the wave of his enthusiasm. "How's your charcoal supply?" she couldn't help asking. "Got enough to hold out?"

"More'n enough, now," he said, slapping a blistered sausage on a split roll. "Ketchup's on the table. Yeah, it was touch and go earlier. I'll tell ya," he said, "that Dan Hawke's a wonder. He picks up the phone and calls someone who calls someone who calls someone, and next thing I know, a traffic chopper's dropping what we need at the airfield. Even I don't got that kinda clout."

Amazed and yet not surprised, Maddie looked around quickly at the other grills, searching for a CNN correspondent in a white chef's hat. But he was nowhere in sight.

Undoubtedly back in his cave.

All innocent, she asked Mickey what he thought of their celebrity neighbor.

"I like the guy," the veteran said with a shrug.

Well, what did she expect? An in-depth character analysis? The man was surrounded by a hungry mob; you didn't chit-chat when your life was at stake.

She took a hungry bite of her food, annoyed at the crowd for being there and annoyed at Norah for making it show up. She wanted everything back the way it used to be: quiet, slow, peaceful, restful.

Dull.

Norah was right. On the whole, Maddie preferred things dull. Dull was the opposite of murder. Dull was the opposite of drink and drugs and teenage sex. Dull was the opposite of . . . Daniel Hawke.

Damn it!

She realized, suddenly, the real reason she'd been going round and round tonight, never stopping for long to talk with anyone. She was searching for Daniel Hawke, and the longer she went without seeing him, the more adrift she found herself feeling. Something had started up on Cranberry Lane on the night before. They'd reached across the darkness to one another and made some kind of emotional contact. She wanted—needed—to make that contact again.

There was only one thing to do, Maddie told herself grimly.

Use his bathroom.

She made her way through the crowd one more time. It was nearly dark. She could hear the murmurs of anticipation: the fireworks would be set off any minute. She didn't have much time.

Maddie knew what she wanted now. She wanted to watch the fireworks with him. It became incredibly important to her that she watch the Very Special Display with no one else but Daniel Hawke. Why this was so, she had no idea. She was going on instinct now, headed straight for the lighthouse like a sailor for a beacon at sea.

"Maddie! For God's sake, I've been looking all over for you."

Her heart sank.

"George? Ah. You made it. Hi, Claire; how's baby? Hi, Mom." Maddie hugged her mother, then hugged Claire and patted her nicely swollen belly. "Traffic was that bad, huh?"

"Where did you set up?" her brother asked. "I'm wiped. I've got to get a beer."

"I didn't set up any chairs," she said with an apologetic look. "There was no place to park this year, as you probably just found out, so I couldn't bring my car."

"What the hell are we supposed to do? Stand?"

Claire jumped in to justify her husband's bad temper. "You wouldn't believe the jam-up on the bridge. We were hoping the heavy traveling would be over by now. That was naive. And you're right about the parking; George ended up leaving the car at Rosedale."

Claire rolled her eyes in the direction of Sarah's mother, tipping Maddie off that Sarah Timmons was having a hard time tonight as well.

In fact, Sarah was on a different wavelength from all of them—distant and sad. "Maddie, honey," she told her daughter in a gentle, tired voice, "I'm too beat after that battle with traffic to enjoy craning my neck at the sky for half an hour. I think I'll just walk back to Rosedale now.''

She did look stiff and more bent over than Maddie had seen her before. And even in the dark, her hair seemed more silver than gray. Sixty-eight—bent and silver? It didn't seem possible.

''Mom, no, don't leave. It's going to be three times better this year. I've been shaking down contributions from every store and business around. I—''

''Oh, I won't miss anything; don't worry about that. I'll watch it all through an upstairs window.''

Ah, no.

''Watch it here!'' Maddie insisted. She came up with a desperate plan. ''You know what? Tracey and a couple of her girlfriends have a blanket. You could sit with them!''

Maddie saw that the idea, awful as it was, had some appeal.

''That might be nice,'' her mother agreed. ''I never see Tracey except on the fly anymore. Where is she sitting?''

Maddie gave her precise directions and then a gentle nudge. That left George and Claire. George was adamant about having a beer before they shut down the stand, and Claire wanted to stay with him, so they agreed that just this once, it would be every man for himself.

''Are you sure?'' Maddie asked her sister-in-law, feeling a vague surge of guilt about her condition.

''Maddie, you act as if I may give birth on the sand. I'm only seven months gone. I just look nine.''

''Yes, but it's all very localized, isn't it?'' Maddie said, grinning. ''You look great, Claire.''

''And I feel it.'' Something in Maddie's manner made Claire suddenly say, ''Now go. You're obviously in a hurry to be somewhere.''

Claire, lovely Claire. Maddie kissed her perceptive relative and ran to join—she couldn't believe it—the line for the bathroom in the keeper's house. It was shorter now; people were positioning themselves for the fireworks. Trixie, flaunting her power, spotted Maddie and directed her to use the upstairs bathroom instead.

Perfect! Maddie took the stairs two at a time, hardly bothering to take in the shabby state of the house, and came to a halt on the dimly lit upstairs landing. There were five doors on it, all of them closed.

She threw open the first door to a room with two metal beds, both unassembled, their stained, worn mattresses stacked up vertically against the wall. The room was dank and had an unpleasant smell, which wasn't surprising. The house had been rented to all manner of free spirits over the years. Not all of them were first-rate homemakers.

The second door opened onto a room that might have been used for a dressing room; it was too small for a bed.

Third door: the bathroom itself, which she ignored.

Fourth: a pleasant room facing the sea, with a neatly made-up bed and sheer curtains on the window. It wasn't a room that looked lived in. Probably a guest room. Not that he ever had guests.

That left what she knew was Dan's room, the one that faced Rosedale cottage, the one whose lamp blinked a mournful code every night, a code she could not fathom. Maddie took a deep breath, prepared to be lost and looking for the bathroom, and boldly opened the door.

Opened it to Norah, looking smashing in a red slip dress and sitting in a reading chair with her legs crossed and a glass of white wine in her hand.

Her presence there seemed so reasonable.

Her presence there seemed so shocking.

"Norah! Hi! I'm looking for . . . the . . . room," Maddie stammered, her rehearsed little speech all shot to hell.

"The bathroom?" Norah said with a wary smile. "It's downstairs."

"No, it's full. Trixie said to come here."

Trixie said? Pathetic!

"In that case, Dan's bathroom is two doors down on the right. The switch is on the outside wall."

"Okay." Maddie began to close the door, then opened it again.

Still there.

"Norah—you wouldn't by any chance be waiting for the lighthouse committee to convene here, would you?"

Norah laughed and said, "Nope."

"I didn't think so. Okay."

Maddie closed the door again and tiptoed away, aware that she had just seen Norah in a whole new mode. This was nothing like everyday flirting Norah. This was Norah hot on the trail. She reminded Maddie of a cat, sleek and taut and entirely focused on the hunt. To Norah, Maddie had obviously been little more than a passing car in her peripheral vision.

Maddie wanted to resent her old friend, but somehow she couldn't, any more than she could resent her cat for hunting birds. Norah was doing what the Norahs of the world were born to do: tracking down men and pinning them to mattresses.

Downstairs, Maddie waved her thanks to Trixie, who'd begun the process of shutting down the line for the bathroom, and then she beat a retreat. She stood outside at the top of the stairs, surprised to see how shaken she was by the encounter with Norah, and ran through possible scenarios.

The good news was, Norah was more scrupulous than most. She'd never take a married man to bed; her rules about that were rigid.

The bad news was, Dan wasn't married.

The good news was, Norah would tire of him soon and shoo him back out to join the rest of the walking wounded.

The bad news was, Dan might not be able to hobble away.

The good news was, Norah was becoming a better, kinder, more thoughtful person as she looked forty in the eye.

The bad news was, she might decide *not* to shoo Dan away. *Oh, damn, oh, damn, oh, damn.*

The sinking feeling was new and scary. Dull was one thing, excitement another, but this was neither. It was wrenching and painful and it left Maddie breathless with anxiety.

Where was he?

"Hey."

She whipped her head to the right. There, at her elbow, he was *there*. After all this, he was right there, close enough to kiss.

Chapter 14

"Hey yourself," Maddie said softly.

Dan said, "I've been looking all over for you."

The relief in his voice was obvious, even to her. Joy bubbled up through her smile. "And now you've found me. They tell me you're a local hero."

"Neither local nor hero," Dan said, deflecting the compliment with his own smile. "Just connected."

"And here I thought you were a loner."

"I will be," he quipped, "unless you agree to watch the fireworks with me."

And fly to the moon right after? You bet.

Maddie glanced around, trying to seem offhand. "Well, somehow I seem to have got separated from everyone else, so . . ."

She shrugged and said, "Sure. I don't mind. Do you want to walk a little farther down the beach?"

"The farther the better," he said in a new, low voice.

Jittery from the sound of that voice, she explained, "It's easier to view the fireworks from a little distance; you don't get such a stiff neck. I feel sorry for my poor m—"

No. Not now. No one else now. Only him. Only her.

They fell in step, and almost immediately the crowd dissolved into a swarm of softly buzzing nighttime sounds. Maddie heard no voices, saw no bodies.

Only him. Only her.

She said, "Really, thanks for getting the charcoal. Mickey Baretsky is so impressed."

Dan laughed and said, "When someone that big says 'jump,' you don't say no, you just ask how high."

"Right."

I like this, she thought. I like walking on the beach with him. A lot.

And suddenly she realized why: she had done it before, on the same beach, with the same man. Their first kiss was on that stretch of beach.

The crowd had thinned out by now, with only occasional dark shadows moving around to remind them that they weren't alone on some island.

He said, "You know what I was just thinking?"

"Maybe," she said, still smiling.

"I was thinking that this is how we started."

"Me too."

"I was thinking how much I'm enjoying it this time as well."

"Me too."

"I was thinking . . ."

He paused, and she did too. "What?" she whispered.

"This," he said, taking her in his arms. His mouth covered hers in a kiss of surpassing tenderness, a kiss that had both less and more than passion in it, a kiss that wrapped itself around her soul and claimed her for its own.

Had she been kissed like that in the last twenty years? No . . . and maybe not ever.

When he released her at last, she said nothing, but only sighed. It was all that was left of her soul; he might as well have that too.

He leaned his forehead into hers. His voice cracked with emotion as he murmured, "I've waited . . . so long . . . for that. My whole life. Maddie . . . my whole life."

She tried to say something, but her own voice was much too torn by longing, a hopeless rag of a voice. So she cradled her hands around the back of his head and drew him to her for another kiss, to express the thoughts she could not say.

The second kiss simmered, then began to churn, then boil, then ended abruptly in a jolting cacophony of thunder and light, color and din.

BOOM! BOOM! BOOM!

The fireworks had begun.

They broke away with awkward laughs, his more forced than hers.

"Post-traumatic stress syndrome," he quipped. "I've covered too much combat."

"I didn't know that," she said, but the rest of her thought was drowned out by the overture.

They dropped where they were to watch. Dan planted himself solidly on the ground, the way men do: legs pulled up, knees aimed skyward, feet flat on the sand. His forearms were looped over his knees, and his hands dangled idly from there. Maddie, who'd watched so many fireworks displays in her life, opted for a more comfortable position. She folded her legs beneath her and leaned back on her hands, angling her upper body to be in line with her head and neck.

Here it was, the show of shows. Was it worth the work and the wait?

Yes. The overture itself was spectacular: Roman candles shooting off their stars of fire; catherine wheels tumbling in blue circles high in the air; suns radiating fire-red sparks out and out and farther out still; pastilles spiraling frenetically upward through them all; and high, high above everything—a magnificent skyrocket, exploding in a colossal burst of silver raindrops over all the color and noise below it.

Welcome, folks, the fireworks said. We hope you have a nice time.

Maddie felt a wide grin of delight plant itself firmly on her face. "Oh! This is fabulous!" she said, though she knew that Dan couldn't possibly hear her.

She stole a quick glance at him and was astonished to see that he was watching her and not the overture. Heat rolled through her, adding inexpressible pleasure to the groundswell of emotions building up inside her.

This is it—what I want. Finally, this is it.

After firing off the sensational sample of their wares, the Domenico Brothers settled down to play a symphony for their entranced audience. The theme was simple—red, white, and blue—but the number of variations on it was dazzling. Ripples of pleasure washed over Maddie with every subtle play of suns and rockets, every rollicking mix of pinwheels and pastilles.

Like everyone else, she sighed and gasped and continually clapped her hands in joy. The pleasure was so fleeting, so intense—each burst of brilliance hardly subsided before it was replaced by the next one—that Maddie became almost frustrated in her bliss. If she could just stop the moment, any one of them, how perfect life would be.

Did Dan feel that way too? "You're not watching," she chided during a spectacular burst of color.

"Oh, but I am," he said, hooking her hair behind her ear.

She laughed shyly and said, "Watching the fireworks, I mean."

Leaning over to kiss her, he said, "Does it matter?"

She was amazed to realize that it did not. All that really mattered was that she was there with him.

Under a shower of radiant silver, they kissed for the third time in two decades. Maddie closed her eyes to the fireworks, to savor the taste of him after all the years without him. His mouth covered hers, his tongue sought hers in an exquisitely familiar way.

"Maddie, Maddie," he murmured, dropping random soft kisses on her cheek, her chin, her mouth again. "It's the same as before, isn't it. Tell me it is."

"Yes," she whispered, "oh, yes. . . ."

And then she caught her breath. "But . . . it isn't," she said, suddenly distressed. "How can it be?"

He kissed her again, more insistently now, holding her close with one arm while bracing himself in the sand with the other. His lips parted hers, his tongue sought hers, all with new urgency. Suddenly he broke off the kiss, his voice hoarse, compelling. "Tell me it is," he said, half in a moan. "Maddie, it is!"

"How can it be, after what happened?" she said in a low cry, averting her mouth from his. "Dan . . . it can never be the same," she forced herself to say. "We have to accept that."

He turned her face back to his and tried to kiss away her objections, but she said, "No, no, wait, please wait—don't you see? It *can't* be the same, any more than you can put your hand in the same river twice."

Why was she trying so hard to break the spell cast over them? She thought it must be from a sense of guilt. But it hardly mattered, because in that instant the Domenico Brothers decided to wrap up the show. They fired off their grand finale, a tempest of blinding colors, riotous displays, and ear-drum-shattering sounds, all of it mixed with the wild cheers and whoops of the crowd that was itself whipped into a frenzy of enthusiasm by the explosions and starbursts above and around them.

It looked and felt like the end of the world, and in a way, it was. Because when Maddie looked away from Dan in confusion and anguish, she found herself face to face with an outraged witness to their torrid encounter: her ex-husband, once a friend of Maddie and of Dan, now estranged from them both.

He was standing not more than ten feet from them. He'd been walking away from the fireworks, and he'd obviously stopped, frozen in midstride, when he saw them. In the bright, blinding burst of the final skyrocket Maddie saw him clearly, saw the demonic fury in his face.

Which meant he must have seen the torment and agony on hers.

She turned back to Dan, already tense from the mass launching of firepower. His gaze was fixed squarely on Michael.

And then the last bright rocket died away, plunging the three of them headlong into a shadowy hell of uncertainty.

The beach was dark now, but alive with humanity on the move. Maddie was just able to make out Michael turning abruptly on his heel and melting back into the crowd.

Dan was obviously affected by the encounter as well. "I didn't expect a handshake from him," he said as he helped Maddie to her feet, "but I could've done without the evil eye."

"He's angry; he can't understand how—"

"You can have anything to do with me?"

Maddie bowed her head. "Something like that."

Dan tucked his forefinger under her chin and lifted her face to his. "I'm far more amazed than he is," he whispered, and then he lowered his mouth to hers in another, more hesitant kiss.

But the image of her infuriated ex-husband was still too vivid for Maddie to be able to respond.

Dan sighed, then released her and said softly, "We'll go somewhere. Where?"

"Oh, Dan—nowhere. I promised—"

"Ah, right, Tracey. Of course."

"No, Tracey has her grandmother with her. It's Norah. She's having a late-night fundraiser at her house, and I'm doing part of the presentation."

"Then I'll go with you," he said simply.

Maddie remembered Norah sitting in Dan's bedroom and sipping wine. Norah would be heading home now, wondering where he had got lost.

"I don't know if that's a good idea."

His laugh was wry. "It's a godawful one. So what? I can't let you go now, Maddie. I can't."

"Dan! It's been twenty years—!"

"I know, I know. But something happened to me recently, Maddie. Something so profoundly, desperately moving . . . I need to tell you all of it. I don't care if I have to tell it between cheese puffs—"

"But why right now? You've been here for weeks—"

"I know that!" he said, sounding disgusted with himself. "I've thrown away more weeks without you—because I didn't know what to say or how to say it. Hell, I still don't!"

He scanned the smoke-filled sky, acrid from charcoal and sulfur, and then he turned back to her for another try. "It's this way: if you'd called the cops when I approached you tonight, that'd be one thing. But you didn't. You walked with me on the beach, and now I've got a right—no, don't look surprised like that—I have a right to be with you. I've always had that right,'' he insisted. "I just didn't know it before Albania."

"Albania?" She was bewildered by the whole rambling speech.

"Yes, Albania," he muttered, frustrated. "When I was there covering the unrest, I was shot—"

"Shot!" she cried, horrified. "How badly?"

"Nothing fatal, as you can see. But the bullet's not the point. The point of the encounter was that I ended up being cared for by a—I guess you'd call her a—"

He sighed and said, "Hell. I was wrong; the story can't be told between cheese puffs."

The crowd, still pumped up from the show, was continuing its mass exodus away from the lighthouse. Maddie and Dan stood fixed to the spot like rocks in a stream while bodies flowed and rippled around them. Maddie, for one, was completely paralyzed. She shouldn't stay; she couldn't go. Dan wasn't much better. He shared the tension of her silence for a long moment.

Finally he said, "To hell with Albania and the cheese puffs; I'm coming with you anyway, just to see your face."

There were so many reasons not to let him. Norah. Michael. The village gossip-mongers. Trixie and her newsletter!

Maddie agonized . . . and then her shoulders lifted in a slow, helpless shrug.

"Okay, but you'd better have a reason. You'd better bring your—"

"Checkbook."

"And a pen."

He laughed out loud and her heart did a somersault; she'd forgotten how much she loved that laugh.

"They can have it all," he said, taking her hand in his.

*   *   *

Still in a rage, Michael leaned on the horn of his Beemer and shouted, "Get the hell out of my way, you moron! Move it!"

The elderly man settled his wife in the front seat of their Buick and hurried to the driver's side as fast as his walker allowed. He folded the collapsible aid and laid it in the back of his car, then gave Michael a timid wave of apology before easing himself carefully into the driver's seat. There was another delay as he belted himself in, started up the engine, adjusted his rearview mirror, and then—for all Michael knew—cracked every one of his knuckles before finally putting the car in gear.

Michael kept his hand on the horn and flashed his high beams on and off for good measure. Christ, what a mistake to think he could escape ahead of the crowd. He hadn't taken into account that some yokel was going to block him in on the grassy lot. For twenty minutes he'd been cooling his heels, his rage keeping pace with his paralysis. For twenty minutes, a single image flashed on the screen of his thoughts: Maddie, in the arms of Dan Hawke, being kissed by him as if she'd done it before.

He remembered every detail clearly: her dress, slid up over the pale flesh of her thigh; her hand, locked around Hawke's wrist as he gripped her shoulder; her head, bent back as Hawke brought his mouth down on hers.

She would pay. Michael didn't know how, he didn't know when—but she would pay.

He needed a drink. His first stop would be at Morty's Package Store; his second, at Norah's fund-raiser.

Chapter 15

The wine and cheese fund-raiser was in full swing.

Norah's house was aglow with carefully dimmed lights that showcased her big house, showcased her fine things, and last but definitely not least, showcased Norah.

Her little red dress was gone now, replaced by a little black dress that managed to be both offhand and chic at the same time. Her only jewelry was in her earlobes: blockbuster diamond solitaires that more than made up for the simplicity of the dress.

The bartenders, both of them, and the servers, all six of them, wore white shirts and black jackets and were much better attired than some of the guests, who already numbered over a hundred. No other house in Sandy Point, and certainly not the lightkeeper's house, could accommodate such a large and lively crowd.

The room where the guests were nibbling and drinking could only be described as ballroom-sized. It featured a long wall of French doors overlooking the sea and glittering with the reflections of two massive chandeliers that anchored each end of the ceiling. Texans in snakeskin boots were reflected in that wall of windows, along with women in slinky dresses, and nautical types in blazers and Bermuda shorts. Each of the guests, whether plain or fancy, had pledged an impressive sum to make it past Norah's front door.

"Rich and eclectic. That's the best kind of support," Dan

said as he scanned the crowd. "Shall we pay our respects to our hostess?"

Maddie said faintly, "Oh, I'm pretty sure she knows we're here."

Who didn't? The reclusive, elusive, damn good-lookin' Dan Hawke had not only deigned to come to a function, but had brought a woman on his arm as well. All eyes were turned to him and Maddie as they stood searching the crush for Norah.

"Ah. There she is," Dan said, oblivious to the stares. He slipped his hand under Maddie's elbow and they began making their way toward their hostess.

He must feel like Moses parting the sea, thought Maddie as guests fell away from them during their trek across the room. People practically scraped the floor with their foreheads in acknowledgment of them. Ingratiating smiles, shyness, averted eyes and just plain gawking—Dan and Maddie got it all in a few short yards.

So this is what it feels like to be a trophy date.

The experience was a little unreal. Maddie had become invisible, except as a reflection of Dan's celebrity. It was a first for her, and only slightly amusing.

Norah turned, saw them together, smiled broadly and waved, all without missing a beat. "Hi y'all," she said, still under the spell of the long, tall Texans. Her glance at Maddie had a mischievous dancing light to it, as if she were saying, "Round one to you, toots."

She kissed the air by Maddie's cheek, and then Dan's, completely without hostility. She wasn't the least bit put out at seeing them arm in arm. To Norah it was all a game, and Maddie had just made it more interesting.

"Where's Joan? Didn't she come with you?" she asked them with perfect innocence, despite the lingering hint of a smile.

Dan said, "The last I saw of her was on the beach, moving through the crowd on tiptoe and trying to see over people's heads for someone."

"Chasing after Maddie's ex, I imagine."

An awkward silence followed. Norah enjoyed it, and Dan was oblivious to it, but Maddie rushed to fill it. "That's a beautiful dress," she told Norah as they lifted chardonnay and shrimp from passing trays.

Norah smiled and said, "What, this old rag?"

Maddie smiled back. "It goes so well with this old house."

Norah had no problem laughing at the quip. She was totally comfortable with her wealth. Still smiling, she said, "Dan, let me steal Maddie from you for a minute, would you?"

He frowned, but she ignored it.

Wrapping her long, slender fingers around Maddie's forearm, Norah drew her gracefully to one side and said, "Do you want him, Maddie? If you do, tell me now."

Maddie choked on her shrimp.

"No, I'm serious," said Norah. "If you want him, I'll leave him be." She added quietly, "I guess I'm just surprised that you do."

"Norah, for pity's sake. He's not a sweater on a sale table," Maddie said in a hushed voice. Even for Norah, the conversation was a little over the top.

But Norah persisted. "Do you?"

"Please, Nor . . . not now," Maddie begged. She stole an uncomfortable glance at Dan, who just then was being buttonholed by Trixie. "I don't know what I want. I know I still have feelings for him . . . but that doesn't mean I have to give in to them. Suddenly everything's moving so fast. This isn't the time to try to decide. Can't we drop it for now?"

Norah shrugged and said, "I'm willing to—but I'm not so sure about your ex."

She nodded in Dan's direction. Maddie swung around in time to see Michael and a tall, silver-haired man talking with Dan and Trixie. Michael looked grim; Dan did too. It didn't take a zoologist to figure out why.

Bringing Dan seemed like such a better idea on the beach.

"Do me a favor, Norah—go play with your Texans and leave us alone for a while," Maddie said, nudging her friend in the opposite direction from the group.

Maddie's heart was high in her throat as she returned to

keep peace between the only two men she'd ever cared for. Please, no scenes, she prayed. Undoubtedly because of the media scrutiny in the aftermath of her father's murder, Maddie had a dread of being in the public eye—and it didn't get much more public than this.

"Well, well, well, here you are at last!" Michael boomed out as she came up to them. His voice had a too-jovial edge to it; she knew at once that he'd been drinking. He introduced Maddie to Geoffrey Woodbine, the director of some kind of research institute.

"I'm sorry," Maddie said, only half attentive, "but I didn't quite catch that. The what institute?"

"Brookline Institute of Research and Parapsychology," Woodbine volunteered. "You've never heard of it," he said without taking offense. "It's been around since 1936—a year after Duke founded their own lab—and yet we're not the household name that they are. We investigate parapsychological phenomena," he explained with a smile. "You know— ESP, telekinesis, remote viewing—that type of thing?"

Maddie gave Michael a single sharp glance. What was he up to now?

He'd always had an interest in parapsychology, and once it had been fun to indulge it with him. But that was before he became convinced that he possessed psychic powers. Maddie was the first to admit that her ex-husband was sometimes extraordinarily perceptive. But he was no mind reader; of that she was convinced.

"I see you're uncomfortable with the idea," the director told her. "Well, it's not unusual for people to be nervous about things they don't understand."

Dan gave him a cool look. "That's a little condescending, don't you think?"

Woodbine looked surprised. "Sorry. No offense," he said quickly.

"And none taken," Maddie reassured him. She had to get Dan out of there or there'd be *two* men challenging him to a duel.

It was Trixie Roiters who ended up warding off bloodshed.

Simply out of curiosity, she switched the focus to the director himself.

"And what brings you here, Dr. Woodbine? Are you interested in the lighthouse?"

"Yes," said the director, turning now to her, "but not in the way you're assuming. Michael told me about tonight's fund-raiser and the reason behind it. It's a worthy cause; these structures should be preserved at any cost.

"However," he added, "I'm here because I have a more academic interest in lighthouses. As it happens, I wrote a doctoral thesis on what are known as 'forms with power.' "

"You mean good-looking women?" Trixie said with a wink at Norah.

The director smiled politely, then explained. "Forms with power are shapes that have metaphoric value for people working psychically. For example, the sword, the circle, the triangle, the cross, the cone—all of these shapes, or forms, have been relied on since antiquity to give guidance or protection to the psychically gifted. They seem to impart some form of energy to these people. At a minimum, such forms are extremely potent symbols."

Trixie seemed to go a little glassy-eyed, prompting Woodbine to cut to the chase. "The lighthouse is a cone form."

That made everyone perk up.

"The tower is a form with power? Power to do what?" asked Maddie.

Like a professor summing up a lecture, Woodbine said, "The lighthouse is a powerful symbol, not only to sailors but to the populace in general. Whether the lighthouse is more than that remains to be seen. I came because I was intent on touring the tower—to get a feel for it, as it were."

"How very interesting," said Trixie, stopping a waiter and lightening his load by three more hors d'oeuvres. "And did you pick up any weird vibrations when you were in it?"

He smiled and said, "I would not call them 'weird.' But did I detect an aura of significance? Oh, yes."

"Great! I'll put all this in the *Crier*."

"I'm sorry?"

"I'm editor of the *Sandy Point Crier*," Trixie explained between bites. "It's a little community newsletter I publish. There are lots of prominent guests here tonight, but you're the only one I've talked to who has a different handle on the lighthouse," she explained, wiping her fingertips daintily on a napkin. "I like that. I'm going to use it."

"I wish you wouldn't," Woodbine said at once, catching them all by surprise. "It's so easy to make a joke of parapsychological phenomena, easy—even with the best of intentions—to distort those truths."

"Oh, I won't distort anything, don't you worry," said Trixie with a cheerful grin. "Cone . . . lighthouse . . . psychic. Got it. Well—must mingle," she said, flapping her fingertips at them. "Ta-ta."

She waddled off and the director turned to Michael. "Is she serious?" he asked, clearly incredulous.

Michael didn't hear him. He was watching Dan with a steady, unblinking look.

It was left to Maddie to answer the director's query. "Trixie pretty much does what she wants; she's an institution in Sandy Point. But I'm sure you have nothing to fear, Dr. Woodbine. After tonight, she'll have much more material than she can possibly fit in the *Crier*. Besides, your theory might be a little too . . . esoteric for her readers," she added diplomatically.

He gave her a tight-lipped smile and said, "If you'll excuse me, I think I'll try to impress on her the impossibility of condensing my theories into a glib sentence or two."

That left Maddie with Michael and Dan. She glanced from one—tall, blond, and hostile—to the other, with his dark brooding eyes and hawkish nose. The air between the three of them crackled with tension. Maddie didn't have a clue whether a cone was a form with power, but she understood perfectly how a triangle could be. Talk about vibrations.

Michael broke into a sudden, ugly grin and said, "So! Here we all are. Gosh. We haven't been together like this since— when, honey? College, would it be? Your junior year—am I remembering it right?"

"Please don't, Michael."

He ignored her and turned back to Dan, punching him with vicious playfulness on the shoulder. "And you were a senior. Hey, man, did you ever finish up that degree?"

Dan said quietly, "It became a little irrelevant."

"You mean—? Well, sure, I guess it would, what with the arrest and all."

"I mean, because it was irrelevant. I didn't need a degree in journalism to carry a camera into a war zone. I just needed to be able to watch my back."

"A useful skill to have," said Michael, in a low, menacing voice. In a lightning change of tone he added, "But you're being too modest, Daniel! You stepped out in front of the camera quickly enough, and you've never really *had* to look back, have you?" he joked.

"I've looked back plenty, Michael. Believe me," said Dan evenly. All the while, his burning gaze was fixed on Maddie.

As much as she tried to control her emotions, Maddie could not keep the color from flooding her cheeks. Flustered, she said, "Michael, did you get a chance to talk with Tracey? I checked before we—I—came here, just to make sure she went straight home after the fireworks. She's there, but of course she's still not speaking to me."

Somehow the word "Tracey" cut through to him. He looked like a man stepping out of a trance as he said, "Yeah, I talked with her. In fact, I promised I'd stop in at Rosedale after this. I said it to keep the Kevins away, but I guess I should follow through on it. You don't have a problem with that, do you?" he added with a sneer.

Definitely, Maddie did. She was afraid that Michael would tell her mother about Dan before she had the chance to, but she was forced to say, "Of course I don't, Michael. For heaven's sake—"

Suddenly his expression changed again, from sarcasm to one of anguish. "Consistent. Isn't that what you said we had to be? Consistent?"

It was a direct plea, but Maddie didn't know for what. Michael was sometimes whipped around helplessly by his emotions, and this clearly was one of those times. In an old, odd way, her heart went out to him.

"Michael, do what you want," she said gently. "I can't make those decisions for you."

She watched in dismay as his emotions turned on a dime one more time. "You're goddamned right you can't," he said bitterly.

He left without another word. Maddie realized that her head was pounding and her knees were shaking from the encounter. She hadn't known how afraid she was until he turned his back on them.

"I'm glad we got that over with," Dan said calmly.

"How can you possibly say that?" she asked in amazement. "Nothing's over with!"

"Every encounter will be easier now," he argued. "The first one is always the worst."

"Is that what they taught you at CNN? Were you listening to him? He basically told you to watch your back."

"Come on, Maddie. You don't believe he's dangerous," Dan pointed out.

"Or I wouldn't trust him with Tracey?" Maddie sighed and said, "I guess you're right. . . . I know he would never, ever, hurt a hair of her head. You might not be safe . . . maybe even I'm not . . . but I think he'd give up his life for Tracey. I really do."

"Be grateful for that," Dan said softly. "I've seen so much worse out there. Infinitely worse."

"I know. I know." She shook off her uneasiness with an effort. They were at an elegant fund-raiser, surrounded by successful and generous patrons of a worthy cause. The evening was a success. She was with the only man in the world she wanted at her side right now. Norah had agreed to give her the space she needed. And finally, Dan was right: the next encounter between the three of them couldn't possibly feel as awkward.

And yet Maddie felt a pall weighing as heavily on her spirits as a fog in July.

Dan was watching her closely. "I'd accuse you of having

pre-presentation jitters," he said, smiling, "but I know you're a dynamite speaker. How 'bout it, tiger? Ready to knock their socks off?"

Her eyes widened. "My speech. Oh my God. I forgot. Oh my God."

Dan laughed and said, "Son of a gun, I was wrong. You're just like the rest of us, after all."

Very shortly and ready or not, Maddie found herself positioned alongside a slide projector, making a pitch to save the lighthouse and its tower.

"I promise to be brief," she told the assembled guests, "because I know that most of you have been to Sandy Point Light and have seen for yourselves how much the beach has eroded recently. In the last three years, we've had five so-called 'storms of the century.'

"Whether it's the greenhouse effect or the whims of Neptune, the storms that keep battering the Cape and islands are gnawing huge chunks of beach and swallowing houses like Pac-Man. Sandy Point Light is living on borrowed time.

"Our lighthouses are a national treasure," she said earnestly. "They're part of the history that marks us as a great maritime nation. Sandy Point Light, like Nauset Light in Eastham and Sankaty Light on Nantucket, can and will be saved from the ravages of the ocean. We have the permits lined up; we have the engineers to do the job of moving it farther inland. The one thing we need—the only thing we need—is money.

"And that, ladies and gentlemen, is where you come in. Your response so far has been overwhelming; our pledge drive is off to a wonderful start. What I want to show you tonight are before and after slides of other lighthouses that have been restored or moved. We've also been able to assemble an impressive archive of historic photographs of Sandy Point Light—the way it looked in almost every decade from the 1890's right through last week. You'll see for yourself how voracious the ocean is. You'll see for yourself why we have to act now, why you have to open your hearts and your wallets. . . ."

Chapter 16

Michael wanted to hurt her, but he didn't know how. Pain, humiliation, anguish—that's what he had felt on the beach, and that's what Maddie deserved to feel now. He drove to Rosedale in a black mood, determined to find the single best way to even the score.

It was Sarah Timmons who opened the door to him. Her greeting was brief; the two had said their summer hellos earlier at the fireworks show.

"Tracey's watching TV," Sarah said, nodding in the direction of the parlor. "It's a little late for a visit, Michael," she added in a gentle scold. "I'm about to go to bed. You'll keep it down, won't you? My bedroom is downstairs in Ed's study now."

Michael flashed his ex-mother-in-law a good-natured grin. "We'll be like mice," he promised, edging past her.

He found his daughter curled on her side in the loveseat, her arm dangling listlessly over the cushion as she watched TV. She was a picture of teenage boredom. He dropped into an old slipper chair and felt a nostalgic surge of discomfort from the coiled springs poking through the flattened down cushion.

"That was a heckuva fireworks show," he said.

Tracey flopped over on her back and lifted a throw pillow from the floor to hug. "It was okay. Not as good as Boston's," she told the ceiling.

"That's because Boston's a much bigger town."

Sighing, she said, "Tell me something I don't know." She reached over for the remote and hit the mute.

"You're really fed up with Sandy Point, aren't you?" he volunteered.

"Like, totally," she said, tossing the throw pillow and catching it in her arms.

"I can't blame you. A person could easily die of boredom here."

"Here I am, on my deathbed."

He laughed indulgently. A plan had sprung up in the trough of their shared resentment against Maddie.

"It's a shame you're not in Boston for the summer," he began. "You could earn some decent money in Boston—not like here, where there's nothing but babysitting for you to do."

"I can't even do that while I'm grounded."

"It's a tough situation," he agreed. "Just the other day I learned about a great opportunity for you. Fascinating work; good pay; and very few are qualified. You would be, although—"

He let the unfinished thought hang there, like bait. Tracey snapped it up.

"Although what, Dad?" she said, sitting up now.

He shrugged. "Although I doubt that your mother would go for it."

"Well . . . she might. What kind of job is it?"

He chose his words carefully. "I wouldn't call it a job, exactly. It's more a series of tests that you'd have to undergo. You know how I've been working with those researchers in Brookline for the past year or so? Well, they're looking for someone your age to do the same things that I've been doing."

Tracey looked intimidated. "*Me?* Oh, Dad—I couldn't! I don't know anything! Not like you!"

He laughed and said, "It's not as if you have to be a nuclear scientist or anything. It's easy, really. You do simple things, like trying to guess which playing card is being held up in another room. It has nothing to do with how much school you've had, or even how smart you are—and you're damned smart, bunchkins. These researchers simply test your natural abilities: how good you are at guessing thoughts and that sort of thing.''

"That's all you do? Huh! You never said." Reassured now, she allowed herself to become enthusiastic. "And they would pay me for that?"

"They'd pay you very well."

"How often would I have to do this?"

"I'd have to check. Maybe only on your weekends with me in Boston."

"But why me?"

"Because you're my daughter."

"Really?"

"That's what they said."

"Cool! Oh, Dad, you have to make Mom let me!" she cried. "You have to!"

He gave her a grave look. "That won't be easy."

He knew there wasn't a chance in hell that Maddie would give her okay to the project, despite the fact that he saw no real danger in it. The simple truth was that he didn't want Tracey hanging around with him in the lab.

All he wanted was to drive Tracey, like a stake, through her mother's heart.

By the time Dan brought Maddie home from the fund-raiser, the lights in Rosedale cottage had been long turned off. Reluctant to part, they sat in the Jeep with the headlights turned off and the engine running.

"After having to share you with contributors all night," Dan admitted, "I don't think much of handing you directly over to your family."

"You never did," Maddie said, smiling. She reached for his hand in the dark. "I loved being with you, even if we never did get a chance to talk about—"

"Albania."

"Among other things," she said softly. "Tomorrow you'll

tell me everything." She sighed and added, "We're in such a hurry to catch up on our separate pasts. Maybe we ought to pretend we've just met and take it from there."

He shook his head. "Can't do it. The past is why I left; the past is why I'm here."

"You speak in riddles, sir," she said, smiling despite the gravity in his voice.

He took Maddie's hand in both of his and lifted it to kiss. For a long, somehow thrilling moment, he held her hand to his lips that way. And then he said, "Maddie. Do you believe in destiny?"

Caught by surprise, Maddie faltered and said, "I . . . don't know. It's such an overworked phrase. Destiny," she said, trying out the word. "Destiny." She was almost afraid of the sound of it.

"Well, after Albania, I do," he said. "Too many forces had to come into play . . . too many events had to occur . . . for me to be here, with you, asking you whether you believe in destiny."

"Albania, again," Maddie said, wondering. "What *happened* to you there?"

"I don't know," he admitted. "Whatever it was—I don't know. I can't explain it to you in twenty-five words or less. I may never be able to explain it to you. But I'm sure as hell going to try."

Someone in the house flipped on the outside floodlight; it poured through the front windshield of Dan's Jeep, blinding them both.

"My mother," Maddie explained, squinting. "She's always jittery now—and she wouldn't know your car."

Dan said wryly, "I guess I should be grateful for that."

He had no idea just how much. Maddie was afraid to be seen kissing him good night in the glare of the yard light, so she said, "See you soon," and scrambled out of the car like a teenager caught by police in a lovers' lane.

As soon as Maddie stepped onto the drive, the floodlight went off; she was left to grope her way down the flagstone path in the dark. No doubt her mother thought she was doing the polite thing. Would she have recognized Dan in the car? Not from the kitchen window, surely.

We'll soon find out, Maddie thought, steeling herself for the coming encounter.

She found her mother sitting at the kitchen table, cradling a cup of tea. The fragrance of chamomile scented the air as Maddie—strictly to humor her mother—threw the bolts on both the top and the bottom of the Dutch door.

"Did I wake you?" she asked.

Sarah Timmons pulled her seersucker robe a little more snugly around her. "You know how it is when it's your first night somewhere; you toss and you turn. Was your night a success, dear?"

"Wildly!" Maddie admitted, hugging herself.

Her mother looked startled by the level of her enthusiasm, so Maddie quickly explained, "The pledges just kept rolling in—the biggest ones from men. I had no idea that Norah was so well connected. I think maybe she's blackmailing these guys; I assume she has videotapes somewhere."

"Don't be flippant," her mother said automatically. "Who was that who dropped you off? I didn't recognize the car."

"Oh! By the way," Maddie said in a clumsy diversion tactic, "did Michael come around tonight? I saw him at the fund-raiser and he said that he might." She edged nearer the hall, ready to make a break upstairs.

Her mother's voice became crisp. "Yes. He did. But he didn't stay long. On his way out he mentioned that you and Tracey were battling about something again. I don't understand how you and the child can keep butting heads," she added. "You and I were never like that."

So Michael hadn't mentioned Dan. Desperately relieved, Maddie smiled and said, "You must have been a much better mother than I."

Ignoring the remark, Sarah said with deadly calm, "I seem to be getting all my news from my ex-son-in-law nowadays."

She paused, then added, "He also told me that Daniel Hawke is staying in the keeper's house this summer."

Maddie's heart plummeted.

Her mother took a sip of her tea and then laid the cup carefully in its saucer. The tiny clink it made was the only sound in the kitchen. All else seemed to be waiting to hear what Maddie had to say next—even the old, wheezy refrigerator, which for once was holding its breath.

Maddie murmured, "Yes. He's staying there."

"Why didn't you tell me this?"

"Would it have changed anything?"

"It certainly would have. I'd never have come down this season."

"Then that's why I didn't tell you."

Among other reasons.

Her mother smiled wearily and said, "Maddie, I know you mean well, but I resent the way you filter the truth for me. You do it all the time—withhold facts to make me do what you think is best."

"You know me, Mom, I'm a control freak," Maddie quipped.

Sarah Timmons was not amused. She lifted her face, so pale without makeup, and looked her daughter in the eye.

"I'm an adult, Maddie," she said with great dignity, "not your little girl. I'm old enough to decide how to grieve and how long to do it. When I'm ready to take up a normal life again, I will. You should respect me enough to let me make that decision."

"Yeah, but sometimes people can get so immersed in a mood that they need to be shaken out of it," Maddie argued. "You know how it was whenever Dad wanted to go on vacation. He wanted to go, wanted to go, but you never did. And then when he dragged you, kicking and screaming, someplace, you'd end up having a wonderful time."

"I somehow don't see me having wonderful times just now," her mother said with a dry smile. "But I promise to think over what you said."

Maddie came back into the room and leaned over her mother, kissing her cheek. "That's all I ask. Good night, Mom."

"Good night, dear," Sarah said, patting her daughter's

arm. Maddie got as far as the bottom of the stairs when her mother called out in a hushed voice, "Oh—Maddie! You never said who that was in the car."

Maddie winced. She could pretend not to hear. She could run up the stairs and hide in her room. She could behave, in short, like her immature, hormone-driven daughter, the one who was driving her crazy.

She came back into the kitchen.

"Dan Hawke brought me home, Mom."

"*Him?* I don't believe it!" her mother said, shocked. Her face went three more shades of pale.

"He was at the fund-raiser and offered to take me home. I was on his way, obviously." It was half a truth—filtered facts again—but better than nothing.

But her mother was wise to her now. "Why didn't you take your own car to Norah's?"

"My car was blocked in our drive."

"Then how did you get there?"

Caught.

Maddie looked down at the checkerboard floor. "Dan took me."

Her mother said in a trembling voice, "He wouldn't dare. He's not that low."

Maddie's head shot up. "Why is it low to want to be seen with me?"

"You know what I mean!" her mother said. "He ruined your father's life!"

"He made a mistake!"

"One that I'll never forgive! Never!"

"That's crazy!" Maddie said, exploding. "That's medieval! We have to be willing to forgive and forget and get on with life. Life's too short—we, of all people, should know that, Mom! Life's too short! It comes and goes in the blink of—"

"Don't tell me about life! My life was destroyed—twice!— by that monster."

"That's a stupid thing to say!" Maddie shouted. "Dan's

not the one who murdered Dad; some demented slug can take credit for that!''

Her mother slapped an open palm on the table in anger. ''Who's to say? Who's to say?'' she cried. ''If your father hadn't been disabled, maybe he would've been able to defend himself.''

''Mom, he was shot! *Four* left arms wouldn't have defended him against a bullet!''

''But we'll never know, will we! We'll always wonder if it would've turned out differently, won't we!''

''You will, anyway,'' Maddie said, ducking behind sullenness.

''*And you will, too, Maddie.* You know you will.''

It was flung at Maddie like a curse. She stepped back instinctively, trying to get out of its way. But she knew that her mother had scored a hit. She knew that whenever she saw Dan from this day forward, she would wonder about it. Was Dan responsible for her father's ultimate fate?

Destiny. Here, surely, was a reason not to believe in it.

''I don't think you have the right to play God, Mom. No matter how good a person you are,'' Maddie said, giving her mother a level look.

She turned on her heel and walked smack into her sleepy-eyed, thoroughly irritated brother.

''What's the matter with you two?'' he said in a hushed growl. ''It's three in the morning, and you're going at it like a couple of fishwives. My God—what will the neighbors think?''

''Go to bed, George,'' his mother snapped. ''This is between Maddie and me.''

''Since I was forced to hear most of the exchange, I'd have to argue the point, Mother.''

He turned to his sister and said, ''Dan Hawke? Are you out of your mind?''

''Oh, not you too. I *have* to listen to Mom,'' Maddie said to her brother. ''I *don't* have to listen to you. Good damned night!''

She fled to her room, exactly the way Tracey would have

done, and threw herself across the bed, exactly the way Tracey would have done. Overwhelmed by a mass of conflicting emotions, she lay without moving, trying to sift her fury from her heartbreak, her frustration from her sympathy.

It was déjà vu all over again, she decided, smiling grimly over the famous quip. She remembered the first time she'd thrown herself across a bed because of Dan, remembered how devastated she'd felt at the news about the demonstrations and the fire, and how angry she was at Dan, and how betrayed by him. Her loyalties had lined up squarely with her family, and yet somewhere under all that grief and rage she'd still felt a terrible, terrible longing for him, and that was the emotion that she had worked for twenty years to destroy.

With no luck at all. Because here it was again, that longing. It hadn't gone away. It had only gone deep. Somehow she had nurtured it and kept it alive—on the sly, without ever letting herself know—and now the longing was back, stronger than ever. The more reasons she had for not wanting Dan Hawke, the more she wanted him. He was the Kevin of her life.

Kevin. Suddenly her heart softened toward her poor, punished daughter. For two cents she'd invite Kevin to Sunday brunch, just to see Tracey's face light up. If only the girl knew how much her mother was identifying with her now. Maddie had an almost irresistible urge to wake up her daughter and tell her.

Almost. But not quite.

Eventually she got up from the bed, too exhausted to sleep, and went over to the one window that had a partial view of the lighthouse. Drawing the curtains aside, she slid the screen up in its tracks and leaned out the window, bracing herself on the sill with her hands. If she stretched, she could just see a slice of the lighthouse. Were the lights on? Was Dan thinking of her, missing her, wanting her, too?

Maddie thought she saw a vague loom of light, but she couldn't be sure. After the long night of ordeals, it seemed inconceivable that he could still be up; but then, it was equally inconceivable that *she* could still be up.

She sighed, then dropped back into the room, feeling as adrift as a paper cup floating on the sea. She wanted to be with him. She wanted to hear his voice, kiss his lips, run her hands all over him. She wanted him in ways she didn't understand, in ways she couldn't know.

Unzipping her sea green dress, she let it fall to the floor, sorry that she was the one doing the unzipping. She wasn't sure how she'd expected the evening to end, but in her most pessimistic moments she hadn't imagined it would end with Detective Bailey back on the case, Michael in a rage, her mother and brother alienated from her for the first time, and Tracey alienated from her still.

The one—the only one—with whom she felt a sympathetic connection right now was Dan. It seemed more than ironic; it seemed inevitable.

Destiny. Had he been right about that, after all?

She undid her bra and tossed it on the dress, then walked over to the closet for the nightgown hanging on the hook inside the door. There it was: cool, demure, and white. Just like her. Her hand hovered over the gown and then came down again.

No. Not the nightgown.

Impulsively, Maddie reached past it for a hanger and pulled a sweatshirt from it, bending the hanger in her hurry. A pair of old jeans was looped on a hook inside the closet; she took those too. In seconds she was dressed and had a plan: sneak out of the house and slip over to the lighthouse and—unlike Tracey—do it without getting caught. Her cheeks burned from the sheer adolescent idiocy of it, but she felt on fire with excitement.

The problem was her mother, tossing and turning in the bedroom on the first floor. That was really, really dumb, installing her on the first floor. Shit. Maddie went back to the window and slid the screen up, then looked down at the ground. Too high. Oh, for the apple tree that had split in half under the weight of wet snow last winter.

It was going to have to be the stairs. Maddie slipped into the hall, grateful to see that her daughter's room had the keep-out sign on it and that her brother's door was closed as well. Grabbing her Keds, she tiptoed down the hall and then down the stairs, skipping two of the treads because they squeaked. She hadn't expected there to be a light on in the kitchen, and she was right. She wasn't as sure about her mother's bedroom, recently the study her father had loved so well. The room had the only wall-to-wall carpeting in the house, and light didn't show under the door.

With infinite care, Maddie tiptoed barefoot past her mother's room. To be caught in the hall carrying her sneakers would be the ultimate humiliation.

Obviously the thing to do was to walk boldly out the front door. She ought to be above this adolescent nonsense. She ought to act her age. And yet something about sneaking around had a wicked appeal.

Déjà vu all over again, she thought, exhilarated despite her jitters. She was definitely punchy.

She was lined up exactly opposite the door to her mother's room when she heard a single sharp click. A lamp? Yes. The big keyhole in the door became filled with light.

Shit!

Maddie didn't move, and after a normal eternity, more or less, she heard and saw the light go off. Safe! It was an easy tiptoe sprint to the Dutch door in the kitchen. She slid first the lower bolt, then the upper, then turned the doorknob carefully and let herself out.

She paused on the other side of the door and gazed up at the stars. The night was less black than before; dawn was on the way. If she were going to be insane, then she'd better do it in a hurry.

Chapter 17

Under fading stars, Dan Hawke stood in front of the lighthouse, holding the last pack of cigarettes he would ever possess in his life.

He'd discovered the cigarettes by accident when he was rummaging through a box of books earlier in the day: a pack of Marlboroughs, the cellophane wrapper still intact. It must've fallen out of his shirt pocket when he was closing up his apartment in Atlanta.

He fingered the wrapper, taking comfort in the fact that it was still unbroken. The cigarettes would still be fresh.

All the more satisfying to throw 'em in the sea, he thought, walking toward the water. There weren't too many things in his life that he had control over at the moment, but this was one of them.

The walk was short; there wasn't much beach between the lighthouse and the ocean, despite the outgoing tide. He pulled away the little cellophane strip—the last time he would ever do it—to allow seawater to soak the pack and take it down to a watery grave. Then he hauled back with his pitching arm and hurled the pack as far as he could over the water.

End of story, he told himself, shrugging off the addiction without a regret. He was too exhilarated to care. Here it was, past four in the morning, and he was as wide awake as a kid at camp. And not jumpy awake, either. He felt too alert, too on top of things, to call himself jumpy.

He would see her at nine. At nine he would see her, hear her voice again, definitely kiss her again. He struck out on a walk along the beach. No point in going to sleep now; he wanted to relive the night. He could still taste her mouth, smell her perfume, hear the ache in her voice as she said his name.

There was still hope! The Albanian crone had been right: all he'd had to do was go back to where he'd made a wrong turn and start over. What if he hadn't listened to the old woman? What if he'd written her off as a crazy lady, drugging him with narcotic tea and muttering gibberish to distract him from his pain?

The Albanian crone! He wished he knew her name. He'd send her a year's wages for the miracle she'd wrought. Wonderful lady! He could picture her so clearly, big pores and all, a babushka on her head and a black shawl around her shoulders to ward off the cold and damp of her hovel. Those eyes! Beady, glazed with cataracts, unfathomable. Without seeing, they were able to look straight through his soul.

He owed her his undying gratitude, that crone. For the maggoty rye bread, for the straw pallet, for the way she jabbered the soldiers into passing on by.

Two years wages! And worth every cent.

Old crone—thank you! he thought, pumping his fists in the air. He made a vow on the spot to find her and build her a new house as soon as Maddie agreed to be his.

Maddie would agree to be his. She had to. A woman didn't kiss a man like that from a sense of nostalgia. And she sure as hell wasn't the type to try him on like a new hat. Maddie, Maddie Regan.

Regan! Wrong name, wrong name. Damn! Maddie Hawke. Right name. His name. Their name. Maddie Maddie Maddie Hawke. God, he was floating on air just thinking about her. He loved her through and through. She was as fresh as the sea: bracing and intoxicating and clear. He hadn't felt this good since Lowell College.

No. That wasn't true. He'd never felt this euphoric before. She'd had him riding high in Lowell College, but even there—hell, he was twenty-four. What did he know about love, back in Lowell College?

No, not true. He was being too hard on himself. He knew enough back then to know the real thing when he saw it. And for the next twenty years he'd wandered through a desert of war and rebellion (maybe trying to get himself killed?) without finding the oasis that was Maddie. It took an old crone to point the way back.

Yes! God, he was happy. It didn't seem possible to love someone this much and not explode. Nine o'clock, nine o'clock. He'd blow apart before then!

A long flat wave nudged an empty beer can in his path. A symbol? Of temptation? To do what? Waste this high in a stupor? No way! He kicked the can ebulliently away from him.

And when he looked up, he saw her.

Or thought he did. He had to be hallucinating. She was walking toward him in jeans and sweats, the same as she had two decades ago. Maddie Timmons back then, twenty years old, an idealist, a *virgin*, for chrissake. He'd never known one before.

And the most beautiful girl he'd ever seen. Beautiful then, beautiful still. Straight-through beauty, not the skin-deep kind.

He humored the vision walking toward him, smiling and charmed by it, and then he stopped dead in his tracks and blinked. The vision had a voice.

"Dan!"

She broke into a run for him and he was so stunned by the reality of her that he just stood there like an ass, like a besotted, enchanted ass.

Still, he had the sense to open his arms as she drew near. And then he was holding her, holding the vision, and she felt and sounded and smelled like Maddie and *was* Maddie, and his heart, at last, was at peace with his soul. For the first time in his forty-four years of life, he was at peace with himself.

"Maddie, Maddie . . . I love you," he said between joyful kisses, because he wanted that out in the open before anything else. "I've always loved you, I'll never not love you, Maddie, I love you."

"I know . . . I know . . . I feel the same, I've always felt the same," she said, interrupting him with urgent, passionate assurances that left him dizzy with ecstasy. "We never, never should have parted, it was my fault—"

"You had no choice," he said, kissing her throat, inhaling her deep into his soul. "It's why you were you, why I loved you . . . I love you, love you. . . ."

It was a dream, it didn't seem possible, it was a dream, and he became suddenly afraid it would end. "Maddie, let me love you here, now, let me love you." He said it in a low moan, tugging her down to the sand. It was cool and damp from the receding tide, and somehow the right place to be, to make love.

"Oh, yes," she said on a sigh, and she fell to her knees.

He did, too, and they lost themselves in one another's arms for a long, rapturous kiss before she lay back, as if on command, and let him remove her jeans. He rolled up her sweatshirt, exposing her breasts, and he caught his breath in agony that he had lived so long without her. He bent over and suckled her breast as if he were a starved thing, and he heard her moan in abject arousal. Her hands were wrapped in his hair, pulling it hard, pulling his mouth hard against her nipple. It left him drunk with satisfaction, wild with desire.

"In me, in me," she said in a low, hoarse cry.

"Gladly, oh, gladly," he said, closing his eyes to savor the sound of her hunger. In his wildest dreams, his deepest fantasies, he would not have imagined them here, at the edge of the sea. He thought, in a garden, with roses . . . honeysuckle . . . but this . . . And yet it was right.

He rolled over on his back and pulled away his khakis and boxers, then sat up and began to haul his T-shirt over his chest. He stopped and pulled the shirt back down, then said to her, "I don't want you to hurt . . . to get sand in you—"

"I'll sit on you," she said, just as she had all those years ago, and it sent a newer, even stronger surge of desire through him. He rolled over on his back again and she took him in her mouth, whipping him to absolute rigidity in a few short strokes, and then she mounted him. The weight of her leg swinging over his torso catapulted him back in time and forward to their future and wrapped him up in a knot of sheer bliss.

In utter silence she fitted herself around him and then went still. She was on him, he was in her, and only the ocean knew—the sad, sighing, mournful ocean, sliding in and then out over the beach. He lifted himself to go deeper still, searching for that last fraction of her, coming home, after all those years.

She let him find her, and then she braced her hands on his chest and drew herself slowly up, then came down . . . up . . . down, the ebb and flow of the sea, the rhythm of their love for one another. He wanted to savor the moment, but the moment had other ideas.

He cupped his hands under her buttocks and began to move, and she didn't stop, and suddenly they were slamming into one another, him up, her down, in a fury of pent-up passion, making up for lost time, for lost years, a whole generation of them. He heard her moan in agony and in joy, and he winced from the passion of it and felt tears sting his eyes. He wanted more than anything to have her forever, but he knew more than anything that he could only be sure of now.

He came before he meant to, before she had a chance to. Part of him felt satisfied, but his soul felt bereft; he wanted her with him on the same plane of ecstasy.

"Stay," he whispered, and pinned her buttocks to his groin. "Wait."

She let out a low, throaty laugh of frustration and he knew that she *had* been waiting, just as he had, all those years. For an exquisitely long moment they stayed locked in their eroticism, listening to the rhythmic approach and retreat of the sea. He knew that he would remember the moment forever: the warmth of her weight on him; the slippery pool of his seed puddling between them; the cool wet lick of a wave as it slid around his ankles and then withdrew as furtively as it had approached.

He would remember it forever.

Suddenly Maddie sighed and seemed to catch her breath, and then she leaned over to give him a scorching kiss. He might as well have been touched by fire. He let out a sharp, animal sound and instinctively rolled over, pinning her under him in the act. He repositioned himself in her, then searched for and found her mouth, thrusting his tongue in it, filling her every hollow with himself, offering himself to her and claiming her for his own.

The hot, quick slide of his flesh back and forth against hers brought him to a new and deeper level of passion. This time, he wanted nothing but to see Maddie satisfied. He made a crazy vow never again to come before she did, because he was crazy in love with her.

He felt her breath grow short and ragged, heard her moan become a series of whimpers, tasted her tears on his lips. He felt her body shudder beneath his. He felt himself go over the edge, and then he felt . . . stillness, a dreamy, tender stillness between them. After all those years . . . stillness. At last.

After a long, long while, Maddie sighed and rubbed her cheek against his hair, wiping away the last cool trail of her tears.

Crying . . . she'd been crying. The thought of tears at a time like this astonished her, until she remembered that she almost never cried when she was unhappy. She mostly cried from joy.

She sighed again, content in her love for him. Dan heard the sigh. Nuzzling her on her neck, he said, "I'm heavier than I was twenty years ago."

"Not much," she said, but he rolled onto his side anyway.

She let out a moan of protest and kept her arms around him, afraid to let him leave her embrace. She'd flung him away once, and had paid dearly for the mistake.

"I love you," she whispered. "I love you."

He stroked her hair away from her face and said simply, "You are my life."

Overhead a gull screeched out a warning: *dawn, dummies! Dawn!*

"It's getting light out," Maddie said, acknowledging the obvious at last.

Dan's voice was wistful: "I guess we can't just stay here?"

She laughed and said, "Not without bottoms on." She sighed, wistful herself, and began the process of brushing sand from her skin.

"Wait," he said, laying his hand on her wrist. "I have a better idea. We can rinse off in the sea."

Maddie smiled and shook her head. "Only in the movies, I'm afraid. In real life someone's bound to come along walking a dog."

"Okay, here's a concession: we keep our sweatshirts on. No one will suspect a thing. And anyway, who'd be out at this hour of the morning?"

A man and a dog, a woman and two dogs, a man running, another man running, and—amazingly—a woman on horseback, that's who. The beach had turned into Grand Central Station. Every time Maddie and Dan began wading back out of the water, Maddie would spy another body on the horizon. By the time the coast had cleared enough for them to make a run for their clothes, they had goosebumps on their goosebumps.

"Geez, doesn't anyone sleep in anymore?" Dan asked while they dressed in record time.

"Can you believe it? I'm so cold," Maddie confessed, "and suddenly exhausted."

Dan wrapped her in a warming hug and murmured in her ear, "Come back to the lighthouse with me, then. We'll huddle there together. Maybe take a nap. Eventually."

Maddie closed her eyes and imagined the two of them holed up in the lighthouse, making love, sleeping, making love again. It sounded like paradise, a dream come true.

But a dream, nonetheless. Maybe Dan could live the life he'd lived twenty years earlier, but that luxury was no longer an option for Maddie. She had a family. She had commitments. For all she knew, her mother was on the phone with the police at that very moment, reporting an abduction.

"It sounds like heaven," she said, holding him tightly

around his waist. "But I can't just run away from home. It doesn't work that way."

Dan sighed and said, "Go, then, though I hate to have you leave my sight. Shower and we'll go somewhere for a meal. I'll pick you up—when?"

"Maybe the best thing is to take separate cars," Maddie murmured, unable to look him in the eye as she said it.

He understood. "Your mother's on to me," he said without a smile.

"Well, what do you expect? She never did like that Harley," Maddie said, trying to keep it light.

He surprised her by staying serious. "What did she say?"

"Oh, you know mothers: they don't say anything; they just give you that look."

"What did she say, Maddie?"

"Well . . . she seemed . . . surprised . . . that you would want to take up with me again."

He smiled wryly. "She thinks I'm a cur."

"Something like that."

"Jesus."

"Oh, don't be shocked, Dan, please don't be shocked," Maddie said, taking his hands in hers and bringing them up to her breast. "My mother is still in agony over my father. She's doing exactly what I did; she's taking out his murder on you. She's frustrated . . . angry . . . grieving. She wants to put the blame on someone. She wants closure, and you're a convenient scapegoat. Trust me on this: I know exactly how her mind is working. Her mind is being led around by her heart, and her heart is bitter right now."

Maddie blinked. She'd formed the theory on the spot, but now that she'd said it, it made a sad kind of sense. She added softly, "Every murderer is really a serial killer, isn't he? When he takes a life, he destroys a whole string of other lives. I'd give anything to know who killed my father."

Dan wrapped his arms around her and whispered, "I know, Maddie." He became quiet after that, lost in his own thoughts.

"I'm sorry," she said in a voice muffled by his shoulder.

"I didn't mean for it to finish up like this. We had such an incredible, wonderful experience . . . that's what I want to take back with me. That's what I want in my heart right now. You."

"Maddie . . . love of my life. If you had any idea . . ." He kissed her again, a profoundly tender kiss that left her in awe. All those years. He'd remained committed to her all those years.

They parted reluctantly, but with the reassuring thought that they'd be together again in a couple of hours. Maddie made her way back to Rosedale cottage with every hope that their escapade would go undiscovered.

She lucked out. Her mother, never an early riser, was still asleep, and so, of course, was Tracey. George liked to get up early, but not on the Cape. Maddie's own door was as she left it: closed.

Once inside the sanctuary of her bedroom, she set the alarm for nine, then fell on her bed as she was and dropped into an immediate, deep sleep. Deep, but brief. The brutal ringing of the wind-up clock would've made her downright vicious if it weren't for the fact that she was so much in love. Tired but almost mystically happy, Maddie showered, changed into a yellow top and a denim skirt, and went to the kitchen in search of caffeine. In two short hours, she'd be back with her lover.

Lover. The word was so joyously inadequate to describe what Dan meant to Maddie. Her life just then was a fairy tale, her sense of malaise, a vague memory. Had she really once been worried and unhappy? It seemed so hard to believe. She had a smile on her face that stayed there through her brother's dry greeting.

"You seem pretty cheerful for someone who didn't get to bed until three," said George pointedly, heading for the fridge to pour himself some orange juice.

Not a clue, then. Excellent!

Grinning, Maddie said to her brother, "We raised ninety-two thousand dollars last night. Isn't that great?" It was a perfectly valid—and true—reason for being happy.

"What a waste of money," George muttered. He stood in front of the open door of the fridge and emptied his glass in one swig, then refilled it from the juice carton. "You know, you might think about making friends with women who have more in common with you," he added in his toast-dry voice. It was no secret that he considered Norah vulgar and Joan much too downscale.

Maddie smiled and touched a finger to her brother's chin. "You missed a spot shaving. And you just dribbled OJ on your shirt."

George looked down his nose at the cream-colored polo shirt and swore. "I'm teeing off in twelve minutes!"

"Most people won't even notice it," Maddie said generously.

He was already on his way back up the stairs. Maddie caught the words "lunch" and "client" thrown over his shoulder.

In other words, George had no time either to lecture her or to deliver a third degree.

Yes! She was on a roll!

Maddie cleaned up the kitchen during her first cup of coffee, and explained the lighthouse project to Claire during her second. By then it was after ten and her mother still hadn't emerged from the downstairs bedroom. Since Sarah hadn't slept well, it wasn't surprising, but Maddie found herself hovering at the door to her mother's room, more worried than not. She gave in to her impulse and eased the door open, just to be sure.

Her mother was asleep, obviously exhausted. She was lying on her back, her mouth slightly ajar. The reassuring sound of her light snoring was tempered by the sight of a bottle of her sleeping pills on the bedstand: Sarah, proud and conservative, had come to rely on sedatives since the death of her husband.

Maddie watched her mother sigh and roll over onto her side, a hint of a smile hovering on her lips. Was she dreaming of her beloved Edward? Maddie hoped so. Leaving her mother in peace, she closed the door silently and went upstairs to Tracey's room.

There, she had better luck. Tracey had showered and was towel-drying her long hair. Mother and daughter exchanged glances in the walnut-framed mirror above Tracey's bureau: appraising glances, on both sides.

Maddie said, "Mind if I come in?"

"Mom! Why would I mind?"

This was new. Bemused, Maddie said, "I guess I got the wrong idea from your 'Keep out!!!' sign underlined three times."

"Oh, that," Tracey said breezily. "I forgot it was hanging." She began untangling her hair with a styling brush, scrunching her face with every pull.

"Here, let me do that," Maddie said, longing for physical contact with her only child. "Did you use conditioner?"

"I'm out."

Which meant she'd refused to use her mother's conditioner. Which meant she'd still been sulking as recently as ten minutes ago. So why the turnaround?

"Your dad was going to stop by last night," Maddie said offhandedly. "Was he able to make it?"

"Uh-huh."

"Well . . . good." Maddie worked at the tangles with short, businesslike jabs as she searched for a way to find out whether Michael had tried to poison Tracey's mind against Dan. He could be so very good at things like that.

But Tracey seemed to have an agenda of her own. "Mom, I wanted to ask you . . . you know how Grandma always talks about your first job, the one walking dogs? If I wanted to do something like that instead of babysitting, that'd be okay, wouldn't it?"

"Well, it's harder work, certainly, and I'm not sure you'd be all that thrilled about the cleaning up part. But if you really were willing to line up the business and follow through on it," Maddie said, fanning her daughter's hair, "I don't see why not."

"Well, maybe not exactly walking dogs, but something like that."

"What, for example?"

Tracey shrugged as she took her brush back. "I don't know."

Mystified, Maddie said, "When you've thought your plan through a little more, we certainly can talk about it."

"Promise?" Tracey's eyes were shining with anticipation, as if all that remained were to cash her first check.

Maddie smiled and said, "Sure."

A wide grin lit up the girl's face, hinting at the beauty that one day would come. Her next words were music to Maddie's ears.

"What's for breakfast, Mom? I'm starved!"

Maddie turned out bacon and waffles for Tracey and left some extra warming in the oven for her mother. She knew that they wouldn't get eaten, since her mother had a lunch date with her old friend Lillian. The waffles were a peace offering, pure and simple.

Stepping outside into brilliant sun, Maddie aimed her Taurus in the direction of Harwich Port, where she planned to have a long, leisurely lunch with Dan. Chatham was prettier, but Chatham was farther. They wouldn't be that interested in the view anyway.

Still, Maddie was aware that the blue, white-capped water of Nantucket Sound looked especially glorious. It was a perfect summer's day, bright and dry, with a stiff breeze from the west. A dozen sailboats dotted the horizon, helmed by sailors with places to see and currents to catch.

She and Dan would have to get their hands on a sailboat of some kind. Nothing big, just a daysailer to go bopping around the bay in. Or maybe something with a cuddy just big enough to sleep two, in case they decided to stay overnight at an anchorage. After all, Tracey spent a weekend every month with Michael. And really, it should have a berth for Tracey, too. Tracey liked to sail—she used to, anyway. Somehow they hadn't got around to it the last summer or two.

Tracey. How would she take to the man who'd replaced her father in her mother's heart? Girls weren't as possessive of their mothers as they were of their fathers, so maybe it wouldn't be too bad. But Tracey and Dan had started off on the wrong foot. Tracey was to blame for that, but Dan had embarrassed her, nonetheless. And girls never—ever—forgot their Big Embarrassing Moments. Tracey could live to be a hundred and twelve; she'd still remember, as if it were yesterday, the night Dan Hawke caught her in the lighthouse and marched her back home.

If it wasn't for Dan . . .

"Thank you, Dan Hawke! I love you, Dan Hawke!" Maddie shouted, and laughed out loud at the sound of her joy.

Chapter 18

Dan's car was one of only five or six in the parking lot of Hollyhocks. Not a big crowd, then. Good. Maddie wouldn't have to feel guilty if they decided to linger over lunch, holding hands and gazing into one another's eyes.

The restaurant was an unpretentious affair a little off on its own, a gray-shingled structure with dark green awnings over the west-facing windows, and windowboxes bursting with pink and white geraniums. The best thing about it was its Fisherman's Platter. The second best thing was its outdoor patio, bordered on two sides by banks of old-fashioned hollyhocks in little-girl pink and racy dark purple.

Maddie parked alongside the red Jeep and eyed the umbrella-shaded tables as she walked past them toward the main entrance. On a day like this, outside was the place to be. On cue, Dan emerged through a side door behind a hostess who was headed for the corner table of the patio.

Maddie did a quick detour, profoundly happy to be with Dan again, thrilled to see a smile light up the depths of his dark eyes as soon as he saw her. A look like that from a Daniel Hawke was more genuine than a hundred easy grins from a Michael Regan.

Dan pulled out a chair for her almost shyly and asked her what she'd have to drink. Too sleep-deprived for wine, Maddie opted for an iced tea. Dan ordered the same.

One other patio table was occupied, by a much younger

couple. They were talking in low, easy voices over the remnants of their meal.

"They can't possibly be as much in love," Dan said, reading Maddie's thoughts.

Maddie nodded. "It's hard to believe we once looked the way they do," she said wistfully.

"Are you kidding? Check out his sneakers. I still can't afford shoes like that."

She laughed at the quip, aware that Dan would never be comfortable with his wealth. How could he, when his career had been spent covering those in the world who had nothing?

"Do you reckon they're married?" Dan asked her.

She shrugged. "People that young don't like to commit any more today than when we were their age."

Dan said in a murmur, "In that case, I feel like going over there and smacking the guy on the head. What's he waiting for?"

They watched as the young man broke off a bit from his hamburger and tossed it to a dog who had been skulking in the shadow of the hollyhocks. The animal, a mutt with some golden retriever in him, was young and skinny and collarless. He ran forward, scarfed up the morsel, and retreated to the hollyhocks.

"I wonder where he came from. It's too early for the summer renters to be dumping their pets," Maddie said. She knew, all too well, how callous some of the groups could be: every September the local shelter became overrun with unwanted cats and dogs. "Maybe he just got loose from someone's yard."

Dan shook his head. "I've seen dogs behave like that the world over. He's a stray."

The guy they were watching dangled a french fry at dog level. The mutt dashed forward, took it gingerly, and returned to his hiding place. Another french fry, and another, and soon the dog felt secure enough to plop down on his haunches, his tail wagging cheerfully at the prospect of a meal, such as it was. He had wonderful, soulful eyes in a sweet, good-natured face.

"Oh, this is sad," Maddie said, distressed. "He should have a home, and someone to feed him and take him for walks on the beach. I'm going to ask the manager if the dog has been hanging around here for—"

Her question got answered before it got asked. A kid in an apron came out from the restaurant to bus one of the tables, took one look at the dog, and grabbed a stone from a small pile on the garden's edge, hurling it at the animal and sending him running off with a yelp.

Dan jumped up and grabbed the boy's arm. "Hey! Pick on someone your own size!"

"We're s'posed to chase him away," the busboy said sullenly. "He bothers the cust—"

The sound of brakes and a shrill cry of pain brought the episode to a tragic close: they turned to see that the dog had been hit by a passing car.

Dan swore under his breath and ran out to the road with Maddie hard on his heels. The animal lay without moving, his head haloed in blood. His gaze, still soulful, was glassy-eyed. The driver of the car that struck him had pulled over and was rushing back, a look of horror on her face. Inside her car, Maddie saw two children.

"He ran out so fast . . . oh, God . . . I never saw him . . . I hit the brakes, but . . ." Tears were streaming down the young mother's face.

The busboy had been hanging back. Now he sprang to life and said, "I'll call the dogcatcher!"

He ran inside. Dan pitched Maddie his car keys and said, "Park my Jeep behind the dog and leave the blinkers on." Maddie ran to the lot to position the car. By the time she got it into place, the young man who'd fed the dog the french fries had come out with the dismal news that they'd got an answering machine and not the animal control officer.

"Oh, for—" Without looking up, Dan told the busboy, "Go find a storm window, plywood, anything." To Maddie he said, "Look up the nearest animal hospital; call and get directions."

By the time Maddie returned with the route scrawled on

the back of a take-out menu, Dan had moved the injured animal onto a plywood stretcher and was loading it, with the help of the others, into his Jeep.

Maddie jumped into the front seat and divided her attention between the wounded animal behind her and the cryptic scrawl of her directions. "Oh, Dan, he doesn't look good," she said, dismayed. The dog's breathing was becoming more labored.

And yet the poor creature seemed to respond to her attempts at comfort, so she kept up a steady, soothing stream of endearments as Dan wove the Jeep through midday traffic until they arrived at the nondescript building that housed the animal clinic. Maddie ran in to warn the staff that Dan had the dog in his car, and an assistant came out to help them bring him inside.

The dog was taken into surgery at once; there was nothing now for Dan and Maddie to do. She said rather timidly, "Do you want to wait?"

"Definitely."

They went outside and sat on a stile fence at the edge of shade being thrown by a huge maple tree. After the burst of activity, waiting now seemed exhausting. Hungry now, and more tired than ever, Maddie watched absently as a sedan pulled slowly into the parking lot. A middle-aged woman climbed out, then coaxed a gray-muzzled, obviously failing setter out of the car and hooked a leash into its collar before walking it slowly to the entrance. It was clear that she cared deeply for her pet; the contrast between her dog and the neglected stray was painful to see.

Maddie's eyes stung with tears. She sighed and said softly to Dan, "You didn't have to take responsibility for the dog back there. But I love that you did."

Through the haze of her sadness, she heard his answer.

"I could relate to him, I guess," Dan said pensively. "Living on the occasional scrap of kindness—it's how I grew up."

She thought about that, and about love and loss and what might have been. After a long silence between them, she said, "Tell me about the fire, Dan. Tell me what really happened."

Her question had come out of the blue, but he didn't seem surprised by it. "Do you really not know?"

She said softly, "I know that the physics building was a converted mansion, and very flammable. I know that the sprinkler system wasn't up to code. I know that my father reentered the building to try to save his files. That he got trapped by the flames but managed to escape. And that he never had a clue afterward how he did it."

Dan took so long to answer that Maddie began to believe she would never learn the truth—the whole truth, anyway. But then, in a voice that sounded subdued and remote, he said, "I'm the one who came up with the plan to occupy the physics building. Understand that."

He looked away from her and fixed his gaze on a place she could not see.

"Some of the students wanted Lowell to reconsider the research it was doing with nuclear energy back then," he began. "They were sincere but disorganized. Hell, their grandparents were doing a better job of demonstrating against the risk of nuclear power than they were. Hollywood made a pretty good movie about it. And I—I, in my infinite wisdom, led the charge to take over a physics building."

"But it wasn't your idea to set the building on fire," she said. "It could never have been."

His laugh was bleak. "No, I can honestly say that the brilliance of that strategy never occurred to me. I still don't know who started it. I wasn't in the building at the time. I'd sneaked out the back to try to set up a meeting with the dean of students. He declined to see me, naturally. By the time I got back, the building was in flames."

"But . . . that means the dean would've been able to exonerate you. Why didn't he?"

Dan shrugged and said dryly, "This is just a wild guess on my part, but I'll bet that by the time the hearings took place, he wasn't feeling all that charitable toward me."

"But still! That's not right!"

Now he turned and looked directly at her, and he was the one surprised. "Maddie, it wasn't right to lead a bunch of firebrands into a building without understanding the risk. I was older and smarter than they were. I should've assumed that one of them was going to run amok. I was the one playing with fire," he said bitterly.

Rebuked, she murmured, "I'm on your side, you know."

"I do know," he said, dropping down from the stile. "It's just that I have to live with it, and it's hard. Especially now."

"It could've been so much worse."

"Yes."

In the pause that followed, a yellow swallowtail fluttered past, an instant of joy in their moment of pain.

"You were in the building, weren't you," she said, somehow convinced of it.

"Yes. It's not as if I've forgotten it."

He sighed, and then he began the unburdening. "I . . . went back into the building through a window, after I heard someone shout that people were still in it, one of them your father. I didn't think about the students. I didn't think about the protesters. I thought only of him. Because of you."

His voice was filled with self-loathing as he said, "Is it possible for someone to behave more selfishly than that?"

She had no answer for him, but let him go on, spilling his heart to the butterfly lifting and falling around them.

"I saw your father face down on the floor, not that far from an exit. He was unconscious. And then suddenly his shirt was on fire. I saw it catch—poof—like that . . . as I was making my way through the smoke. I was driven back . . . I had to drop down and crawl, to be able to breathe . . . it slowed me down . . . and his shirt . . . his shirt, Maddie, it was burning. And then there was a crash—something fell on me, I don't know what . . . heavy . . . hot . . . I rolled out from under it . . . more time wasted . . . it all went so slow, in slow motion. There was a chair in the hall with a loose cushion. I used it to put out the flames, but his shirt, by then it was . . . and then I dragged him the rest of the way out. He'd almost made it . . . so close . . . on his own. The firefighters took him . . . and then I ran. I ran. And I haven't stopped until now. Forgive me. God . . . forgive me."

Overwhelmed with emotion, Maddie sat on the fence without moving, a mute witness to his intensely personal confession. It was not for her to forgive him, she knew. She thought of saying something, but nothing seemed adequate. A long moment passed. And then she saw a tear roll down his cheek.

She'd seen him angry and she'd seen him icy. But she'd never seen him cry.

She bowed her head to give him privacy and said in a whisper, "Can you forgive me for sending you away?"

He turned his dark, brooding gaze on her, and then he gathered her to him, cradling her head to his chest. And there they stood, in the bright sunshine of silence, while God sorted out which of his creatures would live, and which of them would have to die.

Not too long afterward, they found out that the mutt with the trusting eyes was going to live. He had a broken leg, broken ribs, bruises all over and a few less teeth—but he would live. Maddie was delighted. Dan was ecstatic. He wrote a check and left instructions that if no one answered the found ad in the local papers, he would adopt the dog himself.

"I've never had a pet before," he told Maddie as they walked back to his Jeep. "Now that I'm settling down, though . . . gee, this feels good. Ready for that lunch now?"

She laughed and said, "Are you kidding? You're as dead on your feet as I am."

"Doesn't matter," he said, smiling through a yawn. "I have to make up for lost time."

"Not without becoming a vampire." Unable to suppress a yawn of her own that turned into a sigh, Maddie slipped her arm through his and said, "I'm calling this weekend a day, my friend. Let's each go home, crash for a few hours, and then—"

"And then what?" he asked, holding the car door open for her.

Her smile was wistful. "What, indeed," she said on a sigh. "I wish I knew."

He grinned and said, "That was not a deep, philosophical question, m'am. I meant, maybe a pizza?"

"That'd be great." Immediately she checked herself. "I can't," she said, disappointed. "I have to take Tracey to Junior League volleyball."

"Can't your mother do it?"

"I suppose; but I'd have to—"

"Tell her you're with me."

It wasn't posed as a question; he expected Maddie to come clean with her family.

"Well . . . eventually."

"You can't expect to keep us secret this time, too," he said seriously. "Your mother will find out from someone else if not from you."

"Oh, I don't know. . . . My mother doesn't go out much anymore. She stays in touch with a few friends, but—"

"Maddie, tell her the truth. The sooner the better. Anything else gets real tricky, real fast."

"Oh, I know. You're absolutely right. And I will. Only—"

"Not right away," he finished quietly for her. His face showed his disappointment.

"Because I'm so tired, that's all. I can't even think straight. Oh, Dan, this time I want to do it right. I don't want the mess that we had the first time. You don't know my mother—"

"You're right. I haven't had that honor yet," he said dryly.

"She's still so very . . . raw. I can't hurt her more than she's already been hurt. And she can be very unforgiving. I have to take all of it in account and do this right."

"Just tell her the truth, Maddie," he said.

"The truth can hurt, Dan." She knew that from experience. Daunted by his take no prisoners approach, she added, "Didn't you ever slant a story to suit your needs? Maybe played up an injustice or skipped an awkward fact so that you could drive your point home to your viewers? I know that your motives would've been completely honorable—they could never be anything else—but . . . didn't you?"

He grimaced, then sighed and said, "Okay. You win. Tell

your mother about us when you see fit. But, Maddie, tell her soon.''

''Oh, definitely. A little sleep first; that's all I ask. And then I'll be my persuasive, soothing best.''

Dan dropped Maddie off at Hollyhocks, where she reclaimed her car and drove home in a trance, physically aching for her bed. Despite her weariness, her spirits were up. She felt closer to Dan, closer to her daughter. Now if only her mother would let herself get to know Dan and embrace him. . . .

Was it really such a big ''if''? It occurred to Maddie that Dan had a genuine shot at being accepted into the family. After all, he was everything—nowadays—that his mother admired in a man: confident, well-off, accomplished, successful, admired, and much, much more than presentable. Heck, he'd even stopped smoking; no more cigarettes stowed in the sleeve of his T-shirt. What more could any mother ask for?

If only. . . .

When Maddie arrived at Rosedale she found the front door wide open and the screen door unhooked. After a quick check of the first floor and a call up the stairs, she discovered her daughter sunbathing in the back yard, undoubtedly without lotion. The girl was listening to music through earphones, so she couldn't hear Maddie calling her, and she had sunbathing cups over her eyes, so she couldn't see Maddie when she stood in front of the chaise and waved her arms.

To Maddie she looked completely vulnerable, a teenage sitting duck.

The village is safe, the village is safe, Maddie had to tell herself. Don't go to war over this.

She got her daughter's attention by nudging the chaise, but not without startling her as she did it. Tracey sat up, well on the way to yet another peeling nose. Her arms and the fronts of her shins were pink as well.

''Where is everyone?'' Maddie asked her, taking a seat on the edge of the chaise.

''Aunt Claire's shopping in town, and Grandma's still at

lunch with the countess," Tracey said. "I knew you'd freak
if I went to the beach *unsupervised*, so I stuck around here."

"Did you really!" It was a moment to be savored, but
Maddie was—literally—dog tired. She said, "I think I'll lie
down for a bit; I have a splitting headache." It was a lie but
it would have to do.

"And . . . Trace?" she added as she picked up the empty
glass by the chaise. "I appreciate that you stayed around the
house. I know the grounding is hard on you. Why don't you
call Julie and have her come over? You'll have the place to
yourselves until people start wandering back. You can order
a pizza for the two of you. Maybe later on I'll take you both
to—"

Wait. She had her own pizza planned.

"Well, we'll see how it goes," she finished up vaguely.

So this is what it would be like until she told them about
Dan: an ongoing conflict of loyalties.

She touched a forefinger to her lips and planted it on the
tip of Tracey's nose. "Think about lotion there."

"Mom! I did!"

"Uh-huh."

Maddie stood up. She could practically feel the soft down
pillow under her cheek, feel the joy of having a breeze blow
over her as she drifted off to sleep on cool cotton sheets.

Pleased about the cease-fire between Tracey and her, Maddie went back into the house, stopping at the fridge for a glass
of cold lemonade. She was gulping it down thirstily when she
heard a car pull up on the crunchy quahog shells. Seconds
later she heard Sarah Timmons's voice saying a brief good-
bye, and then a car door slam.

Maddie wandered into the hall, pressing the icy glass to
her cheek. Smiling, she said to her mother, "How's the countess? Any good dirt?"

For the rest of her life, Maddie remembered the look on
her mother's face: a mix of shock and loathing, the kind of
look she reserved for grisly murders on the six o'clock news.

Sarah looped her handbag over the hall clothes tree with a
vicious downward jerk, then turned to Maddie. Her voice was

pinched with well-bred rage. "How did you *dare*?"

Something inside of Maddie took a dive. "Dare? Dare what?" she asked with forced ignorance.

"Cavort naked on the town beach with a murderer—can you possibly be my *daughter*?"

Floored by the double blow, Maddie could only say, "Mom—please—don't talk like that."

"Do you deny it? Do you?"

"Yes, I deny it! Of course I deny it!"

"How can you deny it? Lillian saw the two of you when she was walking her dogs!"

The woman in the cowled sweatshirt, walking two terriers. "Oh my God. That was Lillian?"

"What difference would it make, if it was Lillian or the fire chief? Everyone in town knows us. Someone was bound to recognize you. If not you, then certainly a CNN correspondent. What were you thinking? What were you *doing*? I'm not a prude, Maddie. God knows, I've tried to move with the times," Sarah said, her chin beginning to tremble. "I looked the other way when your brother brought women guests here and then crept across the hall to them at night. I sent Suzette and that awful Armand a coffee mill when they decided to move in together on the West Bank. I even forgave your father the one ti—but this! It's insulting. It's hurtful and cruel and beyond my comprehension. You! Of all people, you! The one person in the family who was always above reproach, behaving like some—some tabloid tart! With *him*!"

"It wasn't like that, Mom!" Maddie cried. "Don't say things you'll later regret—"

"I'll say what I want! I'm sick of having to seem blasé about morals. I'm sick of having to believe that times are more difficult now, that people are more stressed, that morality is relative. Times are always difficult! People are always stressed! And morality is *not* relative! When Daniel Hawke led those students into taking over that building, he was wrong. When they set fire to it, it was *wrong*. And when you ignored his past and the harm he'd done to us and went prancing around in the water with him buck naked, *you were wrong*!"

Maddie's head was spinning. All she could say was, "We were not buck naked. We were wearing sweatshirts."

The defense, such as it was, left her mother speechless. Sarah settled for a snort of contempt, then said, "Spare me the rest of that rebuttal. You've dazzled me enough for one day."

She brushed past Maddie on her way to her room, but Maddie rallied and grabbed her mother's arm and swung her around to face her. "He is *not* a murderer and he had nothing to do with the fire! He told me!"

Her mother jerked her arm from Maddie's grip. In an icy fury, she said, "He started the chain of events that's left me a widow. He's a murderer until someone proves otherwise. Now please—get away from me. I have to pack."

Hot tears of shame and anger burned Maddie's eyes as she watched her mother march off with head held high. "Go ahead!" she shouted to her mother's back. "Run! Run away and hide! It's so much easier than forgiving someone and giving that person another chance. That would be work, wouldn't it, Mom? That would take an effort! And we know you have to save your strength for golf and bridge and tennis, and lunches with small-minded friends!"

Maddie was shouting at a closed door. In a rage of her own now, she lunged at the doorknob, but the door was locked. She slammed her hand against the panels and called out, "Listen to me! I love him, and nothing you say or do will change that! I refuse to fall for your power play, and I refuse to feel guilty about it. I've loved Dan Hawke since Lowell College! Do you hear me? He's the only man I've ever truly loved! Everything else has been a sham! My life has been a sham! Do you hear me, Mom? Can you hear me? A sham! And I won't live that way anymore! I won't! Open this door! Deal with this!"

Silence.

Maddie let out an exasperated cry and kicked the door in fury, then turned around and sank, exhausted and with her eyes closed, against it. Suddenly all of it—the fireworks, the fund-raiser, the first confrontation, the escape, the beach, the dog, the relief, the happiness and now this—caught up with her. She was utterly, totally spent of emotion. She felt dead inside. She felt like a woman looking down at her own dead body.

But God or the devil had other plans for her.

When she opened her eyes she found herself staring into yet another pair of shocked and contemptuous blue eyes: Tracey, still in her bathing suit, was standing in the doorway between the kitchen and the hall, watching the drama play out.

Like a fool, Maddie said, "How much did you hear?"

It was Tracey's cue to burst into tears. "All of it," she wailed, and ran up the stairs sobbing hysterically.

"God in heaven," Maddie whispered.

With head bowed low and shoulders sagging, she dragged herself up the stairs after her daughter, but that door, too, was closed to her. She knocked as gently as she had pounded fiercely on the door downstairs, but heard only muffled sobbing in return.

We need a time out, she told herself. All three of us need a time out. Her room at the end of the hall beckoned. She let herself be lured by it, like Ulysses to Calypso's island, and lay down fully clothed on the white quilted coverlet of her bed. She had little thought of falling asleep. All she meant to do was to fashion a strategy, and her body could no longer do that while standing up. She had to lie down in order to think.

That was all.

Chapter 19

The harsh jangle of the phone sent Maddie bolting from her bed.

She hovered in confusion, wondering why they were having a school fire drill in the middle of the night, until she realized that she wasn't in school, there was no drill, and it was the middle of the day.

The caller was Detective Bailey, sounding polite and sympathetic—and oddly excited, for Detective Bailey.

"I was curious to know whether you had a chance to look for your father's address book," he asked after an opening pleasantry.

"Oh, I'm sorry . . . no." She made some excuse about her mother being indisposed.

"Look, Mrs. Regan . . . I have another reason for calling. We may have been given a break in the case. God knows, it's the first one we've had."

No need to ask which case he meant. Fully awake now, Maddie said, "Tell me."

"Okay, here's the deal: we ran your father's plates again, on the odd chance that something would turn up in the computer that wasn't there when we discovered the car. And lo and behold, there it sat: a parking ticket, still unpaid, from April 6. I'm surprised you didn't get dunned about it."

"I'm not sure my mother would've noticed something like that in the mail, not in the state she's been in. Besides, she's ruthless about tossing anything that doesn't have either her lawyer's or her accountant's name on it," Maddie said. Her blood was racing with the thought that finally—*finally*—something might be happening to move them forward. "Where was the ticket issued?" she asked.

"Good for you. It was issued out of Natick. Do you know if your father would have any reason to go there?"

"Nothing comes to mind. I could ask my mother." *But probably not today.*

"You ever been to Natick?"

"Oh, yes, to a mall there."

"Then you know it's not a small town—but it ain't Boston, either. I have hopes. I've just got off the phone with the ticketing officer. The officer was a woman, another big break. They tend to take scofflaws personally."

"But my father wasn't a scofflaw! Just the opposite," Maddie felt bound to say.

"Yes, yes, I know that. I meant, a woman officer tends to remember every little . . . a male officer would write the ticket, all right, but his mind would be on the Celts game from the night before. . . . Not that I'm saying women are vindictive, mind you . . . only that—oh hell, it's a break. Okay?"

Maddie had another thought. "What made you think of running the plates a second time?"

"Truth? Dan Hawke."

"Dan! I don't believe it! How? Why?"

"You tell me. He got in touch a little while ago. Says he's a friend of the family. Says he's been apprised of the case—apprised, hell; he knew as much about it as I did."

"But I haven't told him a—"

"Yeah. I figured. It doesn't matter. Guys like him are networked. He did have one name wrong, which means he's also read accounts in the papers; he wouldn't have got that from us."

Reeling from the news, Maddie nonetheless had the sense to say with conviction, "You can trust him completely. He's a friend from way back. But he's been abroad. . . ."

"I know who he is," the detective answered dryly. "Cops watch shows besides 'Baywatch.' "

"No, I didn't mean to imply—anyway, he has only our interests at heart. And I guarantee that he doesn't have an agenda. He's not going to do an exposé or anything."

"Exposé?" Bailey asked with an edge. "Of what?"

"I don't know," Maddie said, flustered. "Whatever reporters expose. Corruption or ineptitude—but that's what I'm saying he's *not* trying to do." Flustered, she explained, "I'm just trying to say that he'll be totally discreet."

"Oh, good. Then he won't blab about the Ferrari in my garage. I can sleep easy now."

"Please tell me you're just teasing, Detective Bailey. If I've offended you in any way, it's the opposite of what I intended. You're the most honorable, upright—"

"Mrs. Regan, I was pullin' your chain," he said, a little wearily. "The fact is, I wouldn't be working my off-hours if—it's your mother, I guess. I ran into her after the fireworks. She's doesn't seem to be bouncin' back so good. I have a mother her age. If something happened to my pop, well, I don't even want to think about the effect it'd have on her."

In a lighter vein he said, "As for your celebrity pal—we don't let those types get too cozy. This ain't an episode of 'Murder, She Wrote,' and he knows it. Still, it was a damn good idea to run the plates again, and he's the one who had it, and I'm not ashamed to say it."

He took a breath and said, "Anyhoo, getting back to my point: the on-duty officer remembers clearly the day she ticketed your father's car, because she also issued tickets for every other car on the block.

"The street had been slated for a sweeping," he explained, "and signs were posted banning parking. Some kids upped and swiped the signs and figured they were being cute, putting 'em back after cars parked in all the banned spaces. Along comes Officer Geary and tickets the whole street, naturally. That much she remembers. We're looking into the records for the registrations on all the other cars that got nailed that morning. Might be something useful there."

Maddie's mind was racing ahead. "And you want to cross-reference names in my dad's address book with names that you find of the owners of the other ticketed cars?"

"As soon as we put together the list. For that matter, maybe someone in the address book actually has a Natick—can you hold on, Mrs. Regan? I've got Officer Geary on the other line right now."

Maddie waited in agony through an entire Muzak version of "Hey Jude" before Bailey came back and said, "Okay, one question's been resolved, and I don't much care for the answer. So many motorists complained about the tickets issued that morning that the entire batch of 'em was given amnesty. Some of the violations are still in the computer and some aren't, so the records are incomplete."

"How is that possible?" Maddie asked, dismayed.

"My guess is that a shift ended before someone finished expunging the records. So maybe this won't turn out to be such a big break, after all. But it's a break, nevertheless. We really need the address book, Mrs. Regan. We need it soon," he said, pushing her hard.

"I'll start looking immediately," Maddie promised, and hung up.

She went to the dresser to pull out new underwear for after her shower, then slid the drawer closed, knocking over one of the bronze-framed photos that stood on top. She straightened the frame back up and gazed at the photo within: a snapshot from five years earlier of Tracey and Maddie's mother, taken in front of a Ferris wheel. Tracey had Mr. James, already an old bear, under one arm; her grandmother had Tracey under hers.

They were at a carnival that had passed through Sandy Point at a time when Maddie was laid low by flu, so Maddie's mother had pinch-hit for her. It was the first time that Sarah Timmons had ever gone somewhere with Michael and Tracey without Maddie being there.

The day had gone well, much to Sarah's surprise. You could see it in her grin, in Tracey's, too. But then, Michael was a skilled photographer. He'd know just what to say to get them to laugh in just the right way. It was a great shot, one of Maddie's favorites: all bright colors, crazy angles, and high spirits.

Maddie's eyes glazed over, and the picture began wavering and dissolving in front of her. "Tracey . . . Mom . . . how will I ever make you understand?"

She had no answer to that question as she headed for the bathroom down the hall, passing Tracey's open door and empty room on her way. In the bathroom she heard music blaring from the garden: Jimmy Buffet, singing some noisy, innocent song about hamburgers. In ordinary times, Maddie would've had to force herself to sound stern (she liked Jimmy Buffet, too) as she yelled outside for Tracey to turn down the volume.

But these weren't ordinary times.

"Honey, can you turn down the radio? I can hardly hear you."

"Dad, I can't. Someone could listen in on us."

"Tracey, you sound like a spy. You shouldn't be on the cordless phone if you want your conversation to be so private. Now turn down the radio and tell me what's happened. Or at least go to the far end of the garden and talk."

Immediately the girl began to sob. Her breath caught in short, semi-hysterical gasps. She wasn't able to tell him a thing.

Michael was completely frustrated, as usual, because he couldn't comfort his own child by wrapping her in a hug. "Tracey . . . sweetie . . . shhh . . . don't cry. Just tell me what's happened and I'll fix it. Nothing's worth crying over."

"Oh, Dad . . . it was h-h-horrible," Tracey said, collapsing into another series of gasps. With an effort, she pulled herself together and said, "Mom was on the beach with Mr. H-Hawke in the middle of the nuh-hight and . . . and the countess saw them when she was walking her dogs, but they were in the water only with their sweatshirts on . . . and then she told Grandma, and Grandma came back early from lunch and told Mom . . . but Mom, she denied it, at f-first anyway, and then she didn't and not only that . . . but, oh, Dad, she said awful things . . . she said he was the only man she ever loved and that must mean she didn't love you best, and you're my *f-father*, and she was banging on the door and screaming at Grandma and, and Grandma's gone now and Uncle George had to take her h-home but like, they h-had to sneak away because Grandma didn't want Mom to know and now there's only me and Aunt Claire and . . . oh, Dad . . . I don't want to *be* here . . . any-mor-r-re,'' she wailed. "Oh, Da-a-d. . . .''

The wave of jealousy that had been ebbing and flowing in Michael now became a tidal wave of rage. "Goddamn. God-*damn*! I'll kill her," he said, seething.

"*Dad!*"

"No, no, it's just a figure of speech, honey," he said, forcing himself back under control. "No, don't worry, we'll take care of this. Look, this is your weekend with me anyway. I'll come down early, right now—no, I can't, I have something I have to do first—all right, I'll be there by—" He glanced at his watch. "By seven, the latest. Maybe earlier. Definitely earlier. We'll straighten this out. Just sit tight. I'll be there, honey. I'll be there. You won't have to stay there. I'm damned if I'll leave you there after this.''

He *would* kill her!

He made a few more reassurances to his distraught daughter to calm her down, then hung up and immediately dialed the Brookline Institute.

"Dr. Woodbine, please," he said to the receptionist.

He was put through to Woodbine and got straight to the point. "I can't make it this afternoon for testing. I have a family situation down on the Cape.''

Woodbine's voice dropped from cordial to cool. "What kind of situation?''

"My kid's hysterical—with reason. I have to bring her up here. *Now*, Geoff, not later.''

"Are you serious? We're running out of time, man! No, it's impossible. No rescheduling. Be here in an hour.''

"I said I can't make it, goddammit! Do you think I'd be any good in this state? Put it off until tomorrow!" he said, shrill with anger. "If you expect me to go through with this—then put the goddamned test off!"

Woodbine was forced to back down. "All right. We'll re-schedule for tomorrow at the same time. You're screwing me, Michael," he added. "The grant's up for renewal and you're our last, best hope. You understand what's riding on this, don't you? Dammit, man—everything!"

"Bullshit. The Pentagon doesn't know its ass end from a mousehole. You won't get a hard time from them. They've already spent millions. They're not going to stop funding the project now; that's how it works over there. I don't need psychic powers to know *that*, for chrissake."

"Resolve your domestic crisis by tomorrow, Michael," Woodbine said in an icy voice. "Or be prepared for the con-sequences."

Michael hung up without responding. He had to dress and get to the Cape, and get there fast. He went to his closet for a clean shirt and faced an empty rack: he hadn't sent out his laundry in weeks. It angered him still more; if Maddie were still his wife, this kind of thing wouldn't happen.

Making it on the beach with that son of a bitch!

Dan Hawke! He should have known. Even in college there was something about him. Michael saw it, and she did too. The bastard was arrogant and defiant; seedy, and proud of it. Bastard! But you knew, even then, that he was going places.

Were they making it then, too? Christ—of course they were! All these years he'd been assuming that Maddie had been merely intrigued by Hawke, the way nice girls are always intrigued by bad boys. On the few occasions that the three of them had hung out together, he used to catch Maddie sneaking looks at Hawke, but Hawke had always kept his expression bland.

Faking! Hawke had been faking disinterest in her. It was obvious—now. Like a sap, Michael had pursued Maddie and convinced himself that her willingness to be swept off her feet by him was real.

Rebound! He, Carmichael Winthrop Regan III, was a fuck-ing rebound lover for her! The sudden realization overwhelmed him, making him sick. He had a visceral urge to tear Hawke limb from limb and throw the pieces into the sea.

On the beach. Hawke, with *his* wife!

How could she?

A low snarl came out of his throat. His mouth tasted like vomit, his head pounded with fury, and his guts had coiled into a single steel spring.

He grabbed a dirty shirt from a pile on the floor and pulled it over his head, catching a reflection of himself in the bathroom mirror on his way out. Shock: he saw another man altogether than the one who'd shaved there yesterday. His face was red and blotchy with rage and his lips were peeled back, baring his teeth and gums. He'd turned into a wolf— and she was the one to blame.

Blinding shafts of pain were splitting his head in two, like a machete slashing a coconut. He'd taken the drug, expecting the test, but all he had for his effort was pain. Before he got into his car he took a series of deep breaths, trying to calm himself—for Tracey's sake—but it was no use; the rage returned.

So be it. The rage felt good. All he needed was to vent it.

Maddie pulled a dress of cool lavender cotton over her head, then towel-dried her hair and ran a comb through it, too much in a hurry to fuss with the blow drier. The few hours of sleep she'd had had helped immensely, and so had the shower. She felt ready to take on her family again.

She followed the succulent aroma of roasting beef into the kitchen, where she found Claire peeling potatoes for supper.

"Hi," she said shyly to her sister-in-law from the doorway. "Are *we* on speaking terms?"

Claire looked at her with a rueful smile and said, "Idiot. Couldn't you just rob a bank instead?"

Claire, beautiful Claire. Maddie took the potato peeler from her and said, "Make tea for us while I do these. And then sit down. Just because you're the only one left standing after the shootout, it doesn't mean you have to make the meals."

"Your mother's gone back to Sudbury; I assume you know that," Claire told her.

"I figured. She overreacted, you know," Maddie said, peeling a little more fiercely than necessary. "What Dan and I did was possibly stupid—okay, it *was* stupid—but it was hardly criminal. There are whole beaches set aside for nude bathing, you know."

"Lillian doesn't walk her dogs on them. And it sounds like you did more than bathe," said Claire as she filled the kettle.

Maddie let out a nervous laugh and threw the potato into the pot, then picked up another and sighed. "I have to straighten things out with Tracey, too. This is such an unbelievable mess. It was a bad scene, Claire, it really was. But I was so frustrated, so . . . so—"

"Pissed?"

"Pissed that Mom wouldn't listen, that I just lost it. I mean, *really* lost it. I don't even remember what I said, but I know Tracey heard most of it. She burst into tears, the way she always does—"

"You mean, like when you tell her it's her turn to do dishes?"

"Oh, heavens, she wasn't *that* upset," said Maddie, looking up from her potatoes with a smile. But the smile died on her lips as she added, "Seriously—I never should have said those things, knowing Tracey was anywhere around. They weren't for a child to hear." She went back to peeling fiercely.

"Can you smooth things over with her?"

"I think so," Maddie said, frowning in an effort to remember exactly what Tracey had overheard. "She had to learn about Dan and me sooner or later. It's just that right now, I wish it were later. My plate's pretty full as it is."

She told Claire about the phone call from Detective Bailey, and the need to find the address book. Claire, so blonde and pale and pretty, looked uncharacteristically grim as she said with quiet resolve, "I'll help you look."

"Oh, would you, Claire? That'd be great. I'll do all the heavy lifting. I put all of Dad's boxes of papers, books, and even the photo albums in the basement; I wanted the study to be all bedroom for Mom. Anyway, I'll begin bringing them back up and we can go through them one last time. That'd be such a help to me.''

"Consider it done."

"You're a doll. So. Next up: my mother. What can I do about her, Claire?" Maddie asked humbly. "In her mind, Dan as much as murdered my dad. With time, she'll get over the beach episode. But it's obvious that she's never going to get over what Dan did in college."

"For that matter, George isn't too keen on him, either," Claire reminded her. "You Timmons folk have long memories."

"Is that why you're so accepting? Because you weren't there at the time?"

"That's part of it," Claire admitted, taking down a ceramic teapot and a tea tin from the glass-front cupboard. "But it's also that I knew your father so well. If he were alive now, I'm sure he'd be perfectly fine about Dan and you. Your father admired him, Maddie, despite the tragedy.''

"How can you say that?"

Claire lifted the lid from the tea tin and began measuring scoops of loose Darjeeling into the pot. "I can say that, because he and I were watching CNN together once, and Dan came on with a report about the breakup of Yugoslavia. When it was over your dad said to me, and I quote, 'He's a hell of a reporter. He cares about the people, not the politics. Good man.' ''

"Oh, Claire—really? You're not making it up just to cheer me?"

"Not at all," she said in her serene way. "I related the same story to George when he came back up to bed—just before you ran off to the beach?—but he didn't want to hear it. I left it to him to tell your mother, but if I were you, I'd tell her myself.''

Maddie sighed and said, "Assuming she ever talks to me again."

"She doesn't have to talk. She only has to listen."

"I suppose I'll have to kidnap her from Sudbury and bring her back down here somehow. I wonder if they sell handcuffs in town," Maddie said lightly, but she was at a loss about her next move.

She winced again at the thought of the scene earlier. "She's too old for this, Claire. *I'm* too old for this. I need all my strength to ride herd on Tracey. I can't go around throwing hysterical fits in the middle of the day. I never should have done it," she said with a sigh. "Teenage rebellions are best left to teenagers."

"Maybe that's your problem. Maybe you didn't rebel enough when you were young."

Maddie thought about it a moment, and then said, "You know, Dr. Ruth, you may have something there? My dad made sure I was a responsible citizen, and my mother made sure I was responsible, period. I voted and I volunteered; I sent handwritten thank-you notes, never cards, and I got my work done on time, come hell or high water. I was always doing things for extra credit. God. I was a complete failure as a teenager."

"You never ran with a wild crowd?"

"Never," Maddie said, running water into the pot of potatoes. "Dan Hawke was the one wild thing in my entire life. But my parents never knew it. No one did—except maybe the groundskeeper at Lowell College. I wish now that they had . . . especially my father. But I guess I was too afraid of my mother."

Claire said softly, "The way Tracey is, you mean?"

Surprised, Maddie looked up at her sister-in-law. "Tracey's not afraid of me. She's much too busy defying me."

Claire shrugged and poured the boiling water slowly into the teapot, then snugged a quilted floral cozy over it. Her silence was more eloquent than any argument could possibly be.

It had a direct, immediate impact on Maddie.

"I'm going out to talk to Tracey right now," she said suddenly, wiping her hands on a towel. "And—Claire?"

"Hmm?"

"I hope you're wrong."

"You wouldn't be a mother if you didn't."

Chapter 20

Maddie found her daughter in the most secret place of the yard: a small nook, tucked in the northwest corner behind an ancient clump of lilac, that Michael had paved with a few flagstones one summer. Tracey had liked to hide there when she was a little girl, and now that she was a bigger girl, she liked to hide there still.

She'd hung a miniature set of chimes from one of the lilac branches; they tinkled in a delicate, enchanting way at the slightest hint of a breeze. The chimes were silent now, like Tracey.

She was sitting cross-legged in a twig chair that doubled as a scratching post for every cat in the neighborhood. One of the cats, the neighbor's calico, was curled up in her lap at the moment as she sat with an utterly blank look on her face.

"You look so sad," Maddie said as she lifted a branch and stepped inside the nook, sending the chimes carolling. "Do you mind if I visit a bit before supper?"

Tracey pressed her lips together and shrugged. Permission was neither denied nor granted.

Maddie repositioned the unused footstool and then sat down gingerly on it, hoping it wouldn't collapse underneath her and create an unwelcome diversion. Somehow, some way, she had to get through to her daughter, because the chasm between them had just widened again. Both of them knew that Maddie had Dan, but that Tracey wasn't being allowed to have Kevin.

"I don't know what to do about us, Tracey," Maddie said softly. "We used to be such great friends. But somehow I've gone from being your mom to being your jailer. And you know what? I'd rather go back to being your mom. Do you think I could do that?"

Tracey hadn't expected the question; that was obvious. Maddie could practically see the disk drives spinning inside her head as she searched for the right rebuttal. Finally she sighed rather violently and said, "I never said you couldn't."

"True."

Stroking the chin of the neighbor's cat, Tracey continued to look straight ahead at nothing at all. She looked exhausted; it was wrenching to see.

"Well, here's the thing," Maddie began. "I know that when your dad and I decided to—"

"Divorce."

"—divorce, it was hard on you."

"*You* decided; not Dad."

"Whatever. And then when Grampa was . . . was—"

"Murdered."

"It made it even harder for you to deal with your feelings. I know that, honey. I can't tell you how bad I feel that you were gypped of your childhood. It doesn't seem fair. And the fact that a lot of other kids are also gypped in the same way— as incredible as that may seem—doesn't make it any better. It's unfair, it's awful, I wish it could be some other way, but there it is. Nothing we can say or do will bring Grampa back . . . and nothing we can say or do will bring your father and me together again."

"Don't you think I know that?" she said, becoming more rigid in her exhaustion.

"Yes," Maddie murmured. "You certainly do, after this afternoon. I'm sorry you heard everything that you did. I lost my temper and I said things that I never should have."

Tracey shrugged and, still staring somewhere past her mother, said, "I'm cool with it."

"Are you, honey? I don't see how you can be," Maddie
admitted. "It's an awful lot for a kid to have to deal with. I
guess what I'm saying is, I really, really want us to start over,
beginning today, because Mr. Hawke is going to be a part of
my life now. . . ."

At the mention of his name, the look in Tracey's eyes became even more blank, if possible. She looked as if she'd
been abducted into an alien cult.

Maddie had to force herself to stagger forward with the
burden of her apology. "I loved him very much back when
I was in college," she said softly, "and now I care for him
again."

"Still, you mean!" Tracey said, flashing her mother a look
of fury. But in a typical lightning shift of mood, she went
back at once to being a zombie again.

"Okay, yes. Still," said Maddie, aware now that her
daughter understood the distinction.

"Even though he did burn down some building," Tracey
added venomously.

"He wasn't the one who started the fire," Maddie said,
wondering when that bit of history had leaked out. She had
a vague idea that her mother had shouted something about it
during their argument, but the whole exchange was still a blur
in her mind.

She said, "Mr. Hawke made a huge mistake in college,
and he and I made a pretty dumb one last night. It just goes
to show that you're never too old to use poor judgment. Anyway, I have a peace proposal. Would you like to hear it?"

Maddie saw a flicker of interest in Tracey as she turned
her head a fractional amount in her direction.

"Okay, here goes. You think that I was being too hard on
Kevin, and I think that you're not very inclined to like Mr.
Hawke. Am I right?"

No answer, just a resounding snort.

"I'll take that as a yes," Maddie said dryly. "Okay. Suppose I agree to put you and Kevin on probation. He—and his
brother, and Julie, whatever—can come here, or I'll drive you
all to a show or the mall or an event we agree on. I'll be able

to look him over a little more thoroughly, and we'll take it from there. In return, all I ask is—"

She wanted to say, "That you please not spit in Mr. Hawke's face when he shows up here," but she confined herself to saying, "That you give Mr. Hawke the same chance that I give Kevin."

She was surprised when Tracey didn't jump up and down with joy. This was *Kevin* they were talking about.

"This isn't something I have to do, honey," she prompted. "After all, I'm still bigger than you are, plus don't forget I've got the law on my side," she added lightly.

She waited and watched as her daughter's gaze slowly refocused from the lilac bush to her bare feet.

"Well . . . okay," Tracey said, raking her dusky blonde hair away from her face. "If that's—no!" she cried, her voice going from thoughtful to shrill in a heartbeat. "No, that's not what I want!"

"Not what you want?" asked Maddie, blinking. "What *do* you want?"

"I don't know! I don't know!"

Immediately Maddie felt guilty of bribery. Had she done the wrong thing? Had she dangled Kevin like a bone before her daughter, trying to distract her while she indulged her own wild yearnings?

"Tracey, I was trying to be fair, that's all," Maddie said.

She *was* trying to be fair, damn it! But maybe the whole point of being a parent was that you couldn't be fair, shouldn't be fair. She just didn't know anymore.

Upset though she was, Tracey glanced at her watch. The gesture puzzled Maddie. "Oh dear, am I wrecking your schedule?" she asked with mild irony.

"No! No, I was just sitting here anyway. Okay, I'll do what you . . . what you said. I'll give Mr. Hawke a chance." She seemed to be reading from a script that only she could see.

"Well . . . good," Maddie said, still puzzled. "And we're both going to be on our best behavior. Agreed?"

"Uh-huh."

The girl seemed curiously detached from the conversation.

"Tracey? Is something else bothering you?"

"No, nothing."

"Because now would be a really good time to talk about it. I'm in a negotiating mood," Maddie said with a smile.

The smile that she got in return seemed a little preoccupied, which was understandable. Maddie had thrown a curve ball that had sailed right past her daughter's bat. It was time to leave Tracey alone so that she could think about all that her mother had said.

Maddie stood up to leave, then impulsively bent over to give her daughter a quick hug, which she accepted with less than her usual squeamishness.

"Supper will be in half an hour," Maddie said, and then she left, sending the chimes on one last fling of merriment.

Back in the house, Claire had poured Maddie her tea and placed a saucer over the cup. "How'd it go?" she asked as Maddie sank into a chair across from her.

"Okay, I guess," Maddie said thoughtfully. "But somehow Tracey seemed to act, I don't know—guilty."

"She was just embarrassed."

"I suppose. Boy. That conversation would've been a heck of a lot easier ten years from now."

Claire laughed and said, "Ten years from now, you wouldn't have been guilty of a roll in the sand on the town beach."

"You're right," said Maddie, sipping her tea, now lukewarm. She decided to zap the brew in the microwave for a few seconds. "Actually," she said after she punched in the command, "you're not right. Ten years from now I could see us pulling the same stunt all over again."

"Maddie! Is it that serious between you?"

"Let me think about that," Maddie said with mock gravity as she pulled out her tea. "Uh-huh." She grinned and said, "Doesn't it show?"

The phone rang. Maddie looked around and said, "Who took the cordless?" and ended up answering the phone on the wall.

Dan's voice sounded sleep-filled and intimate and sent Maddie into an instant state of arousal. She felt her cheeks flush from the sheer pleasure of her reaction. "Hey-y," she said in a voice as low and intimate as his. "You're up."

"Up, standing, call it what you like," he quipped. "I saw you moving around at the window. How's everything in your neck of the woods?"

"Oh-h-h, you'd be surprised, I think."

"Can't talk?"

"Not about that. Oh, but I can tell you that Detective Bailey called. Why didn't you tell me you'd contacted him?" she asked.

"For one thing, I thought he might just blow off my suggestion," Dan admitted. "But he didn't; he actually ran the plates again and then called me back to thank me. I was impressed. He's a good man."

"Funny, I just heard that expression used about you," she murmured, twisting the phone cord absently around her finger. She wandered back to the window above the sink and gazed out at the lighthouse. So close. So far.

Dan's voice became huskier. "Maddie, I wanted you in my bed when I woke up just now. I wanted you big time. This is crazy. We should be together now. When can I see you? Find an excuse. Use the sugar excuse. That one works."

She laughed, giddy and confident and in love. She wanted to tease him, to talk dirty, to make him climb the walls of the lighthouse with frustration.

And only then show up with the empty sugarbowl in her hand. "That's not a bad idea. I may try it," she said cryptically. She glanced over her shoulder. Claire, considerate Claire, was trying to top off her tea and get out of the kitchen as fast as she could.

"Oh, hell!" Dan said suddenly. "I see Norah and Joan driving up to your house. Don't let 'em in, don't let 'em in; you'll never get rid of 'em. Oh, God, I can't believe this," he said with a groan. "I may as well be in love with the old woman who lived in a shoe."

Maddie skipped right over the old woman part of his sentence and homed in on the "in love with" part. "You haven't told me that lately," she murmured.

There was a pause.

"I haven't said I love you? There's something drastically screwed up about this courtship, in that case. If we could just—I love you, dammit—if we could just get past all the friends and worthy causes and wounded creatures and mothers and daughters, not to mention the ex-husbands and dogged detectives and . . . Maddie, this is nuts! I love you, for God's sake. I've loved you for twenty years. When do we get to go out on our first freaking date?"

Car horn beeping, doors slamming, Norah calling out hellos all over the place, Joan and Claire in happy talk about babies and big bellies—Rosedale had suddenly turned into a noisy madhouse and a perfect example of what Dan meant. And meanwhile Tracey was hiding in the garden, mulling over Maddie's explanation, and Sarah was hiding in Sudbury, hoping to avoid Maddie's explanation, and Maddie still didn't have a clue where the godforsaken address book was. Dan was right: Maddie *did* live in a shoe.

Still clutching the phone as Dan tried to nail down a time when they could meet, Maddie took the yellow bag of Domino sugar out of the cupboard above the stove and threw it in back of the one above the fridge, then emptied the sugar bowl into the garbage can and put the empty bowl on the table just in time to wave hi to Norah and Joan.

She turned her back to them and whispered, "Dan? Ten minutes," then swung around, hung up the phone, and smiled radiantly at her impromptu visitors.

Norah, dressed in a black T-shirt and form-fitting pants and decked out in clunky gold jewelry, said, "Joannie wanted to go out for supper and we decided to shanghai you into coming along. You too, Claire. Come on; it'll be fun to get away from George for a couple of hours."

But Joan lifted her nose and sniffed the air. "We're too late; their dinner's in the oven."

Norah said, "For goodness' sake, Joan, it's a roast, not a soufflé; it'll keep for sandwiches."

."It might be an expensive cut," Joan argued.

"What difference does it make?" said Norah exasperatedly. "The point is to go out and have a good time."

"You're welcome to join us," said Claire. "There's plenty of food."

"Oh, but if they want to go out and have a good time. . . ." Maddie argued.

"We can have a good time here," Joan said in an oddly poignant voice. "It's cozy. I like Maddie's kitchen."

"No, this is entirely too . . . domestic," said Norah, looking around her with a visible shudder. She frowned fiercely at Maddie, apparently trying to send her a signal of some kind. "Besides, George will be here. He's a male. It alters the chemistry."

Claire explained that her husband wouldn't be back until the next day, at which point Tracey came in and was apprehended by Norah, who tried to make her join them too. Tracey seemed horrified by the thought, which prompted her Aunt Claire to begin nudging Maddie out the door with assurances that Tracey would be perfectly fine staying home with her. Tracey said quickly, "That's a good idea, Mom. You go." And Norah said, "Finally! It's all settled. Maddie, put on some lipstick. Are you wearing that dress?"

The plan was *not* going according to plan.

In desperation Maddie blurted, "Wait! We're out of sugar!" and grabbed the bowl from the table. "I'll just go borrow some and then I'll feel better about leaving poor Claire in the lurch. I'll be right back."

"Maddie, don't be silly. I don't need any—"

Too late. Maddie was out the door and in her car, fleeing like an escaped convict, feeling terrified and exhilarated at the same time.

She had to see him, had to. If she didn't see him, hold him, hear him, she would go absolutely mad. She was wild, she was crazy—she was compensating for a lifetime of doing the right thing.

I did it! she realized as the lighthouse hove into view. She brought the Taurus to a skidding halt and jumped out, leaving the engine running and the car door open.

Dan must have been watching her getaway attempt. He was standing in the open doorway with a look on his face that was half amused, half amazed.

"Inside, inside!" she urged him, waving the sugar bowl as she rushed past him. "I only have two minutes!"

Grinning, he closed the door behind them, then took the bowl out of her hand and slapped it down on the hall table. "Two should do it," he said, taking her in his arms and giving her a kiss that she felt down to her toes.

"Oh, criminy," she whimpered, "oh, I love you, Dan; I can't go without you anymore." She returned kiss for kiss, moan for moan: both of them were breathless, frustrated, hot.

"No need . . . no need . . . to go without, love," he muttered distractedly. He hiked her dress up over her waist and tore at her underpants. "Two minutes . . . ye gods . . ."

He glanced around and said, "Couch!"

"Yes!" she said, holding her dress up and making a run for it. She pulled off her pants, then lay on the sofa, feeling scratchy polyester under her buns as she waited the few quick seconds it took for Dan to shuck his trousers and shorts.

He dropped on top of her, fitting himself into her at the same time that he kissed her savagely. She lifted herself toward him in a fierce lunge, causing herself pain, reveling in the sheer brute rawness of it. No foreplay here; it was sex on the run, quick, fast, wet—an act of primal mating, over as soon as begun, and it left them both panting and stunned.

In a husky, breathless voice he said in her ear, "Next time . . . a bed, by God."

"Yes, next time," she said, wiggling out from under him, still dizzy from her orgasm. He hopped out of her way and she slid her underpants back on, then shimmied her dress back down and raked her hands through her unstyled hair.

"How do I look?" she asked, aware that it couldn't be good.

Dan just stood there, with an odd, strained look on his face.

"That bad?" she asked, embarrassed.

"Oh, my darling," he said, coming close and cradling her face in the palms of his hands. "Like a dream version of my recurring dream. I love you so very much."

He kissed her in a gentle, touching way, sending new shivers all through her, or maybe just keeping the old ones going. The desire to stay with him was so strong that Maddie scarcely heard the blaring horn of Norah's Mercedes, urging her back to Rosedale.

"I have to go," she moaned.

"Tell your family about us, then; tell them," he said as they walked to the front door together. He opened it and she stepped outside.

"It turns out I won't have to tell them," she admitted, trying to sound offhand about it. "The lady with the two terriers? She turned out to be Lillian Lebonowicz, a countess, no less, and a friend of my mother's. We've been outed."

She saw the frustration in his eyes turn to something else. Relief? "Oh boy. What did your mother say about that?"

"Not a whole lot. She's in Sudbury now, giving me the Amish treatment."

He shook his head and said, "That's too bad. What about the rest of your family?"

"Well, George was more than willing to drive my mother back to Sudbury. I'm taking that as a nay vote. As for Claire—Claire's like Switzerland. She sympathizes, but would never take a stand one way or the other."

"Tracey?"

Maddie winced and said, "I might be making some progress there, but it doesn't feel quite right. Well, thanks for the—"

"Shit! The sugar!" he said, grabbing the bowl and handing it to her.

Between them, she was the one with the presence of mind to notice that the bowl was still empty.

"Oh, geez," he said, taking it back from her. "Pray no one's watching this fiasco," he said on his way to the kitchen.

"Trust me, they're watching," she yelled after him.

He came back, after a too-long absence, with the bowl only

a third full. "I had to empty some packets of Equal I found in the cupboard. I think my sister left them here, so they shouldn't be too old."

Maddie rolled her eyes and said, "This'd be funny if it weren't so pathetic."

"*We're* pathetic, Maddie," he said, his cheeks flushing with the realization. "Maybe I should just have it out once and for all with your family."

"Don't do that," she said quickly. "I'd be so humiliated. I'm not a child, Dan; you have to let me handle this. One way or another, they now understand what you mean to me. And if my mother and brother don't accept that—so be it," she said stoically.

She searched his face for understanding. Except for a sister, he had no family of his own. Did he grasp what she was prepared to give up for him? Christmases and Easters and birthdays and babies, and all the joys and sorrows and history that bound a family together?

"I know," he whispered, answering her thoughts. "I know, and I love you the more for it. Call me when you can. I love you, Maddie. Keep me in your heart this time."

It was a plea, a scolding, a threat—it was all those things, and more. She gave him a sad, sweet smile and said, "This time, I will."

She turned and ran back to her car, its door wide open, its engine still running.

For all her reluctance, Maddie was glad she'd followed Norah's signal and let herself be hauled off to the restaurant, because as it turned out, Norah had found Joan in a deep melancholy when she dropped in on her that afternoon. Getting Joan out of the house had been the only solution that Norah could think of, but having her spend the evening in Maddie's cozy, sweet kitchen didn't seem like the right antidote.

So, voilà: dinner at the Pink Fancy, a New England restaurant with a funky Caribbean decor. You couldn't help but smile at the over-the-top decorations, and that had been Norah's brilliant intention from the start. Fake palms, dried co-conuts, fishing nets strung across the ceiling, posters of Bob Marley and Jimmy Cliff, stuffed parrots, tanks of live tropical fish for viewing and live lobsters for eating, and a steel-drum band that insisted on playing "Yellow Bird" every third song, gave the place a charmingly hokey air. Not only that, but the food was supposed to be good.

They had settled in with their drinks when Joan excused herself to go to the ladies' room.

"I don't get it," Maddie said as soon as Joan was out of earshot. "She was in a fine mood when I saw her last."

"She's sick of being alone, that's all," said Norah with a shrug. "Personally, I think she should adopt."

"That's one solution," Maddie said, taken aback.

"Or maybe she just needs more sex."

"And there's another."

"Speaking of which—how was your quickie?"

Yipes!

Maddie said primly, "I don't know what you're talking about."

"It's a sin to tell a lie, darling. When you came back to the house from Dan's, you had a certain glow. I know it when I see it."

Norah folded her perfectly defined arms over one another on the table and leaned forward. "Don't misunderstand me," she added, flashing a good-humored grin. "I'm incredibly impressed. Even *I* have never kept friends and family waiting while I got it on with someone. My beeping the horn didn't slow him down at all?" She swirled the remains of her Scotch, a pensive look on her face. "I'm just so impressed," she repeated, downing the last of the drink.

Maddie took the paper umbrella out of Joan's piña colada and closed it, laying it neatly alongside Joan's napkin. "Do you think anyone else noticed?" she asked, memorizing the umbrella.

"Nah. You have to have done one to know one. Joan's not the type, and as for Claire—George isn't the type. Your secret is safe with me."

"Norah, I don't know what's happening to me," Maddie confessed. "I see him and . . . I want him. I don't mean, just for sex. I want *him*. All day, all night . . . I haven't felt like this since Lowell College. No, that's not true; I've *never* felt like this before."

"You had a scare," Norah decided. "You lost him once. You don't want to do it again."

"But this is so crazy. Am I just another baby boomer reliving my youth? Is this all about nostalgia? Is it one last grab at wild romance before I turn once and for all into . . . my mother?"

"Darling, bite your tongue."

"I'm so overwhelmed by him, Norah. I'm wondering how far I'll go for him." She stared at an especially bright angelfish in the nearby tank. "I'm beginning to think, pretty far."

"Family's not jumping on the Dan Hawke bandwagon, I take it?"

"Hardly," Maddie murmured. "They're trying to shoot out the tires."

She gave Norah a brief version of the beach episode—too brief for Norah—as well as of the blowup between her mother and her afterward.

"It's as if we're frozen in an earlier decade," Maddie summed up. "I was hoping that his celebrity status would help him with them. If anything, it's made it worse."

"Of course it has. Your people have no use for townies who make good. It gives the lie to all the myths they hold so dear about breeding and training."

"We're not talking horses, Norah, for pity's sake."

"Worse. We're talking Bostonians."

Even Maddie had to laugh. No single word described her mother better than that one. Proper, starchy, Puritanical, and exclusive came close—but "Bostonian" said it all.

"Joannie!" cried Norah in warning as their friend approached. "Drink up; your piña colada's melting."

Joan, dressed in too much pink, sat down and lifted her glass in a toast. "I've been thinking. I can't remember the last time I got ripped. Whaddya say?"

"I'll drink to that," said Norah, clinking her second Scotch against Joan's glass. "Maddie?"

Maddie hesitated only a very brief instant before touching her glass to theirs. "Count me in." It might be just what she needed after the roller coaster week she'd just had.

As it turned out, no one was much good at getting ripped. Piña coladas were too filling; chardonnay was too pleasant; and Scotch, while potent, had little effect on a woman known to possess a hollow leg. Still, everyone got a little buzz on, and everyone felt a little better for it. The food was to die for: flying fish pie and callaloo soup, chicken calypso and curried goat. Maddie personally toasted Norah's good judgment at least three times, and Joan decided to buy a house at once in the Virgin Islands.

When Maddie's cell phone rang in her purse, she almost didn't hear it; they were all laughing too hard at a fund-raising story that Norah was telling with her usual flair.

"Maddie? It's Claire," said her sister-in-law, automatically raising her voice to be heard at the other end. "It sounds like you're having a really good time; I'm sorry to bother you during dinner, but—"

"No, no, it's fine, Claire," said Maddie, trying to shush her friends. "Tracey wants special permission to do something, right? I knew she would."

"Well, sort of. Actually, Michael's here. He came down for the day and—well, can you talk to him for a moment?"

She was giving Maddie a chance to beg out of it, which Maddie appreciated. She said, "Thanks, Claire, but it's okay. Put him on."

Chapter 21

Michael kept the smile plastered to his face as he accepted the phone from Claire. He'd had to do a backflip out of his rage when he found her at the cottage alone with Tracey, and he wasn't sure she'd bought his act.

She was watching him now, warily.

He stayed in the role of Mr. Congeniality as he said, "Maddie, hi. Listen, I had to drive down to an emergency in my condo this evening and I'll tell you, traffic was unbelievable. I dread going back, knowing that I'll have to do it all over again tomorrow to pick up Tracey for my weekend. Would you mind if I took her today? I know I'm springing this on you out of the blue . . . if I'd had any brains I would've called before I left Boston, but who knew? The roads were actually better on the Fourth."

He could tell she didn't like it. She hesitated, and he took advantage of the pause to beat her black and blue with more congeniality. "The Cape's overdeveloped, and that's a fact. Of course, I should talk; I'm part of the problem—with my newly built condo—right? And by the way, your garden looks great. Tracey took me for a tour of it. You have a way with roses, Maddie, like nobody else."

"I don't know, Michael. What does Tracey say?"

"You know how she is—doesn't want anyone to go to any hassle over her."

"I'd really rather she didn't leave before I saw her. Things got a little—I'd like to say goodbye to her, Michael.''

Bitch.

''Oh. Well . . . then maybe we should just forget about it,''
he said, sounding cool. ''I've already been hanging around
for almost an hour and—''

''Michael, it'll take her another half hour to pack. You
know that. I could almost be home by then.''

''Actually, she's all packed. Her suitcase is in the hall.''

''It is?''

The next pause was long, and, to Michael, eminently satisfying. He had her now.

Maddie said, ''All right. But let me talk to her first.''

''Sure,'' he said with a thumbs-up sign to Tracey. ''Here
she is.''

He handed the phone to his daughter who had six words
to say: yes, no, uh-huh, okay, and goodbye. She added a
''Mom?'' but by then Maddie had hung up. Good. No chance
for either one to have second thoughts.

''Well, kiddo? What do you say? Ready to hit the road?''

''I guess so,'' Tracey said uncertainly, looking around as
if she were missing her car keys.

Michael could've done with a little more enthusiasm from
her. But he reminded himself that it didn't matter. He knew
that after three days of letting her run free with her Boston
friends, and three nights of shows and concerts, Tracey would
look back at her time in Rosedale the way she would a prison
term at MCI.

Claire had her arm around Tracey as she walked them to
the door. She said, ''That's a big suitcase, honey. What on
earth do you put in there?''

''Just . . . stuff. I never pack it very tight,'' she said, looking at Michael in a panic. She was a lousy liar. It pleased
him somehow; he didn't know why.

Claire hugged her and seemed to let go reluctantly.

''I might be gone back to Newton by the time you return,''
she told her niece. ''But I'll be down for your birthday. Is
there anything special you want this year?''

Tracey stood there in the twilight, unprepared for the question and unwilling to leave without answering it. She looked like a little girl again, a little girl of four, standing in line for Santa. It seemed like only yesterday. He had to look away.

In a voice so young that it caught at his heart, she said to her aunt, "Like, did you ever see those clogs with the stars around the front part of the sole? The heel is, like, wood? They're really cool. I saw them in Filene's."

Claire smiled and said, "Maybe a gift certificate from there, then. So you get the right size."

Michael lifted the two-ton suitcase and dropped it in the trunk of his car. "Let's go," he told his daughter. "And, Claire—"

"Yes?"

"Say hi to the gals for me," he said with a wink.

Bitch.

Maddie had left her banana flambé still flambéing, but she wasn't in time to see her daughter drive off for the weekend. All she found was Claire, sorting through a box of Edward Timmons's papers that she'd hauled upstairs from the basement.

Claire wasn't surprised to see Maddie so quickly, but she was surprised to see Maddie alone. "What happened to Joan and Norah?"

"I told them to enjoy dessert and then take a cab," Maddie said, disappointed that she was too late. She slumped into one of the dining room chairs. "How did Tracey seem?"

"Still a little edgy, I think."

"And Michael?"

"You know him better than I do. How did he sound on the phone?"

Maddie shook her head. "He seemed okay. Too okay. At the fund-raiser I thought he was acting jealous of me and hostile to Dan. Could I have been that wrong?"

"Maybe he was just lining up with your mother and George."

"You mean, hostile to Dan but *not* jealous of me?" asked

Maddie, smiling wryly at Claire's diplomacy. "You could be right. Dan has me so puffed up about myself that I've begun to assume that men are lining up outside my door."

"You? Puffed up? Maddie, you're the most unassuming woman I know. You could do with a little more ego, in fact. Borrow some of Norah's. God knows, she has plenty to go around."

Maddie laughed, then pointed to her father's papers and said, "And who told you to go lifting heavy boxes, by the way? That wasn't very smart. You were supposed to wait for me."

She was dismayed when her sister-in-law agreed. Claire stood up rather slowly and rubbed her big belly. "I've felt a couple of . . . twinges," she admitted. "I wonder if maybe I did overdo it."

Now Maddie was alarmed. "Claire, get up to bed and lie down this minute. My God. Should I call George?"

"Don't be silly. He's already wasted enough—no. He'll be here tomorrow afternoon. That's soon enough. If I don't feel quite up to speed, I can always go home then."

Nonetheless, she gave Maddie no argument about going to bed. They exchanged good nights and Maddie added the new worry to her basket of old ones. It didn't seem possible that a family could be in such disarray as theirs. Nothing seemed to be going right, and now this. Twinges. Pregnancies were filled with odd creaks and strange pangs, but . . .

Maddie shook off her murky thoughts, afraid to have anything to do with them.

She'd had such hopes for this year's summer at Rosedale. The previous summer, coming hard on the heels of her father's death, had come and gone with all of them still in shock. Maddie and George had opened up Rosedale for the season, but no one had bothered to use it. This summer was going to be different. This summer Maddie had made sure that her condo was rented to another faculty member; that way, she'd have no choice but to tough it out at Rosedale. It had begun exactly according to plan.

And then came Dan.

And there went the family.

And the worst of it was, Maddie almost didn't care. As long as she had Tracey and she had Dan—they were the only ones, at bottom, she needed to survive and to be happy. She could never say so to anyone, of course. But in the deepest recesses of her heart, she knew that if God ever told her to pick two people for that desert island, they were the two she'd pick.

She gravitated to the phone and was dialing Dan's number when she heard a two-thunk knock at the kitchen door. She turned and there he was, her desert island wish come true, standing on the other side of the opened Dutch door. He was dressed in jeans and a black T-shirt and looked fit enough and sexy enough to scare the bejesus out of her mother still.

Maddie unhooked the screen door and Dan came in and pulled her toward him with a hard, silent kiss, then cocked his head, obviously listening. "It's quiet in the shoe," he said, surprised. "How come?"

Maddie explained all the various comings and goings and added, "Joan and Norah should be back soon, although for all I know, they're square dancing in a Veterans' Hall somewhere."

"We can but hope," he said wryly.

"I know you're okay with Joan," Maddie said, slipping out of his arms and getting him a beer. "Is it Norah who bugs you?"

He accepted the can from her and popped the lid. "She assumes," he said with a shrug.

Maddie laughed and said, "Still your same old sociable self, I see. I probably shouldn't tell you this, but I found Norah waiting in your bedroom right before the fireworks. She was wearing a little—a very little—red dress and I think she had plans that involved bedposts."

Again he shrugged. "As I said: she assumes."

Maddie slipped her arms around his waist and snuggled close. "I can't believe this," she murmured, inhaling the scent of him. "I can't believe you're really, really mine."

Dan put the beer on the counter and wrapped his arms

around her. He cradled the back of her head, rubbing it absently, tenderly, as he pressed her close and kissed the top of her hair. "Believe it, Maddie," he said. "Yours, and no other's."

It was heaven, being held by him and with the echo of his promise floating through her head. Maddie had no desire for anything else, anyone else, just then. She sighed heavily and tried to lock the moment in her memory, because she knew that when she was old and at the end of her span, this would be a remembrance she'd return to again and again, and again. Her heart welled up from this new, profoundly deep awareness. "I love you, Daniel Hawke," she whispered. "I truly do."

"Then be my wife," he said, tipping her chin upward. "Because without you, I can't, anymore. Maddie, be my wife."

"Dan. . . ."

When first they'd been together, neither had ever spoken of marriage. It wasn't cool; Dan had big plans; she had vague fears. And then without warning came the protest crisis and they found themselves being swept downstream on the rapids of trauma, ending up on opposite shores. It took two decades for him to find her again. But he had. Miracles did happen.

"Yes," she said. "Yes."

Could they be happy? Would the Fates allow it? Would her family? Maddie had no answer to those questions, so she simply swept them from her mind.

"I have no ring," he whispered, kissing the finger that should've been wearing one now.

She smiled and said, "I can't imagine you in a jewelry store. You've probably never been in one in your life."

"Sad but true. We'll go together."

She knew that there would be no mother's trinket or grandmother's gold wedding band to pass down. When she'd asked him about his family, he'd simply said, "Gone. A while ago."

Had he tried to find them? Yes, he'd told her. But he'd been too late.

A new ring, then, for an old love. It was oddly fitting.

He kissed her softly, sealing his pledge, and then let out a baffled laugh. "I'm new at this. How do we make our intentions known? Wedding banns? Town crier?"

"Who needs a town crier? We've got Lillian."

"Ah, the countess. I forgot." Smiling, he let his arms fall lower and caught Maddie under the curve of her buttocks, pulling her closer to him. "How's this for an inspired thought? We spend the night at the lighthouse," he suggested with a look she remembered well.

"That's almost a perfect idea," she answered, "except . . ."

She explained her nervousness over Claire's condition and Dan agreed immediately that leaving her would not be wise. He added, "I'll bring up the boxes myself while I'm here. Maybe by then your two pals will have come and gone and I'll be able to sneak into your room. You may recall that I'm pretty good at that."

"The sorority house! Oh, Dan—we were so *young*," she said, astonished that they weren't still.

"Young, shmung. You're much more beautiful now."

"Stop," she said, blushing. "Before you go completely over the top."

"I mean it." He bent his head in a playful lunge for her throat. "I vant you," he said in his best vampire voice, backing her against the refrigerator. "And when we finally do manage to get into a bed—wherever the hell it is—I'm going to lick you until you're a whimpering puddle of lust."

Maddie arched her neck, exposing it to him. "Go on, I dare you."

"That's not what I—well, okay," he said, chuckling, and took her up on her dare, alternately nibbling and licking her neck, and, in between, muttering cheerful thoughts about belfries and coffins. The electric surge that initially shot through Maddie dissolved into a series of giggles as she tried to fend him off with little success. They were tangled up like two paper clips when the doorbell rang, ending the comedy of seduction.

"I suppose it was too much to hope that they'd step directly from the cab to her car," Dan said with a sigh as he tucked his T-shirt back into his pants.

"Love me, love my shoe," Maddie told him, yanking his shirt back out again on her way to answer the bell. She felt a little disheveled herself as she opened the door.

Apparently it showed. Joan and Norah took one look at her, and then Norah stuck out her hand and said, "On second thought, I want my cab fare back. Twenty-five bucks, please."

"Put it on my tab," Maddie said, grinning.

Joan was making little hops, trying to see over Maddie's shoulder. "Aren't you going to let us in?"

"I am not." Maddie thought about telling them the news, but the news was still too new; she wanted to savor it alone with Dan. She promised to call them tomorrow and slammed the door as politely as she could in their faces.

She went back to the kitchen, which was empty. Her first thought was that maybe Dan had fled to the lighthouse, but then she noticed the basement light on. She found him at the workbench, where he'd piled half a dozen boxes of her father's books and papers and had begun the process of going through them.

He looked up as she turned the corner on the wood stairs. "What color was it? Burgundy, you said? What size?"

From vampire lover to Sherlock Holmes in two minutes flat: the transformation took her by surprise. Immediately she fell in with his more somber mood. "I'd say five by eight. It was bound in flat plastic spirals, I think. Old, but not that old. The police went through my dad's study, and then I kept an eye out for it as I packed all this away. I don't see how we could've missed it."

"Did you look behind the drawers of his desk? Behind the bookcases in his study?"

"We had to take out the drawers to move the desk, but no, not behind the bookcases."

He nodded absently as he continued searching quickly through the magazines, obviously not finding anything beyond tightly packed periodicals. "Your father could've folded a magazine closed over the address book and then put it away," he speculated, but he didn't sound hopeful.

"I'll look," she said. "You stack."

"Right."

Dan brought down a high counter stool from the kitchen for Maddie and fed her a steady supply of boxes as she forced herself, one more time, to rummage through the remains of her father's intellectual life. When Dan wasn't moving and packing, he searched other boxes of odds and ends from the study, not necessarily for the address book.

After an hour or so, Maddie took a break to check on Claire, sleeping peacefully, and then brewed some coffee for Dan and her. They sipped as they searched, speaking in half sentences and unfinished phrases, the way they used to, without having to explain their thoughts in detail. The basement—unfinished, poorly lit, dusty and cluttered—made it easier to focus on the job at hand. It was not the place to think thoughts of love or to give in to melancholy musings. It was a place, simply, in which to get the job done and then get out.

Dan was on his last box when he said, "Huh!" and held up a covered plastic tray filled with floppy disks. "Someone has a computer?"

"Oh, that," Maddie said, looking up. "Does the label say 'backup'?" Dan nodded, and she explained. "The police took the original disks and my dad's PC and then read the disks, looking for evidence. I don't know who actually did it; apparently one of the homicide detectives is a computer geek. They didn't find anything incriminating, so they gave it all back to my mother. My dad must've left the backup disks here the summer before."

"I have a laptop," Dan said. "Mind if I run through some of these?"

"Why should I mind?" she asked, yawning. Dan had been reading freely from her father's longhand work all evening.

He shrugged and said, "It could be awkward to find, say, a diary of his most secret thoughts."

"Dan—my dad had no secrets," she said firmly. "He was

aboveboard and blunt to a fault. It used to make my mother crazy; she's no big fan of letting it all hang out.''

''Now you tell me,'' Dan said with a wry grin. He stood up and stretched, bumping his fist into the joists above his head. ''Well, I'll go check behind those bookcases now—''

''Oh, no-o-o,'' Maddie said, slumping forward melodramatically. ''Can't that one wait until morning? We've been *so* good.''

Dan walked over to her and slid his hands under the back of her hair, rubbing his thumbs into the base of her neck and drawing away some of the tightness that had pooled there. Maddie sighed and let her eyelids droop down, shutting out the dreary light overhead. She might have been lulled into sleep where she sat if it weren't for the sound of a car pulling into the drive alongside the basement window.

''That's George's Acura,'' she said, snapping to attention. ''What's he doing here?''

''Maybe Claire called him after all,'' Dan suggested.

It was too late—she was too tired—for another confrontation. She considered throwing a tarp over Dan, but he saw the panic in her eyes and warned her off with a look. ''Steady, girl. You can do this.''

He was too calm by half. She didn't like it when he was too calm by half. It meant he was prepared to push back.

''Let's go upstairs!'' she said, sliding off her stool. Anything to get Dan closer to an exit.

''He knows we're down here,'' Dan said, motioning her to stay where she was. ''We're not breaking any laws.''

''Technically? I'm not so sure. My father's stuff all belongs to my mother, after all.''

Laws were not uppermost in Maddie's mind, in any case. Uppermost was the memory of George and Dan rolling around on a courtroom floor. It was the last spontaneous thing she'd ever seen George do, proof that his feelings ran bitter and deep. But Dan wasn't in handcuffs now, and there were no bailiffs to separate them. And in the meantime, what was all around them? Tools. Weapons, pure and simple—every last hammer and wrench on the pegboard.

Her mind was still picking through bloody scenarios as George descended to the basement. He saw Maddie, standing at the foot of the stairs and poised for flight. And he saw Dan, leaning back on the workbench with his arms folded across his chest.

He addressed his sister first. "You're getting pretty nervy, don't you think?"

Maddie decided to take it as a compliment and said, "Why, thank you, George. I have to work at it."

He's wearing his Armani, she thought. He won't risk ripping it. Nerves were one thing, a thousand dollar suit another.

George turned his surprisingly steely-eyed gaze on Dan. "Would you mind telling me what you're doing, poking through my father's effects?"

Dan's voice slowed to a streetwise drawl. "I reckon you've summed it up nicely."

"Let me rephrase, then," George said in lawyerly tones. "Why are you poking through my father's effects?"

Irritated, Maddie said, "We're looking for clues, George, what do you think? That this is our idea of a hot date?"

He resented their ganging up on him; she could see it in the way his cheeks reddened and his jaw clamped shut. Poor George. His grandstanding days were definitely behind him. He was thicker in the middle, thinner on the top, richer all around. He was going to be a father soon. He was too successful to make a fool of himself; Maddie could see that now.

But that didn't mean he couldn't be huffy.

"I'd like you to leave now," he said, like a librarian ejecting the high school quarterback from the reading room. He all but pointed up the stairs.

Dan smiled and shoved himself away from the workbench with a lazy gesture, his dark eyes glinting with dangerous amusement. Maddie stepped back, giving him room. Dan's foot was on the bottom tread when he stopped and turned to say something to her.

George wasn't expecting it; he flinched, as if he were about to be hit, and both of them saw it. It was more humiliating for him than taking an actual punch.

Dan pretended to pretend he didn't notice. "You'll take care of it, then?" he asked Maddie.

She nodded, clueless, and then she realized he was referring to the box of disks. "First thing tomorrow," she promised. "Good night," she added with irrepressible cheer. They were going to be married. Married!

"Good night, Maddie . . . George," said Dan pleasantly. He ascended the steps, worn down in the middle by generations of summer colonists, while Maddie resisted the urge to chase after him and pinch his tush.

She heard the screen door whack closed and turned to her brother. The recklessness that seemed to be part and parcel of being in love with Dan Hawke seized her once more. "That's my fiancé you just threw out," she said triumphantly. "You'd better hope he doesn't take it personally."

George looked shocked, as if she'd announced she was marrying Jack the Ripper, and then he glanced at her finger.

"We haven't bought the ring yet," she explained. "But we will."

"Bullshit."

Maddie knew that upstairs, Claire was wearing their grandmother's ring, an exquisite diamond and sapphire affair. But Claire's ring—alas—had come with George attached. All in all, Maddie would rather have Dan at her side and a cigar band around her finger.

Her happy, punchy mood was lost on George. He scowled and said, "If you think Mother is going to stand for this, you're crazy. Do you have any idea how outraged she'll be?"

The trouble was, Maddie did have an idea. Some of her bravado evaporated.

"George, George, let it go," she pleaded in an entirely different tone. "It was such a long time ago. Claire told you what Dad said after they watched Dan on TV. If Dad forgave him, why can't you? What gives *you* the right to act as judge, jury, and hangman?"

Her brother became tight-lipped. "That son of a bitch wrecked Dad's career and now he makes more money than Dad could ever dream of—"

"But Dad wouldn't care!"

"He makes more money than *I* ever will, goddammit! And I *do* care!"

And that, at bottom, was what George was all about: money. Who had it, and how they got it. If Dan had inherited it, George wouldn't have blinked an eyelash. But Dan had earned it, by virtue of his skill, wit, and personality. And for that he would never be forgiven.

Maddie looked deeply into her brother's blue eyes for some small sign of relenting, if not right then, then later. On their wedding day, perhaps . . . or if God let them have a child . . . or on their silver anniversary. As long as it was someday.

But she came up empty.

"I'm so sorry you feel that way, George," she said, feeling him slip away from her outstretched hand. "You know that I love you, and I love Claire, and I love your unborn child. I want us all to stay a family. But I want, more than anything, that you accept Dan into it."

She turned and walked halfway up the old, worn steps, and then she paused and looked down at her brother. She saw the top of his balding head, the first cruel hint of the mortality that lay in wait for him and them all.

"I'm so, so sorry you feel that way, George," she whispered again.

But George had nothing to say.

Chapter 22

The first crack of thunder was absorbed into his dream, a harrowing flashback to his months in Albania. He was in the port of Vlore again, when a box of munitions stolen by rebels from an Army depot exploded, sending a storage shed near him sky high.

The second crack of thunder was worse. It turned into the bullet that grazed the back of his head—fired at one of Berisha's thugs by an insurgent with a rotten aim.

But it was the third crack of thunder that woke Hawke up, because the third crack of thunder brought rain: sheets of it, wild and furious, driving against the lightkeeper's house, forcing itself through the window screen and bouncing off the sill onto Hawke's face as he dreamed.

He sat up in his bed, relieved that he was holed up in a lighthouse and not still tagging after a rebel band, and hastily shut the window, fully awakened by the pings of cold rain that stung his bare chest.

His mouth felt dry. It was the rain; it was making him thirsty. He padded down the hall to the bathroom for a glass of water, pausing at the small window to look out at the sea. He couldn't see anything, really; it was still dark. But he was able to feel the violence of the wind on the water, ancient allies in a dance of destruction. Would the lighthouse survive? It would this squall, certainly, and many others like it. But somewhere down the road a hurricane named Betty or Fred or Virginia was going to roar up Nantucket Sound and swallow what was left of the beach, knocking the lighthouse down, pulling it under. It was only a matter of time.

Another wild gust slammed into them. The house shuddered, like a frightened old woman locked out in the street in a bad neighborhood, and he actually found himself patting the bathroom wall to reassure it.

They'll get you to safety as fast as they can, he said, beaming his thoughts to the frail, imperiled structure. Hang on, old girl.

It was odd: he had bonded, really bonded, with the lightkeeper's house and its tower. They deserved a better fate than to be pounded to splinters and rubble. He wanted to see the tower lit again and sending comforting winks to sailors out there who were tired and cold and confused. What would it take to get hold of an old fresnel lantern? he wondered. It was almost guaranteed that the Coast Guard had one in an attic somewhere. He tried to think: did he know anyone who knew someone? He remembered getting drunk with a rear admiral once; he'd have to search around for the guy's card.

Hawke was awake now. On a whim, he decided to go up into the lighthouse itself. He stepped barefoot into a pair of moccasins and pulled a sweatshirt over his pajama bottoms, then went down to the first floor, crossed through the breezeway, and entered the tower itself. The noise from the pelting rain was horrendous. It was like being in a drum going over a falls, he thought. He flipped a lightswitch and began to ascend the spiral staircase, wondering why he felt impelled to do it in the middle of a thunderstorm.

Was the lightning rod intact? God only knew. He remembered reading somewhere that early New Englanders objected to the idea of lightning rods on the towers because they considered the rods sacrilegious. Pity the early New England lightkeeper, if that was the case.

Ignoring the flashes of lightning and cracks of thunder, he crept to the top, still not sure he wasn't going to end up toast, and walked around the deck of the lantern room. With the lantern dismantled, the chamber had the look of a giant socket with no bulb in it. Two of the safety-glass windows that used to surround the lantern were broken and gone now, boarded up with sheets of plywood. And the sashes of the windows that did remain were decayed. One of the curtain rods was still intact; rusty curtain rings hung on it, the fabric drapes mere shreds of rot.

The tower was in pretty sad shape—but standing there in the fury of the thunderstorm, Hawke had to admit to feeling a rush. What would it have been like to be a keeper of the flame in days gone by? Most of the keepers were dead and gone now, replaced by automatic beacons and radio signals and satellites. To modern technology, there was no such thing as a dark and stormy night. Cold, hungry, tired, scared— instruments never felt any of it. But the poor devil who used to have to force himself to refill the lamp oil with half-frozen fingers while his mariner counterparts struggled in the rigging on a storm-tossed sea . . . *those* were the days.

Christ, you're getting sappy with nostalgia for a life you never knew, he told himself. Chalk it up to being moody in love. He gazed into wet, driven darkness toward the charmed place where Maddie was sleeping now, hopefully dreaming of him.

When she stepped aside in the basement earlier to let him pass instead of coming up the stairs with him, she was sending him a signal: *I have business to finish up here.* Had she had it out with her brother after he left? With no brothers of his own—that he knew of—it was hard for Hawke to imagine the emotional fallout that might result.

God knew, it hadn't cost Hawke much to break with *his* family—at the time, anyway. It was only a decade later that he let himself think about his parents with anything like homesickness, and by then it was too late; they were both dead. But his search had led him to a reunion with his sister, and she became the single spot of joy in his life. Until now. Until Maddie.

Madelyn, my Madelyn.

He sighed, then laughed at himself. He was pining like a medieval troubador for her.

He was still peering through one of the lantern room windows into the slashing rain, trying to make out the gabled roof of Rosedale cottage in the distance, when suddenly the night sky was split by a blinding flash of light that knocked him to his knees and sent every hair on his body standing straight up. The noise from the thunderclap was as excruciating as the pain from the electrical surge. This was Zeus in all his fury, sucking out the air from Hawke's lungs, the life from his body. He couldn't hear and he couldn't see—but he could smell, and what he smelled was burnt hair, the sickening smell of his own burnt hair.

He was thrown back to the day he forced himself into a burning physics building and came out with Maddie's unconscious father, delivering him to firemen on the scene before he himself escaped into the crowd and made his way to an emergency room to be treated for his burns.

Oh hell, oh hell, oh hell, he thought, too dazed this time around to do anything except lie there. Oh, hell.

A moment later, the smell of burnt hair became overwhelmed by the smell of smoke. Somehow Hawke staggered to his feet. He was appalled to see that behind him the roof of the lighthouse—the keeper's dwelling, *his* dwelling—was on fire. The lightning bolt, Jesus Christ, had hit the house, not the tower!

Ignoring the numbness in his knees, Hawke hobbled down the spiral staircase, fighting a nauseating wave of vertigo as he wound down in record time, then ran through the breezeway into the kitchen. He stabbed at the phone and punched in the nine, the one, and the one in what seemed like slow motion before he realized that the phone—obviously, of course, what a stupid asshole he was—was no longer in service. Fried!

Too far to a neighbor; someone else would have to call it in. He grabbed the coiled garden hose from the breezeway and ran up the stairs with it and hooked it up with rubbery hands to the old-fashioned sink in the bathroom. From there it was a stretch up the attic stairs, but he was able to poke the nozzle into one end and aim vaguely in the direction of the flaming wood around the center chimney.

Too much smoke. Just like the physics building, too much smoke. He was driven back, hacking and coughing and searching for a rag to wet and put over his face. He found a towel and gave it a shot and lasted longer this time before he was driven back down the stairwell. Somewhere during the struggle it came to him in another blinding flash that he was going to spend his afterlife burning in hell: why else have two close encounters with fire and brimstone? He knew karma when he saw it.

The welcome sound of sirens broke through his maniacal preoccupation. This time, like the other time, the fire brigade came to his rescue. This time, like the other time, he wanted to fall on his knees and thank the Lord.

"Hey, pal, you okay?"

For an answer the firefighter got a violent spasm of choking; Hawke felt fairly sure he'd coughed up his small intestine. Someone slapped an oxygen mask on him and told him to breathe easy, which was all very well. . . .

"But I'm temporary keeper of the flame, damn it! This is not what the expression means."

"Don't talk; breathe. Don't talk; breathe."

"Maddie, I'm fine. No kidding—I'm fine."

Maddie was hovering over him like a mama duck in early summer, alternately horrified and soothing. "I saw it all . . . I was getting a glass of water and I saw it all . . . I can't believe it . . . a lightning bolt, hitting the house . . . my heart . . . when I saw it, my heart . . . it could've been so much worse. . . . It struck the antenna, they said. If you'd been changing channels, you could've been electrocuted. You could've been dead now! Oh, my darling . . ."

He ended up soothing her. The trauma was a throwback for Maddie, too; Hawke knew that all too well. To distract her, he said, "You remember Professor Woodbine's theory about 'Forms with Power'? Well, by cracky, I think he's on to something there. Damned if that cone shape didn't protect me from—as you keep pointing out—an agonizing, hideous death. Shoo, I could've been switching from early news to a 'Gilligan's Island' rerun. *Then* what?''

"Very funny," she said, whacking him in the chest.

He pretended to fall into a fit of coughing again, which sent her into a spasm of concern until he wrapped his arms around her and held her close, on the beach, in the light, in his pajamas, in front of the departing fire department and an assortment of town busybodies, including Trixie Roiters— there with her trusty Canon A-1 to record it all for posterity— as well as the Countess Lebonovicz, passing through with her two black Scotties for an update on the latest village scandal.

The lightkeeper's house, fortunately, came through its ordeal of fire and rain with minimal damage. The rain had beat back the blaze until the firefighters could finish the job. A rafter would need to be sistered, and some sheathing and shingles replaced. It could've been worse. It could've been a Betty or Fred or Virginia.

"As for me, it's lucky I own nothing of value," Hawke told Maddie after a quick check through the house. "The TV's been zapped into oblivion, of course, and I can forget about having cold beer until the fridge gets fixed. The landlord's dryer was busted anyway, so that's no loss. My laptop was on its battery pack and should be okay—by the way, did you bring those disks?''

"Gee, no, it must've slipped my mind," Maddie said with an incredulous look at him as she went from window to window, opening them to air out the house.

It hadn't occurred to Hawke until then that the house really smelled. He took a deep whiff and said, "Is this place habitable?''

"Not up here, for sure," she said, wrinkling her nose. She looked up at the plastered ceiling of his bedroom and added, "That looks ready to fall any time now."

She was right; he was disheartened. "I was planning to insist that you move in with me," he said, rubbing the back of his neck. "I had a speech all ready."

Her gaze went from the ceiling to him. When she was

pleased, her eyes had a way of becoming more sparkly, somehow. They were shining now. The breeze lifted strands of her golden brown hair as she sat back on the low windowsill, bracing herself on it with her hands. Beautiful, he thought, aware of an old, familiar ache.

She said with a wistful smile, "I have a teenage daughter."

"I forgot. So help me God, for a while there, I forgot. I was on a high."

"I know," she said softly. "Tell me your speech anyway."

"Anyway?" He scraped his unshaved chin and realized that he must look like hell. She looked like an angel. How could he hope to approach her and lay his proposition at her feet?

He compromised by not approaching her at all. He stayed where he was, planting his hands on his hips and his feet wide apart, while he stared at a knot in the pine plank floor. If he didn't look into her eyes . . . if he didn't let himself get blinded by the integrity he saw there, the goodness that radiated from there . . . maybe then he could make his case.

"Somewhere between your basement and the thunderbolt," he began, "I realized that we hadn't set a date for the wedding. Now, the date can be as soon as the next plane that touches down in Vegas; that's fine with me. But it seems to me that you deserve more. *We* deserve more. We've waited so long . . . we've loved so long. I want the world to know that you and I are going to be wed at last. I want you to wear a beautiful dress, and I want flowers everywhere, sweetsmelling roses and honeysuckle that remind me of you. I want us to draw up a guest list together and then keep adding names to it. I want a band! I can't believe I'm saying this, but I want a band."

He risked glancing up at her—would she think he was bonkers?—but all he saw was a vision of what he held dear. She started to say something, but he held his hand palm out like a traffic cop and plowed on, unable to hope, unwilling not to.

"And meanwhile, you're living in enemy territory," he said, grimacing at his own blunt choice of words. He tried to keep the bitterness out of his voice as he added, "and every night that I draw breath without you at my side is one night closer to oblivion. I'm afraid, Maddie," he confessed. "I'm afraid to be without you anymore."

He compressed his lips into a stoic smile and said, "So that was my speech. It never occurred to me that you had to set a moral example for your kid." He snorted and added, "Can you tell that no one ever set one for me?"

He had to stop himself from saying anything more. He was a loner by nature and by training, and he wasn't used to spilling his guts to anyone, even to her. Twenty years in the field had taught him to keep his own counsel. Twenty minutes with her, and he was babbling like a sinner on his deathbed.

It wasn't a bad comparison.

Maddie didn't know what to say. Her eyes were filled with sympathy—not quite the emotion he was trying for—as she came up to him and slipped her arms around his waist and pressed her cheek to his chest. "We can elope," she offered in a poignant voice. "We'll bring our own honeysuckle."

He shook his head. "Eloping is a good idea only for the ones who don't have to. For us it would feel too much like skulking. You deserve more," he said doggedly, rubbing his hands in an idle motion up and down her back. "I don't want us to sneak around in the shadows the way we did then. This time I want—"

"A band. You're right," she said in a feistier voice. "So do I. We'll have a real celebration and we'll invite our friends and family, and whoever comes, comes. And in the meantime I'll sign Tracey up for pottery lessons and cake decorating and—I don't know—model shipbuilding. I'll figure out some way to get her out of the house under supervision so that I can come over here."

He had a thought. "What about summer camp? Aren't you people big believers in it?"

"Rosedale *is* our summer camp," she told him. "Or at least, it used to be."

He nodded. "When I was a city kid—this is when I was seven or eight—I used to wish that someone like you would invite me to spend the weekend," he said, remembering how he'd hang out on the beach in Southie and dream.

Maddie leaned back in his arms and said, "Well, I'm inviting you now. You don't have electricity or hot water or a phone or even a dry roof over your head. It's the only neighborly thing to do."

He was definitely surprised by the offer. "I can afford a motel, you know."

"As if you could find one, this time of year. No, you'll stay at Rosedale, at least until Tracey gets back. We'd do it for anyone else. And it sounds like Mr. Mendoza is counting on you to get the repairs arranged. Wasn't that the deal?"

"That's what he said when I called. He won't be back from the Azores until the end of the month. Look, Maddie—I appreciate what you're trying to do, but . . . what's the point? Old George would have a conniption."

"Old George can go suck an egg!" she said, showing a flash of anger that was new. "Rosedale belongs to all of us! This has nothing to do with you and me and the past. This is about a fire and a neighbor who needs help. Period! Now pack a bag and come *on*."

Hawke was able to convince Maddie to return to Rosedale ahead of him. He packed his duffle in a leisurely way, allowing her time to break the news to old George.

Part of Hawke believed that her plan wasn't all bad. A fire in the neighborhood tended to bring out the best in people. He'd seen it happen more than once, neighbors rallying around the victims. On the other hand . . . well, Hawke getting screwed by a fire. Could it get more poetic than that? George might just rub his hands in glee and let it go at that.

Hawke locked the door, hiked the strap of his duffle over one shoulder, and struck out along the beach. He had no desire to drive; it was far too fine a morning. The thunderstorms had scrubbed the sky a new shade of blue and the sand was cool and clean. There wasn't a scrap of litter around from the town's party on the Fourth; the volunteer crews had done their job well.

Considering the early hour, Hawke was surprised to see people already on the beach: two young mothers setting up with their toddlers; a family of four with chairs, multiple coolers, a playpen, and an umbrella; a couple with a blanket stripping down to their swimsuits. If you only had a week, he surmised, then you damn well had to make the most of it.

It's what he wanted to do with what was left of his life: make the most of it. He was inexpressibly happy that Maddie felt the same way.

The rest of the way to Rosedale, it was their future that he thought about, and not their past.

That changed, once he drew near the picket-fenced cottage on Cranberry Lane. He saw George loading a smart leather suitcase into the trunk of his Acura, and Maddie hugging her attractive, pregnant sister-in-law on the brick walk in front of the house.

Okay, I got two choices here. I can pass, or I can run the ball into the end zone.

He opted for the touchdown. He walked up to the house, unhooked the latch in the knee-high gate of the picket fence, and, feeling oversized for all that charm, entered the diminutive garden that led to the cottage. He'd never approached through the front before; it made him feel less like a servant and more like . . . like what?

A Fuller brush man, damn it, he decided as he returned George's condescending stare.

He tried hard to keep it civil. Apparently—he didn't see any cops around—they were going to allow him entry. He went up deliberately to Maddie's brother and held out his hand.

"George, I appreciate this," he said evenly.

Maddie's brother permitted himself a glance at Hawke's outstretched hand before he closed the trunk and said to his wife, "If you're ready."

Not much progress on that front, Hawke could see. He shifted his duffle strap to a new position on his shoulder, as if he were a sailor on shore leave checking out a boarding house that might or might not have a ban on booze, and then went up to Maddie and Claire.

"M'am," he said, nodding his good morning to the attractive blonde.

Maddie jumped in and introduced them. Claire was as gracious as Maddie claimed she was, and about as neutral.

"I'm so glad to meet you. I'm sorry we have to leave," she said, all with a perfectly straight face.

Leave? Hell, it was an out-and-out evacuation! Hawke had no doubt that if he checked their bedroom, he'd find the drawers still open and hangers on the floor. They'd have hung around longer if he'd had leprosy.

"Have a good trip," he told Claire with a jaunty look.

Maddie stepped around them and went up to her brother with some last parting words, which Hawke couldn't hear. He did hear George mutter, "Do what you want. You won't be doing it for long."

Chapter 23

Maddie was far more jumpy than she'd ever thought possible, having Daniel Hawke as her guest. She wanted to prove that she really *had* acted out of kindness when she put Rosedale at his disposal. The only way to do that was not to be in the same room with him, and preferably, not on the same floor.

So she laid out her thickest, softest towels in the upstairs bath and while Dan showered, she stayed downstairs making a big breakfast for him. When he sat down to eat, she disappeared into the living room to clear a space for him at the small desk there. When he sat down at the desk to call repairmen and contractors, she returned to the kitchen to wash the dishes. And when he came back into the kitchen and picked up a towel to dry the dishes, she went upstairs to strip the linens from Tracey's bed, where he would spend the night.

"I have a question," he said from behind her as she plumped the pillows on her daughter's iron bed.

Maddie jumped; she hadn't heard him approach. "Uh-huh?" she said, glancing at him over her shoulder as she worked.

He was standing in the doorway with a book in his hand and an odd, pensive smile on his face. "Where are you keeping my candlesticks? In the closet with the oil portrait of the ugly aunt?"

"Oh . . . Dan, I gave them away," she admitted, more embarrassed than if he'd caught her stealing them instead. "I had to. They were exquisite," she added, as if that helped.

His nod of enlightenment was mostly ironic. "Oh, okay, that explains it, then."

"I know how precious they were," she told him as she gathered Tracey's old sheets into her arms. "I'm sure you went through every antique shop in London before you finally decided on them."

"You know me much too well," he admitted, looking rueful about it.

"But I couldn't keep them to use and enjoy . . . or exchange them . . . or even sell them. I couldn't take advantage of them in any way. You know? It wouldn't have been right."

"So like you, Maddie," he said softly.

She bowed her head and stared at one of the pink cabbage roses on the sheets. "I donated them—anonymously—to an auction benefit, and now I wish I hadn't. It would've been something we shared from our first life together."

"I was thinking along those same lines," he said, but in a much more cheerful voice than hers.

She looked up to see a sheepish grin on his face. For that single moment in time he was a student again, raw and intense and amazingly shy when it came to social niceties that she took so much for granted.

He came into the room and laid a worn, utterly shabby book on top of the laundry that she held in her arms. The covers of the book were water-stained and warped, the gold-leafed title illegible. Puzzled, Maddie picked up the slender volume with her free hand and read the spine: *Pre-Raphaelite Poetry: A Selection.*

For a brief second she drew a blank, and then she made the connection. "I used to read these aloud to you on the campus green!" she said, thrilled that he still remembered.

Dan was pleased, too. She saw it in the half-smile on his lips and in the flush of emotion that settled over the high, chiseled bones of his cheeks as he watched her closely for her reaction.

" 'Her eyes were deeper than the depth / Of waters stilled at even'," he quoted.

"Rossetti!" she guessed at once. "Oh, Dan—"

"Read the inscription," he told her.

Nestling the book in the crumple of bedsheets still in her arms, she opened the cover and read:

> *Fall, 1979*
> *For Maddie.*
> *No other love,*
> *Dan.*

"Of course, like me, the book was in a lot better shape at the time," he explained with that same half-smile. "But we've been around the globe more than once since then."

It was the gift of the book, ultimately, that did Maddie in. How could she treat Daniel Hawke like an ordinary houseguest, even for a day, when he was the most un-ordinary man she'd ever known? She tried to say something, but an overflow of emotion rose up and drowned the words as they formed.

She took a deep breath, forcing back every other thought but one: "I love you, Daniel Hawke. I love you."

He took the book from her and laid it gently on Tracey's pine dresser, then took the laundry and tossed it aside on the rag rug.

With infinite, tender care, as if he were lifting a veil to a secret place, he slid his hand under Maddie's hair and held it away from her neck, kissing the warm skin underneath, making it warmer still. Maddie closed her eyes and let him have his way—let him kiss her neck; nibble her earlobe; test her resistance and find out for himself how lacking it was.

"We haven't been . . . in a bed together . . . since my basement apartment," he murmured between soft tugs at her lower lip. "Don't you think . . . it's time?"

"I remember that bed," she whispered. "It was made of . . . water."

The waterbed leaked; it was an old one, left over from the

hippy era. But on the concrete floor it hadn't mattered; Dan used to mop up the water now and then and top off the bed with a hose, and it would be good as new.

"Will we have one again?" he asked her, slipping her pink shell up over her head and adding it to the laundry pile.

She caught the hem of his polo shirt and reversed it over his torso. "They're supposed to be good for bad backs," she said gravely, "and general aches and pains."

"Glad to hear it," he answered with a grin as she tossed his shirt, "because I have a hell of a hard-on right now."

To prove it he caught her close, letting out a low chuckle, the same wonderful sound that had excited her as they sloshed around to the make-love beat of the Stones.

In a sly voice, she said, "For now, I guess we're just going to have to make do. So-o—which bed do you want?" She slid the palms of her hands up his back in a sinuous motion. "Mine's the biggest."

"This one's the closest."

"Sounds good to m—" She stopped in the middle of the leisurely excursion over his back with her hands. Something new, something different had been built into the corded surface there. "Turn around," she said, curious about the odd grooves and patches she'd felt.

The smile faded from his face, but he did as she commanded.

Maddie sucked in her breath when she saw the scarred skin: a pale patch, obviously from a burn, that covered an area from the top of his right shoulder down over his wing. "Dan! How did this happen?" she cried, running her hand as tenderly over it as if the burn were new.

He turned around to face her—or to turn his scar away from her—and said with a shrug, "I got a little too close to a burning oil well in Kuwait."

"Truly?"

"Shh. Don't ask so many questions. Shhh. Just let me *love* you," he said, and his voice seemed suddenly more urgent than ever before.

"But—"

He stopped her with a kiss, a hard kiss that had his tongue seeking and probing hers until she thought, Yes, why do I ask so many questions? and let herself be carried away in the passion of his embrace. The scar was from the burn he'd suffered saving her father, obviously—the scar of a hero, whether or not he wanted to admit it.

Her response became more fevered; she felt a rush of wet heat as he hooked his hands under her buttocks, pulling her close again.

He fumbled where her zipper should be until he realized that her jeans had a button fly. He whispered hoarsely, "Are you kidding me?"

Her laugh was dizzy as she hurried to explain. "The jeans I was wearing got sooty from the fire. This is the only other flattering pair I have."

He groaned and said, "Maddie, you could be wearing a sackcloth for all I care—as long as it had a zipper."

They ended up stripping themselves of their own jeans, then sat on the side of the bed in their underthings.

This part was harder for Maddie. Before the baby, she used to think that she had a decent shape: fairly firm, reasonably curved, not too much or too little of anything. After Tracey, all that changed.

"I'm not a kid anymore," she felt constrained to remind him.

"Who is?" he answered with a wry smile. He dropped his chin to his chest and pointed to the back of his head. "See that thin spot?"

"Where?" she said, fanning through his hair with her fingers. "I don't see any thin spot."

He lifted his head back up and said, "When you see my brush in the morning, you'll know," which made her feel overjoyed at the prospect.

The bra she was wearing unsnapped in the front; she was able to see his face as he unfastened it and beheld her breasts in broad daylight for the first time in a long, long time.

"They're lower now," she said with a wince. "I've nursed a child."

"They're a woman's now," he answered softly, and leaned over with something like reverence to kiss the pale skin of each breast in turn.

"It gets worse as you go down," she added, trying to sound gay.

He laughed and said, "We'll see about that," as he guided her onto her back. He slipped off her panties as she pressed on with her extended apology for not being twenty years old anymore. "I had to have an emergency C-section. See?" she asked, patting her stomach above and below the scar. "Maybe you didn't notice. The top part somehow doesn't match the bottom part the way it used to."

Dan ran his forefinger with exquisite tenderness along the line of her scar. "A badge of honor," he whispered.

"Well, now you've seen all of me," she said, oddly elated by the fact. "Am I still waterbed material?"

"Oh, my darling, are you ever," he murmured in a voice that sounded eminently satisfied to her.

Maddie was aware that he had changed little. Some of the black hairs on his chest had gone gray, and maybe—maybe—he was a little thicker in the waist. He was no longer lanky, in any case. Solid? Yes, that was the word that came to mind. And sexy; that was the other word.

He bent over her on all fours and she was very, very aware that one part of his anatomy was still exactly the same.

"What do you want?" he asked in that same husky voice. "Tell me; show me."

"Dan, *you* know," she said archly.

"Tell me. Tell me where you want me."

Shameless now, she closed her eyes and said with a sigh, "Start at the top . . . work your way down."

"Consider it done."

"Do you want me here?" he murmured, teasing and kissing her nipple until her breathing came faster and shorter and finally dissolved in one long, ragged sigh. "Do you want me here?" he said, sliding his tongue to a spot between her breasts, inhaling her scent with a deep sigh of pleasure, then drawing lazy circles with his tongue. "Or . . . maybe you want me here,'' he said, deftly drawing the other nipple with licks of his tongue into the same erect state.

''Oh . . . oh, either is good . . . both are . . . good,'' she said, rippling in response, amazed that she still had the capacity to lie there with no other desire than to soak up the pleasure he was willing—eager—to give her.

''Wait, the little spot inside your elbow; I almost forgot about that spot,'' he said, going off on a side trip down memory lane with a kissing caress.

And so it went, with him revisiting every charmed place and secret haunt of her youth, marveling that they were all still there, just the way he remembered. He stopped in at her navel, went back to her midriff, wandered back down again, and was delighted to rediscover an easily missed spot where her thigh joined her torso, just outside the soft brown nest of her pubic hair.

And Maddie? She was like a burbling brook, being rushed along in parts, slowed down in other parts, but aware that every bend and curve was bringing her nearer to her destination. When he focused with his tongue at last on the small nub of flesh between her thighs, alternately licking and sucking and making her wild, she knew . . . she knew. Rapids and white water, and then over the precipice she went, falling, falling, falling, into a deep, deep pool: a serene, utterly still, totally . . . fathomless . . . pool.

She floated in that pool for a small eternity, perfectly content, hardly aware that someone she loved was standing idly on the shore, waiting for her to come out.

Someone got a little impatient. ''Hey, miss,'' he whispered, touching his lips to hers in a feather-light kiss. ''Mind if I join you?''

Maddie smiled and opened her arms to him, inviting him in. He was her playmate, her lover, her friend from way back. And an excellent guide: no one else knew the way to the pool.

The kiss she gave him began in simple gratitude but quickly escalated into something ardent. Dan got all of the credit: he had that profound power over her, to know what she wanted more than she knew herself. Stroking her tongue with his, he coaxed her along, breath by breath and sigh by sigh, until he had her panting in his arms again, and then he slid his hand down to her mound, probing the depth beneath with his middle finger.

"More of this, Maddie?" he asked in a raspy, guttural drawl. "Only better? Bigger?"

"Oh, yes . . . oh yes, yes, yes," she answered, submitting all over again to the profoundly sexual hold he had on her. "*Yes.*"

He came into her then, sliding easily on the slick of her spend, filling her, driving her forward with the varied pace of his movements, and finally—when he knew she was ready—driving her home, and then collapsing himself on her breast.

Again she floated, with him this time, in the pool.

Chapter 24

"So what did your mother have to say?"

"She said, as long as the party was supervised."

"That's all? She left two messages on the machine, and when we got back you were on the phone with her a pretty long time. What about?"

Tracey made a face and said, "You know Mom. 'Don't do this. Don't do that.' Just the usual."

"I forgot to ask: *Is* the party supervised?"

"Dad! The Wiltons' au pair is going to be there, and Rick Wilton. He's Chris's older brother—way older! But . . . I kind of told Mom you'd be there for part of it, too."

"And how'm I supposed to do that, when you know that I'll be driving to Brookline, doing hours of testing, and then driving all the way back to pick you up? I'll be lucky if you don't end up having to spend the night with the pink flamingos on the lawn while you wait for me."

Tracey giggled and said, "There aren't any flamingos here, Dad. Stop teasing."

Her eyes were bright with anticipation as she watched the mob of kids converging on the main house, most in their own cars but some being dropped off by indulgent parents like him.

Michael lasered in on a model-gorgeous blonde wearing a dress that barely covered her ass. She was standing under the portico and hanging on the arm of some quarterback type.

The guy, a steroid hulk with a chest fairly bursting through his rugby shirt, was pumping his fist in the air at the rest of his teammates, all of them charging across the lawn at the moment and making animal sounds.

Michael turned back to the beauty and her beast. "So who's the charming couple?" he asked his daughter.

Sounding surprised that he didn't know, Tracey said, "That's Frieda, the au pair? And Rick, of course. They are, like, *so* cool. Frieda came to school once to meet Rick, and we're all like: she's *awesome*."

"Are you kidding? You're as awesome as she is," Michael said stoutly.

"As if!"

He smiled and said, "Okay, outta the car, Your Awesomeness. I'm late already. Be good, now."

"*Da-ad.* You sound like Mom!"

She wriggled out of the car, slammed the door, and didn't look back. His little girl, growing up fast. He watched her fall in with a couple of shrieking girlfriends who seemed much less nervous and yet somehow much more hyper than Tracey.

All day, Michael had watched bemused as his daughter prepared for the big event. After their early hit-and-run shopping trip downtown, she'd spent an amazing number of hours silvering her nails and mixing and matching every piece of jewelry she owned with every scrap of clothing.

As near as he could figure, she hadn't been able to make up her mind, because she walked out of his condo with two earrings in each ear and a dozen bangles on each arm. As for the dress she was wearing, it was too damn short—but still a lot longer than Frieda's. Since Tracey ended up looking more or less like her two girlfriends, Michael assumed that she was happy with her outfit, even if he was not.

A blaring horn from the car behind him on the circular drive sent Michael hastily throwing the Beemer in gear. He glanced in the rearview mirror and saw a snot-nosed dipshit letting out a carload of other snot-nosed dipshits and then peeling rubber trying to impress them with his drag racing skills. Feeling suddenly old, Michael glanced over his shoulder in time to see his daughter enter the doubled-doored entry under the massive portico of the brick colonial.

She'll be fine, he told himself.

She'll be fine.

A four-car pileup on Route 93 played havoc with Michael's schedule as well as his mood. By the time he pulled into the parking lot at the Brookline Institute, he was in the grip of another crushing headache and feeling downright psychotic.

Geoffrey Woodbine wasn't pleased.

"I've been trying to reach you for hours," the director said, walking around to his desk and picking up the phone. He punched a button, then waited.

"I told you," Michael explained, as reasonably as he knew how. "I had to take my daughter to a party. It was vital that she be fashionably late." He stroked his temple. The pain there was relentless.

"He's here," Woodbine said into the phone. "Give us ten minutes to get it together . . . I don't care what you tell them. Ten minutes!" He hung up the phone, then turned to Michael and arched a silver eyebrow.

"Fashionably late?" he said with an icy stare. "Was that necessary?"

Michael exploded. "Jesus, man, don't you remember what it's like to be fourteen? Those things count, you know!"

Woodbine glanced at the open door to his office, then walked over to close it. In a more jocular voice, he said, "Why the devil didn't you pick up on your car phone, in that case?"

"I junked it," Michael said.

Actually, he'd hurled it out the window of the Beemer after calling Rosedale and having her not pick up. She was there. He knew she was there. She was there with *him*. She'd monitored the machine, and she hadn't picked up. Were they in the middle of it? Lying in their sticky afterglow? He'd find out. He'd find out, or he'd die trying.

"Michael? Are you hearing what I'm saying? I am pointing

out to you that we have three gentlemen *from the Pentagon* sitting in a small, very stuffy sender booth and staring at their watches. They will not be returning after today. Michael? They will make their recommendation to fund or not to fund based on the results of today's testing. Do you understand?''

In fact, Michael had to make a real effort to register what Woodbine was telling him. He looked up in sullen response. ''Why bother going through with the test, in that case? It sounds like they've made up their minds not to continue.''

''You're being defeatist, Michael. That is not good. As you know, the last time anyone bothered to check, the CIA had paid consultants over twenty million dollars to try to locate the whereabouts of MIAs, plutonium in North Korea, and Omar Qaddafi, among other missions. What method did these consultants employ? Remote viewing, Michael. As you know.

''What you do not know,'' Woodbine went on to say, ''is that one of the men sitting in the sender booth used to work in the CIA. It's because of him that this project was funded in the first place. He's more than willing—''

''To throw our tax dollars around?''

''Cynicism is counterproductive,'' Woodbine snapped. ''You need to go in there and concentrate. I want you to forget about everything else on your mind,'' the director added with a meaningful look. ''*All* of it. It's idle distraction. Concentrate. And—just as we've discussed—I'll take care of the rest. Can you do that?''

Still balking at the do-or-die stakes, Michael said, ''It's these drugs, Geoff. They're killing me.''

''Nonsense. The drugs you're taking are natural memory enhancers. Their use is widespread in Europe; the side effects are minimal. I suggest to you that your headaches have nothing to do with the drugs, and—perhaps?—everything to do with your reluctance to carry out your part of our bargain.''

Michael's mood turned hostile again. He wanted to slit Woodbine's throat. He hated him, hated everything about him, from his imperious manner to his clipped, vague accent. ''You're full of shit,'' he said. ''I practically black out sometimes.''

"Take the drugs and have them analyzed by a lab, then," Woodbine suggested. "You'll find the ingredients available in health food stores both here and abroad."

"Oh, sure, have a lab analyze them. And how do I do that between now and the test? Psychokinesis?"

Michael hated the way he sounded to himself: whining, sneering . . . afraid. He wasn't afraid. Whatever else he was capable of, it wasn't fear. He'd come too far, done too much, to bow to fear.

With a massive effort, he pulled himself back together for the forthcoming test. "Let's go," he said, standing up. "I'm ready."

Woodbine gave him an appraising look. Laying his hand on Michael's shoulder, he said, "I believe you are. Good."

They walked together toward the lab, down halls of a building that seemed eerily quiet. "It's like a ghost town in here," Michael quipped, trying to ease the tension he felt.

Obviously relieved to see the effort, Woodbine smiled and said, "It's Friday evening; they're all at the bars. So—your daughter is at a party," he added, making a connection that Michael didn't care for at all. "They grow up so fast, don't they? I still can't get over how very much she resembles you. A bright girl, quite intuitive. The resemblance is striking, really."

"So they say," Michael answered, dismissing the subject. He was trying to keep himself focused.

"And she's staying on the Cape with her mother for the summer?" Woodbine asked pleasantly. "I envy them, getting out of the city for so long. I enjoyed myself last week. Which reminds me. Have you thought about bringing in your daughter for that interview? I've been interested in doing this project, as you know, for well over a year. If only you had allowed me to—well, never mind. But now that the funding is a reality, I need to move immediately on finding suitable subjects for the study."

"It's up to my ex-wife," Michael found himself saying.

"And how does she feel about it?"

"She's my *ex-wife*, damn it! Didn't you hear me?"

"I'm sorry," Woodbine said, taken aback. "It was a simple question."

"It amazes me that you had to ask it! You were at the fund-raiser. Did it look as if Maddie and I were best friends?"

Woodbine gave him a cool look and said, "I got the distinct impression that there were still feelings between you."

"Did you! Gee. Maybe you're actually psychic, after all."

The sneering remark caught Woodbine off guard. He gave Michael a sharp look and said, "Let's just stick to the script, okay?"

Fifteen minutes later, Michael was isolated in the test area, hooked up to the EEG, and ready to begin the final remote viewing experiment. In the adjoining room were the targets of the test: fifty photographs of everyday objects scissored at random from a J. C. Penney catalogue and sealed in individual envelopes.

Michael had wanted to test in early evening because that was the time of day when distractions fell away for him. In early evening he could focus. In early evening, he had a much better chance of imagining the contents of a sealed envelope in another room.

But it was late evening now. He didn't like that, and he was unhappy at his distress. Still, unhappy or not, he had to shut out the negative vibrations. He had to concentrate. Woodbine was absolutely right about that.

The pad of drawing paper sat on the table in front of him, daunting in its blankness. Three pencils without erasers were lined up like an honor guard alongside the tablet.

Concentrate.

He knew that Woodbine, in an effort to pander to the government observers, had departed from normal procedure by letting them—and not the Institute's staff—choose the objects from the catalog and then seal them in the envelopes. Woodbine himself was not present at the time the selections were made, just before Michael's scheduled arrival. Amazing, how that one degree of separation had jolted Michael's confidence.

Concentrate.

He could hear Woodbine's voice saying it.

The test was not complicated. After each envelope was opened, a buzzer was to sound. Michael, alone in the subject enclosure, was to envision the object from the envelope. He was to draw a rough approximation of that object on the pre-numbered sheets of the tablet in front of him. If he was not able to envision the target, he was to "pass" by drawing a line through the sheet.

Concentrate.

He tried to sweep away thoughts of the day: Tracey, jumping up and down when he said she could accept the last-minute invitation. *Thank you, Daddy, thank you.* Maddie on the phone, bothered that Tracey was under his control for the weekend. *Remember our pact, Michael; we have to be consistent.* The animal sounds of the teammates charging across the lawn. *Whoo-whoo-whoo.* Maddie on the machine, her voice cool and remote. *No one is in now, but if you'll leave your name and number . . .*

Concentrate.

Someone was in her now; who was she kidding?

Concentrate.

The buzzer sounded. It caught Michael by surprise. How long had it been? He looked at the clock. He looked at the blank sheet. I'm number one, said the sheet. Guess what I am?

Concentrate.

After a fierce effort, too fierce, he began to scrawl a—a what? A tine? A dinner fork?

A pitchfork. He drew a handle on it, bold and big, and tore the sheet from the pad, then placed it face down in the plastic bin on the table. He pressed his buzzer; he was into it now. Next?

Almost immediately, the buzzer from the experimental room signaled him again. He repeated the process but tried to slow down, to push less, to let the images come at their own pace.

Something in a bathroom. . . . A sink? . . . a towel? A toilet!
Toilet humor! He could hear Tracey saying it: "Ee-yew! How
totally gross!"

How totally Pentagon.

The fog that was lurking offshore all day rolled in sometime
after supper, wrapping its clammy arms around Rosedale and
its garden.

Inside the cottage, Maddie and Dan had finished turning
the rooms inside out in their search for the address book, and
were focused instead on the computer disks in the plastic
storage case marked "backup." Dan was at his laptop, me-
thodically examining each and every file on each and every
disk. It was slow, tedious work, but Dan had the discipline—
and the computer background—to keep at it.

Maddie, on the other hand, had little to do. She felt frustrated, but also subdued: the fog had dampened her mood
much more than the failure to find the missing address book.
Without an immediate goal, she found herself wandering from
window to window, staring into nothingness, occasionally
pinching off a spent bloom from the pink geraniums rioting
in the window boxes.

She gazed into the fog where the lighthouse should have
been and said pensively, "If the tower were lit, I'd feel better
somehow."

"How long has it been?" asked Dan, tapping commands
into the keyboard.

"Oh, gosh—I was, let me think, Tracey's age when the
Coast Guard decommissioned it. I guess there wasn't enough
boat traffic to justify the operating expense. We were all so
sad the day they dismantled the lamp, boarded up the house,
and moved out. My dad took pictures—hey, I'd forgotten
about those! I could've used them for my talk."

"I'd like to see them sometime."

"I'll drag out the albums; I packed them away to go back
to my mother's. Anyway, eventually Mr. Mendoza bought the
lighthouse at auction for a pittance. He lived in it for a few

years with his family, then moved out and began renting it for the season.''

"Lucky for me.''

She turned back to him with a smile. "And me.''

But her mood continued its slow slide into melancholy. It was the fog, Maddie decided. It was so completely capable of swallowing things whole: boats . . . beaches . . . houses . . . gardens. . . .

Children. "Do you think it's foggy north of Boston?'' she asked after a while.

Dan looked up from his computer and saw her face. "Why don't you call her and ask how it went?'' he said softly.

It sounded like such a reasonable suggestion.

She shook her head. "It doesn't work that way. On their weekends, you have to trust . . . to seem to trust, anyway. You don't just call.''

"Hell, I would,'' he said, tapping on the keyboard. He frowned at something, then tapped some more.

"You mean, because she could be in trouble?'' Maddie asked. It wasn't what he meant at all. She knew that, but she wanted to be reassured.

He looked up again, infinitely patient with the mother side of her. "Call her because you miss her, not because you're worried.''

"The *last* thing she wants to hear.''

"No—the second last,'' he pointed out.

She had to laugh at that one. "Actually, I can be just as devious as a fourteen-year-old. I told her to call me if she got in early.''

"So if she doesn't call—''

"It means she got in late. I'm assuming that if she *is* late, she'll call anyway and say she forgot to call earlier. Not the best scenario, but at least I'll know she's home and safe.''

Dan hesitated, then said, "Michael would let her get away with that?''

Maddie shivered, then closed the window behind her. "I know he wants to win the war for Tracey's affections,'' she said.

"Are you at war over them?"

"No. But he thinks we are. That's what matters." She wandered instinctively to the painted mantelpiece, where an array of framed family photographs was lined up—even one with Michael.

"Why must she be so devoted to Michael?" Maddie asked plaintively, picking up the photo of Michael and Tracey at her eighth-grade graduation. "It makes me feel like such a skunk."

"Maybe that's why."

Shaking her head, she tucked the frame behind another one so that Michael's face didn't show. "You think she uses him to get back at me. She doesn't. They've always been close. No, the problem with Tracey is our divorce. And I have to take responsibility for that."

Dan took off his reading glasses and tossed them on the desk. "Stop it, Maddie," he said quietly. "Stop beating yourself up over Michael's infidelities. He's a womanizer. I've seen the type a million times. It doesn't mean he's evil; he just doesn't belong in a marriage, that's all."

Her sigh dissolved into a shiver as she said, "How come I couldn't figure that out before I said yes?"

Dan thought about saying something, but stopped himself. She knew what it was. "You were going to say that you could've told me that, right?"

Dan shrugged. "He's always had a roving eye."

"I guess I didn't want to know," Maddie admitted. "I never told my family about his flings, Dan. It was easy to tell you—but not them. It was none of their business, for one thing. And besides, it was too humiliating. All I told them was that we had irreconcilable differences. My mother is much too well mannered to have asked what they were, but I know she thinks I rushed into an unnecessary divorce. It's part of the ongoing friction between us," she said glumly. "No one wanted that divorce except me."

Dan got up from the desk and came over to her, encircling her from behind. "You're cold," he said, rubbing her upper arms. "Why don't I make us a little fire? We can curl up on the couch and spin devious strategies while you wait for Tracey to call.''

''No, let me make the fire,'' she told him. ''It'll give me something to do. You can finish up that disk so you don't lose your place.''

''Deal.'' Dan reached for a framed snapshot, taken by Maddie's father, of a grinning Tracey proudly displaying a hefty bass that she'd caught in Maine.

''Something about her reminds me of you,'' Dan told her. ''It's hard to pin down.''

''Miss Teen Rebel? Are you serious? The bass is more like me than she is.''

''No, really, she's not the rebel you think she is,'' he said, propping the photo back up. ''You set strict standards for her, right?''

''Tracey seems to think so.''

''Then she's got nothing to rebel against. Maddie, I know all about rebellion. People think it's a reaction against authority. It's not. There was absolutely no one in authority over me when I was a kid. If I wanted something, I took it. If I didn't have it, I wanted it. And I got away with it for a long time. I've thought about this a lot: I was anti-authority because I resented the fact that authority existed, but not for me. I didn't want anyone else to have what I couldn't.''

Maddie turned around in his arms to face him. ''Excuse me? You were jealous of people who felt answerable to authority?''

''Uh-huh. Kinda makes you wonder, don't it?''

''Okay, Geraldo,'' she said, slipping her arms up behind his neck. ''What about Tracey, in that case?''

''She's in a phase, not a lifestyle. Tracey's just feeling her way. It might be a different way from yours, but she'll get there just fine. You're doing your part; that's all you can do.'' He kissed her forehead. ''How about getting that fire going? I won't be long.''

Maddie left him to his computer and went out through the mudshed, unhooking the woodbag from a nail as she went.

She picked her way through thick fog to a woodcrib that was filled to the top with seasoned firewood: it could get cold and clammy on the Cape during all but the dog days of summer, so fires were a year-round treat.

After filling the bag with the smallest pieces of the split wood, she retraced her steps down the pea stone path to the house. The Cape Cod cottage, with its shuttered dormers and soft lights shining through multipaned windows, looked especially cozy snugged down in the fog. As always, Maddie felt a surge of affection for the quaint and tattered gray-shingled cottage; she'd never known a summer without it, and hopefully never would.

Will they let us stay? she wondered. Surely the rift would heal. Families really were like trees. Branches died, others broke off, still others grew to replace the ones that were gone. Through it all, though, a tree stayed a tree. Maddie could not—she would not—give up the belief that her family would remain a family.

She dumped the bag on the hearth in the cozy parlor that the family somehow squeezed into on summer birthdays and anniversaries. Dan, still at the mission-style desk that Maddie had dragged home years earlier from a yard sale, peered at her over his half glasses.

"I've found a file of personal letters your dad wrote," he said. "Nothing as private as a diary or anything, but—do you want me looking through them?"

"Of course," Maddie said as she laid the wood in a criss-cross pattern on the iron grate. "I've decided that secrecy is a lot more destructive than candor. This is an investigation, after all." She glanced back at him. He still looked uncertain, so she said, "You have my leave to read the letters without guilt, sir."

"I'll scan," he said.

Maddie had arranged the logs and shoved a dozen sheets of crumpled newspaper under the wood when Dan said behind her, "Uhhh, this is interesting."

"Really?" She struck the match and set it to the paper,

then moved the folding brass fire screen back in front of the flames and turned to him. "What'd you find?"

"A letter from your father, threatening to kill someone named Joyce."

Chapter 25

"Don't be silly," said Maddie, marching right over. "You're misinterpreting something."

Dan swiveled the laptop a hundred and eighty degrees to face her, then tipped his oak chair back on its hind legs while she read.

> Joyce,
> You're cuckoo, you know that? But there's no law against being cuckoo. What amazes me is that you've become involved with Michael now. Where do you think this will go? Can you honestly see potential there? Are you merely naive, or just plain stupid?
> I suppose what you and Michael do is your business. But if it reverberates in any way on my daughter or my granddaughter, then it becomes my business. And I would sooner see you dead than that either of them is hurt. Remember that.

The letter hit Maddie with the force of a bus.

"But what does it mean?" she asked Dan.

She read it again and looked at Dan again, begging him this time. "What does it *mean*?"

He said, "Do you know anyone cuckoo named Joyce?"

"I don't know anyone cuckoo or sane named Joyce," she murmured, and meanwhile, something was clicking not so far down in her subconscious.

I even forgave your father the one time . . .

The one time what? Her mother had blurted that much and no more in the middle of her angry litany of the family's sexual indiscretions. Maddie hadn't thought of it again until now.

Oh, please, no. Not Dad, too.

"I never knew anyone in the physics department named Joyce," she told Dan, distracted by the memory. "But it could've been a student, I guess."

"You don't want it to be, I can see that," Dan told her.

"I can't begin to tell you how much I don't," she admitted. She read through the letter again and shook her head, completely in denial. "This can't mean what I think it does."

"What do you think it means?"

"I can't even say it," she whispered, but she forced herself. "When he writes to her that she's involved with Michael now, doesn't it seem to imply that my father was involved with her first?"

For a moment Dan said nothing, and then he asked, "Do you want to stop here? Pretend we never poked around in the disk?"

She leveled an angry look at him. "No! I told you, no more running away from the truth! We follow this trail wherever it leads!"

"I'm sorry, Maddie," Dan said softly. "I know this is hard for you."

"Okay, whatever," Maddie said, squaring her shoulders back. Out of sheer tension, she began pacing the small parlor, back and forth in front of the merrily blazing fire.

"The thing is, I only just found out something about my father that I never knew. You know that really horrible fight I had with my mother? Well . . ."

She told Dan that Sarah Timmons had upbraided them all for having loose morals and had included Edward Timmons in her tirade. "It never occurred to me to ask my mother what exactly she meant by that," Maddie said dryly.

"You'd make a lousy reporter," Dan decided, bringing his chair upright with a thunk.

"Probably. Between my upbringing and the way the press intruded in our lives after the murder. . . . The thing is, it probably wasn't a real affair," Maddie said, veering back to defend her father. " 'That time,' my mother said. One time. Maybe my dad drank too much at a faculty party, or drove someone home and somehow . . ."

She stared briefly out at the fog, blinking back her disillusionment, then turned away and began to pace again.

"I guess I can accept a one-time lapse on my father's part. But I can't believe that this woman went after my husband next." She stopped to read aloud from the computer display: *What amazes me is that you've become involved with* Michael *now.*

"Not only involved, but she expected to land him!" Again Maddie read aloud: *Can you honestly see potential there*? "If she did see potential," Maddie said caustically, "then she *was* cuckoo."

An ember shot from a log with a loud pop, making her jump. "I mean, who is this Joyce?" she asked, raking a hand through her hair. "Some sexual predator? Did she have it in for our family? Was this her way of taking revenge on us? After all, my father and Michael are nothing alike; they couldn't both be her type."

Dan said quietly, "And you're thinking that this Joyce is the one who actually murdered your father?"

She turned the question around on him. "Is it possible?"

"Physically? Yes. Your father was shot in his car, in the passenger seat. The murderer would've used his or her feet to push out his body. A woman could've done that as well as a man."

Maddie stiffened at the matter-of-fact recital. Dan was a reporter, she knew, but still. . . . She let out a little wounded sigh and Dan said instantly, "Maddie, maybe we should stop. I can't watch you as I do this; it's too painful. But I can't discuss a murder any other way. This isn't the place to speak in euphemisms."

"I know, I know," she said in distress, making two fists and shaking them like baby rattles. She was determined to keep up with him as he forged ahead. "What do *you* think?"

"Well, for starters," he said, turning the laptop screen to face him again, "if Michael was still your husband when this supposed affair between Joyce and him took place, it had to have been over four years ago. In which case, either this Joyce dropped Michael, or your dad was just blowing smoke when he made that threat."

"Oh. Oh! How stupid of me! I never noticed when the letter was dated. That's what's important. When was it?"

Dan shook his head. "No date. A whole batch of letters was apparently consolidated into one big file on the same day: March 20—a couple of weeks before April 6. Your dad seems to have skipped the date, inside address, and signature when he copied each letter into this master file, which is maddening. The letter before this, though, is a complaint about a roofing job—"

"That was six or seven years ago!"

"And the letter after it is, let's see . . . it's a request to Carnival Cruise Lines for a brochure," he said, looking up quickly at her.

"They never went on that cruise," Maddie murmured. "They never got the chance."

"All right," he said, sighing. "We can't confirm when the letter to Joyce was written. Not from this disk. Suppose we try to find the originals."

"Oh, but they'd all be with—"

"Your mother. You'll have to ask her. And, Maddie?"

"Yes?" she said, knowing what was coming next.

"You'll have to ask her about Joyce, too, if you're serious about following this trail wherever it leads."

"Oh, Dan . . . no. I couldn't. That's incredibly personal."

"So was taking your father's life," he said, glancing up at her with the first flash of impatience she'd seen. He was in reporter mode now; she could see it in the way his attention stayed on the computer screen as he continued scrolling through the file.

"You're right," she conceded. Her mind raced ahead to the scene that would take place between her mother and her.

"God . . . my mother is screening my calls now through the answering machine—if it weren't for Claire, I wouldn't even know if she was dead or alive—and yet you want me to knock down her door and demand that she tell me all about Joyce."

"Mm-hmm," he said, his gaze still locked on the screen.

Maddie walked back to the desk, lifted the laptop out from under his fingertips, and started walking away with it.

"Hey!"

"Ah-ah . . . this is a laptop computer. It's designed to work on a lap. The least you can do is move the lap in question closer to the fire. I'll curl up next to you, and we can read through the files together."

The stern look on his face softened as he said, "Leave it to a woman to find a civilized way to fight crime."

Maddie waved the computer in a sinuous ballet over the slipcovered sofa, and when Dan sank into the down-filled cushions, she laid the instrument on his lap and got up to poke the fire. In the thirty seconds it took to do it, he was gone, lost in the digital halls and rooms of the small gray box.

The fire could go out and the moon fall down the chimney; he wouldn't know. He was completely engrossed in the hunt. For Maddie, it was different. Part of her didn't want to find out any more than she already knew, because every revelation so far had brought pain.

First there was the April 6 note, the first real indication they had that her father actually had an appointment with his murderer. Then, the news that he hadn't been in Cambridge at all, but in Natick. And now, Joyce. Who was this Joyce who preyed on two such different types of men? Did Maddie really want to know about Joyce? Did she want her mother to know *more* about Joyce?

And there was something else. In an unlit corner of Maddie's heart was the fear that an investigation might come too close, scorching them all with its intensity, like an asteroid that brushes a planet. It might even score a direct hit, taking them all down in flames.

So she sat in a state of hushed ambivalence, wanting to know the truth, afraid of what the truth might do to her and the ones she loved.

She read the letters over Dan's shoulder, but mostly they were mundane—stuff about conferences and seminars and glowing referrals for bright students. Once in a while a letter to a news editor would scroll up: some wry and indignant blast over a zoning variance or proposed tax increase. Those letters she liked, because they were written in her father's voice—crusty, honest, candid.

Who was this cuckoo Joyce?

Dan broke the silence just once to ask, "Was your mother possessive of your father?"

"Somewhat," Maddie said pensively, "but not wildly so. In any case, it didn't bother my father at all. He accepted that women were jealous and possessive of their mates. He was an awful chauvinist that way."

And that was their only exchange until the telephone rang at 2:00 A.M.

Maddie wanted so much to believe them both, but by morning she was forced to admit the obvious: her daughter and her ex-husband had conspired to lie to her.

Maddie felt utterly downhearted. She and Dan had spent their first night together in twenty years, and she'd blown it by brooding in his arms for the greater part of it.

Tired from her sleepless night, she propped her cheek on the palm of her hand as she stirred extra sugar into her coffee. "Why didn't I just go along with the don't ask, don't tell philosophy? I'd be so much happier now," she said, sighing.

"Are you that certain they weren't telling the truth?" Dan asked as he dropped two slices of bread in the toaster.

"Tracey's a rotten liar, and Michael's a great one. If you'd heard either of them last night, you'd know," Maddie told him.

She watched him as he moved easily around the kitchen, filling his coffee cup, tending the eggs, searching the cupboards for dishes and jam. It was a small thing, his wanting to make breakfast, but she loved him for it.

"I don't deserve you," she said with a wistful smile.

"Hell, who does? But you're stuck with me anyway," he quipped.

They heard a thunk, the unmistakable sound of a newspaper being bounced off the front door. Dan grinned and said, "A night with you, and there's the *Times*. I can die happy now."

She watched him pad barefoot toward the hall to retrieve the paper. On his way out of the kitchen, he grabbed his T-shirt—undoubtedly to slow down the gossip. It was another small thing, but it was another reason to love him.

I feel as if we've been together all our lives. As if, like Rip Van Winkle, I've awakened from a long nap and am picking up where I left off.

She loved him so much, trusted him even more. He was the only one, she realized with a jolt, that she *could* trust. No, that wasn't true. She was being unfair. But Michael . . . Tracey . . . even her father. . . .

She looked up to see Dan entering the kitchen with an altogether sheepish look on his face. In the next instant, she saw why: Norah and Joan were tiptoeing in behind him.

"Good *morning*," said Norah, giving Maddie a sly smile that only she could see. "We just happened to be in the neighborhood."

"Don't you two *ever* knock first?" Maddie asked, amazed at their tenacity.

"Puh-leeze. We tried that once and you barred the door," Norah reminded her.

"Yeah," said Joan, pulling out a chair. "From now on we ransack first, get permission later."

Behind them, Dan winked good-naturedly to Maddie as he said politely, "Can I get you ladies something?"

"Coffee, thank you, black."

"Coffee, two sugars. Cream if you've got it, otherwise milk."

Norah seated herself with languid grace. She looked

smartly turned out, as always, this time in nubby white linen shorts and a silk tank in impressionist pastels. Maddie admired her—as always—and yet for the first time, she noticed something missing, something wanting, in her friend's strikingly beautiful face.

Joy? Maddie knew that she herself must look like hell in her oversized T-shirt and Levi cutoffs, and yet she felt pretty. More than pretty. She felt sexy. Surgery scar, puffy eyes, unset hair and all.

Sounding brisk, Norah cut through her revery. "I really do have a purpose here, other than catching you two barefoot." She glanced at Dan and added from under lowered lashes, "Although I have to say, stubble becomes you."

Dan reached for his chin and actually blushed, which prompted Maddie to step in. "Suppose you tell us why you're here, then, because right after that we plan to kick you out again."

Joan and Norah exchanged a ritual raising of eyebrows. Joan turned to Maddie with comically pruned lips and said, " 'We?' 'Us?' Excuse me, but when did you begin making decisions in tandem?"

Dan glanced at Maddie. Now? his look said. Are we going to tell them now?

Yes, Maddie decided. Why not? She gave him a look that said just that.

His face lit up like a high-school band. It gave Maddie incredible pleasure to realize how much he loved her, how much he wanted the world to know that he loved her.

Grinning like a dope, she blurted, "We're getting married!" She meant to sound dignified. She failed so badly.

There were squeals and screams, giggles and hugs. Three women, all of them entering middle age—and they sounded like teens hiding in the bathroom during their first social.

Norah said, "The wedding will be at my house, of course."

"It will not," Joan said, instantly getting her dander up. "It's got to be at Rosedale!"

"We haven't even talked about where we're going to—"

"Uh . . . how about the lighthouse?"

"It might be on rollers and in transit soon; the money's pouring in for the move. When is the wedding, by the way?"

"Waitamminit! Where's the ring?"

"We haven't decided on a date . . . have you, Mad?"

"Obviously I'd like it at Rosedale. But things have to smooth out with my family first."

"So what else is new?"

"I do not see a ring."

"We'll be your bridesmaids, of course. And Tracey will be a junior bridesmaid."

"Omigod. I'll have to lose twenty pounds."

"My little girl, a bridesmaid. That's amazing to me."

"I know a divine caterer. Just don't let him roll over you, Maddie. They can be petty dictators—"

"It's true that I'd love to be married in the garden. . . ."

"What's wrong with *my* garden?"

"It's lovely, Norah, don't misunderstand. It's much more organized and striking than mine. But mine is—well, mine. And it's fragrant."

"The ring?"

"When does honeysuckle stop blooming, anyway?"

"Oh, y'know, Dan—that's a problem. I think the maple next door starts shading our garden in late summer, and the honeysuckle hardly ever flowers on the second bloom."

"Maybe we should get married while it's in the first bloom."

"I need more time than that! And if you two even think of eloping, I swear, Maddie, I'll have you dragged behind a buckboard all the way back from the chapel."

"That's what I told her. I said, no way will we elope. I want a band."

"You'll never get Peter Duchin at this late date. Although, I heard a fabulous band at an affair last week. Not well known, but they can play anything, from swing to Strauss. They might have a shorter cancellation list. I'll make a call."

"I hope you're not going to be one of those modern couples who refuse to wear rings—"

"Do you suppose your neighbors'd let us cut down their

maple? I feel fairly adamant about that honeysuckle."

"Dan, a minute ago you were willing to have the wedding at the lighthouse, where there's no honeysuckle at all."

"Yeah, but now that I think about it."

"Ooh, their first fight, and here we are to see it! Norah, is your video camera still in the trunk? I think we should record this for—"

The phone at Joan's elbow chirped and she reached for it automatically. Still grinning, she answered with a cheery, singsong, "Rosedale cottage!"

And then her grin dropped away, replaced by a forced little smile. "Oh. Michael. Sure. She's right here."

Chapter 26

Maddie said quickly, "I'll take this in the other room," and left the three of them standing around in sudden, awkward silence.

Behind her she heard Norah speak first. "I came here to pick up the lighthouse slides that Maddie used in her presentation."

"She's just remembered some new photos; ask her about 'em."

And then Maddie was out of earshot, left to deal with a call that seemed out of the Twilight Zone.

Michael got straight to the point. "Well, well. It sounds like you're having a merry old time over there, so I won't keep you. I just wanted to 'fess up. Last night I had business that ran over schedule. I wasn't able to pick Tracey up from her party until much later than I'd planned, and then when she told me she'd promised to call you, well, I panicked. I told her to fudge the time we got back. I'm sorry. But I didn't want you getting your nose out of joint the way you always do—"

"So it was *your* idea? *You* got her to lie to me?"

Oh, how she didn't want this call!

"All I'm saying is don't blame Tracey. She was doing it for me, Maddie. To protect me."

"And you're telling me this—why? To make me feel better about your parenting skills?"

She couldn't help it. The sound of his voice, the perennial excuses, the candid, whining dishonesty—she was sensitized, no doubt about it.

And now came the petulance. "I *said* I was sorry," he muttered through obviously gritted teeth.

Mentally, Maddie was throwing up her hands. "What exactly do you expect me to do about this, Michael?"

"Nothing! That's the point! I don't want you taking it out on Tracey!"

"Then why put her in a position to lie in the first place?"

"I *told* you—! Oh, shit, you're not listening to a thing I say. Never mind."

She could feel her exasperation with him bubbling over. She didn't want to take potshots at him; ideally, she wanted nothing to do with him. Over the last four years she had made an effort, and had succeeded, in letting go of her anger at him. But he was still Tracey's father; she had no choice but to keep engaging in the same weary dialogue, call after call after call. They were prisoners of a failed marriage, bound to one another by the shackle of their child.

"I was prepared for Tracey to wheedle you into letting her stay late," Maddie said, dropping her voice low. "I was even prepared for her to lie about when she did get home. I wasn't surprised when you seemed to back her up. But I have to admit, Michael, it never occurred to me that *you'd* be the one to force *her* to lie."

He answered in one of his typical nonsequiturs. "What did you expect her to do?" he said. "Take a cab?"

"Where were you that you couldn't get her back until two in the morning? Obviously you weren't chaperoning the party. God only knows who was!"

She was assuming he'd been with a woman and was surprised when he said, almost eagerly, "I've been working on this project with Geoff Woodbine. It's a big, big deal and it went pretty well last night. The bunch of us went out for a few drinks afterward to celebrate."

"Oh, well! Why didn't you say so in the first place? I feel

a lot better now! Geoffrey Woodbine? What in God's name have you got yourself into, Michael?''

The sound of his silence thundered in her ears.

''Calling to apologize was a mistake, I see,'' he said at last in a wounded voice. ''I wanted to do the right thing . . . I wanted to be aboveboard . . . and this is your reaction. Screaming at me like a banshee.''

''Michael, believe me, I'm not screaming.'' In fact, she was whispering. She'd be mortified if anyone in the kitchen overheard her end of the conversation. ''Can I talk to Tracey, please?''

''She went off with a couple of girlfriends to the Common,'' he said sullenly.

''Michael! You let her go off on her own?''

''For chrissake, why not? It's broad daylight out!''

''That's not the point; she's supposed to be grounded except under supervision!''

''That was your idea. You raise her your way and I'll raise her mine! Damn! Why did I bother calling you? Because I was feeling bad . . . feeling bad . . . so I thought—''

He hung up. Without a good-bye, without having a clue what Maddie was trying to say, he hung up.

She really *had* fallen into the Twilight Zone, and now she found herself groping, trying to get out. On the one hand, everything Michael had said sounded more or less reasonable. On the other hand, it all *felt* desperately false and wrong. Was it her or was it him?

Despite the jarring call, Maddie wanted desperately to salvage some of the happiness she'd been sharing with Dan and her friends, so she took a deep breath, fluffed up her hair, and marched back out to the kitchen.

But it was obvious, even before she entered the room, that the mood had shifted. Norah, Dan, and Joan were speaking in quiet murmurs, the way they would at a wake for someone they didn't know well.

''Hey, sorry about the interruption,'' she said with a kind of brazen cheerfulness. ''Where were we?''

It didn't work.

"Actually, we're going to leave you two lovebirds in peace," Norah said, setting her coffee mug in the sink. "I've invited a couple of fat cats over to my house for lunch, and before I shake them down for contributions, I thought I'd give them a special showing of the lighthouse dog-and-pony show. I'll need the slide carousel?"

"Oh . . . sure . . . it's on the desk in my bedroom. Dan, would you get it for Norah? And I'll run down to the basement and bring up my dad's photo album. I can't believe I forgot about the snapshots there."

By the time Maddie came back upstairs, Norah had the carousel in her arms and was standing with Joan at the Dutch door, acting as if she had a plane to catch. Maddie laid two thick photo albums on top of the slides and said, "The shots of the lighthouse being closed up are in one or the other of these; that year was a two-album summer."

Norah tried to lighten the mood by saying, "Your father was an amazing man. I don't know where he got all the energy—or the film."

Nonetheless, some of the pall that Michael's call had thrown over the group lingered as Norah kissed Maddie on her cheek, and then Dan. She had one hand on the screen door when she turned back to them and said in a pensive voice, "Don't you wonder why we're bothering to move the damn thing? It was in tough shape even before the lightning and the fire . . . and when you get right down to it, the entire Cape will be washed away in a few thousand years in any case."

After they left, Dan said, "Wow. Talk about mood swings. What just happened here?"

"Two words," Maddie said, whacking one of her hard-boiled eggs on the Formica counter. "Michael. Regan." She began peeling the shell away with tense little jabs. Her hand was shaking.

"They didn't want him to rain on our parade, I guess."

"Well, he did. I swear, the man truly is psychic. He knows exactly when I least want him around. Five'll get you ten that was him calling all day yesterday and then hanging up."

The egg had waited too long in its shell; it didn't want to peel gracefully. Maddie tore at it, muttering, "You sadistic little ovum—!"

"Here, here . . . let me," Dan said, lifting the egg from her grip. "Sit down. Relax. You're angry and upset."

"I am, I am!" she admitted. She folded her arms across her chest and gnawed her lip as she stared at the checkerboard floor. "Oh, and I don't want to give in to it. I don't. You don't know how hard I've worked to put him behind me. Every minute I used to spend being angry at him was a minute less I could be happy about something else. I knew that. I know that. So why am I so helpless at times like these? Why do I let him still get to me?"

"Tracey?" Dan ventured as he shucked the egg of its shell. He dropped it in a bowl and started on the second.

"Tracey," Maddie agreed with a sigh. "Until she's grown up and making her own decisions. . . ."

And then, because it was Dan standing there and not anyone else, she confessed to a truly dark wish. "If I just had total custody of her . . . or if his weekend could somehow be supervised. . . ."

Dan turned and gave her a sharp look. "Is this still about his lax standards, or are we talking about something else?"

"I don't know," she had to confess. "I can't pin it down . . . he's just . . . different . . . lately. Mood swings? It's almost an understatement to describe him. You saw how he was at the fund-raiser. He was that way just now on the phone. He's been plagued by headaches lately . . . and he sometimes seems confused."

"So you're thinking . . . what? Drugs?"

"I hope not," she said with a grim look as she took the bowl from him. "Here's what's *really* bothering me: he's involved in something with Geoffrey Woodbine."

"Woodbine! Like what?"

As she poked halfheartedly at her cold breakfast, Maddie explained Michael's lifelong fascination with the paranormal, and his fondness for pursuing different paths to self-discovery.

"His special fascination was with self-hypnosis," she told Dan. "He said it made him fully realize his talent as an artist. It sounded reasonable to me. I tried self-hypnosis myself a few times, but all I ever felt was relaxed. But Michael was into it in a very serious way. He said . . ."

She felt uncomfortable talking about Michael's private side with someone else—even Dan—and had to force herself to continue.

"Michael said that he could go anywhere when he was self-hypnotized. Into his . . . his past lives, as well as to other places in the present. I think they used to call it 'astral projection,' but now it's called 'remote viewing.'"

She expected Dan either to laugh or act alarmed and was surprised when he did neither. She added, "His—I don't know what to call it—hobby? used to bug the hell out of my father. But then, my dad was a scientist."

"A natural adversary," Dan agreed. "They'd view things differently."

"Then you don't think Michael's crazy?" she asked, taking comfort from Dan's mild reaction.

For an answer, Dan took her by both hands and pulled her up into his arms. He held her there a long time without saying anything. Finally he murmured, "I think we should go for a walk on the beach."

The morning had undergone a mood swing of its own. The sun was nowhere in evidence, hazed over by gray, muggy air sulking over a listless sea. Brooding: the ocean was bothered by something. They could see it in the way its shoulders lifted and fell in a series of heavy sighs as it rolled onto the beach and then slid back, clawing at the sand on its way out.

"There's a storm offshore," Maddie said uneasily as they walked barefoot along the tide line. "I wonder how bad it is. I haven't watched a forecast since the Fourth when it mattered so much."

Dan skimmed a pebble over the rolling swells; it bounced once before diving into the murky depth. "You're right," he said. "I generally get four or five skips out of a stone."

They resumed their slow amble along the beach. Most of the people there had begun to pack up, convinced that the sun was done for the day. Soon the two of them would have the beach—their beach—to themselves.

"You asked me if I thought Michael was crazy," Dan said, slapping his shoes against his thigh as he walked. "I never answered your question."

"I thought you did," she said, looking at him quickly.

"Nope."

They walked a little farther along in silence before Dan began again. "There was a time when I would've said, hell, yes, the guy's mad as a hatter. I would've said, astral projection? Get real! But that was before Albania. Maddie, something happened to me that I still can't explain. I've told nobody this," he said, picking up another stone. "Not even my sister."

He rubbed the stone between his fingers, gauging its flatness, and then sent it hurtling across the sea. Two skips this time.

He was definitely stalling, but she didn't know why.

"Okay, here's the thing," he said, looking somehow embarrassed. "I've told you how I was wounded in Albania, and how the old crone told me to go back to where it all began. What I haven't told you is . . . that I did."

"Did what?" she asked, prompting him when he seemed to run out of steam again.

He cleared his throat. "When I was in that old woman's hovel, I . . . ah . . . I would have to say . . . that . . . well, I left my body. Okay? I left my body physically, left it behind, and I came here."

She stopped and stared at him. "Here? How?"

"Well, that's the part that's a little hard to explain. My guess is that I flew. You know, like this," he said, making an arc with his arm. "From Albania to Sandy Point. Nonstop. Non-airplane."

"You mean that you dreamed you flew."

"Oh, no, I don't think so. I flew. I mean, I've told myself that I was delirious—that it was from the tea. Or maybe from the mushrooms in the stew. From loss of blood. From stark raving fear that Berisha's gorillas were going to find me after all.''

He kicked away a strand of seaweed that had wrapped itself around his ankle in a receding wave and said, ''Don't you think I'd rather have a rational explanation than a freaky-flyer one? But Maddie, no kidding, this was the genuine article, an out-of-body experience.''

He was antsy and wanted to walk; she fell in beside him again.

''It was nothing like some long tunnel ending in white light and a heavenly chorus welcoming me,'' he explained. ''There was no bliss in it at all. It was more like a feeling of, 'Well, so this is where I screwed up, and this is what I have to do to make it right, okay, I got that, the lighthouse, okay, that's doable.' And then I reentered my body and got on with it. I started mending; I rejoined the insurgents; and I got hooked back up, through them, with my camera crew. Then I flew back to Atlanta—on a plane this time—closed up my apartment, took a leave from my job, and moved into the lighthouse. Where, as you know, I suffered a temporary but complete form of paralysis before I got the guts to approach you in your cottage.''

She stopped again. ''So it all came down to the lighthouse?'' she asked, openmouthed. ''What if it had been rented?''

''It wasn't.''

''What if we'd sold Rosedale?''

''You hadn't.''

''What if I were still *married*?''

''I'd have done my best to break it up,'' he confessed. ''Or should I be keeping that to myself?''

Dazed, she said, ''Why start now?''

''All right; I know this is—this is hard for you, especially after Michael. I can't tell you how depressed I was when you told me that he's into this stuff. Well, all I can say is, I'm not. I just did this one . . . this one trip. But man, I truly was airborne. I hovered over that lighthouse like a spaceship. I saw the rock that I used to sit on to have a smoke—I saw the water at its new high level!—and I saw Rosedale down the road. I saw you, Maddie. You were as real and as tangible and as . . . as of the earth as you could be. You were in your garden, on your knees, planting something in a big hole. You were wearing jeans and a heavy sweater, a blue one. I saw you from my perch in the sky and I knew; I knew that I loved you in a way I would never love another human being in this lifetime, or any other, for that matter.''

Maddie gaped at him. ''Oh, Dan—oh my God,'' she said. ''I *did* wear jeans and a blue sweater—in April! I came down alone to plant a rose; it was to commemorate my father's death.''

''I know that,'' Dan said with supreme confidence, dropping his shoes on the sand and taking her in his arms again. ''It was on April 6—three days after I was shot.''

She reached up behind his head and touched her fingers to the narrow scar where the bullet had grazed him.

''But what does it all mean?'' she said, overwhelmed.

''It means that I'm not gonna be the one to call Michael crazy,'' Dan said in a wry voice. ''I'll leave that to someone more grounded—so to speak—than I am.''

Hands linked, they fell back in step, walking the thin line where eternal sea met ephemeral sand. They were silent for a while, and then Maddie said in a musing tone, ''Do you know the name of the rose that I planted?''

Dan chuckled softly and said, ''Sorry, I couldn't read the label from up there.''

''Celestial,'' said Maddie with a timorous smile.

''Huh. Now *that's* funny.''

Chapter 27

By the end of the weekend it was obvious to Maddie just how much she'd lost touch with the elements. A tropical storm spinning over a wide spiral and packing fifty to sixty knot winds was expected to slam into the south shore of the Cape—from the southwest—in the predawn hours on Monday.

The outer Cape lived in fear of winds from the east, but it was winds from the south that made the Sandy Point waterfront cringe. Those were the winds that sent residents scurrying for food, water, candles, and batteries. Maddie was among them, standing in line at the small general store in the center of town.

"Tropical Storm Dot. It sounds so little," said Trixie Roiters, standing behind her. Her red plastic basket was filled with milk, bread, and M&M's. "How much damage can a storm named Dot do?"

All Maddie had to say was, "Remember 'Bob?'"

Trixie winced. "Maybe I should have Henry drag out the plywood and board up the windows. Are you battened down?"

Maddie nodded. "Dan did the water side for me this morning. He's securing the keeper's house now, working with a couple of contractors."

The mention of Dan's name brought Trixie's attention front and center. "That poor, poor house. How much more can happen to it? The roof is covered with tarps and the chimney's a pile of rubble. And now this. The keeper's house—is it even habitable?'' she asked, obviously fishing to know where Dan was biding his time.

''It's habitable, more or less,'' Maddie said vaguely. ''At least the phone works and the electricity's back on.''

''Ha. That won't last.''

She was right. Sandy Point lost power at the drop of a thunderbolt. After Hurricane Bob swept through, they'd been without electricity for two weeks.

Maddie looked over her own basket, filled with lamp oil and candles. ''I just hope the phones keep working,'' she said, aware that she had a dread of being out of contact with her family, especially now.

It was anyone's guess whether Michael would be able to make it across the flood-prone roads to drop Tracey off in the morning. Maddie should've insisted that Tracey come back early; but they had an agreement, and she, at least, was determined to keep her word.

''How is your mother, by the way?'' asked Trixie. ''I understand she's gone back to Sudbury already? She didn't stay very long this time; I never even got to say hello.''

''It wasn't much of a visit,'' Maddie said in an understatement. ''I had planned to go up there today, but now with a storm imminent, I'll have to stay here and house-sit.''

The one good thing was that the approaching storm had forced all of them to stay in contact. When Maddie called Claire to find out how she was doing, George actually got on the phone to ask whether she'd boarded up the windows. It wasn't much, but at least he was civil. And Maddie had left a message on her mother's machine asking her the name of the new insurance agent, just in case. Her mother had returned the call and had left a terse answer on Maddie's machine. Again, not much, but . . .

It saddened her that all they had in common at the moment was an old house. But then, some estranged families didn't even have that.

''Maddie, you look like your cat's been run over,'' said

Trixie, laying her hand on Maddie's arm. "What's wrong, dear?"

Her voice was so achingly sympathetic that Maddie wanted to blurt, "My family's disowned me and my ex is a nut." But none of it, apparently, was true, so she said, "Oh, you know how it is when a storm's barreling down: hurry, hurry, wait, wait."

Trixie said, "That reminds me—a radio battery. Not that there's a chance in Hades that they'll have one here."

She turned on her heel and dove back into the crowded aisle anyway, and Maddie let her mind obsess on the trivia of her own checklist. Take in the lawn furniture, fill up the tub, fill up the rainbarrel, fill up the car, turn up the fridge— Pringles!

She dropped out of the line and headed for the snack food aisle.

By nightfall they could feel the first sharp gusts of wind from the south-southwest slicing through the oppressive calm like labor pains well in advance of a painful birth. The storm had been bumped up to possible hurricane status; everyone was waiting for the nine o'clock report. Although few of the houses on Maddie's side of Cranberry Lane were boarded up, most of the ones across the lane that faced the ocean were shuttered tight.

Maddie took a portable radio with her on her walk to the lighthouse to check on Dan's progress there. He and the contractors had decided that the blue plastic tarp covering the burned-out roof would never hold up to the forecast winds, and so they'd spent the day furiously sheathing and shingling the damaged section.

Maddie had brought them supper earlier in the evening. Dan, like the other two men, was drenched in sweat, filthy, smelly—and pumped. Like most men, he was more than willing to take on Mother Nature in hand-to-hand combat. The three were in crisis mode, working feverishly and enjoying every minute of it.

"We'll have the roof buttoned up by dark," he had told

Maddie as he wolfed a monster-sized sandwich in half a dozen chomps, then washed it down with a quart of milk from the carton. "If the winds don't come in any worse than forecast, we should be okay. All we need now is daylight."

But now it was dark and as she approached, she could still hear faint hammering mixed with the sound of curling, breaking seas a hundred yards out from the beach. Already, she was forced to walk above the normal high-water mark to keep her sandals dry—not a good sign. The storm was expected to come ashore on an astronomically high tide—more bad news.

The lighthouse has stood here for a hundred years, she reminded herself.

The problem was, there used to be a decent-sized beach between it and the ocean.

Rosedale, too, was closer to the sea than ever. Her father used to joke that if he lived long enough, he'd be the owner of waterfront property yet. It hadn't happened that way, but Maddie was beginning to wonder whether she wouldn't see the day.

She hurried along, chilled by the warm gusts that seemed to whoosh out of nowhere, sending up sand in her eyes. The beach was peopled with the usual stormwatchers: inland folks, out for a thrill, and those who who lived close enough to make it home quickly as soon as the weather turned truly foul.

Ahead of her, standing apart from a group of teens hanging together and flirting with one another, Maddie spied her daughter's star-crossed love. Kevin had his hands in his hip pockets and was staring out at the water, reveling in the imminence of the storm. Was he attracted to the beauty of it or the violence of it? she wondered. Probably both.

She passed close to him with a "Hello, there," wondering whether he'd acknowledge her. He didn't—until she'd gone by.

"Mrs. Regan!" she heard him call.

She stopped and turned.

"I just wanted to say, uh, thanks. For not tellin' my old man about the tower."

It would've been pointless. The boy's father would've screamed at him and maybe beat him, and then gone back to the tube and his bottle. Maddie had tried a different strategy: talking to Kevin herself when she'd seen him in town. She'd kept a firm grip on the handlebars of his bike as she laid out a vision of his future that covered the spectrum from rosy to bleak. Had any of her pep talk sunk in? Hard to tell; he'd stared at the clock on the village green the whole time.

Now, she thought that maybe it had. The boy did seem grateful.

"I meant what I said about giving you a second chance, Kevin. You're welcome to stop by our house anytime."

Kevin looked away at the sea. It had a greater hold on him than she did, that was certain.

A fisherman or maybe the Coast Guard, she thought, if he straightened out in time.

"Yeah, well, I ain't seen her around, anyway. She's not on the beach tonight," he said offhandedly.

"No, she's with her father in Boston."

"Like I said. She ain't around."

Maddie smiled and said, "You can stop by anyway, Kevin. Especially if you need to make a little extra cash. All the shutters need sanding and painting. Let me know if you're interested."

"Yeah. Maybe I will."

They parted on better terms than they had in the village green. Justifiably or not, Maddie felt uplifted from the encounter, which showed how tenuous her faith in herself as a parent had become. All Kevin had to do was refrain from out-and-out mugging her, and she was able to walk away feeling like Mother Teresa.

She arrived at the lighthouse in time to see the contractors taking the ladder down by the light of their truck's headlights. Dan hailed her as she came near. He was still exhilarated—and drenched with sweat.

"We had a change in the game plan," he explained. "Matt was walking across the roof after supper and poked his leg through another hole, this one from rot. Lucky for us, the guys had extra material in the truck."

"You could use a good hose-down," she said, wrinkling her nose as she lifted a lock of his dripping hair.

He laughed. "Yeah, I'll shower and then come over to Rosedale later. I have a few things more to do inside, and after that the house and tower are in God's hands."

Another gust, this one sharper than any of the others, flattened his sweat-stained tank top against his chest. Maddie felt the wind at her back and told herself that she'd felt far worse, but a feeling of dread had her locked in its grip.

"I don't like this, Dan. I don't know if it's me or Dot, but something feels wrong. This doesn't feel like a garden-variety tropical storm."

"We'll see what the weather update has to say. Hey! You two want a beer before you go?" he asked the other men.

Young and muscular, the men decided to pass in favor of a local hangout. Dan tipped them a hundred dollars and they threw their big-wheeled truck into a U-turn, deftly avoiding Dan's Jeep as they took off at regulation contractors' speed of ninety miles an hour.

"Look at 'em," Dan said, grinning. "They worked twice as hard as I did, and now they're gonna go off and party all night. Geez, I wish I was young again. *We* could party all night."

Maddie shook her head. "I'm telling you, this doesn't feel like that kind of storm."

Something in her voice made Dan say quietly, "Turn on the radio, then. It's time."

The NOAA forecast was a surprise to Dan but not to her: a sharp increase in the average wind speed, a sharp drop in barometric pressure, and a shift in direction which, if the eye came ashore as predicted, would put Sandy Point in the dangerous semicircle of what was now Hurricane Dot.

"Whoa, Cassandra," Dan said lightly, "see if I make fun of *you* again."

"They're going to want us to evacuate," said Maddie. "I've been through this before."

"Are you going to?"

"I don't think so," she confessed. "It's still a minimal hurricane. The house is very sturdy, and it has a low profile. Cape Cod houses are designed the way they are for a reason."

"And Dot's the reason?" he said in a gentle pun, then added more seriously, "Are you sure you want to stay? I waited out a typhoon once in Bangladesh, Maddie. It scared the pants off me."

"I know, but . . . somehow I just don't want to evacuate this time." She knew what the reason was—proximity to a phone—but she was too embarrassed to tell Dan that.

"Okay," he said with a smile. "But make the popcorn early, just in case we lose juice."

He kissed her lightly and they parted company. By the time Maddie made it back to Rosedale, the gusts were coming at quicker intervals—those labor pains again. If Dot were actually about to have a baby, they'd be putting her toothbrush in the suitcase and thinking about calling a cab.

Inside the cottage, Maddie hooked both screen doors to keep them from ripping off their hinges later, but she kept the inside doors wide open to allow a breeze to move through. She had another reason for keeping them open as long as she could. The truth was, she got claustrophobic whenever the south windows were boarded up; it felt too much like an entombment.

Maddie set thick candles on fat stands in several of the rooms and put matches next to the hurricane lamps. The flashlights were handy, the rechargeable batteries topped off. All she had to do now was wait.

And wait. Despite her deep conviction that the storm would be a bad one, the wind stayed fairly steady for the next hour or so. The gusts, when they came, no longer seemed like premonitions. They were simply welcome relief from the muggy stillness of the boarded-up rooms.

In the meantime, Maddie was going just a little bit stir-crazy.

She would have liked to call Claire or George or her mother, but she had no real excuse for doing so; everything was depressingly under control. She'd already talked with Tracey. It was a strained conversation, to be sure. Maddie had suggested that they put off any discussion of Friday night until Tracey came home the next day; the girl was more than willing to do that. Maddie had talked with Joan, too. Joan was riding out the storm at Norah's house. She'd talked with most of her neighbors, many of whom had chosen to stay in their homes. There was literally no one left to talk to, nothing left to do.

Except wait. And so Maddie wandered from one room to another, returning to the cable weather station every few minutes to see if there were new developments. The message to the Cape was the same: batten down and then get out. Maddie glared at the weatherman. "Easy for you to say," she muttered.

And then came the news that the big bridges on the Cape had been shut down. She was glad to hear it, grateful to have an end to her second-guessing the evacuation option.

Finally the phone rang, and she picked it up eagerly. It was Dan, and he sounded tense. "Maddie—I'll be over later. There's a sailboat aground a hundred yards out; we're gonna see if we can get them off. I gotta go."

"Be careful!" she said, and then he was gone.

One more reason to pace. Although she'd wanted Dot to come ashore and get it over with, now Maddie prayed that the hurricane would sit out there long enough for Dan to complete his mission and come home safe to her. Damn it, damn it, damn it. Was it possible for the ones she loved to be any more scattered to the wind?

She listened with growing dismay as the gusts blended into one long howl. Finally, unable to bear any more inaction, she slipped into a foul-weather jacket and was on her way out the back door when the phone rang. She pounced on it, expecting it to be Dan.

It was Michael—the one person she had absolutely no interest in talking to.

"Tracey and I had a long, serious talk today," he said, ignoring the impatience in her voice. "I know it's late to call, but by tomorrow you'll be too distracted fussing over your trampled garden to listen to what I have to say. Is lover-boy there?''

He was trying to hurt her. It seemed bizzarely inappropriate with a hurricane bearing down. She considered simply hanging up on him, but she didn't dare, so she said in measured tones, ''What is it, Michael? What do you want?''

''Tracey, that's all; I want Tracey.''

''But you already ha—''

She realized then that he wasn't talking about the weekend, or spring break, or the week between Christmas and New Year's. He was talking about tomorrow and the next day and the next. Stunned, she pulled out a kitchen chair and sat down on it, still in her yellow slicker, and tried to clear her brain of every other thought but him.

''What exactly do you have in mind?'' she said, pressing the palm of her hand over her left ear to drown out the wind.

He made a tisking sound and said, ''See? I told you you never listened. Tracey. Can I say it any clearer than that? *Tracey.* T-r-a-c-e-y. You know—the daughter that you and I created in an act of passion? Or wasn't it passion, Maddie? Were you faking it all those years—hmmm?''

She tried to shut out the lascivious sneer in his voice. ''Why are you doing this, Michael? Why?''

''Why am I doing what? Behaving like a concerned father? Isn't it obvious? Because you're a bitch and a slut, that's why.''

''*Michael*!''

''Don't get prim with me, bitch! You were faking it, weren't you? You were waiting for him. All those years I didn't have a goddamned clue that you were waiting for him. What a fool I was. Oh, yeah, I can admit it now. I was a fool. Standing meekly at the door after you threw me out . . . standing there hat in hand, waiting to be let back in again. Taking whatever crumbs you threw at me. Ohh, you made me want you . . . that was your revenge, wasn't it? Making me want you. Holding me at arm's length and leading me on, leading me on. . . .''

"I wasn't leading you on, Michael," she said, beating back a wave of nausea. "I wasn't. I wanted us to be civil for Tracey's sake. If you misread that, I'm sorry. Truly I am."

He seemed not to hear her. "How was it on the beach that night, hmm? Good? Was it good? Was he good? How were you? Were you good? Were you good together? You didn't hold anything back from him, I'm willing to bet. Not if you had to have it on a beach. *We* never had it on a beach. How come, Maddie?"

He didn't want answers; he wanted only to rant.

Maddie said, "Please, can I talk to Tracey now? Just for a minute." She was terrified that he'd done something to her.

"When I'm done!" he snapped. He laughed softly and said, "You shock me, Maddie, really you do. On a beach! Prim and proper Maddie Timmons Regan. Timid Timmons, romping bare-assed on a beach. Your mother's not too happy with you, did you know that? Ah, of course you did. She told me she made that very clear to you. We were over there this afternoon, Tracey and I—did you know that? Sarah and I had a long talk, a *long* talk, when Tracey was at a neighbor's. Sarah's not happy with you at *all*."

A terrific gust of wind slammed the house, rattling the kitchen windows. Maddie turned away from them, trying to focus on Michael and not on the storm, trying to make out his nearly incoherent muttering. It was a futile effort: she could hardly hear him over the pounding of her heart.

"My mother's entitled to her own opinion," Maddie said, just to say something.

It seemed to snap him back to a semblance of rationality. "Yes, she is entitled, isn't she. And your mother's opinion is—ta-dah!—that under the circumstances, Tracey belongs with me. Now ain't that a hoot? She thinks I'm a better parent than you—for the time being, anyway. With all due modesty, I would have to agree. I'm friendly, well mannered, and presentable. I'm not running around—anymore. I've got money and I don't need to work. I adore my kid and she—well, let's face it, Maddie. She prefers living with me. A court pays attention to stuff like that."

A court!

"You can't do that, Michael!" Maddie cried.

"Why not? You did it to me. See how it feels, hmm?"

"Tracey would never want that," she said vehemently.

"Aw, a mother in denial—is there anything sadder?" Michael said, oozing with sympathy. "I admit, Tracey was a little confused about her own power. But I explained to her that fathers got custody all the time nowadays, and that she was old enough to have a say. And now that she knows her grandmother's going to back me up—and that she can go there whenever she wants—she's a lot less nervous about the whole thing."

"Bring her back right now, Michael. Bring her back or I'll have the police at your doorstep so fast—"

"Don't threaten me, bitch!"

"Let me talk to her. *Now*."

There was a pause. He ended it by saying, "You know, I think I'll do that. Go ahead—alienate her once and for all. Threaten to have the police drag her from her father's hearth. Hold the specter of psychiatric evaluation over her head. She'd like that, I know. Yeah, talk to her, Maddie. Finish this off nice and clean. Hold on; I'll just go wake her up—"

"Michael, wait!"

Maddie was shivering under the oilskin jacket, even as the sweat trickled between her breasts. She felt faint, she felt enraged, she felt completely unequal to the sudden challenge to her role as custodial parent. Even as she felt all of those things, she felt something else: a conviction, deep inside, that Michael was negotiating. What did he want? To screw her on the beach and even the score? Whatever it was, it was bound to be cruel and humiliating. Nothing less would satisfy him.

"I'm waiting," he reminded her, almost amiably. "Do you plan to tell me what I'm waiting for?"

Not me, please, not me, she thought. "What will it take," she asked him humbly, "for you to give up this fight?"

Chapter 28

The pause this time was much longer.

Finally she heard him let out a long, thoughtful sigh. "What will it take?" he mused. "Obviously not money. Hmm. What will it take," he said again. "Well, you could always come back to me. Tracey would have both her parents then. Problem solved. But frankly? I don't think so. You'd make my life hell, wouldn't you, my darling. Let's think of something else."

He was so incredibly sick. She had to get Tracey away from him.

"Hey, here's a thought!" he said with perverted brightness. "Blow off Daniel Hawke! No, wait, let me rephrase that," he added with a merry chuckle. "Tell him—firmly is best—to get the hell out of your life. Without Hawke around, I think I'd feel—we'd all feel—that Tracey's environment was much more wholesome."

For a moment Maddie went absolutely blank. Twice? Twice in one lifetime? "I can't do that, Michael," she whispered. "Please don't ask me."

"Oh, Maddie—of course you can!" he said cheerfully. "It would please Tracey, who's had a grudge against him ever since the tower. It would please Sarah; we know how far back *her* grudge goes. And George; it would please him no end. But most important—it would please *me*, Maddie. It would please me!"

Her breath was coming shallow and fast; she rocked back and forth in her chair out of sheer nervous agony. "But if Dan can't have me and you can't either—I don't understand, Michael," she said, closing her eyes, trying to will him away. "What's the point?"

"*You're* the point, bitch!" he said with sudden savagery.

She understood, then, that he didn't want to humiliate. He wanted only to inflict pain.

"So what's it gonna be, bitch, hmmm?"

Give him what he wants; he has a hostage. That thought, and that thought alone, drove Maddie to say, "All right. All right. I'll end it. Just . . . bring her back. Right now. Tonight."

"How am I supposed to do that?" he asked, sounding genuinely baffled. "You know the bridges are closed."

Obviously he knew it, too. "Yes . . . no, of course . . . I know that. Take her to my mother, then!" she said suddenly.

"Now? It's nearly midnight." His voice became suspicious and hostile again. "What's the matter? Don't you trust me with our own daughter? For chrissake, Maddie, you know I'd cut off my painting arm for her!"

"No, of course, I trust you. It's just that I thought—I don't know. I wasn't thinking. Can I talk to her, please? Just for a minute?" Maddie was begging him now. "It's getting really bad out," she said as another blast of wind rocked the house. "I don't know how much longer I'll have a phone connection. Please, Michael."

"Yeah, okay. We have an agreement, though—right?"

She assured him that they did.

"If it was anyone else but you—but I trust you, Maddie. You hear me? I'm taking you at your word. If you break it, I'll know. Believe me. I'll know. Do . . . *not* . . . break your word."

"Yes. Please . . . let me say good night to her."

It took a wrenching moment before Maddie heard her daughter mumble sleepily, "Mom? What?"

"Hi, honey. Um . . . we have some big, big stuff to talk about, but it's late and you're asleep. The hurricane is going to come ashore soon, and you know what that means: no electricity. We might lose the phone, too, so—''

''Hurricane?'' she said, her voice wavering higher. ''I thought it was just a storm.''

''It is, really, just a biggish storm. But I wanted to say good night. I wanted to tell you that I'll be up th—''

No. He might take off with her. Better not to say.

Completely unnerved with second-guessing herself, Maddie said, ''Good night, Tracey. I love you.''

She heard her daughter hesitate and then say simply, ''G'night.''

It was a blow, but Maddie hardly had time to feel the pain from it. There was too much to think about, too much to plan. Overwhelmed by the horrible combination of circumstances, she tore off the sweltering vinyl jacket, then drank down a tall glass of water, fighting the urge to throw it all up. Sick with apprehension, she slapped both hands over her mouth and circled the phone, her mind racing in circles of its own. Who to call? Her mother, the police, George, anyone at all?

Was he dangerous? That was the first thing. *Was he dangerous.* Yes, obviously—but to Tracey? Maddie honestly couldn't say yes to that one.

But it didn't stop her from calling the Boston police.

She was put through to the officer on duty in the Fourth District and quickly explained the situation. The officer was less than enthusiastic about intervening—exactly the reaction she'd feared.

''He's not in violation of the custody agreement,'' the officer said. ''He hasn't done or said anything that you consider a threat to your daughter's safety. He has attempted, you say, to blackmail you, but again, what goes on between ex-spouses isn't always pretty. Let me ask you: did he in any way prevent you from talking to your daughter?''

The answer, most dismally, was no.

''Did he indicate that he was going to bring your daughter back down to the Cape tomorrow? Which, by the way, might be difficult if not impossible.''

''Yes, he's going to bring her—but only if I give up the

man I'm involved with!" Maddie said, exasperated by the officer's calm manner.

"Whatever. Until he's actually in violation of your agreement, I'm afraid there's nothing we can do. At that time—if he does go into violation—then you would come down and file a police report, which would be referred to court. I wish I could help you, ma'am."

Maddie hung up more frustrated than ever.

Where was Dan?

The hurricane was lapping at the edges of Sandy Point. Outside, a gust of wind attacked with a vindictive shriek, shaking the house to its rafters. The rain had arrived as well: it came in sporadic, battering squalls, swinging wildly in its fury, then easing long enough for Maddie to see another broken limb lying in the yard, another layer of torn-away leaves covering the ground. The house was shuddering nonstop now. It was old. It knew all about hurricanes, and it feared them more as it grew more frail.

Maddie was staring out the kitchen windows—from a safe distance back—when the power went out, plunging the house and the spotlit yard into murk. She'd been expecting it, and yet when it happened she let out a sob of despair. She picked up the phone: dead. She was apart from the ones she loved, and trapped in a rose-covered tomb.

Where was Dan? He couldn't possibly be on the water still. If they hadn't been able to free up the sailboat, then that boat was as good as lost. Surely its owner and crew had abandoned it by now. Quickly she lit a kerosene lamp, stumbling with the match in the pitch-black house.

I can't stay here any longer; I can't, she realized. The waiting, the uncertainty, the horrifying scenarios that seemed much too willing to play out in the theater of her imagination—all of it made her want to run screaming into the night.

Was she losing her mind? Anything seemed possible in the chaotic unraveling of events. One thing Maddie knew: she had to find Dan. Unable to bear a minute more of inaction, she donned the clammy jacket again and made herself wear the pants as well, to protect against flying debris. Dunned by the incessant roar and shriek of wind and rain, she groped her way through the unlit hall to the front door. Not until she had her hand on the doorknob did she realize that the door was pumping in place. She laid her other hand flat against a panel. It was pulsing, like a heart beating wildly in a chest. If she opened the door now, it would break her arm.

She cracked open a couple of windows to relieve the pressure inside the house, then ran to the back door, determined to make a break for it. *Was* she insane? Very possibly. But if she stayed, she had no doubt that she'd break down completely. She got a good grip on the doorknob of the massive Dutch door and pulled it open. It swung away without fuss, giving her hope. It only sounded bad out, she decided. All sound—no fury.

In the yard, in the lee of the house, it wasn't too bad—horrendously noisy and windy, but bearable. Heartened, she felt her way carefully over branches and flattened shrubs until she turned the corner onto the shell-lined drive.

First surprise: her neighbor's maple tree was draped across her Taurus. Second surprise: the wind wanted to tear her face off. Gasping, she turned her back instinctively to the force of it and pulled the drawstrings of her hood more tightly across the front of her chin. Then she turned, leaned into the fury that was Dot, and began plowing forward. Foot by foot by foot, Maddie made her way to the lane, then turned left in the direction of the lighthouse.

Nothing; she could see nothing. If only the tower were lit! Sheer blind instinct drove her on. She had no idea where the horizon was, where the lane ended, what had happened to the picket fences that used to line its sides. All she knew was that the lighthouse was ahead of her, and where the lighthouse was, Dan was. She drove herself forward, whipping her determination, telling herself that she wasn't crazy, that this was the way to life everlasting, that this was the way to Dan.

Something hurtled past her with the speed of a well-aimed missile. In the next instant, the next missile—sharp, abrasive, a roof shingle?—caught the edge of her hood, searing a path across her cheek. She raised her hand to the pain and felt warmth. *Oh, damn—blood. Another scar.*

She plowed on.

The rain came again and still—thick, blinding sheets of it, stinging and brutal and cruel. She hated the rain, she couldn't see through the rain, and yet she knew it was so much kinder than the sea was going to be at high tide. She was completely disoriented now; for all she knew, she could be headed back to the cottage. She raised her head and opened one eye a slit's width, trying to peer ahead and get a bearing.

She staggered back, rocked off balance not by a gust of wind this time, but by the sight of what lay ahead.

The tower was lit: a glowing green luminescence shone feebly through the chaos of rain and wind and swirling atoms of sea. The tower was lit. God in heaven, the tower was lit! She held up her arm to visor her eyes, afraid that she was hallucinating. No. It was lit. She was forced to look back down: salt spray was needling the wound on her cheek and stinging her eyes. Sobbing with determination, she forced herself on. He was there, somewhere, and she would find him.

The sandy beach had disappeared, lost to the continuous roiling seas that piled up one upon another. The fragile, submerged dune grass catching around her ankles was her only reference point; to her left apparently was the road, awash now, with worse to come. She stumbled along with her face down, her clothes drenched and clinging to her body under the vinyl slickers. Her lips were briny with salt. Her eyes burned from it, prompting tears that were helpless to wash it away. Her running shoes caught continuously in the wet, swirling sand. The blackness was impenetrable now: the green light was no longer visible. Cold hard fear wrapped itself around her soul, and yet she staggered on, compelled by a force as powerful as the sea itself.

"Mad-day! Maad-day!"

It was Dan's voice, a faint echo of the howl of the storm. She listened again, heard nothing. She cupped her hands to her mouth and called out his name, and then strained to hear him call hers.

"Mad-day! Maa-a-d-daa-ay!"

"D-a-an! Dan-niel Haw-w-wke!"

She pushed ahead, screaming his name, in agony listening for her own. For a hideous span of time she thought she'd never hear his voice again, and then she saw him just a few feet away. How she found him, she never afterward knew. He was on the beach—what used to be the beach—perhaps halfway between the lighthouse and Rosedale, and he was in danger of being dragged into the sea.

He was crawling toward higher ground, but his gear was obviously too sodden, his boots too heavy to let him break free of the ocean's grip. She saw him struggle to his feet, then get knocked back down from behind by a crashing wave that had no business being so high on the beach. The hissing of the retreating sea sounded venomous, diabolical—as if Neptune himself had decided to make an example of Dan and drown him like a junebug.

And then the earsplitting din of the storm fell away and the hurricane became all fury and no sound. All Maddie could hear, all she wanted to hear, was Dan calling out her name. In the total silence of that fierce desire, she staggered through the dune grass and grabbed the shoulders of Dan's jacket while he was still on all fours, trying to stand. Her strength just then was obviously greater than his. With her to anchor him, he was able to resist the pull of the sea and stumble over the low dune and onto the road. There, the water was up to their knees still, but the footing underneath was more sure.

Now the storm, cheated of its prey, rose up in newer, louder fury than before. Maddie felt Dan's weight bear down on her as she struggled to support him on their way back to Rosedale, but their progress was pitiably slow.

"Your boots . . . we have to get them off!" she shouted in his ear. Was he lucid? She couldn't tell. "Your boots!" she shouted again.

"BOOTS!" he shouted back. He nodded in comprehension, then dropped down on his rear end. He was his own little rock in the ocean; the seas swirled around him shoulder high as Maddie struggled to pull the open-topped, rubber-handled monstrosities from his feet.

Where had he found them? They weren't sailors' boots at all, but firefighters' boots, made to get into quickly and capable of holding gallons of water. No wonder he hadn't been able to move. Somehow between them they got them off. Maddie threw them aside, then helped Dan back on his feet. Freed of the encumbrance of the water-filled boots, they were able to make better progress than before, wading slowly but purposefully down the asphalt road that was now a vast black whirlpool, strewn with floating debris.

Plywood floated around and into them, and resin lawn chairs, and broken-off pickets and neatly split firewood, as they waded the interminable distance to Cranberry Lane. Exhausted and traumatized as she was, Maddie was still shocked to see that the sea kept tagging along with them down the lane: it flowed through the pickets of her front garden, killing with salt as it went, and was lapping at the bluestone stoop of Rosedale cottage.

Please, God, let this be the surge; let this be the worst of it.

They passed through the opening in the picket fence where once the gate had been. With the last of her adrenaline, Maddie led Dan around the fallen maple to the back of the cottage, then unhooked the key from the side of the Dutch door and unlocked it. Despite the hellish conditions outside—or maybe because of them—the kitchen, by lamplight, looked snug and welcoming. The painted checkerboard floor danced with their dripping shadows as Dan began to shuck himself free of his gear.

Maddie beamed a flashlight on the night watchman's clock that had sat on the same kitchen shelf her whole life long: half past three. It was high tide, pushed violently higher by the storm surge.

"The question is, is the surge still surging?" asked Dan, expressing the thought on both their minds.

"Ten more inches," Maddie said tersely, turning off the flashlight. "And then it'll be in the house."

"Not to seem like a pessimist, but maybe we should start moving furniture?"

"The hell with it," Maddie said, collapsing onto the nearest chair. She peeled off her jacket and let it fall on the floor; she was too tired to get rid of the pants. Now that the immediate danger was over, she found herself utterly without resources. Talking was an effort, and so was thinking. Worrying. Grieving. All she could do was sit on the kitchen chair with an utterly blank look on her face, the perfect reflection of the state of her mind.

Dan wasn't much better. He hooked his jacket over the back of a chair and laid his pants over the jacket with the same precision that a visitor uses to fold a hand towel in the guest bath. Then he, too, collapsed.

"I hate when I do that," he muttered.

"What?" she said dully.

"Use up another one of my lives. I'm down to just a couple, now."

She wanted to smile, but for so many reasons the smile wouldn't come.

After another gap, Dan said, "The boots didn't work out too well."

"No."

"I found them in the breezeway. Maybe someone used them to garden."

"Maybe."

"They seemed like a good idea at the time."

Another long gap.

"Thanks, Maddie," he said quietly. "I wouldn't have made it."

"No problem."

He sighed. "We couldn't save the boat."

"Oh."

"But we got the people off okay."

"Ah."

Again he sighed. "One of the men helping out almost got crushed between the sailboat and the launch. No boat's worth that. Men do stupid things in a crisis."

"Mmm."

"Not only men. What were you doing out there, missy?" he asked, reaching across the table for her hand. "Not that I'm not grateful, but what the hell were you doing, strolling along a beach in a hurricane?"

She let her hand lay limp under his. "I wanted to be with you," she said, staring without seeing.

He laughed softly and lifted her moribund hand. "Yeah. I can tell."

She saw him force himself to stand, then come around to her side of the table and take her hands in his. "C'mon, Miss Nightingale," he said. "The storm's gonna do what the storm's gonna do. We can't see out the ocean side anyway. Let's go upstairs to bed."

To bed. "No," she said, shaking her head slowly. "I can't."

"Too many stairs, huh? Okay, then let's curl up on the couch and huddle together like two orphans in a storm. I haven't felt this sorry for myself since the day I gave up smoking."

Again she shook her head. "I don't think so."

"Maddie?"

She heard it in the way he said her name: the first tremor of alarm. Déjà vu, all over again.

Could she put them through it, all over again? It didn't seem possible. Did she have a choice? It didn't seem possible. Nothing, in her present state of exhaustion, seemed possible.

"Okay, the sofa," she said, simply to put off the impossible.

"That's probably better. If the water starts seeping through the door, we can . . . we can . . ."

She gave him a look of pure despair. "We can what?"

He shrugged. "We can lift our feet. Honey, it's not the end of the world," he said softly. "Roofs can be fixed; floors, refinished. Honeysuckle grows back. Listen!" he said, cocking his head toward the windows. "Doesn't it sound like the wind's abating?"

He was trying so hard, though he himself was exhausted.

She could see it in the gauntness of his face, in the hollows under his eyes. Even in the lamplight he looked worn and used up. He'd worked furiously into the night on the roof, then helped rescue a foundering crew on a boat, and after that—obviously dehydrated and weak—had still tried to drag himself through a hurricane to reach her.

"I love you," she said, not even trying to hold back the tears.

He pulled her up slowly into his arms and kissed her, then nudged away a rolling tear with his lips. "I can't tell you how scared I was on that beach," he said in her ear. "Not because I'm that afraid of dying—but because now, when I have so damn much to live for, it would be really tragic to check out. Let's promise one another not to do anything stupid for the next half century or so."

What could she say in response to that? Nothing. She didn't even try, but only held him tight.

He released her, reluctantly it seemed, so that she could change into dry clothes. When Maddie came back downstairs, he was sitting on the couch in his damp khaki shorts and T-shirt.

"Call me crazy, but I'd feel goofy sitting around naked if the roof blew off," he said with a beguiling, goofy grin.

Maddie herself had changed into shorts and a sweater and had brought down a soft cotton sweater of her father's for Dan to wear. He peeled off his T-shirt and put on the sweater instead. So now they were salty but more or less dry and warm, with nothing to do but huddle and wait. The one good thing was the complete state of their exhaustion. Hers was more emotional; his, physical.

It would suffice.

Chapter 29

They dozed in one another's arms while Dot hung around, ranting and raving like a homeless psychotic left to wander the streets without medication. The hurricane shrieked and threatened and bullied, but the worst was clearly over: no saltwater seeped under the front door.

Still, every time something cracked or broke outside, Maddie would emerge from the tumble of her dreams with a start. Then she'd feel Dan's arms around her, remember Michael's threat, and sink into the merciful chaos of her subconscious again.

A line of especially violent thunderstorms passed over them on the tail end of the hurricane, making sleep, even dozing, impossible. Maddie jumped with every explosion. She used to love the awesome power of a thunderstorm, but she was sensitive now. She cowered in Dan's arms, praying for the ordeal to be over, knowing that when it was, a new and worse one would begin.

They'd said little since they curled up on the sofa together. Now, between thunderclaps, Maddie had to know. "Did you call my name when you were making your way over here?"

"Out loud?" Dan said, absently rubbing the fleece of her sweater. "No. Why?"

"Did you see a green light burning in the tower?"

He laughed softly. "Definitely, no. I'm not *that* crazy."

Was she? Had she simply heard what she wanted to hear

and seen what she wanted to see? Was that the definition of crazy? What about Dan and his mystical experience? Yesterday she would've compared notes with him. Today, she lapsed into silence.

The last of the thunderstorms passed over them like the muted drumroll of a distant marching band. Maddie could see that the parlor was a lighter shade of black now; dawn had arrived to shine a light on the wanton destruction that Dot had left behind.

"I suppose we have to go see what's out there," she said, sitting up with bone-tired reluctance.

He pulled her back close. "Part of me is afraid to know," he confessed, "and the other part doesn't care. Let's just stay here."

She shook her head. "Life doesn't work that way."

Dan sighed and said, "Okay—but I'm not putting any roofs back on until I've had my coffee." He stood up, circling his upper arms out of their stiffness, then arched his spine. "Ow, ow. I take it all back. My roofing days are over."

They followed the trail of daylight to the kitchen windows and looked out at what used to be the garden. Dan groaned. Maddie simply stared. Every shrub and tree within view had been stripped of its leaves, which were lying in a thick soggy blanket over the ground. Underneath the leaves were the flowers, apparently: in any case, they were nowhere to be seen. A patio table—not theirs—lay upside down in the middle of the yard next to a section of a roof, also not theirs. A Sunfish had sailed in under its own power: the yellow and blue striped sail swung jauntily under a clearing breeze from the northwest. A bundle of pink cloth lay in a heap in a corner of the yard. In her present frame of mind, Maddie was convinced it was wrapped around a drowned body, until Dan pointed out that that it was a blanket, probably off a neighbor's clothesline, lying over a shrub.

"Incredible," Dan said in awe. "What will the beach side be like?"

Maddie had stepped into the on and off sunshine of the

yard for a closer look when she heard the telephone ring. It sounded amazingly shrill.

Dan was behind her, still in the kitchen. "Want me to answer it?" he offered through the screen door.

"God, no!" she cried, and ran inside to pick it up. If it was Michael. . . .

But it wasn't Michael or anyone else. It wasn't even a dial tone. It was a dead, dead phone, one more brief skirmish in the overall war on her nerves.

"They must be working on the phones already," Dan said, trying the phone and then laying it in its cradle again. "That's good news."

Good news? Terrible news. Michael would know. Somehow or other, Michael would know if Dan was there. He'd find out from the neighbors, or from Trixie, or from their daughter, if and when he did return her to Maddie.

Overwhelmed by the need to tell him about Michael's vindictiveness, Maddie blurted, "Something's happened, Dan!"

Dan snorted. "Yeah, a frickin' hurricane's happened."

"Something else. Something worse."

"Worse'n Dot?" he joked, still milking his beloved pun. But underneath the light tone, he was heeding her anxiety. "Is this what's been bothering you, above and beyond the hurricane?"

She nodded and swung away, unable to bear up under his sharp scrutiny.

Déjà vu, all over again.

Dan came up behind her and turned her around. "All right, it's Michael. That much I can see in your eyes. What about him?"

"He . . . he has Tracey," she said, looking away again. She stared at the hell that had once been her paradise. "He's keeping her."

"Well, he doesn't have much choice," Dan said mildly. "Water Street may be torn up. If not, it'll be buried under sand and debris. It's going to take a little while to clear this mess."

Biting her lip, she shook her head.

"Longer than that?"

"Permanent custody," she managed to get out. "He wants it."

Dan's reaction was succinct. "The guy's an asshole! Look ... Maddie ... don't worry. It'll be fine. He's an asshole, he's jerking you around—that's all. He's jealous, and this is his response—dragging you through a custody review. Hell, he's not going to go through with it. He wants you to suffer, that's all. He wants you to think about him—and he'll take any thoughts he can get."

"It's true," she said faintly.

"Don't give him the satisfaction," Dan urged, trying to take her in his arms. She turned away again.

He came around to face her. She saw that his cheeks were flushed with emotion. Anger? Panic? Both?

"Don't let him get to you, Maddie! If you do, he's won. You know that. Don't let him."

"You don't understand—"

"Sure I do! I know his kind! They claim to care about everyone, but they care about no one—no one but themselves! People will see that. A judge will see that—assuming it ever gets to a judge. Michael's an ex who wants revenge. Everyone will see right through his motive."

"Tracey doesn't."

"Oh, Tracey—she's a kid! What does she know?"

"She's told him she wants to stay with him."

"You're not going to believe him when he says that, are you?"

"Tracey's told me that, too."

She saw Dan flinch. It was the beginning of the end.

"It doesn't mean anything," Dan said, taking another tack. "Kids her age change their minds every five minutes. Tomorrow she'll decide she doesn't like the view out the bedroom and she'll want to come back home."

"He knows about the beach—"

"Big deal!"

"And—oh, God, I still can't believe this—my mother is willing to back him up when he goes to court."

Now it was Dan's turn to stare. "Your mother? Your own mother?"

Maddie lowered her gaze and nodded.

"She can't hate me that much," Dan murmured, stunned.

"She thinks it's best, temporarily," Maddie added, trying to soften the blow.

"She said that to you?"

Maddie shook her head. "Michael told me."

"Then how do you know, Maddie? How the hell do you know?"

Throwing up her hands, Maddie said, "Well, I can't very well ask her, can I? For one thing, the damn phone is gone—and for another, she refuses to talk to me! Doesn't that tell you something? Besides," she added, beginning to pace, "Michael sounded too smug to be lying."

"He's lying! He's a lying shit! I'll wipe that smug right off his face—"

"Don't even think about it!" she said angrily. "It would just give him more evidence to take with him to court. Everything becomes evidence now!"

"That's crazy! That's stupid crazy! You're in love with another man—you're going to marry another man—that doesn't mean you're an unfit mother! Why make it sound like you're selling your body for crack? Jesus!"

Maddie suddenly stopped and brought her fist down hard on the kitchen table. "It's *everything*, don't you see? It's your past, it's my family, it's our scandalous behavior on the town beach, it's first and foremost Tracey's *choice*!"

"Fight it!"

"And what? Alienate her forever? All I'm saying is, I have to do this slowly . . . gingerly; I can't make a single false step now. Can't you see that?" she pleaded.

Dan walked away from her. With his hands flat in his back pockets, he stared through the windows at the destruction outside. In the silence that followed, Maddie heard a lone hammer. People had already started to put their lives back together again.

In a dull tone, Dan said, "Well, okay, you know best, I

guess. I'm not a parent. I can't say what's right or wrong in your approach. Personally, I think you're wrong—but I'm not a parent.''

Eager to smooth things between them, she said, ''You're right that he just wants to hurt me. I've hardly even had a date since the divorce . . . so this has hit him hard. I think with time I can make him see reason. I wish there was a better way . . . it will be horrible, not being with you—''

Dan turned around slowly. ''Not what?''

''Not . . . not . . .'' And then it hit her that she'd omitted one small detail of Michael's plan: that to get Tracey back at all, she had to give Dan up. ''Not being with you,'' she repeated faintly. ''If I . . . if I see you, he'll begin the proceedings. That's what he said.''

The look on Dan's face became part of her permanent memory: the dark brows, pulled down in disbelief; the unshaved chin, locked in grim repose; the total stillness of his being as he forced himself to comprehend the terms she was laying before him like cards in a game of blackjack.

At last he said, ''You're going to spit on his threat, right?''

''Oh, Dan—how *can* I?'' she asked him in agony. ''For all the reasons I've just said. I'm her mother, Dan! And Michael is, and always will be, her twisted, twisted father.''

The silence was as long, as brutal, as any that had ever occurred between them.

''I can't argue with that,'' Dan said at last, looking away again. After another long pause, he said, ''So. The wedding's off.''

''If I marry you,'' she explained gently, ''I may lose my child. I wouldn't have believed it a month ago. Now I do.''

''And you want me to—what?''

''Wait?''

He swung back around. ''How long? Weeks? Months? Years? Until he walks Tracey down the aisle? Until your first grandchild is born? How long, Maddie? How long this time?''

''You've loved me this long, Dan. . . .'' she whispered.

His jaw was clamped down tight; she could see the muscles working in his temples as he considered her entreaty.

Finally he said, "You're asking too much, Maddie. Too much of any man. Even me."

He turned to leave. His hand was on the screen door when he suddenly pulled off the cotton sweater she'd lent him and flung it at her. "Here—your father's sweater," he said in disgust. "The curse goes on."

Cranberry Lane looked like a war zone. Hawke was in no mood to take in more than that general impression. He'd walked out of her cottage in such a seething rage that he hadn't even noticed if Rosedale still had a roof or not; presumably it had. Very quickly, though, the extent of the widespread damage became clear, even to him.

A house was flattened, another one, half gone. Where it had gone was anyone's guess, but at least some of it had wedged in the lane. Dan picked his way barefoot around the debris and cut between two houses down to the beach, where he saw home after home split open and laid bare for all the world to see. A kitchen, a living room, a master bedroom— once those rooms had had a view of the ocean. Now the ocean had a view of them.

It was bad. Whatever the ocean hadn't pushed forward, it seemed to have dragged back. The beach was littered with furniture and deck planking and the broken bones of boats that had washed ashore. People wandered everywhere, most of them in awe. Some wept. One elderly couple, holding one another, simply stared in silence at the remains of what was once a tiny cottage covered over with climbing roses. He wondered if it had been theirs.

It was impossible not to feel their collective misery, but it only made his private one worse.

We should be together now. We should be sharing this together.

He couldn't believe that she'd done it again: sent him packing. After all the vows, all the tears, after all the phenomenal satisfaction of making love—off y'go, mate; that's a good boy.

Unreal! This couldn't be happening. He felt dazed by her

response, and the disaster on the beach only made it feel that much more unreal.

The sound of sobbing pierced his reverie. He turned to see a middle-aged woman sitting on the deck of her home, sobbing over a framed photograph that hung limply in her hands. And yet her house looked pretty much intact. Had she lost a pet? Her grief seemed deeper than that. A relation? It occurred to Hawke, really for the first time, that people undoubtedly had died in this storm: a surfer, a resident, a motorist, a fisherman. Dot had to have fled with blood on her hands.

Maddie could've died in this thing. She had forced her way through hell to find him and bring him home safe—and then had booted him out again. Unreal!

"She really kicked ass, didn't she?"

Dan looked up, inclined to agree.

A deeply tanned beach-bum type grinned at him from the deck of a sailboat lying on its side, high and dry. "I hear Hyannisport's a disaster, man."

He seemed too happy by half. "That your boat?" asked Dan, convinced he was looting it.

"Nah. It's my buddy's. We're taking what we can off it. It's a total."

"It looks fine to me," Dan said, still not convinced about the guy. "The sails didn't even unfurl."

The beach bum cocked his head at Dan. "You blind, man? You could drive a truck through the hull."

Only then did Dan see that the side that lay on the sand had a hole in it big enough—well, to drive a truck through.

"Huh. You're right," he said, and he moved on, relating to the boat in an intensely personal way. Totaled. That's exactly how he felt.

He walked over hard wet sand the rest of the way, jumping nimbly when debris sloshed back and forth in the flattening seas that still broke on the beach. As far as he was able to tell, the keeper's house and the lighthouse were still standing. It was only when he got directly between them and the water that he saw the change: the tower's foundation had sunk into the sand and it was now leaning, just like the one at Pisa. Not good.

The keeper's house, on the other hand, was still intact. Some—many—shingles were missing and some windows blown out, but all in all, the keeper's house was in better shape than the lighthouse itself. Dan was proud to see that the roof had held. He counted it as the single accomplishment of his stay in Sandy Point.

So. Back to square one. No phone, no electricity, no running water. It was a lot like being in Albania again, except without hope. The realization sliced through his gut like a rusty saber, infecting him as it went. He closed his eyes, willing away all thoughts of Maddie. She'd made her choice. Twice. You couldn't get more certain than that. He'd given it his best shot, but destiny and biology had other ideas.

In any case, the thought of waiting any longer was completely repellent to him. Weeks, months, years—any wait at all was unacceptable. He was going to have to get on with his life, hopefully without bitterness. He had to forgive, and somehow to forget.

It'd be a lot easier to do that with a drink and a cigarette, he thought, plucking a strand of seaweed from his Jeep. He was going to have to figure out how to get both.

Chapter 30

As hurricanes go, Dot was no Hugo. But half a dozen towns on the mid-Cape's south shore had taken it on the chin—Sandy Point hardest of all. The village was laid flat on its back for almost two weeks while Com Electric replaced rows of poles and reels of cable, and bulldozers shoved bits and pieces of houses from the roads. The only vehicles allowed to traverse the town's torn-up streets were emergency ones—chief among them the water truck. Chainsaws and generators whined nonstop during the daylight hours, wearing on people's nerves.

But at night, when the equipment was shut down, a quaint serenity prevailed. Sandy Point became a sleepy Victorian watering hole once more. No TV's blared, no stereos throbbed; neither fan nor air conditioner hummed. Oil lamps and candlelight glowed through wide open windows and doors, and neighbors gathered on porches and decks, rehashing the scary parts of the storm and wondering when they'd have their electricity back.

The ocean, too, stayed oddly meek—embarrassed, no doubt, by the fit it had thrown in front of everyone. It ebbed and flowed quietly now, over much less beach than before. Two feet less beach, to be exact; that's how much was missing from the front of the lighthouse. Coastal engineers said that the sand had shifted to the east, to someone else's shore.

"Not that it matters where it went," Norah told the ad hoc

committee that she'd assembled at the lighthouse. "We've got to move the lighthouse *now*. The contractor needs at least thirty feet of beach to maneuver his equipment around it. We have about thirty-four at high tide."

The ad hoc committee was Norah's idea—a sop to flatter the six top contributors into coughing up the balance of the quarter million needed to move the tower across the road. If time and money permitted, the keeper's house would be moved as well. But it was the lighthouse that was now the more urgent concern.

Hawke watched with grudging admiration as Norah explained the moving procedure in expert detail to the five men and one woman clustered on the sand. Step by step, she laid out the arduous process of moving the historic structure—the cutting of the concrete floor, the hand excavation inside and out, the installation of the cribbing and steel beams through holes cut in the foundation, and the jacking up of the lighthouse to transfer it to the dolly system on which it would be driven across the road to its newly acquired site.

The hurricane had flattened morales all over town, including Hawke's, but Norah seemed to have been energized by it. She'd arrived at the lighthouse less than an hour after he returned to it on the morning after Dot's rampage, and she'd spent every daylight hour there since. A great deal of her time was spent with town and state officials, contractors, and engineers.

And the rest of it was spent with Hawke. Thrown together in the lighthouse crisis, they'd become friends in the last twelve days. Despite his foul mood and his desire to get out of Sandy Point, Hawke had ended up letting Norah talk him into pitching in to make the latest repairs to the keeper's house. One job led to another, and his mood began to improve. Soon he found himself going through his shoebox of business cards, looking for contacts that might be useful in the effort to speed up the relocation.

And now, after the last committee member piled into the car that Norah had waiting for them, she and Hawke settled back in plastic chaises for sundowners on the beach. It was their fourth or fifth evening in a row, a nice little ritual by now.

"They'll definitely come up with the cash," Norah told him with typical confidence. "We'll be able to sign the contract for the move this month."

Hawke lifted an icy Coors from the cooler she'd brought and popped the lid. "How long before the actual move, do you think?"

She shrugged her bare shoulders and said, "The contract will run for four months. The move itself will only take about a week. It's the preparation that's time-consuming. And everything will depend on the weather. Didn't I hear someone forecast half a dozen major hurricanes this summer?"

"Ah, what do they know?" Hawke asked, squinting into the evening sun. There were shadier places to set the chaises, but here they were out of sight of Rosedale. He didn't want to be reminded of it. Ever.

Norah stretched languidly, like a cat, then lay back and closed her eyes with a smile. "I love this time of day," she said. "The way everything winds down and people go home, but I don't have to. I always feel both self-indulged and sad, as if such a beautiful dream can't possibly go on."

He laughed and slugged his Coors. "I don't have a clue whether that makes you selfish or humble."

She rolled her head in his direction and batted her eyes once, slowly, at him. "Right now, I feel both."

He didn't back down from the look he saw there. Definitely, there was a scent in the air. Did she know about the breakup? He hadn't once alluded to it, but it didn't take a rocket scientist to know there'd been a change in his status.

She raked her red mane of hair over to one side; the setting sun danced and played over it, revealing a whole spectrum of russet tones. Spectacular, Hawke thought. He was startled to realize that he'd noticed.

Because he was genuinely curious, he said, "How is it that a gorgeous thing like you is sitting on plastic chairs with an unemployed bum like me?"

"Because you refuse to come lounge on the fancy chaises around my pool," she said with a smile.

It was true. He'd stuck to washing himself from a barrel of rainwater rather than take advantage of her generator-equipped villa. Right about now, he was asking himself why.

He had hung around Sandy Point for eleven days longer than he'd planned to do after he walked out of Rosedale. Not once had Maddie made an effort to contact him. No visits, no smoke signals. She meant what she said. Hell, he should've known that from the first time.

A wave came up a little higher than the rest, lapping around the legs of their chaises. Hawke felt a corner suck into the sand, setting him ever so slightly off balance.

"Ask me again," he told her softly.

Michael Regan was in a well-earned rage. Two weeks had passed since he'd single-handedly secured new government funding for the remote viewing project—and he still hadn't been paid. Woodbine was screwing him good, putting him off with all kinds of excuses about procurement procedures and black contracts and some kind of security inspection before the funding would be released. Enough was enough. Tonight he was going to physically shake the damned money out of Woodbine if he had to.

It didn't help Michael's mood that his daughter had come back more mopey than ever from a five-day visit to her grandmother. Despite all the attention, despite all the freedom—despite all the money!—he'd given Tracey, she missed her mother. She claimed not to, but he could see it coming; soon she'd want to go home.

It infuriated him to know that there were now two people who preferred someone else's company to his: his wife—and his own daughter. He felt like a pariah. Him! The most sought-after guest at a party, the most popular teacher on campus.

He didn't let the aggravation show as he knocked on Tracey's bedroom door and said cheerfully, "All packed? The train's leavin' the station. Whooo-whoo!"

His daughter came out of her bedroom with a backpack over her shoulder and a glum look on her face.

"What's *this* all about?" he said, tucking a playful fist under her jaw.

She lifted her chin away as he did it and said, "Dad, don't."

"Hey! I thought you were looking forward to this sleepover thing."

"It's not a sleepover; it's just a bunch of girls getting together."

"And yakking all night. Yeah. A sleepover."

"Have it your way," she said, walking ahead with her shoulders drooping.

Oh, yeah. She wanted her mommy, all right. Damn. Maddie must have made inroads during the couple of phone calls she'd managed to put through. What would happen when power was restored and Rosedale was habitable again?

He dropped Tracey off at her friend's house, telling her he'd pick her up at noon the next day, and then he backtracked to Brookline, where Woodbine would be working late. The very distinguished, very hard-working director invariably worked late at the Institute on Friday. It was quiet then, Woodbine liked to tell people. A man could hear himself think on a Friday night.

A man could also alter data on a Friday night. Michael had no illusions about what went on at the Brookline Institute, and he didn't care. If the project results were tweaked, what did it matter? It was all a gray area, anyway. He knew his powers were real. If the government wanted them to be more real, fine. That's where a Woodbine came in handy.

He arrived ten minutes early and sat in his car in the parking lot, waiting for the director to unlock the door for him. Exactly on time, Woodbine appeared in the lobby, glanced at the BMW, and walked up to the imposing double doors. By the time he had one of them unlocked, Michael was on the other side, glaring at him through the glass.

Woodbine said curtly, "Let's get this over with," and led the way to his office.

Michael fell in beside him. "You took your sweet time returning my calls. I'd be surprised if your secretary isn't on to us."

"There's no 'us' to be on to, Michael," Woodbine said with icy reserve.

"Yeah, right. Just give me my money. I've waited long enough."

"Obviously you have absolutely no idea how long it takes for government funding to make its way through channels."

"So hire a channeler; you must have a few on your staff," Michael quipped.

Woodbine declined to respond.

They went into his office. Woodbine didn't offer him a seat and Michael didn't avail himself of one. As always when he was there, he felt edgy and angry. As if on cue, the first sharp stab of a headache appeared, reminding him that he hated the Institute, hated the Director, and wanted no more part of their program.

Woodbine opened the top drawer of his elegant mahogany desk, took out a clasp envelope, and tossed it on the desktop. Pleased to see that it had a satisfying bulge to it, Michael reached for it and said, "For a job well done. You never did tell me how well I scored, Geoffrey."

"In a word? You sucked."

Michael's hand froze on the envelope where it lay. "The hell I did," he said, flushing with anger.

The director shrugged and said, "A mailman could've done better. A nurse. A janitor. Anyone who could tell the time and follow a few simple directions. A buzzer sounds, and all you had to do was look at the clock on the wall, determine which ten-second sector the buzzer sounded in, and correlate that sector to a room of a house. We agreed beforehand. One to ten seconds: the kitchen. Ten to twenty seconds: the bath. Twenty to thirty: the garden. And so on. Your chances of guessing the object—or a thematically related one, which is nearly as good—would skyrocket. Was that so hard, Michael? Apparently it was."

"I did do that!"

"Half of the time. The other half you ignored the clock

and guessed the object based on—what? Your intuition? Don't make me laugh."

"What did you expect?" Michael shouted, feeling humiliated. "I was in a *zone*, Geoff! I couldn't just pull out of it and focus on some dumb-ass clock. I was focused! Ask Michael Jordan if he can turn it off just like that; ask Mike Tyson."

Woodbine leaned over his desk, palms flat on the surface. "Those are hardly compatible zones, either with one another or with yours, Michael. Quite simply: you're a deluded fool. You drew a bed when I signaled the garden; you drew a teapot when I signaled the bathroom. You're a fool and an idiot. The only reason we got that funding was because I was able to capitalize on the few times you did manage to follow the plan. Next time, I'll buy myself an engineer; at least they can follow instructions."

"You son of a bitch!" Michael shouted.

Woodbine reached into the top drawer of his desk. Michael threw himself across it, slamming the wide drawer hard and catching Woodbine's left hand in it. With a cry of pain Woodbine yanked it out, holding it hard against his chest with his other hand.

"Sonovabitch—you've got a gun in there, haven't you?" Michael cried. He vaulted over the desk and pulled the drawer all the way out, revealing a revolver at the back of it. Snatching it up, he felt his first real surge of power over his despised mentor.

"This is the one, isn't it?" he said to Woodbine, hardly containing his glee at having the upper hand. "This is the gun you used to blow away my father-in-law."

Woodbine's breath was still coming fast. "I don't . . . know what you're . . . talking about, you freak."

"April 6. You agreed to see him April 6," Michael said, pointing the gun at him. "You thought I didn't know that? I knew that. And not because I'm psychic. *Because he told me, you moron.* He found out that you were interested in testing Tracey, that you'd been asking me about her. Okay, he found out because I told him that you had—but that's me all over, isn't it? Dedicated to the pursuit of parapsychological truth. And am I appreciated? No. Not by you, not by my family—well, screw you all.''

Without taking his eyes from Woodbine, Michael groped the top of the desk for the envelope and dragged it closer to him. "How come you never told me about your colorful past, hmm? How come I had to hear it from Edward Timmons instead? I thought we were better friends than that, Geoffrey—or should I say, Clive?''

"You're more prone to fantasy than I thought," the director said, eyeing him warily.

"Uh-huh. Y'know, I don't much care what you did or did not do. All I really want at this point is the money. I'm mad, I'm tired, I need a vacation. Besides, it's the principle of the thing.''

Michael struggled to open the clasped flap of the envelope with one hand, then jiggled it lightly so that some of the money eased part of the way out.

He glanced down. "Twenties?" he said, stunned. "*Twenties*?'' He dumped the rest of the envelope on the desk: all twenties, no more than a few thousand dollars' worth.

Woodbine took advantage of the distraction to make a lunge for him, knocking him back into a bookcase. They locked in an uneven struggle over the gun; Michael was younger, stronger, uninjured. The gun went off with a deafening sound and the director staggered back, his eyes wide with shock. He grabbed his stomach, then fell to the floor.

Michael stood there, paralyzed by the sight of the blood oozing from the wound. He dropped to his knees and felt for a pulse. If there was one, he couldn't find it. He stood up. His mind went blank. Then he seized the gun and he ran.

Heart hammering, head pounding, he tore down the hall through the lobby and grabbed at the handle of the glass entry door. Locked! He turned and ran down the nearest aisle, looking for another door. He found a fire exit, then pushed the door open, setting off a shrill, mind-bending alarm. His pace was frantic now, his breath exploding in his chest. He circled back to the parking lot, dropped into the front seat of his car, and with violently shaking hands, got the key into the ignition slot. He sped out of the lot and down quiet residential streets and didn't look back until he was merged into the Friday night metro mess on Route 9.

Convinced that he was being pursued by police, he took a roundabout route from Brookline to his condo on the Back Bay, then parked in his rented carriage stall, where he checked obsessively for blood. He searched his hands, his clothes, the leather upholstery of the Beemer. No. He was clean. The car was clean.

Once he was safely ensconced in his kitchen, he poured himself a huge Scotch, still with shaking hands, and tried to assess. He was okay. He was okay. He hadn't been followed, hadn't been seen. He was okay. Most importantly, he had remembered to snatch up the gun. It lay on the table in front of him; he'd have to heave it off a bridge or bury it deep.

It wasn't until the Scotch had settled nicely in his brain that he was able to re-assess. For one thing, his fingerprints were everywhere. The chair, the desk, the handle of the lobby door—those were all legitimate and easily accounted for. But the fire door? The money envelope?

What about the struggle itself—what other evidence of himself had he left behind during it? He held his arms up and scrutinized them front and back. Scratches, not enough to draw blood—but this was the age of forensic miracles. Had he left his skin behind, under Woodbine's nails? Oh God, of course he had! He kept his arms extended rigidly in front of him, his hands gripping the edge of the kitchen table. Slowly, painfully, his alcohol-soaked mind focused on a white band across his otherwise tanned wrist.

His watch.

Where was it? Had he been wearing it? He jumped up and ran around the apartment like a scalded cat, checking his dresser, his bureau, the low table where he ate while he watched TV. Nowhere. Yes! He'd been wearing it, he had! He remembered checking the time by the overhead light when he got to the parking lot, because the clock in the Beemer was shot.

He collapsed on a chair at the kitchen table in front of the gun and dropped his face onto his hands, gripped by sudden despair. He'd left money and his watch, and fingerprints on everything. The gun that lay before him now—*was* it the one that had killed Ed? Would he be blamed for that, too?

He jumped up; he had to go back.

No. He couldn't go back. He couldn't get in, for one thing, and for another, the fire department had undoubtedly responded to the alarm. By now they knew.

The pit of his despair grew deeper still. He remembered that the Institute had a copy of his fingerprints and a photo on file; they were required for classified government work. It was only a matter of time, then. How much of it did he have?

He tried to make himself think, but his mind drew a blank as thorough as anything he'd ever achieved during meditation. He sat at the cluttered table for a terrifying length of time, trying to come up with something—anything—to break him out of his paralysis of fear and get him moving again.

It was a neon pink newsletter folded in three that finally caught his eye; it lay on top of the day's mail, all of it still unread, on the table next to the gun. His gaze fell on the masthead of the pink missive: *The Sandy Point Crier*, Trixie Roiters, Editor.

The banner headline was visible in the tri-fold: *Hurricane Batters Sandy Point*. So was the head to one of the twinned stories underneath it: *Lighthouse Damaged*. He tore through the staple and began to read.

Hurricane Dot, packing top winds of 110 miles an hour, caused serious erosion to the town beach, undercutting the foundation of the Sandy Point Lighthouse. The lighthouse, which now leans noticeably to the east, has been the focus of a recent fundraising effort to relocate it inland across Water Street. The keeper's house, which was unoccupied for the duration of the hurricane, sustained moderate damage.

Michael read no further. *Unoccupied.* The word throbbed like a raw wound in his head. *Unoccupied.* If Hawke hadn't been in the keeper's house for the duration of the hurricane, then where had he been?

With Maddie, of course. Had he been there while Michael was talking to her on the phone? Had he appeared at her front door while the phone was still warm in its cradle?

That lying, lying slut. She lied. She promised, and she broke that promise. She lied. She was with him now. She lied then and was lying still and would always lie.

This is all her fault. Once that simple realization coalesced, his brain immediately cleared and he became energized. It was all Maddie's fault. If she'd stayed married to him, none of this would've happened. His life was in ruins, he was going to prison, and it was all Maddie's fault.

That thought, and only that thought, sustained him for the rest of the night as he made his plans.

Chapter 31

Hawke had his first shower in eleven days, and he had to admit that it felt good. As he rubbed his hair dry with a sinfully thick white towel, he tried to figure out what perverse motive had made him turn down Norah's repeated offers of hospitality.

On balance, he decided that he had wanted to feel sorry for himself, which was easier to do when he was living in a state of primitive hygiene. If he'd had any other motives, he preferred not to think of them now.

He stuffed his dirty workclothes into his duffel and walked barefoot through the guest suite down to what Norah called her gathering room. Everything, upstairs and down, was done up in shades of white. Pity the kid with dirty feet who tried to run free in *this* house.

While he waited for Norah to shower and come down, he helped himself to a bourbon from the sideboard, then walked through one of half a dozen French doors that were opened to the night breeze. He was on a deck that ran the length of the house and overlooked a turquoise pool with underwater lighting. Norah was right: her chaises were fancier than his.

The sea was ahead of him; he could hear it. The town was somewhere off to the left; he could sense it. Sense her in it. To the right was new development—big houses like Norah's, built on stilts and with their own huge generators for awkward times like these. At the moment they were all lit up like Las

Vegas, doing their best to stick it to the older, humbler part of town.

He turned his back to the sliding, hissing sea and gazed into Norah's gathering room. Everything was very elegant, very understated. He liked the Tiffany lamps; they gave all the white a much needed shot of warmth.

Yes, indeed, a man could get used to a life like this.

Even as the thought was shaping itself in his mind, Norah glided in, dressed in a simple black tunic over long bare legs. Like him, she was barefoot. Was she just kicking back, or was she making things easy? He heard a compact car start up in the driveway and then drive out: Tanya had just been given the night off was his guess.

Norah smiled and beckoned him in. "There's food," she said, waving to a plate of nibbles on a low table.

Hawke was hungry, so he took her up on her offer and dropped into one of the white chairs that surrounded the glass-topped, iron-legged table. "What happens when someone spills grape juice in a joint like this?" he asked, helping himself to a thick wedge of cheese. "Do you just zip off the slipcover and throw it out?"

"Something like that. I have a closet full of spares," Norah said, reaching down in front of him and knifing some beluga onto a thin white wafer.

Her tunic had a deep vee that fell away from her unbound breasts. He didn't gape, but he didn't look away, either. He hadn't played this game since before Albania. It interested him to know that it was a lot like riding a bike: you never really forgot how.

He said, "Why do you call this a gathering room? What do you gather? Scalps?"

"No-o, money for worthy causes."

Chastised, he said, "Yeah, well, you've done a bang-up job there. You're saving the lighthouse almost single-handedly, as near as I can tell."

"Don't go all sentimental on me, Mr. Hawke; it's not your style," she said, biting through the caviar with straight white teeth.

"Nope, that's where you're wrong," he said with a hapless smile. "Right now I'm feeling downright maudlin."

"You know what cures the blues?"

"No, but I'll bet you do."

"A really good bottle of wine. I'll get one."

"Don't make it too good," he said as she headed out of the cavernous room. "It'll be lost on me."

She paused and gave him a look over her shoulders. "In that case, I'll see if I can dig up some muscatel."

He laughed and she disappeared from his view. He stood up, edgier now than when they'd arrived. Something was out of whack. He wanted this to happen; he really did. On the way over he'd made up his mind, just the way he'd made up his mind a thousand times before in his life.

Had Norah made up hers? He didn't feel as certain about that as he had on the beach. Maybe Norah had more scruples than he. Maybe she really *was* just offering him a hot shower and a snack. Hell, he didn't know. He felt so screwed up right now. . . .

He wandered around the room, trying to walk off his restlessness. What did he want? What the hell did he want? It wasn't Norah. When he came right down to it, it wasn't Norah. How could it be, when there was Maddie?

This was pointless; he was lashing out at Maddie by hitting on one of her best friends. More embarrassed at his juvenile response than ashamed of it, he began to walk out to the kitchen to stop Norah from popping the cork.

He never made it that far. As he passed a glass-topped console near the hall that led to the kitchen, he saw the photo albums that Maddie had lent Norah. One of them was opened to two pages mounted with snapshots of the keeper's house being boarded up and the fresnel lens being removed from the lighthouse and loaded onto a truck. Maddie was in a couple of the photographs: a kid of thirteen or so, with skinny legs and a flat chest, wearing a two-piece bathing suit that nowadays would be considered laughably modest.

Hawke would've known her anywhere, in any life, at any age.

His heart constricted painfully in his chest; it was like being shot again. He realized that he'd never seen a photograph of her as a young girl before. The things that lovers and spouses took for granted had always been unavailable to him—simple things, like family albums. He began to leaf hungrily through this one, trying to make up for a lifetime of deprivation.

His face relaxed in a melancholy smile as he gazed at Maddie on a horse . . . Maddie with George and it must be Suzette . . . Maddie with her father, a man who clearly had adored her. They weren't very artistic shots, but there were a lot of them: page after page after page of Edward Timmons's kids. What must it feel like to love children that much? he wondered. It was an emotion he'd never known—the fierce love of a parent. He thought of his sister, how crazy she was about her own two kids.

For the first time, some of what Maddie had been trying to tell him sank in. He was astonished to realize that his eyes were glazed over with tears.

"Ah—you've found her," said Norah, stating a profounder truth than she knew.

"Indeed," Hawke said in a choked voice.

He kept turning the pages, utterly captivated by the images of the only woman he would ever love. "You never had children," he said to Norah without looking up.

"Oh, my gosh, I must've forgot," she said dryly.

Now he looked up. "I'm sorry. That was personal. I guess . . . it's hitting me that I haven't had any, either."

"If that's a proposition, it's the oddest one I've ever had," said Norah, placing a stemmed glass next to the album.

He laughed softly. "Not that you're not propositionable, but . . ."

"But your heart lies with another."

"For all the good it does me."

Norah leaned back on the console and sipped her wine. "How *are* you going to handle this thing with Michael?"

So she knew. Hawke shrugged and said, "My old job's still open."

"You're going to cut and run?"

"Hell, no, I'll offer it to Michael," he quipped, unable seriously to face the prospect himself.

"How do you feel about unsolicited advice?"

"Believe me, I'm soliciting it."

"Stay in town. This will work itself through."

"I guess I've pretty much made that decision," he murmured, more to himself than to her. "Not that it matters if it works itself through or not. I couldn't leave her now if . . . if . . . Well, I couldn't; that's all."

He kept turning the pages, slowly, compulsively, as Norah watched from alongside.

"Ah, here they are in London," he said, instantly recognizing the landmarks. There was a shot of three kids on the bank of the Thames, lined up according to height by their doting father. Three kids, feeding the pigeons in Trafalgar Square . . . gazing up at Big Ben . . . waiting at one of the gilded gates to Buckingham Palace.

Not all of the photos were taken in London; there were four pages devoted to photographs of the three children at what was undoubtedly a university, probably Oxford, judging from the Gothic spires. Yes . . . here was a clipping from a newspaper, yellowed with age, recounting Edward Timmons's lecture at a conference there.

"It's nice that he took his family along," said Hawke, pleased by the fact. He could never have taken his own kids to a war zone—another disappointing epiphany for him.

He was about to turn the thick, heavy page of the album, but something had snagged in his brain like a burr on a sock. He looked at the clipping again.

Dr. Edward Timmons, an American scientist distinguished for his research in particle theory, spoke here on Monday at the invitation of the University.

Hawke read it through and found nothing more than a nice, respectful piece about what a respected presence Edward Timmons was in the scientific community. He was about to shrug off the odd sensation that had gripped him when his gaze fell on an adjacent article, one that hadn't been completely scissored out. Ah. It must have been the dateline that had caught his eye: Woodbine, Oxfordshire. Woodbine; it was an unusual name. He kept reading.

A local minister, the Reverend Peter Tolley of Christ-at-Woodbine Church, has filed civil charges on behalf of his congregation against Dr. Clive Joyce, a self-proclaimed spiritualist who is alleged to have defrauded members of the church in a deception known as "billet-reading," in which the performer purports to divine the contents of a note in a sealed envelope.

Joyce, it is claimed, waived his usual admission fee in favor of a voluntary collection by members of the congregation. At least one parishioner, an elderly widow, is alleged to have donated £50 at the

And that was all. There was a photograph—part of a photograph—of a man standing with what looked like adoring fans. *Dr. Clive*, the caption read; the Joyce part of the name was cut away.

Hawke went back to the face in the photo. No doubt about it: Dr. Clive Joyce, the guy with the movie-star looks, was none other than Geoffrey Woodbine a quarter-century earlier. The face, with its dark wavy hair and square jaw, was easily recognizable. Movie-star types were like that.

If he needed a clincher, Hawke found it as he turned the page, looking for the rest of the article. Edward Timmons's long-sought address book was wedged there, no doubt forgotten by him in his own excitement at making the Joyce-Woodbine connection.

Hawke turned to the "W" page in the address book. The last entry there was for "Geoffrey Woodbine, aka Clive Joyce." It included the Institute's address, business phone, and fax number. Edward Timmons was nothing if not methodical.

Trying to mask his excitement, Hawke turned to Norah. "Does your phone work?"

"It's the one thing that does," she said, pointing to one in the hall. "We never lost service at this end. Who on earth do you plan to call?"

"Too long to go into," he said, walking straight to the wall. He tried to remember Detective Bailey's home phone, blew it on the first try and got it right on the second. It was late, after ten. The wrong number had been very annoyed; Bailey was not.

Hawke brought him up to speed on the discoveries in the album.

The detective heard him out and said, "Okay—who the hell is Woodbine?"

Hawke told him what he'd learned about the director at the fundraiser, then said, "He's not on your list of motorists who were ticketed that day in New Bedford? He's *got* to be!"

"No way. I've memorized the names. Although—wait a minute. There was a car registered to a company in Brookline. Uhh, lemme see, I got the list right here—yeah. BIRP. Which you're saying could be—"

"Brookline Institute of Research and Parapsychology."

"Hold it; let me write that down. Great. Now tell me why this guy was in Timmons's family album."

"Pure serendipity," Hawke said. "If someone had clipped the article on Ed Timmons properly, we wouldn't have had this scrap of information. But they wanted to keep the clipping square, maybe to allow the paper's name to show. Obviously the Clive Joyce story with its Woodbine dateline had sunk into Ed Timmons's subconscious over the years."

"I've had that kind of thing happen to me," the detective agreed.

"When Timmons found out through his son-in-law that a guy named Woodbine was doing psychic research, it must have rung a bell. Timmons was a physicist, after all. He'd look at parapsychology with a jaundiced eye in the best of times—and he knew, from the article still attached to his own, that this guy was a con to boot."

"And when Timmons found out that Woodbine was interested in his granddaughter, he naturally would've gone ballistic," said the detective, building on Hawke's theory. "Timmons would've threatened to expose him. Woodbine-Joyce couldn't have that; he's the director of a big deal research institute—well, you got your motive right there. Hint of scandal, the funding dries right up. Was there a photo?"

"Not a great one. But he's a striking man; the photo's good enough. Besides, Timmons could have done a little research on his own. It wouldn't take much to finger Woodbine as Joyce. Match the accent, match the age, match the subject interest, and Bob's your uncle."

"What?"

"It's a British expression; I have no idea what it means," Hawke said with a laugh. He was ecstatic. This was it, the break they'd been looking for. Serendipity, hell. This was destiny.

Hawke said, "When do you want all this stuff?"

"The sooner the better. We have software that can recover files that have been deleted; maybe there's something else useful on the backup disk."

"I'll bring everything first thing in the morning."

"Good. And we'll bring this guy in for questioning second thing in the morning."

"You got it."

Hawke hung up, his adrenaline flowing now. If he could nail Woodbine, justice would be served on more levels than one. He'd vindicate himself with Maddie and with her family, and, oh, by the way, Michael Regan's a kook, hanging around with a fraud psychic. No judge in the land would let him have custody.

He tried not to think of whether or not Tracey's heart would be broken in the bargain. He knew that Maddie was the infinitely better parent; you didn't have to be one to know one. King Solomon would consider this a no-brainer.

He came back into the gathering room and scooped up the album, then turned to leave.

"What is going on?" Norah asked, barring his exit with outspread arms.

"You've helped solve a crime and you've saved my life,

that's what. Norah, I'm forever in your debt. Thank you for the shower. Thank you for the wine. Thank you for the phone. And thanks for not—you're a doll.''

He kissed her cheek, ducked under her arm and left her in her cavernous room of white. Grateful that he'd brought his Jeep, he threw it in gear and made his way back from the bright lights of Norah's neighborhood to the dark streets of town. He wanted desperately to pound on Maddie's door and tell her what he'd discovered, but it seemed the more prudent thing to get the investigation off and running first.

But as he drove down Water Street past Cranberry Lane, something made him pull over. He parked his Jeep at a cock-eyed angle a little off the road, and approached Rosedale on foot. He had no intention of letting Maddie know he was there; he simply wanted to be as close to her as he could get, if only for this one exultant moment.

Cranberry Lane was cleaned up but still pitch-black, and he had to pick his way slowly down it. Eventually his eyes adjusted to the dark and he was able to see that the downed maple had been cut up and cleared away from Maddie's drive. So had her crushed Taurus. She had a new car there now, a Voyager that was maybe a rental. The plywood had been pried from the south side of the cottage, and an oil lamp burned on a low flame in one of the opened windows.

It was all very quiet, all very quaint. He thought of Maddie, sleeping upstairs, and his heart settled down to a reassured, steady thump. He gazed up at her bedroom window in the tiny dormer and whispered, ''Please hurry up, Maddie. Don't wait until I'm an old man.''

And then he left.

Chapter 32

Tracey stepped over her girlfriends' sleeping forms, tiptoed over to the nightstand, silently lifted the cordless phone from there, and sneaked down the hall with it to the guest bathroom. The grandfather clock on the downstairs landing tolled seven times as she punched in her father's phone number. She didn't dare wait any longer; what if he went out for breakfast?

The voice that answered didn't sound like her father's at all. It was sleepy—well, that wasn't surprising—but it sounded funny, like a snarl.

"Dad?" she said, because she really wasn't sure.

"Yeah, what."

"Dad? It's me, Tracey," she whispered, confused.

"What do you want?" he asked in a growly voice.

Really, it didn't sound like him at all. It made her favor all the harder to ask. "Dad, I know you're s'posed to pick me up at lunchtime, but, like, could you come get me sooner? Like . . . now?"

"Now? What the hell for?"

She swallowed hard. "Well, I was thinking . . . I was up all night, just thinking, and . . . like . . ." She sighed, unable to phrase her request in a way that wouldn't hurt her father's feelings. "I want to go home," she said plaintively.

"I'll bring you home later. That was our plan."

"No, I don't mean home to your place, Daddy. I mean home . . . to Mom. *Home* home."

Her father said nothing. Nothing at all. She sighed, distressed that she had ended up offending him after all, and after she had tried so hard not to. "I kind of miss Mom, Dad, you know? And I don't care if there's no electricity in Rosedale. I really don't, even if you do tease me about being spoiled. I can take showers at Aunt Norah's. I thought you could take me to Rosedale now, before there's a lot of traffic. That would be pretty easy, wouldn't it? Dad?"

Her father didn't even think about it.

"No!"

It felt as if he had slapped her in the face. Her cheeks burned from the answer. She felt all hot and upset inside. "Dad, why not?" she said, stunned.

"Absolutely not, God damn it! We made a deal!"

"But it was only temporary! Dad, I want to go home!" she said. Her voice sounded much too high and loud; someone was bound to hear her. With an effort, she made herself calm down to a whisper. "Dad, *please*."

"You heard me, Tracey. We stay with the plan. Go back to sleep."

Over her protests he hung up, leaving her pleading with empty air. Tracey began to punch in his number again, but she knew her father well enough to know that he must be in the grip of one of his vicious headaches. Or maybe he wasn't. Maybe he just didn't want her to go back home because down deep he hated her mother for what she'd done with Mr. Hawke. She never should have told her father about that. Now she was trapped, and it was her own fault.

She held the phone next to her breast and rocked back and forth as she sat on the side of the tub. What could she do? What could she do? Tears sprang up, the way they always did lately. She brushed them away, determined to act like a grown-up. What would a grown-up do?

Dial 411. It came to her in a flash of determination. When the operator answered, she said, "The number for Yellow Cab, please?"

*　　*　　*

Hawke arrived at the station in Millwood, one of the jumble of small towns that arced around Boston, not long after Bailey's shift began.

The detective offered him coffee, and Hawke, sleepy after a sleepless night, took him up on it. He leaned on a wall and sipped while Bailey studied the clipping and photo.

"Yeah, that's him, all right," Bailey said, laying the clipping in its plastic sheet protector flat in front of him. "We've got a request out to the village or hamlet or whatever it is of Woodbine in England for a police report, and Scotland Yard as well. I want to know just how far this guy had been willing to go when he defrauded little old ladies."

"Had been?"

Bailey's round face sagged. "You heard me right," he said glumly. "Woodbine was murdered last night. A little before you found this, in fact," he added, tapping the plastic sheet with his middle finger. "Maybe you can find some humor in the timing. I sure as hell can't."

Neither could Hawke; he turned and slammed his hand against the wall, spilling his coffee in his anger. "I don't believe it! Shit! I don't believe it!"

"Hey, hey, cool it! How do you think I feel? You don't have anything at stake here."

"Yeah, right," said Hawke, bitter in his irony. "How did it happen? Where?"

Bailey filled Hawke in with what he'd learned so far. "There was a brief struggle in the office—nothing long or violent, which is surprising because Woodbine looked to be pretty fit for his age—and there was some kind of penny-ante payoff involved. Or maybe another 'church' collection: they found an envelope stuffed with small bills."

In the same dejected voice, he said, "There are prints everywhere; they're running them against the staff's now. But there was no gun. The gun might have belonged to Woodbine. Apparently he owned one. They're searching the area for it now. And—this is all strictly off the record, you got that?—the shooter left his watch behind, unless Woodbine was wearin' one on each wrist when he got popped.''

The detective plunked his elbows on his desk, bent his head down, and ran his hands through what was left of his hair. "This is such a pisser," he mumbled. "We'll get this guy— whoever did it was a hack—but that doesn't help *my* case none. My only hope is that the bullets match up between the two victims. 'Course, even if they match, we have to allow that the gun could belong to the shooter. Or that he got his hands on Woodbine's gun a while ago and shot Timmons first with it. We'll probably never know.''

"I don't suppose Woodbine left behind a full confession or anything," Hawke said dryly.

"No. But look on the bright side," Bailey said, dragging his hands over his face. He smiled grimly and said, "You yourself have a damn good alibi. Me."

Hawke said wryly, "I appreciate the vote of confidence. Okay. Well . . . you need me for anything more?"

Still staring at the clipping, the detective shook his head in silence.

Sighing, Hawke got up to leave. "Keep in touch. Sooner or later I'll have a phone again."

"Yeah. Thanks anyway."

"Sure," Hawke said, giving the detective a tired thumbs-up.

He returned to his Jeep a different man than he'd left it. Much, maybe all, of his enthusiasm was gone. What was he going to tell Maddie? Gee, we think we had your dad's murderer, but he slipped through our fingers and got himself killed, so now we'll never know? That ought to impress the family, all right.

Bailey had ticked off the possible gun scenarios with depressing thoroughness. There were too damn many of them. The only way to prove that it was Woodbine who shot Edward Timmons was to come up with yet new evidence. They could feel reasonably sure—maybe very sure—that he was guilty. But would the family be satisfied with that? Would they see that a crude sort of justice had been done? Hawke couldn't say. All he knew was that *he* sure as hell wasn't happy.

He considered stopping for breakfast somewhere on the road, but the morning was getting on, and he was anxious to get back. For better or worse, Maddie had to be told. He was surprised at the depth of his reluctance to tell her. Something was sitting uneasily at the pit of his stomach. Whether it was too much coffee or a sense of foreboding was hard for him to say.

He kept coming back to Michael Regan. When all was said and done, Maddie's ex-husband was the obvious link between Woodbine and the Timmons family. He could be an innocent, deluded pawn of Woodbine's—or he could be more implicated than that.

The fact that Michael had made no secret of his involvement with Woodbine made it seem as if he had nothing to hide. On the other hand, he apparently had come into some money. Supposedly it was an inheritance. Maddie had infrequent contact with his family, so she hadn't been able to say for sure that it was; all she had was Tracey's version of her father's version of events. That was too many removes for Hawke's taste.

But an envelope of small bills not amounting to much— that didn't fit in with either a blackmail or a bribery scenario. If Michael's "inheritance" was a fat first payment, what was the church-sized one all about?

Conceivably Michael had ended his association with Woodbine by now anyway. Whatever the project was, it had been completed, apparently successfully, two weeks ago.

Where Michael was concerned, Hawke didn't trust his own instincts at all. He had too deep a grudge against the man for having married Maddie. Still . . . he didn't like the gnawing feeling in the pit of his stomach.

He rolled down 495 with relative ease, then became more and more frustrated as traffic slowed on 25. What was it with Massachussetts? Was there nowhere to go on a weekend but the Cape? He turned on the radio and searched for a news

station, curious to know whether the murder had made it to
the airwaves yet.

Ten minutes later, he had his answer. "The murder of
Geoffrey Woodbine, director of the Brookline Institute of Research and Parapsychology and a prominent lecturer on the
international circuit, was discovered late last night by firefighters responding to an alarm there," a newscaster intoned.
"Dr. Woodbine is believed to have been shot in his office at
about nine o'clock last night. Police confirm that they are
seeking a possible suspect for questioning."

A possible suspect. The adrenaline that had drained so completely from Hawke came back like a raging river. He had to
call Bailey, but where was a phone? He kept driving, sometimes forced to a crawl, looking for either an exit or a phone
booth. Why the devil hadn't he got himself a cell phone the
minute the electricity went out? He would have had enough
battery power to handle an emergency like this.

Finally—an exit. He pulled off the highway and pulled in
the first gas station he came to.

Bailey, fortunately, was at his desk and up to speed on
developments. "Michael Regan," he answered without being
asked the question.

Hawke wasn't at all surprised.

"The facility is apparently involved in government work,"
Bailey explained. "They have a security clearance, so everyone who works there is photographed and fingerprinted, including the subjects in their research. Identifying the prints
was almost too easy. Like I said: the guy's a hack. The watch,
which a lab assistant recognized, was just frosting on the
cake."

"Have you picked him up yet?"

"They're doing it now. I can tell you this: he's planning
to skip the country with Tracey this afternoon. He's charged
two tickets to Paris in their names to his Visa. Worse case,
they'll be apprehended at the gate. He's not going anywhere.
Not with her, and not without her," the detective said grimly.

"You'll traumatize the girl," Hawke said, bothered by the
scene that was playing out so vividly in his mind.

"Yeah, I'm aware. But there's not much we can do about it, and it probably won't come to that."

"If it does, I'll bring Maddie to Logan. She should be there, so give me the flight information. If I don't hear from you by—damn! I don't have a phone. All right. I'll be at Rosedale, either inside or out of the house. If you don't pick him up at his condo, send someone from the Sandy Point station to me at Rosedale, and I'll get Maddie up to Logan. Make sure you give me enough time."

"Okay. Wait there to hear from us. And pray this goes right."

Hawke wrote down the terminal, the gate, the flight, even the seat assignments. His thought was that the data would be something concrete for Maddie to cling to. It was going to be the toughest day of her life, tougher than anything else she'd known so far. And that was hard, even for him, to believe.

Minutes later, Hawke got snared in the traffic jam from hell. The traffic report blamed it on an accident in the rotary before the Sagamore Bridge. He was trapped on Route 6 with no way out, and he wouldn't get off if he could. It was the only road to the Cape.

Chapter 33

"Hi, come on in," Maddie yelled in answer to the knock on the front screen door. "I'm in the kitchen."

Joan walked in cradling an armful of daisies, zinnias, and snapdragons, and handed them to Maddie. "I know you miss your garden," she said. "There was a truck in town selling these. I couldn't resist, which is why I'm late. Of all the days to walk. Don't look for rhyme or reason in the color scheme," she added defiantly. "I just bought two of everything."

Grinning, Maddie said, "They're fabulous!"

"And, they don't need refrigeration."

Maddie handed Joan a green hobnail vase and said, "Here, dip this in the water barrel—halfway is enough—and arrange the flowers while I finish making breakfast. A hot brunch. I'm so excited. Praise the lord for Coleman stoves."

"You didn't have to go to all this trouble, Maddie. We could've just had Danish."

"It's no trouble, and besides, I really appreciate your agreeing to be here when my mother arrives this afternoon," Maddie said. She added wryly, "There's strength in numbers, you know."

"Uh-oh. I take it a little tension remains?"

"Actually, not too bad. Currently I resent her more than she resents me. I like playing the martyr; it frees me of guilt," Maddie quipped.

Joan pulled an Asian lily out of the bouquet and stuck it

like a flagpole in the middle of the vase. "I'm glad to see you're handling this with such aplomb."

Maddie sighed and said, "You want the truth? I cry myself to sleep every night. I'm afraid of the dark—I feel so alone then—so I leave an oil lamp burning all night. If I had TV, I'd watch the shopping channel till dawn. In short, I have all the symptoms of someone who's grieving. And yet I don't dare let my mother see it. Or Tracey. Or George or even Claire. It's my only hope: that they see me having so much fun without them that they want to be around me again."

"Wow. Did you get that out of a book?"

Smiling sadly, Maddie answered, "Yeah. What was the title again? Oh, right: *The Book of Life.* Have a seat, Joannie. I'll bring in our food."

Maddie went out into the yard where she'd set up the stove on her beloved HMS *Bliss* shop shingle—whose name seemed on the ironic side nowadays—and returned with the plate of blueberry pancakes that she had been keeping warm. Bacon, cantaloupe, strawberries, and hot coffee. "Things could be worse," she told Joan as she poured coffee from a thermal carafe. "Don't you feel almost normal right now?"

"Excuse me—normal?" said Joan, drowning her pancakes in syrup. "We're flushing our toilets with buckets of sea water and reading by candlelight. I'm showering under a black plastic bag that's hanging from a clothesline. Normal? I'm tired of washing my clothes in a bucket with a plunger. I'm thinking of forfeiting the summer and going back home."

"Joannie, no, you can't do that!" Maddie said, dismayed. "I really would miss you. You *have* to stay."

Joan seemed shyly pleased to be wanted. She smiled and said, "Oh, all right. But you have to promise me brunch now and then, pioneer woman."

"Deal."

"How about Tracey? Any chance that she'll be returning soon to paradise?"

"Not until paradise has running water," Maddie said, trying to deal lightly with the painful question. She added, "Sometimes I think she sounds homesick. But as soon as I say anything at all about Rosedale, she changes the subject.''

"Is she staying out of trouble, do you think?"

Maddie winced. "Who knows? It's so bizarre, being es-tranged from a child. I'm not handling it at all well. And even after a good call, like the last one, I end up being furious at her for what she's putting Dan and me through.''

"Which brings me to my next question," said Joan, biting a strawberry free of its stem.

"He hasn't left," Maddie said softly. "I have no right to expect him to stay, and yet . . . I do. It's not so much that he has to be with me or die, as that he can't be with anyone else anymore. It's the same with me.''

She laughed self-consciously and said, "I know that sounds weird, but I've thought about this so much: either we're going to live the rest of our lives together, or we're going to live them out alone. There's no in between for us; no making do with someone else ever again. Not after this.''

Joan's dark eyes were filled with sympathy. Somehow, more than anyone else, she came closest to understanding. But even she felt bound to say, "It sounds so romantic—and yet you're so miserable.''

Maddie smiled wanly and said, "Just don't tell my mother that.''

They moved on to other subjects. Half an hour later, they were wiping the dishes as clean as they could with paper towels before using precious water on them, when they heard a car pull into the drive. Maddie's ears pricked up. "That sounds like Michael's car.''

Joan ran to the window and said, "It's Michael, all right.''

"Is Tracey with him?" Maddie said instantly.

"No, he's alone. He's bringing a box of Dunkin' Donuts.''

"Shhh. Move away from the window," Maddie said, wav-ing Joan back. "I don't want him to know I'm home.''

Unequal to the task of facing him, Maddie sat without mov-ing while they waited for him to go away. Instead, they heard Michael let himself in through the front screen door, calling Maddie's name cheerfully as he walked through the house.

"I'm in the kitchen, Michael," Maddie said, dismayed that

he hadn't bothered to knock. Where was Tracey?

He turned the corner from the hall. "Joannie!" he said, surprised. "Long time no see. How you doin'?"

"I'm okay, I guess," said Joan, clearly uncomfortable.

"Where's Tracey, Michael?"

"I didn't expect to see you here," he said to Joan, ignoring Maddie's question. He set the doughnut box on the counter along with the pink and white bag. "I would've brought three coffees instead of two. Cream and just a touch of sugar for you, Maddie," he said, lifting out a paper cup and then a second one from the bag. "Milk, no sugar for me."

He slid Maddie's half full mug of coffee to one side, then set the paper Dunkin' Donuts cup in its place, carefully peeling back the sipping tab for her.

"Michael, will you please answer my question?"

"Actually, I should've brought three coffees in any case," he said, returning to the counter and the box of doughnuts. "Because the chances were good that I'd find Dan Hawke hanging out here—I'm right, am I not?" he asked with a bright smile.

His voice didn't match the look in his eyes. Nothing could match the look in his eyes. The lids were too intensely open, as if he were keeping them propped that way with sticks. He frightened Maddie. This was not a Michael she'd ever seen before.

"What have you done with Tracey?" she said, more desperately now.

"Didn't she tell you? She's at a sleepover. Oh, I know: adult supervision, yadda, yadda, yadda. Don't worry; the parents were home."

"She's up there now? But ... couldn't you have brought her with you—at least for the day, since you're down here anyway?"

He looked delighted to be asked the question. "Funny you should ask. Tracey *wanted* to come down, sweet wife of mine. For good. Oh, yes; she's ready to come back home. She phoned me at seven this morning—our Tracey, awake at seven!—to inform me of this latest whim."

"Whim?"

"What else could it be? I told her that it wasn't convenient; that it absolutely did not fit in with my plans for now."

"What . . . did she say to that?"

Michael sipped his coffee and smacked his lips. "Ahh-h-h . . . good. By the way, did she tell you the latest? She has— she *had*—the chance to make really big bucks. Geoff Woodbine wanted her for testing. A brand new project, a brand new grant, a brand new scam: kid psychics. Doncha love it?"

His revelation, hard on the heels of the news that Tracey was ready to come home, had Maddie reeling. "Michael, what're you talking about? Tracey didn't say a word about that. She talked about . . . about walking dogs," Maddie stammered.

"Dogs! That's rich! But don't worry; something tells me the Woodbine project's not going to fly."

Even as he said it, Maddie made a connection that had eluded her up until now.

"Geoffrey Woodbine! He's the one who called Tracey here at the house! He called, and when he heard me pick up another phone, he hung up on her. It wasn't the first time he tried to reach her. I'm sure it wasn't!"

Michael got an odd look of distaste, as if he'd eaten bad meat. "I'm not surprised. He was a fool. And a con. And, alas for your family, a murderer. *Where is he*?" he said with sudden violence, and Maddie knew they weren't talking about Geoffrey Woodbine any longer.

"Dan's not here," Maddie said, her voice gone so faint that it sounded as if she were lying. She tried to put indignation into it. "Why *would* he be here? You made your terms clear."

"Yeah, right." He seemed not to hear her; he was looking down into the box, picking over the contents, searching for— what? A jelly doughnut?

He lifted out a gun.

And aimed it at her.

Joan had been backing away from him steadily, drifting toward the hall.

"Stay right there!" he barked.

Joan froze, and he turned back to Maddie. "Now. Where were we? Oh, yes. Hawke. Where is he, sweet love of my life?"

"He's not . . . here, Michael," Maddie said, staring at the gun. She had the insane idea that if she kept her eye on the barrel, she could duck when the bullet came out. "You know he's not here."

"He *was* here, damn you! He was here during the hurricane. You broke your promise, Maddie. Why did you do that, Maddie?" he asked, cocking his head. "Huh? Why?"

Unable either to answer his question or deny it, Maddie said instead, "They'll hear the gun, Michael! It's as quiet as a church around here." Even as she said it, the loud racket of someone's generator rang in her ears.

"Hey, guess what? I don't care!" he answered cheerfully. "If I get away, I get away. But I . . . don't . . . *care*. That's the beauty of this plan, Maddie. It's win-win. You see? I've worked it all out. I spent the night working it all out. I admit, I blacked out there for a little while, or I would've been here earlier."

He swung the gun in Joan's direction. "If I *had* got here earlier, you wouldn't have been here and Dan Hawke would. It's really too bad. All I can say is—I wish you were Dan Hawke. But you know what they say: 'If wishes were horses, beggars would ride.' Sorry 'bout that, Joannie."

"Oh, no . . . please . . . please. . . ."

Dan Hawke was in the hall, hoping to God that Michael wouldn't hear him breathing or smell the sweat running freely from every pore. The sight of the BMW in Maddie's drive had made Hawke's heart go flying out of his chest, and he'd been dizzy with fear for Maddie as he reconnoitered the cottage. This was it, his one best shot, with no time to think of an alternate plan.

He was about to charge into the kitchen when a car pulled up outside. Hawke glanced out the screen door and saw, improbably, a Yellow Cab in the lane. He was amazed to see

Tracey emerge from the back seat and walk slowly toward the front door, staring at her father's car as she passed.

Jesus Christ! Dan cocked his ear toward the kitchen. Joan was still pleading with Michael. If he hadn't fired the gun yet, then he wasn't necessarily going to. It gave Dan hope.

Tracey swung the door wide, saw Dan, and opened her mouth to say something. He silenced her with a fierce look and tried to make her stop where she was by holding his hand palm out. Instead, she came toward him as if he were some kind of Pied Piper.

He frowned and shook his head and tried to shoo her away, but she heard her mother's voice inside the kitchen saying, "Michael, don't do this! Don't, Michael!"

The girl let out a sound of alarm. Hawke grabbed her and spun her around, intending to hurtle her toward the front door and safety, but he never got the chance. A bullet rang out behind him, shockingly loud, and tore through his flesh, sucking the breath out of him as it went. He heard screaming from the kitchen at the same time that he felt Tracey slump forward in his arms. Dazed and wounded, he was aghast to see that the same bullet that had ripped through his side had gone on to hit Tracey. Unnerved now, he lowered the child to the floor to examine her wound.

He heard another scream, this one from Maddie, and looked up in time to see her rush toward them and fall to her knees beside her unconscious daughter. Behind her stood Michael, a look of baffled horror on his face. Was he still dangerous? Who knew? Without thinking, Hawke lunged for Michael from his awkward angle, knocking him back but not down. The gun went flying behind them, sliding across the red and white checkerboard floor of the kitchen.

Michael's grunt of surprise from the body slam turned into a bestial snarl as he rallied his wits and fought back. Hawke himself was furious now: furious from the pain, furious from the scare, furious that Michael had hurt a woman and then a child.

It became primal between them, ugly and vicious and battering. Strength held its own against street smarts, and a wounded Hawke realized that he could not prevail. They were in the kitchen and he was on his back fighting for his life when he felt the gun underneath his left side. With a last, exhausting effort, he rolled with Michael to the right, then grabbed the gun and aimed for Michael's head, wanting nothing less than to blow out his brains.

He missed. The bullet carried away Michael's earlobe, but that was all. Still, it had an effect: Michael was stunned into submission at last and lay docile on the floor.

Faint and losing strength fast, Hawke said to Maddie, "How is she?"

"Barely conscious . . . bleeding," Maddie answered in anguish. "I've called an ambulance and the police."

"How?"

"Cell phone."

"A phone! Are you serious?"

"Yes. Are you—?"

"I'm . . . okay," he told her, trying to sound okay. "Go. Stay by her." He could see that Maddie was in agony over him as well. "I promise not to take offense this time," he added, smiling through the pain.

Without even glancing at Michael, Maddie went around the corner to tend to her daughter in the hall. Where were all the neighbors? Hawke wondered. Probably on their boats, where the amenities were. He kept the gun aimed at Michael. He could do that for five lousy minutes. He peeled back his shirt and winced. There was blood, but he could feel it pooling more inside than out. He'd so much rather it were out.

He heard Joanie somewhere, sobbing uncontrollably.

Four minutes to go, with any luck. The gun in his hand felt like a cannon. It seemed to him that Michael was looking livelier now. He was sitting up—slowly, to be sure, but definitely the general direction was up. He didn't miss that earlobe of his one damn bit. Hell, why should he? He didn't wear earrings.

And meanwhile Hawke himself was sloping more and more heavily to the right. The cupboard door handle jabbed him in his back and it was really, really more annoying than the hole in his side. Michael was eyeing the gun now. Was it Hawke's imagination? Or was Michael reaching over for it, the way he might for a salt shaker at a picnic table.

In slow, slow motion, Hawke watched Michael reach, reach, reach and he thought, I'd better keep track of the time and *one* elephant *two* elephants *three* elephants *four* elephants and then the red and white squares on the checkerboard floor became very, very bright with white and with blood and a horrendous sound, oh, shit, a bullet; and that was all.

He opened his eyes to bright light and flowers in the air. They floated all around him, all the same ones, fat white roses climbing pale green trellises.

Heaven.

"I know this wallpaper," he said to the nurse.

"You ought to; you've been here for three days," the nurse said, grinning.

"This room's too . . . nice . . . for a hospital."

"That's because it's a cottage hospital. You stay right here," she said after she checked a monitor. She hurried out of the room.

"No, wait—"

Gone. He lay there feeling a little like after the tea in Albania, only more anxious. He needed answers, needed faces—one face—and he kept his gaze fastened on the door, waiting for the one face.

A forty-year-old physician came in, wrong face, and then the nurse again, two wrong faces now.

And then, after a long time and pointless testing of his vital signs—the right face. She came in with her eyes all red with flowing tears and her mouth all crooked with trying to keep the tears back and he'd never seen such a beautiful, beautiful face in his life.

He smiled his own version of her crooked smile. "Maddie."

She seemed to float, like an angel, and drifted down into a chair alongside his bed. He thought that maybe he was in heaven, after all. Whatever. As long as she was there with him.

She took his hand in hers and he felt her warm flesh under his hand and over it; so they must be in heaven on earth.

Whatever. As long as she was there with him.

Maddie said, "It didn't look so good for a while there."

It was news to him. "It couldn't have been *that* bad," he murmured, smiling. "I didn't even have a near-death experience this time."

She smiled, but tears rolled out anyway. "Don't joke, don't joke," she said, and lifted his hand to her lips.

He realized that she was holding his gunslinging hand, and some of the horror came back. "The last thing I remember . . . was a shot," he said.

Maddie nodded and said, "You shot the clock as you passed out, which brought Sergeant Millhaus and Billy—Officer Smith—storming into the kitchen, guns at the ready. That was all."

"How's Tracey?" He knew from looking at Maddie that her daughter was all right, but he wanted to hear that out loud.

"She's fine," Maddie said with a pretty brave smile. "She'll be discharged before you will, in fact; she hasn't lost as much blood."

"The resilience of youth."

"You saved her life, Dan. She knows that."

He shook his head, because it seemed to him that he should have done better, and he said, "How is she handling this?"

"I don't see how she can ever—"

"She will," he said firmly. "In time."

"The resilience of youth?"

"That's my theory, and I'm sticking to it," he said, prompting a wan smile from her. After a pause, he added, "What about Michael?"

Some of the light and all of the smile left Maddie's face. "At first they thought he was having a psychotic episode as a result of some kind of prolonged drug use. But it's worse than that. They did an MRI scan. The drugs, they're what caused some of his behavior—but not all of it, Detective Bailey told me. It doesn't look good. They said the tumor's inoperable.''

Hawke said softly, "I hope your family's there for you and Tracey."

Maddie nodded. "It took a major crisis . . . but yes, we're starting over."

"Starting over," he said, closing his eyes and sighing. "I like the ring of that." He gazed at her face, strengthened by the very sight of her. "I'm willing, Maddie. You?"

For an answer she bent over him and dropped an angel's kiss on his lips. "Willing, and able."

Epilogue

Three years later.

"Is my cap on straight?"

"Who's going to notice?" said her stepfather, tugging on her tassel. "They'll all be too dazzled by your smile."

"I'm *so* nervous."

"You're going to be the best valedictorian in the history of Mount Fidelis School for Girls. Knock 'em dead, tiger. I've got to get back to my seat. Your mother wants every second of this on video."

He took a couple of steps away, then came back and straightened her mortarboard. "There. Now it's straight."

He melted into the assembling crowd of families and faculty, and Tracey—in between bursts of excited conversation with her friends—went over her speech. She had so much to say and her heart was so full; but with a stepfather in television and a mother in teaching, she felt more pressure than she'd ever felt before, more even than during the debate for the state championship.

The graduates were given the signal to line up in order, and somehow that settled her nerves. By the time Tracey stood at the podium, she had herself under control—which she had better be able to do, if she was going to be a TV news reporter.

Tracey scanned the audience for her family and friends.

She found Norah first, wearing a wide-brimmed white hat and sitting next to Joan and her fiancé. Next to them were all of her family. Everyone was waving and smiling, even her stepdad as he videotaped her at the podium. He had the zoom all the way out on the camera, so she definitely couldn't cry; it would be so uncool.

She hugged herself with her elbows and lifted the corners of the first page of her speech. Her hands shook as she held them, and her voice started out a little wobbly, but she gained confidence with every sentence, because she believed so much in the words she had written on those pages.

"It's customary," she said into the microphone, "to begin by thanking our parents and our teachers, our mentors and our coaches, for all that they've done to get us here in one piece. But I want to back up a little, and thank our parents for having had us in the first place.

"It couldn't have been easy to make that decision, not with all the dangers and pitfalls and time-consuming demands and, yes, expenses that are involved in bringing up a family. It would have been so much easier for them not to have bothered. But they did bother, not only to have us, but to stick with us, and agonize over us, and pay for us, and at all times, to love us.

"Many of us—most of us—are from blended families. Even more activities, more expense, less time, more stress: that's what parents in a blended family have to deal with every day of their lives. So to our mothers and fathers, to our stepmothers and our stepfathers—thank you, from all of us. Each of you has contributed in some way to the fact that we're here and ready and eager for the next phase of our lives."

Tracey looked up from her notes at the sound of a child's shriek; she knew it well. "I think my baby sister wants me to get on with this, so I—Mom, don't you cry, too! If you do, I will, and that'll ruin Dad's video for sure. . . ."

Sarah Timmons was seated at the picnic table in Rosedale's garden, holding her three-year-old grandson on her lap.

George Junior was everything she could ever hope for in a grandchild—a beautiful, fair-haired boy who was perfectly content with whatever amusement he was offered. At the moment he was scribbling with a crayon in a coloring book. As far as Sarah could tell, he had no artistic talent at all, which pleased her: perhaps he would go into business.

She smiled as Tracey approached, holding the hand of her two-year-old stepsister Emma. Behind them, tail wagging as usual, trotted the dreadful stray mutt that Dan had rescued during that awful summer.

"Grandma, a bunch of us are going across to the beach," said Tracey. "Aunt Claire said that we could take Woody, too."

"Tracey, dear, I've told you before; please call him George."

"But he likes the name Woody—don't you, you widdle George Sherwood Timmons?" she cooed, crouching down and rubbing noses with the boy. "Want to go wading with us?"

Young George scrunched his face and rubbed his nose, and went back to his coloring book.

Tracey shrugged and said, "Okay, Emma, it's just you and us." She looked down at the girl and said, "Ready to go wading, Emma? In the big water?"

Emma's gypsy eyes went round with excitement as she nodded vigorously, then broke from Tracey's grasp and ran around in a big circle, screaming a wordless cheer.

Sarah sighed and shook her head. "Will she *ever* talk? Considering that her parents are such great communicators. . . ."

Tracey ran after the toddler and snatched her up, blowing raspberries into her fat bare belly and sending her into shrieks of joy. "Emma doesn't need words, do you, sweetie? Come on, let's go by the big water."

Sarah said, "You'd better watch her every single minute, Tracey. You know how she is."

"Yes, Grandma."

Still unhappy at the prospect, Sarah said to her granddaughter, "Emma, would you like to stay here and color in the book, hmm? With George?"

Little George frowned and pulled the coloring book closer to him. Emma said, "No, no, no!" and made a grabbing gesture with her fist over Tracey's shoulder toward the sea.

"See, Grandma? She knows some words," said Tracey, and off they went.

Dan was taping it all with his camera. Now he zoomed in close on Sarah and said, "Say something for posterity, Sarah, on this momentous occasion."

Sarah cringed at the thought of the close-up of her face. She was feeling her age more than ever; maybe it was the sight of so many new beginnings unfolding around her. She resisted the urge to smooth her hair or compress her lips to bring color to them, and instead looked directly at the camera and said, "Congratulations on your graduation, Tracey. We are all very, very proud of you."

Dan grinned and shut down the camera. "Thank you, ma'am," he said. "Only fifty-two guests to go."

He went off to capture his wife on film as she supervised the cleanup from the barbecue. Maddie shooed him away, but it didn't work; she ended up in his arms again.

"Someone ought to tell those two to get a room," John said, laughing, as he dropped on the bench next to Sarah.

John Gunderson, resident keeper and tour director of the Sandy Point lighthouse, never missed the chance for sexual innuendo.

Sarah tried to give him a cool look, but—as usual when he came up with one of his insinuations—she felt her cheeks burn pink. "Hello, John. I'm surprised you're not out sailing. It's a fine day for it."

He arched one grizzled eyebrow at her and said puckishly, "And miss a free meal? Not on your life."

"You like to tease," she said evenly.

"I like to tease *you*."

Her cheeks burned hotter. He was an odd duck, this John Gunderson—a man who'd sailed around the world and come back home only after a bout with gangrene in Thailand cost him his leg below his left knee. At Halloween he actually replaced his prosthesis with a peg leg, strapped on an eye patch, and handed out Three Musketeers bars to kids trick-or-treating at the keeper's house. He was famous for miles around.

And he liked to tease Sarah.

"More than anyone else," he said aloud, reading her mind.

She stared at the scribbles in young George's coloring book for a long time while John sprawled at ease with his back to the picnic table, his elbows supporting his weight, and scanned the horizon for sails.

She took a deep breath. "I was just about to get myself some cake and coffee," she said.

"And so was I. You sit, Sarah. You sit. I'll take care of us both."

From across the yard Maddie nudged her husband in the ribs and said, "Are you getting this? Are you getting this?"

"I am," said Dan, zooming in on the couple with his videocamera, "but don't expect your mother to be thrilled about it."

"Someday she'll thank me. After they're married."

The seaman stumped off to the dessert table and Dan shut down the camera, then turned to his wife. "You honestly think that can happen? Since when are you such a hopeless romantic?"

Maddie slipped her arms around him and said, "Since you came back to me. Oh, Dan," she added with a happy sigh, "it doesn't seem possible to feel this much joy."

He grinned and caught one of her hands in his, then began sliding it from behind him to his front. "You wanna feel joy? Here, I'll let you feel joy."

"Dan!" she said, lowering her gaze and looking around her. "Someone will see!"

He laughed. "Okay, let's tell 'em all to go home, then." He kissed her fleetingly, but the kiss had a burning edge to it, one she knew well.

She dropped her voice even lower and said, "I know I've

been busy planning the party, but it's only been—"

"A week and two days!"

"Nine days," she said through a reproving smile. "Is that so very long?"

"It is when you look so good and act so happy," he whispered close to her ear. "How about it? Would anyone miss us?"

Scandalized, she said, "Dan! Definitely!"

He sighed and said, "Yeah. I guess they would. Ah, well. Back to the taping." He kissed her lightly and wandered off, joking with the guests and warming them up for the camera.

Maddie watched him, handsome and at ease as he recorded the graduation event for his stepdaughter. He was, beyond a doubt, the most beguiling, wonderful, devoted . . .

She watched him wander past Sarah Timmons and John Gunderson and say something funny enough to make Sarah laugh out loud. An amazing man! And he belonged to her, Maddie Hawke. It didn't seem possible.

Her heart welled up and she felt a surge of that old, old ache for him. Life was short. He wanted her, and she wanted him, and what did a few people around them really matter?

She caught up with him and stood on tiptoe. "Upstairs," she whispered in his ear. "Five minutes."

He flashed her a million-dollar grin and said, "That's how much time we get, or that's when I should go?"

"Scram," she said, laughing.

Maddie spent the next five minutes backing into the house and then through the kitchen, fielding guests like ping-pong balls. Suddenly everyone had something to say to her; but she didn't care. The single most important thing that she wanted to hear was that Daniel Hawke loved her, and the best way to hear that was in his arms.

But first, the alibi. She went into the upstairs bathroom, turned on the light and the fan, and stepped back out into the hall, closing the bathroom door behind her.

The door to their bedroom was already closed; she sneaked down the hall and tiptoed into the room like a burglar. She assumed that Dan would be naked and on the bed—he was reckless enough—and was surprised to see him, still dressed, standing at the gabled window and looking out. He had drawn the lace curtain aside and held it pinned to the window frame as he stared out at the distance.

"Hi there," she said, suddenly shy.

He glanced over his shoulder and gestured her over with a smile, then wrapped his free arm around her shoulder. "Look out there," he told her. "What do you see?"

"I see roses, lots of them . . . roofs . . . and beyond them, the sea," said Maddie. "I see a strip of beach. I see—ah!—I see all that we hold dear."

Dan chuckled and said, "Look at her run . . . well, you wouldn't really call it a run . . . more like a bowlegged waddle . . . but the sand is slowing her down. She'll be fleet as the wind someday."

"Couldn't you just squeeze her?" Maddie said, biting her lip through a grin. "How were we so incredibly lucky?"

"I don't know. . . . I don't know. Look at her chase after Tracey. . . . God, she adores her. What's she going to do when Tracey goes off to college?" He turned to Maddie and said with a sudden, hapless look, "What're *we* going to do?"

Maddie said lightly, "The way I look at it, it's a wash. We gain some privacy; we lose a sitter."

He gave her a sideways, good-humored look. "Baloney, a wash. You're going to fall apart completely when she packs up for Cornell this fall."

Sighing, Maddie said, "I will—but not in front of her. I'm just too happy for her. Between the two girls, I don't know who's the greater miracle. Dan . . . we're so incredibly lucky."

"I know . . . I know. Isn't that Kevin throwing the Frisbee?"

"Mm-hmm. He's signed up for the Coast Guard, did you know?"

"It's where he should be," Dan agreed.

"Mmm."

Arm in arm, they watched the scene on the beach in loving silence. Eventually Dan smiled and said softly, "Hey, dollin', it looks like our five minutes are up. We'd better get back to our guests.''

He kissed her on the top of her head, but Maddie had other ideas. She lifted her face to his, fluttering her lashes closed, and said, ''I love you, Dan Hawke. For everything, I love you.'' Her mouth parted for his kiss.

The lace curtain dropped back into place, casting crystals of sunlight on the cool white sheets of their bed.